Penny Jordan has been writing for [...] and has an outstanding record: ov[...] five novels published, including the [...] *Perfect Family, To Love, Honour & Betray, [...]* and *Power Play*, which hit the *Sunday Times* and *New York Times* bestseller lists. She says she hopes to go on writing until she has passed the two hundred mark—and maybe even the two hundred and fifty mark.

Although Penny was born in Preston, Lancashire, and spent her childhood there, she moved to Cheshire as a teenager, and has continued to live there. Following the death of her husband she moved to the small traditional Cheshire market town on which she based her Crighton books.

She lives with her Birman cat Posh, who tries to assist with her writing by sitting on the newspapers and magazines Penny reads to provide her with ideas she can adapt for her fictional books.

Penny is a member and supporter of the Romantic Novelists' Association and the Romance Writers of America—two organisations dedicated to providing support for both published and yet-to-be published authors.

PENNY JORDAN

Pride

MILLS & BOON

Mills & Boon, an imprint of Harlequin (UK) Limited,
Eton House, 18-24 Paradise Road, Richmond, Surrey TW9 1SR

PRIDE © Harlequin Books SA 2011

Rocco © Penny Jordan 2009
(originally published as: *Captive At The Sicilian Billionaire's Command*)
Alessandro © Penny Jordan 2009
(originally published as: *The Sicilian Boss's Mistress*)
Falcon © Penny Jordan 2009
(originally published as: *The Sicilian's Baby Bargain*)

ISBN: 978 0 263 88757 0

010-0511

Printed in the UK
by CPI Mackays, Chatham ME5 8TD

CONTENTS

ROCCO

PROLOGUE

ROCCO threw down the hard hat he had been wearing whilst he showed the 'suits' and potential investors round the new complex—a luxury spa and holiday resort here on Sicily—pushing an impatient hand into the thick darkness of his hair as he held the mobile to his ear and said laconically, 'You wanted me, Don Falcon?'

If his elder brother was irritated by Rocco's mocking use of his title he didn't say so, announcing coolly instead, 'We've found her. Here is her address in London. You know what you have to do.'

Falcon had ended the call before Rocco could say anything, leaving him to retrieve his hard hat and stride towards the Porta cabin that was currently serving as his on-site office.

CHAPTER ONE

A LOUD bang from a noisy exhaust somewhere in the street had Julie glancing over her shoulder and then checking automatically to see that her shabby shoulder bag was tucked in against her body. This was a down-at-heel and often unsafe neighbourhood. Only the other day she had been warned by the woman in charge of the nursery never to leave any personal documents in her flat as there had been a spate of robberies, with passports especially being targeted. As a result, she was now carrying their passports with her in her handbag.

'Ms Simmonds?'

Julie gasped with shock. She had been so busy looking over her shoulder that she hadn't seen the man who was now standing in front of her, blocking her way to the entrance of the converted house where she rented a small flat.

One look at him, though, told her that this was no thief. Not with that expensive car parked right next to them, which she hadn't noticed before and which she suspected must be his.

Warily she nodded her head.

'And this is *your* child?'

Now she could feel herself tensing, hesitating, as she held on tightly to her orphaned baby nephew whilst she fought off her feeling of apprehension. Josh *was* her child –

after all—now. The icy March rain that had started when she had left the local eight-until-ten shop where she worked part-time to walk to the nursery to collect Josh had soaked through her thin coat, turning the fine silver-blonde silkiness of her hair into lank rats' tails whilst the cold had left her skin blue-white and bloodless, and now she was trapped here on the street with a man who was asking her questions she did not want to answer. The weight of Josh, plus his nappy bag and her handbag, were already making her thin arms ache.

'If you're a debt collector…' she began. Her voice might be thin with disdain and exhaustion, but it was fear that was making her heart thud so painfully. Josh *was* hers. There was no reason for her to feel that this man—this stranger—somehow threatened her right to call Josh her child, even if she wasn't actually Josh's birth mother. That was what living a hand-to-mouth existence and constantly fearing the arrival of another demand for money did for you: it made you feel guilty and on edge even when you had no cause to do so.

If it *was* money that this man was after then he was wasting his time. Julie's chin unconsciously lifted with the pride she knew he would believe she no longer had the right to have. There was no point in anyone sending in any more bailiffs as there was nothing left to take. Even Josh's buggy had been claimed against her dead sister's debts. There was no point feeling sorry for herself or wishing that her parents had thought to make a proper will. Ultimately, as their now only surviving child, she should inherit something—enough, she hoped, to clear all Judy's debts and buy a small house for herself and Josh. But according to her solicitor a final settlement of everything could be some time away, given the complications of the situation.

The fact was that her parents, her sister, James—her sister's fiancé—and his parents had all died, along with twenty other people in the same fatal train crash. It had been such a terrible shock, and had left Julie with the task of supporting herself and her late sister's child whilst being hounded to pay Judy's debts. And, of course, cope with James's death.

The funerals had been in their way even worse than the news of the deaths itself. She, of course, as the only adult living member of her own family, had had to make the arrangements for the burial of her parents and her sister. She had thought that maybe Judy should be buried with James, but Annette, James's elder sister and only relative, had refused to entertain the idea, insisting that James was buried with their parents.

With the funeral two days after her family's, Julie had been able to attend—and she had found that Annette was exactly as James had once described his elder sister to her. Polished and expensively dressed—her husband was a banker—and very cold.

'Keep that child away from me,' she had said sharply, stepping back from Julie. 'My coat cost a fortune, it's pure cashmere.'

James had told Julie that Roger, Annette's husband, desperately wanted a family but that Annette flatly refused to entertain the idea. They had a smart townhouse in Chelsea, where Annette entertained Roger's colleagues and clients. She was very much the corporate wife, and according to James was very ambitious for her husband. James. Julie blinked away exhausted tears. Her one and only love. Her one and only lover. It only things had been different. If only *she* had been the one to conceive his child. If only…

Losing him still hurt so very much. Only with his death had she admitted that somewhere deep inside herself she had been cherishing the foolish hope that one day he would come back to her.

Rocco watched the shadows come and go in the woman's unusually expressive dark grey eyes. The only part of her that looked anything like alive. He had never seen such a washed-out-looking female.

'A debt collector?' He gave her a haughty look, before adding dryly, 'You could call me that,' he agreed, answering Julie's bitter question. 'Although what I'm here for is more properly a matter of repossession.'

Repossession? There wasn't anything left in the flat to repossess. The bailiffs had taken it all. She tried to look braver than she felt as she looked at the man.

The harsh street lighting gave his features a Byzantine quality of polished arrogance allied to cruelty, gilding the olive skin drawn tight over the high cheekbones. It was the face of a man without mercy or compassion—the face of a man whose heritage was rooted in the alien and the dangerous, Julie recognised.

It was hard for Rocco to see what could possibly have attracted his young half-brother to this pale plain English girl. She was thin to the point of malnourishment, whey-faced, and so far as he could see without charm or personality—but perhaps he was being unfair. Given enough champagne and the illegal party drugs his late half-brother had favoured, maybe she had sparkled in the tawdry manner in which Antonio had liked his women to sparkle.

Distaste filled him—for his late half-brother's way of life, for the morals of the woman standing in front of him, but most of all for the duty that had been imposed upon him by his own birth and his elder brother's conscience.

He had been against this whole thing right from the start. A child's place was with its mother. But Alessandro had pointed out that the child *would* be with its mother, at all times, and would continue to remain with her since Rocco's task was to bring them both back to Sicily with him. In fact, now that he had seen the circumstances in which the pair of them seemed to be living, Rocco acknowledged that his intervention in their lives could only be of benefit—to them both.

She was so cold, and she must get Josh inside—but *he* was still standing in front her. Josh still wasn't over the nasty cough he had caught at the beginning of the winter.

Poor baby, he had had so many problems since her sister had given birth to him three weeks early, in January. First there had been the fact that Judy had never wanted him in the first place. Then there had been his inability to feed properly, followed by the discovery that he was slightly tongue-tied... That had led to a very minor medical procedure, after which—perhaps because Judy had not been careful enough—he had contracted an infection, which in turn had led to further feeding problems. And then with one blow fate had robbed him of his parents and both sets of grandparents.

But somehow Julie would make it up to him. She would love him and look after him. He was, after all, all she had left of James and her family, even if he hadn't already been precious to her in his own right.

When they had come to tell her about the train accident which had killed so many people, including her own and

Josh's family, she had made a silent vow to the man she loved so much to love and protect the child he had believed was his.

James had been so proud and excited when he had discovered that Judy was pregnant…

Rocco was getting impatient. He was a Leopardi after all. The Leopardis had ruled their lands and dispensed their own form of law in Sicily from the time of the Crusades onwards. Rocco had grown up in an environment where to be a Leopardi meant that one's word was law.

'I don't know what it is you wish to repossess,' Julie began tiredly, 'but my…my baby is cold, and I really need to get him inside.' She didn't really want to have to open her handbag in front of this stranger, but she needed to get her keys so that she could let herself into the flat. It wasn't easy, trying to surreptitiously open her handbag and at the same time hold Josh safe, and when she saw the way the man was looking at her, with a mix of male irritation and impatience, she knew that her attempt at discretion had been a waste of time.

'Let me hold the child for you.' The cool assurance in the male voice combined with the unexpected offer caused Julie's eyes to widen in astonishment. He sounded as though he was perfectly at home holding young babies.

'You've got children of your own?' Julie's face burned as she realised how personal and inappropriate her question was.

His terse 'No' compounded those feelings, which hardly inspired her to hand over Josh. But then her ineffectual scrabbling one-handedly in the bag suddenly caused it to tilt upwards, disgorging some of its contents onto the wet street, including her purse, an assortment of bills that belonged to Judy, her keys and their passports—Josh's a sad reminder of the honeymoon her sister had been so excited about, their first holiday as a family. Rocco frowned as he looked down at the wet pavement and saw the passports amongst the other detritus that had spilled from the woman's handbag.

Ignoring Julie's gasp of protest, he bent down to retrieve her possessions, picking up the now wet bills and the two passports before casually flicking them open. Both passports were in his hand—a providential accident or a potent sign that this task might after all be simpler and easier than he had thought? What kind of woman carried passports around with her? he wondered, and then grimaced as he found the answer to his own question.

Obviously the kind who expected that the opportunity to leave the country might occur at any time and wanted to be prepared for it. He imagined it was the kind of thing that would be quite common where high-class hookers were concerned.

But this pathetic and unappealing-looking woman couldn't have looked less like anything high-class. Rocco reached for her purse, frowning as he felt its emptiness, and then picked up her keys.

He was handing everything back to her, including her keys. Julie exhaled shakily in relief. She wasn't sure just what she had been fearing, but now she admitted she did feel a bit more relaxed—or at least she did until he said autocractically, 'The baby needs to be out of this rain and wind.' He put his hand on her arm, nodding in the direction of his car as he told her, 'My car's over there.'

Had she moved of her own volition, or was it a combination of the wind and his hand on her arm that had somehow brought her so close to his car that she was standing with it on one side of her and him on the other, hemming her in? Julie shivered.

What were his intentions? What did he really want? Not her. Not a man like this one, whose every movement and expression suggested a certain contempt for everything and anything that was not of the very best—including the speed with which his hand had dropped from her arm. All she needed to do was simply ask him to move. She could even push past him. Her hand was beginning to feel numb from clinging on to her possessions, and Josh was an increasingly heavy weight on her arm, despite his slightness. Carefully she tried to adjust Josh's position to ease her arm.

'Let me take him.' He was reaching for Josh, Julie recognised immediately, all maternal anxiety, his hands long-fingered, lean and tanned against the baby's shabby suit.

'What is it you want?' she demanded. 'Who sent you here?'

'No one sends me anywhere,' he told her coldly. 'And it isn't *who* I am from you should be asking, but where.'

'Where? I don't understand what you're talking about.'

'No? Try this, then. I'm from the country and the family to whom the boy belongs.'

Julie's eyes were as grey and drained of warm blue as London's March sky, and they registered shock and then fear as the meaning of his words slammed into her heart, causing it to thud so heavily that she could hear its beat in her own ears.

'You're from Sicily?' she guessed.

'I'm from Sicily,' he agreed.

Of all the possibilities she might have envisaged, this

had not even come close to being one of them—and that alone was enough to fling her headlong into mindless panic as she demanded, 'Who are you?'

Rocco wasn't used to having his identity questioned. He looked down at her contemptuously from his six-foot-three height, folding his arms across his chest. The fine wool of his handmade Italian suit moved with him as easily as though it was his flesh.

'My name is Leopardi—Rocco Leopardi. And now that I have answered you perhaps you will be good enough to give me the child—my nephew—and get into the car?'

His *nephew*. So this was not Antonio—the rich, louche Sicilian playboy with whom her sister had had an affair in the South of France early last May, which may or may not have been responsible for Josh's conception—a fact which she had forced Julie to promise to keep a secret from James. A feeling akin to relief which there was absolutely no justification for her to feel warmed the icy sting of Julie's rain-chilled body, temporarily making her drop her guard and momentarily relax her tightly protective hold on the sleeping baby.

Fearing that she was about to drop the child, Rocco immediately reached for him, lifting him bodily out of Julie's arms before she could stop him and then opening the rear passenger door to the car.

'What are you doing?'

Fresh panic and fear filled Julie as she watched Rocco place Josh into a baby seat in the back of the car. Everything about the way he handled her nephew was gentle and protective of the small, vulnerable life, but for some reason the fact that he was being so careful, so caring, actually increased Julie's fear. For herself and her own position in Josh's life?

'I'm simply putting the baby out of harm's way whilst we talk. You almost dropped him.'

'No, that's not true,' Julie denied. 'You're trying to take him away from me, aren't you?' she guessed. 'You're trying to steal him.'

Rocco gave her a tight-lipped look. He might have known she'd be the high-drama hysterical type.

Fear and panic had seized Julie. Did he know that she wasn't really Josh's mother? Was he going to try and claim that she had no rights where Josh was concerned? He was the kind of man from the kind of family who would stop at nothing to get what they wanted, and if they wanted her nephew… Julie's heart was thumping frantically. She could see a man and a woman coming towards them on the opposite side of the road. She opened her mouth to call out to them for help, her instinctive need to protect her relationship with Josh overwhelming her normal dislike of any kind of scene.

'Look—' Rocco had begun intending to point out that she was overreacting, only to stop when he saw that Julie was looking across the road at a couple who were walking towards them. Instantly guessing what she was going to do, he reacted immediately. She was already standing close to the car, so it was easy to hold her there in his arms, and easier still to silence her planned cry for help with the pressure of his mouth on hers.

Normally the last thing he'd have contemplated doing was kissing a woman like this one. She appealed to him almost as little physically as she repulsed him morally— thin, blonde, pale-skinned, and ready to have sex with any man who asked her just so long as he was rich.

Rocco liked strikingly attractive, intelligent women,

who showed their pride in themselves in everything they did and were. His father might be the head of one of Sicily's oldest aristocratic families, and he himself might have a courtesy title, but Rocco was a billionaire in his own right, through his own endeavours, and he took pride in that achievement. When the time eventually came that he was ready to settle down—which most definitely was not yet—he wanted a partner who was exactly that: a woman who was equal to truly being his partner. Someone who understood the demands that came with his birthright but who at the same time had made her own way in the world and knew the value of having done so—a woman who was equally at home in society as she was in the corporate world; a woman who held herself aloof from the cheap sexual thrills beloved of his half-brother and his cronies, and who disdained them and everything they represented as much as he did himself; but at the same time a woman who understood and shared his own deep-rooted core sensuality.

One thing she must not do, though, was fall in love with him or expect him to fall in love with her. Bitterness gripped its ever-ready fist tight on his emotions. His mother had loved his father and that love had destroyed her. That was never going to happen to him, nor did he want to be responsible for the pain of it in someone else. He had no intention of becoming either the victim his mother had been or the callous enforcer of that victimisation that was his father.

The child's mother had stiffened in his hold, and he could feel the frightened race of her heartbeat.

Frightened? Of what? Not him? Rocco was outraged. The thought of creating fear within anyone, but especially in someone weaker and vulnerable, was totally abhorrent to him. How could a woman who had given herself to his depraved late half-brother possibly be afraid of him? From what he knew of Antonio, a woman who was frightened of a man's touch was hardly his style. And from what Falcon's sources had discovered about her, this one had been very much Antonio's style—a so-called glamour model. Not that there was anything remotely glamorous about her now...

And yet somehow her lips were unexpectedly soft and full, and her slenderness within his arms disarmed and distracted him, making him want to hold her close, tempting his tongue-tip to explore the shape and tease apart that closed line of denial.

Rocco wasn't used to women who denied him.

The reason why Julie had ended up in Rocco's arms had become buried beneath a surge of other feelings and a very different kind of panic. James was the only man she had ever wanted to hold her like this and kiss her like this, Julie thought painfully, but somehow—either through exhaustion or fear or both—she could feel her will to resist him giving way to the warmth emanating from him. It was as though her weakness was irresistibly drawn to his strength, her woman to his man, the softness of her lips to the hard command of his mouth, until the determined male pressure of his tongue was melting her resistance as easily as the heat of a Sicilian summer sun could melt winter snow. Her starving senses were betrayingly greedy for the sensual pleasure of his kiss.

This was how she had once dreamed of James holding her and kissing her—before they had become lovers, before she had lost him to Judy.

It had been bad enough having to listen to James telling her gently that, whilst he liked her and valued their time together, he had fallen in love with Judy, but it had been even worse having to listen to Judy confessing in a drunken moment that she was not sure who was the father of the unwanted child she had been carrying.

It could, she had admitted, be the wealthy Sicilian playboy with whom she'd had an affair but who had since ditched her and was refusing to answer her letters. But she was going to tell James that it was his—because, as she had told Julie smugly and with open malice, it actually could be, seeing as James had rushed her into bed the minute she had returned from Sicily.

Having to listen to Judy telling her about them making love had been pure torture. Julie clung fiercely to Rocco. It had been *her* kisses she had wanted James to long for, her touch, her body... Lost in her own emotions, she felt the man holding her become James, and the intensity of her emotions dictated her actions, so that she was kissing him with all the fierce longing and pride of her love for James.

Julie's sudden passion caught Rocco off guard. She was pressing her body into his, opening her mouth beneath his, and her breathing was altering to become as unsteady as her heartbeat.

Unaware of the reason for it, instinctively he responded to it, shaping her body to his own, taking the sweetness her parted lips were offering, and letting the soft moan of assent she gave at the first thrust of his tongue be the signal that brought his hands sweeping down her body to bring her intimately close to his own flesh.

The sensation of hard male thighs pressing against her jolted Julie back to reality.

This man was not James.

As soon as he felt her struggle Rocco stopped kissing her, sliding his hands back up over her body more out of habit than desire, as distaste for his own actions filled him. Since when had he ever wanted Antonio's leavings?

It was unthinkable that he should want a woman like this one—a pathetic excuse for a real woman.

He had stopped kissing her, but he was still holding on to her, Julie recognized, shivering in his hold. Why had she kissed him like that? He wasn't anything like James. The couple she would have called out to for help had now, of course, gone.

As much as he wanted to turn his back and walk away from her, and from his own momentary betrayal of himself and his values, Rocco knew that he could not do so. On this occasion his duty to his family must come before any duty to himself.

'There are matters we need to discuss,' he told Julie coldly.

'I will not let you take my baby away from me,' Julie warned him fiercely, blinking back the tears caused by the overload on her emotions.

Rocco frowned at her.

'You are being ridiculous. There is no question of anyone wanting to take your child. This is simply a matter of you both accompanying me to Sicily so that the legal complexities of a certain situation can be dealt with. All that is involved is a stay of a week—ten days at the most— and then you will be free to return here if that is your wish. I give you my word on that.'

Julie looked at him. His giving of 'his word' should have sounded theatrical, something for her to question and even mock, but somehow instead she found herself reacting to his words at some deep psychological level—as though a contract had been made, a promise given, a vow, almost. She could feel her breath leaking from her lungs and she knew that the slight inclination of her head was an acknowledgement of that contract—just as powerful a commitment from her as his words had been from him.

She had relaxed slightly, but a woman like this one, who had no conception of honour or what was due to a man's given word, was all too likely to cause the kind of public display she had already tried to cause once, Rocco decided, making up his mind that the sooner they were on their way to Sicily the better. Since she had their passports with her, he could see no sense in prolonging their departure. His personal jet was on standby, with its flight path filed. There was nothing to be gained by delaying things. Once she was in the car, she could argue with him all she wanted.

'Now, if we can both get into the car and out of this rain,' Rocco continued, opening the passenger door of the car for her.

Julie was still hesitating.

'I assure you that, far from suffering any harm, as you seem to think, ultimately both you and the child stand to benefit financially,' Rocco told her coolly.

Benefit? Financially? What did that mean? Julie's heart started to beat too fast.

Ah, now he had found the key to unlock her resistance, Rocco thought cynically.

'But why? I mean, I know that your brother...' She could not bring herself to say that she knew that his brother might be Josh's father, because that meant admitting to herself that Josh might not be James's son, and she longed so much for it to have been James who had fathered him, even though Judy herself had told her that she was not completely sure about who the father was. It was Josh she must think of now, though, she warned herself, and if the family of the wealthy playboy with whom her sister had had a fling were prepared to make some kind of financial provision for Josh, what right did she have to deny her nephew that benefit?

A fresh fear struck her. What if Antonio Leopardi wanted to claim Josh and take him from her? What if that was what this was all about?

The car, long, shiny and expensive, was parked beneath a streetlight, and she could see quite plainly the contemptuous look in the slightly hooded golden-amber eyes as he turned towards her. The eyes of a predatory hunter. Leopard's eyes.

'Antonio was my half-brother, not my brother. He was Sicilian, therefore this child—his child—is also Sicilian, and as such is entitled to his inheritance. That is the law of our blood and our family.'

The whole sentence was seamed with warnings as dark and ancient as Sicily's own history, but initially it was the first three words he had spoken that Julie focused on.

'Antonio *was* Sicilian?' she repeated. 'What does that mean?'

'It means exactly what it always means when one speaks of a person's life in the past tense,' Rocco told her curtly. 'My half-brother—your lover, the child's father— is dead. However, whilst the Leopardi family does not have another Antonio, and most certainly will not supply you with a replacement lover—' another even more derisory look, designed to strip whatever pride she might have left from her much in the same manner that one of his ancestors might have ordered that a criminal be flayed alive, followed the first one '—it does take its responsibilities towards those of its blood very seriously.'

She was almost mentally and emotionally numb now, as well as numb with cold, and the hardship of these last months was abruptly taking its toll on her. It was hard to remember now that she had ever been a confident, successful young woman, with a promising career in local government in front of her—never mind that it was less than six months since she had been smartly turned out, well fed, a stone heavier, with glossy hair and a growing circle of new acquaintances, sharing a comfortable apartment with three other young female graduates who, like her, had jobs in local government.

The thought of sharing the responsibility for the safe upbringing of the child she loved so much with a proper family, with a man with shoulders broad enough to carry that weight easily and safely, filled her with unexpected relief. How much easier all those decisions that would need to be made down through the years would be if there were others to share them with her, for her to turn to, others who—unlike James's sister—would not reject her nephew.

Rocco Leopardi might not reject Josh, but he was making it plain what he thought of *her*, and instinctively Julie wanted to defend herself and refute his accusations. She began to say indignantly,

'But I am not—' and then wondered if it would be wise to tell him that she was not Josh's mother. He might have given her his word that she and Josh would not be separated, but that word had been given to her as Josh's mother, not his aunt—even if, as his aunt, she was also his legal guardian. Julie had no idea why she felt the need to conceal her true relationship to Josh, only that instinctively somehow she did.

'You're not what? Distraught at the thought of Antonio's death? No, I can see that,' Rocco observed as he held open the car door for her to get in. 'But then it was hardly a long-standing relationship that you had with him, was it?'

As she sank into the luxury of the blissfully comfortable seat Julie dipped her head, knowing that she now had to either accept his insults or confess that she wasn't Josh's mother.

'What happened to…to Antonio?' Julie had no idea why she was asking. She had not even known the man, after all, even if the news of his death had come as a shock.

'He died as he lived,' Rocco told her curtly. 'Believing that nothing and no one mattered apart from himself.'

Now Julie looked at him, taken aback by the contempt she could see in his gaze.

'He was showing off, driving a car he did not have the skill to control far too fast.'

Judy had said that she and Antonio were two of a kind, and from what Rocco had just told her it sounded as if she had been right, Julie acknowledged.

'However, if the child is of our blood,' Rocco continued curtly, 'then no matter how carelessly he was conceived he is of us—a part of us, Leopardi.'

Instinctively Julie wanted to tell him that there was no way Josh could be a Leopardi, and that it was James who was his father. She had been so determined to believe that Josh was James's son that she was still in shock from the sudden appearance of Rocco Leopardi, with his unwanted reminder that not even her sister had known just who Josh's father was.

The look in the leopard eyes whilst he had been speaking had been all fiercely proud severity and intent. He really meant what he was saying, Julie recognised. His words revealed to her the centuries-old proud belief of a family who prized their blood and honoured their responsibility towards it above everything and everyone else.

It was slowly beginning to sink in for her just what it would mean if Josh *was* Antonio Leopardi's son. A part of her wanted to state that she knew beyond any shadow of a doubt that Antonio could not be Josh's father—but, even if Rocco Leopardi would accept that claim, how much damage might she be doing to Josh if she were to deny him his right to a heritage that might be his?

It was his need and his well-being that she must put first from now on, until the day came when he was old enough to make such a decision for himself. After all, she loved him for himself equally as much as she loved the thought of him being James's son.

Just as she could not and must not refuse to go to Sicily and reject whatever financial advantage for Josh that visit might bring about, so equally she must not deny the fact that he could be, as Rocco Leopardi has so emotively put it, 'of Leopardi blood'.

It was obvious that Rocco Leopardi did not know about her sister's death and thought that she was Judy. Julie's lips twisted in a small sad smile. If he had known her sister he would never have mistaken them. Both of them had disliked the fact that their parents had chosen such similar names for them, but it had been Judy who had complained about it most frequently when they had been growing up, stating that it was silly when they were so different and she was so much prettier and more popular than Julie.

'What will happen when we reach Sicily?'

'Our family doctor will do a DNA test.'

'But that could have been done here,' Julie protested.

Ignoring her outburst, Rocco continued, 'It will be at least five days before it is possible to have the results of this test. If it should prove that the child was fathered by Antonio then naturally that will mean that your son is part of our family.'

'And if they do not prove that?' Julie asked huskily, unable to bring herself to look at him as she made what she knew in Rocco Leopardi's eyes would be an admission of her lack of morals.

Rocco frowned. Her behaviour was not what he had expected. He had anticipated that her manner would be more coy—cloyingly so—with many protestations of love for Antonio and her conviction that her child *must* be his half-brother's. It seemed out of character that she should talk so openly about the possibility of the child not being Antonio's.

'Then you will be financially recompensed for agreeing to travel to Sicily and given a substantial sum of money in return for your discretion.'

Julie's eyes widened.

'You mean that you will buy my silence?' she guessed shrewdly, watching as Rocco inclined his head in agreement.

How unpalatable and sleazy the whole situation was, Julie thought uncomfortably. She wished desperately that she and Josh did not have to be part of the whole unpleasant situation, but for Josh's sake she had to ignore her own distaste.

'Of course if you already know the father is not Antonio…?'

'No, I can't be sure,' Julie had to admit.

She was telling the truth, Rocco recognised.

The interior or the car smelled of expensive leather mixed with a hint of equally expensive male cologne. Julie turned to look at her sleeping nephew, thankful that she had taken the time to feed and change him before she had left the nursery.

Josh was such a quiet baby. Too quiet, Julie often worried, and the lovely new doctor at their busy local practice had agreed when Julie had raised her concerns with her.

Initially Julie hadn't wanted to betray her dead sister by telling the doctor that she had often worried that Judy neglected her baby, but Josh's health was her responsibility now, and more important to her than any loyalty she might owe a sister whose attitude to life had been opposite to her own and who had often treated her so unkindly.

The sad truth was—as Julie had feared and the doctor had gently confirmed—that poor little Josh had been neglected and malnourished by his mother during the first weeks of his life. Because the infection he had picked up had been left untreated it had compromised his immune system, which had then struggled to combat the winter viruses other babies could throw off. Emotionally too he had suffered—from maternal neglect. Julie had sworn to herself that she would make up for the sad early weeks of his life, and ideally she would have liked to be with him herself twenty-four-seven. But that, of course, was not possible since they were dependent on her income until her parents' estate was settled.

Slowly Josh had started to recognise her and respond, and earlier in the week for the very first time he had smiled at her and held out his arms to be picked up. Just thinking about that precious, wonderful moment now as she looked at him brought a lump of emotion to Julie's throat.

Everything about this car was expensive and new and clean, including the baby seat, and so very different from the shabby second-hand things that were all she had been able to afford once she had realised that many of those to whom her sister had owed money expected *her* to pay off her sister's debts.

Rocco started the car's engine and eased away from the pavement, causing Julie to look at him and demand, 'What are you doing?'

'I'm driving us to the airport,' he told her with exaggerated patience, 'where we shall board a plane to take us home to Sicily.'

Sicily? Now? When she didn't have so much as a change of clothes for Josh, never mind herself, and she hadn't even agreed that they would go—at least not properly.

'We can't do that,' Julie protested wildly.

'Why not?' Rocco asked her.

'There are things I need to do, people I need to tell— my landlord, and the crèche, and where I work. And we… Josh needs…we both need clothes and…and his…'

'You can telephone everyone you need to speak with here from the car. As for everything that the child might need, you may leave that to me.'

Quite plainly he was a man who did not like wasting time, Julie thought weakly, her eyes widening as Rocco pressed a button on the steering wheel of his car and a mobile phone slid out from the dashboard.

It gave Julie a feeling rather like deliberately swimming out of her depth to make the phone calls which were in effect committing her to accompanying Rocco to Sicily.

She was just finishing leaving a halting explanation on the message service at the crèche when a small whimper from the back of the car had her concluding her message quickly, so that she could turn to look at Josh, who was now awake and grizzling.

'Could you stop the car, please?' she asked Rocco, elaborating when he frowned, 'I want to sit in the back with Josh.'

Rocco had pulled over almost before she had stopped speaking, getting out of his own seat whilst she was still unfastening her seat belt to come round to her door and open it for her. He placed his hand beneath her elbow as he helped her out.

His manners certainly could not be faulted, Julie admitted, along with his kissing technique. They were in a class of their own.

Julie froze, hardly daring to breathe, the blood suddenly flooding her face in a rich tide of guilty colour. What on earth had made her think that? She felt shocked and mortified, reduced by her own confusion to stammering slightly as Rocco opened the rear passenger door of the car for her, allowing her to get inside.

She couldn't—dared not—look at him, so she busied herself instead with removing her coat and fussing over Josh, who had stopped crying now but was still awake, whilst from the front of the car she could hear Rocco speaking in what she assumed must be Italian, using the hands-free phone she herself had just used.

As he explained to an exclusive concierge service exactly what he wanted, Rocco watched Julie discreetly in his rearview mirror, and then frowned. He hadn't expected her to be as devoted to her child as she obviously was. That, like the fear of him she had displayed earlier, sat uncomfortably with his pre-assessment of her.

Only now that the decision was made, and its execution taken out of her hands, could she admit to herself how exhausted she felt, Julie admitted. The debilitating and often frightening feeling that it would be easier to crawl than walk, easier to lie down than do either, had been growing steadily these last few months, inexorably stalking her until at times she came face to face with it and realised how much stronger and more powerful it was than her.

The peace and comfort of the car, along with its steady movement, were lulling her to sleep, but she must not give in to her aching need to close her eyes. She must think of Josh. She must put his needs first....

Rocco glanced in his driving mirror to see if Julie was still asleep. It was nearly an hour now since he had seen her eyes close, and she had fallen asleep with the speed of a child. But even in sleep her hand rested protectively on the side of the baby carrier. No one else could touch it or the child in it without waking her, Rocco suspected.

The smell of cheap wet wool being warmed by the car's heating system reached his nostrils. His fastidious eldest brother would quickly have shown his displeasure, Rocco reflected, but he was more down to earth. In the construction industry one had to be.

His father had been furious when he had learned what

Rocco planned to do with the land left to him by his mother's uncle. A resort with its own private airfield on what should have been Leopardi land—it was unthinkable, an abomination, a betrayal of everything that the name Leopardi stood for: tradition, continuation of the male line, pride and secrecy.

'On my *mother's* land,' Falcon had corrected his father, stepping in to shield his younger sibling from their father's wrath, just as he had done so many times during their childhood.

They said that blood was thicker than water, but it was the Leopardi blood he shared with his brothers to which Rocco was loyal—not the Leopardi blood of his father.

The lights of the airport, gleaming on the wet tarmac, shone up ahead of them through the winter night, and as Rocco brought the car's speed down Julie woke up, not knowing just where she was for a few seconds, and then— when she did—looking anxiously at Josh, relieved to see that he was still asleep before glancing self-consciously towards the front of the car. She could see Rocco's hands resting on the steering wheel, and for some reason the sight of them made her heart jerk against her ribs. It was an effort to drag her gaze away from him to look out of the car window instead.

They were turning off the main access road, swinging round down a smooth road and up to a checkpoint, where Rocco produced a plastic card for the security guard—who saluted him before raising the barrier.

The car picked up speed, and Julie's eyes widened in disbelief as she realised that, no, she wasn't seeing things. Rocco *was* driving right up to the sleek silver jet parked on the tarmac in front of them.

* * *

'Good evening, sir.'

Rocco smiled at Nigel Rowlins, the first officer of his private jet, as he opened the door of the Mercedes.

'Good evening, Nigel. All set to go, are we?'

'Yes, indeed, sir. Flight plan's logged and approved, the deliveries have arrived and have been loaded. Passport control's on alert.'

Rocco nodded his head.

They were flying to Sicily in a private jet? Why hadn't she realised that that might be the case? Because she wasn't used to people whose lifestyle included private jets, that was why, Julie answered her own question wryly.

She had been banking on them going through the departure area so that she could at least buy some necessities for Josh—luckily his bottles and heater were in the nappy bag, along with a couple of changes of clothes. And she needed a change of clothes for herself—the cheaper the better, since she only had a tiny bit of cash on her. Now what was she going to do? She realised that Rocco Leopardi had said that he would deal with things, but she neither expected nor wanted to him to buy anything for them. There was no way she wanted to feel beholden to him. No way at all.

Perhaps he had forgotten what he had said? Perhaps she should remind him?

She took a deep breath and said quietly, 'I was hoping we'd have some time to buy clothes.'

The soft, quiet voice was at odds with the intent behind her words—which said quite plainly that she'd been expecting him to take her on a shopping spree.

'You will find everything you are likely to need is already on board,' Rocco told her dismissively.

'Everything?' Julie queried uncertainly. How could that be? He hadn't so much as asked her what Josh might need.

'Everything.' Rocco confirmed grimly. What was she expecting? *Carte blanche* at Heathrow's duty-free designer shops? Tough, he decided unsympathetically as he got out of the car, effectively putting an end to their conversation, and going to open the door nearest to Josh. He reached in to lift him out of the baby seat, leaving Julie to gather together her coat, the baby bag and her own handbag, and follow him out onto the tarmac.

It was dark now, and cold, causing Julie to shiver.

The shock of the cold air after the warmth of the car woke Josh, and his thin, fretful cry jerked on Julie's heart-strings. It was too cold for him out here, and he needed feeding.

Rocco Leopardi was still holding Josh. Turning away from her, he strode towards the plane, taking the steps two at a time with easy, relaxed energy, leaving her no option other than to hurry after him.

If the uniformed steward waiting in the luxuriously furnished cabin was surprised by her appearance, or the fact that his boss was holding a shabbily dressed crying baby, he was too well trained to show it, simply offering to take Julie's coat from her and asking her what she would like to drink.

'Something hot rather than something alcoholic, Russell,' Rocco Leopardi was answering on her behalf, and the fact that he was not allowing her to make her own decision filled Julie with an unfamiliar and foolish desire to insist that actually she wanted champagne, even though in reality she rarely touched alcohol.

Instead she gave the steward a diffident smile and asked uncertainly, 'If there is somewhere to heat Josh's bottle?'

'Of course. I've got a choice of formula in the galley for when you want it, and the cot and everything else has been set up in the sleeping cabin.'

'It's no wonder he looks so whey-faced and undersized, since you obviously aren't feeding him yourself.'

Rocco's criticism, voiced the moment the steward had disappeared with the bottle Julie had removed from the shabby nappy bag, caused her to stare at him. The colour came and went in her face as she searched and failed to find a response that would have the effect of putting him in his place and ensuring that he knew just how seriously she took her responsibilities towards Josh.

'I have to go out to work,' was all she could think of to say, and she prayed that he wouldn't make any comment about expressed breast milk being better than formula.

Ignoring her response, he continued, 'As Russell just said, you'll find everything you need in the inner cabin. It will be a three-hour flight, so feel free to snatch a couple of hours' sleep yourself, if you wish.' He frowned when he saw the wariness in her eyes, demanding, 'What's that look for? You are perfectly safe. I can assure you that I'm not desperate enough to lower myself to make use of Antonio's leavings.'

Dangerously, the repugnance in his voice actually hurt her. Why? There had only ever been one man she had wanted to desire her, and that had been James. He *had* desired her— until Judy had bewitched him and taken him from her. She certainly didn't desire Rocco Leopardi, and she never would.

The steward had reappeared.

'We'll be taking off soon,' he told her. 'If you'd like to come with me, we've got a sky cot set up for the baby in the sleeping compartment.'

Obediently, Julie turned towards the door he was indicating. That was the trouble with her, James had once told her. She was far too responsible and law-abiding, What he had meant, of course, was that compared to Judy—who had been spectacularly good at taking risks and getting away with taking them—she was dull and boring.

But she was also alive, Julie reminded herself sadly, whilst Judy, James and two sets of loving parents were all dead. And all because Judy had wanted a big candyfloss wedding in a fairy-tale castle. The same castle where a well-known glamour model celebrity had married.

As the steward opened the door into the sleeping compartment, Julie saw that Rocco Leopardi was busy working on a computer which had appeared almost magically at the touch of a button on the desk in front of him.

What the steward had referred to as a sleeping 'compartment' was far from being the utilitarian and small space Julie had imagined. It was, in fact, the most luxurious bedroom she had ever seen.

Thick pale-coloured carpet covered the floor, merging with equally pale walls. The bed—surely the widest Julie had ever seen, and equally surely, she decided, with distaste, intended for the sort of sex games and romps her sister had freely and boastfully indulged in rather than merely for a good night's sleep—barely filled a third of the floor space.

'The controls for the bed are here,' the steward was telling her. 'You can raise it to read or watch TV.' He pressed several buttons on the remote he was holding in demonstration, causing one half of the bed to tilt up as though it were a chair, whilst almost magically a huge TV screen appeared from a narrow cupboard on the opposite wall.

'We've set up the sky cot here,' he added. 'Right next to the seat you'll need to strap yourself into for take-off and landing. It pulls down out of the wall, like so. The bathroom and dressing room are through that door next to the bed. I've unpacked a few things for you and the baby, and hung them up. I'll be serving dinner in about half an hour. If Rocco follows his normal form he'll want to work as soon as he's had dinner, so you might want to think about getting a few hours' sleep. We'll be landing shortly before one in the morning. I don't know what the baby's exact routine is, but I shall be on standby if you need me for anything. I'll bring the heated milk as soon as we're airborne.'

Julie would have liked to tell him that she'd rather eat her food on her own, and as far away from Rocco Leopardi as possible, but she didn't—because she didn't want to cause the steward any extra work.

A light above the door started to flash.

'Take-off,' the steward told her briskly.

Two minutes later Josh was strapped into his sky cot and Julie into her seat.

CHAPTER TWO

'HERE'S the baby's milk, and I've brought you a pot of tea.'

Julie nodded her thanks to the steward. Their take-off had been smooth, but even so it had left Josh fretful, and he was grizzling as Julie lifted him out of the sky cot to feed him. She tested the heat of the formula and then settled down with him. At first he sucked greedily, but then to her dismay he suddenly rejected the teat, crying in pain and drawing his legs up towards his body.

He was having an attack of colic, Julie recognised anxiously as she tried to comfort him, gently rubbing his torso the way the doctor had shown her.

To her relief, almost immediately he started to relax. The disruption to his routine meant that this feed was late. He must have been so hungry, poor baby, that he'd tried to take it too fast. He was tired as well.

Ten minutes later, when he had only managed a third of the bottle, Julie admitted defeat, putting the bottle to one side and lifting him against her shoulder to wind him. Almost immediately he was sick, covering both himself and Julie's jumper with sour-smelling sticky formula.

He was crying again now, and Julie felt a bit like crying herself. It was so important that he got the nourishment he needed, but the attacks of colic he suffered meant that feeding times had become a nightmare of anxiety for her—

even though the doctor had assured her that she was doing everything correctly.

He felt so light. Lighter than he had yesterday? Was he losing weight instead of gaining it?

She'd have to change him and then try again, Julie acknowledged, replacing the bottle in the thoughtfully provided insulated container before carrying Josh through into the bathroom.

Mirrored walls gave back to her an unprepossessing and unwanted image of her own too-thin body and wan face. The pair of them looked half-starved, pinched, and with too-sharp features, she admitted, as she stripped off Josh's soiled clothes and placed him down on his changing mat.

To her astonishment, the steward had told her that there were clean baby clothes and nappies in the drawers in the dressing room, along with clothes for herself. How Rocco Leopardi had managed to arrange that she had no idea— but perhaps when you were a Leopardi everything was possible. She suspected that Rocco would believe that being a Leopardi meant that it *should* be possible.

It would be a long time before she could forget the feel of those hard hands on her body, and even longer—if ever—before she could forget the feel of his mouth on hers. As an adult woman who earned her own living, she found the thought of wearing clothes bought for her by someone else made her body stiffen in angry rejection— but, whilst she might be able to afford the luxury of pride and self-denial for herself, she couldn't do that to Josh.

When she found the carefully folded baby clothes she looked at them with a mixture of anger and pain. Designer label baby clothes. What a shocking waste of money. All Josh or indeed any baby needed, surely, was simply clothes that were warm and clean and fitted? Even so, it was hard to stop herself from drawing in a small breath of delight as she removed a complete matching set of baby boy's clothes in soft blue, cream and beige. The little shirt had an identifiable designer check, the beige trousers were vaguely 'cargo' style, and the cardigan was blue and trimmed again with the same check—like the socks that completed the outfit. Even the babygro to go under everything had its own designer logo, and the disposable nappies were not only the right size, but were also 'boy' nappies—a luxury she had never been able to afford, and which she had told herself was little more than a cynical marketing ploy designed to add yet another expense to being a parent.

It was impossible to even think of touching such exquisite clothes whilst she was still wearing her formula-encrusted jumper—which, of course, would have to be washed and somehow dried in time for her to put it back on before she left the plane.

In the bathroom, Josh had started to cry. Quickly Julie pulled the jumper over her head. She needed a shower every bit as much as Josh needed a bath, so she might as well remove her skirt and her tights as well.

If there was one thing Josh did enjoy it was his bath, and with all the splashing around he did she'd be better off bathing him wearing only her bra and knickers.

It was amazing what wealth could do: nothing that Josh might need had been forgotten—right down to a baby bath and luxury products that smelled deliciously of vanilla.

Lifting Josh out of the bath, Julie wrapped him in a towel and carried him through into the bedroom, where she finally managed to coax him to take a bit more of his formula.

He was falling asleep as she put a clean nappy on him and then fastened him into a brand-new, deliciously soft sleep suit patterned with floppy-eared rabbits.

Kissing him tenderly, she put him in the sky cot, making sure that he was secure and safe before returning to the bathroom, where she washed out her jumper, cleaned up the baby bathtime mess, and then finally—blissfully—stepped into the shower.

In the main salon, Rocco finished writing thee-mail he was sending his elder brother and then tapped the 'send' button, mentally reviewing the events that had led to the search for Antonio's child.

Rocco hadn't planned to spend Christmas with his father and his brothers. He'd intended to fly to Colorado to stay with friends and ski, but then his eldest brother had telephoned him with the news that their father was terminally ill, so Rocco had flown home instead.

Home. Rocco lifted his arms to link his hands behind his head, exhaling as he did so. He was naturally strongly built, but the hard physical labour he had done during his teenage years, when he had preferred to work on a building site during his summer holidays rather than be financially tethered to his father, had honed and developed his muscles in a way that had left a legacy Rocco's tailors deplored and his lovers adored. Happily, one of the benefits of being a billionaire was that he could afford to have his shirts hand-made and made to measure, to accommodate the powerful muscles of his chest and upper arms.

Falcon, aesthete that he was, tended to look down his long, proud nose at what he somewhat derisorily termed

Rocco's 'prize fighter torso'. Alessandro, his second brother, was less critical.

'Who says that Father is dying?' Rocco had asked Falcon cynically. 'Because if it is the old man himself…'

'It isn't. I've spoken to the specialist myself. He gives Father a year at the most. I see no point in any of us pretending that we're grief stricken,' Falcon had continued coolly. 'At least here amongst ourselves we can be open and honest without being judged as uncaring.'

From the high windows of the ancient fortress that had been their childhood home it was possible—just—to see the summit of Mount Etna. Etna, like their father, breathed bellicosity, fire and danger—and like their father it was a symbol of power. The kind of power that could be cruel and destructive.

Their father's power, though, was waning, if Falcon was to be believed, and his eldest brother had never given Rocco reason to do anything other than believe him.

It had been a solemn moment. Their father—the head of one of Sicily's greatest, most powerful and rich aristocratic dynasties—was dying.

At thirty-four, a billionaire in his own right via his own endeavours, and the least loved and favoured of his father's three living sons, Rocco acknowledged that he should have been the last person to be swayed by the deathbed plea of a man who had spent his entire adult life manipulating others to his own will, and who was responsible for the death of Rocco's own mother. No more children, their father had been told after the births of Falcon and Alessandro, but he had ignored that warning, and his delicate wife had died within hours of giving birth to her third son.

Her death had left a bitterness and a canker at the heart

of the family, dividing father and sons, and that bitterness had been driven deeper when their father had married his long-term mistress within a year of their mother's death.

However, tradition was burned deep into the hearts of the Leopardi family, handed down from generation to generation from the time when the Saracens had been driven from the land by the Normans and the first Leopardi had taken as his wife the daughter of the Saracen lord who had owned the vast, rich tracts of land that had passed with her to her husband. Those traditions involved putting the family and what was best for it first, rather than any individual member. They had held fast and become so tightly woven into the Leopardi culture that they were bred into their blood and souls.

As Falcon had said after he had spoken with them, despite their lack of love for their dying father they could not simply turn their backs and walk away from the duty he had imposed on them all.

They had been summoned to their father's bedchamber—a lofty, feudally styled room, hung with the banners of past battle glories—where their father had been lying almost in state in the vast double bed.

It had been in this bed that they had all been conceived, including Antonio, their late half-brother—who, if their father was to be believed, had confided to him before he died that he had fathered a child.

'There is a child—born to an Englishwoman. And that child is a Leopardi.'

Their father's long thin fingers had curled round the silver head of his cane and he'd rapped it hard on the floor.

'It is Leopardi and Sicilian by its father's blood. He or she belongs here at Castello Leopardi, with this family.'

'And the mother of this child?' Alessandro had asked.

'Antonio did not have time to say her name.'

Rocco remembered thinking that Antonio probably hadn't even been able to remember it.

The old Prince's retort had been typical of his way of thinking and his way of life. 'This woman, in carrying Antonio's child and keeping it from us, his family, is guilty of theft. The child must be brought here. It is his birthright and ours. Antonio was my son.'

And his most beloved son. They had all known that.

'This child belongs here. It was Antonio's dying wish to me that this should be so.'

'Having no doubt refused flatly to accept any responsibility whatsoever for it during his lifetime, knowing our dear late half-brother as we do,' Alessandro had murmured dulcetly to Rocco, out of earshot of their father.

'That is all very well, Father, but we do not know the identity of the mother of Antonio's child,' Falcon had reminded their father, 'since Antonio neglected to tell you her name.'

Their father had refused to listen.

'The child must be found.'

That had been the Prince's living will and his dying demand, and in the end they had had no honourable option as Leopardis other than to concede defeat.

Two weeks later they had all been back in their father's bedchamber, to hear the results of the investigations Falcon had put in hand.

'We now know that out of the multitude of women Antonio appears to have disported himself with last summer, only one went on to have a child,' Falcon informed them all. 'This woman was a British holidaymaker, attending the Cannes Film Festival at the time. Not entirely surprising, since Antonio had a taste for a combination of blonde hair and loose morals. However, there is no guarantee that it is this child to which Antonio was referring. It is true that it was conceived at the right time, but the only way we can be sure that the child is Antonio's is via a DNA test, and for that we shall need the mother's cooperation. In my view the simplest thing would be to approach the mother and—'

'The child belongs here.' Their father had interrupted Falcon angrily. 'But only the child. The mother is nothing—little more than a slut who tempted and tormented my poor son until in his craziness his life was stolen from him and he was stolen from me. My beloved and most precious child—your brother. Your youngest brother. Where were you when he needed protecting from this harlot, whoever she is? You, Falcon, were in Florence, presiding over copyists and their fake works of art. You, Alessandro, were buying yet more jets for your airline— and you, Rocco, were too busy overseeing the rebuilding of Rome in the middle of the desert, for tourists to go and gawp at. No doubt flown there by your brother's airline and decorated by Falcon's copyists.'

They had all been aware of his angry contempt. But then they had all been aware of their father's contempt for them all their lives. They were, after all, the sons of the woman their father had been forced to marry against his will.

Oh, yes, their father had been passionate in his contempt for them—expending energy he did not have in his determination to inject every bit of passion and persuasion into his voice as he extracted from them their reluctant promise that they would find the Englishwoman who had carried their dead brother's child and that they would bring that child back to Sicily to be raised as a Leopardi.

Antonio himself could not be restored to their father since he was dead—killed in a senseless, stupid accident, showing off in his new car. So typical of him and so unacceptable to their father, who had adored the son of his second wife—the woman who had been his mistress during his marriage to their own mother.

If Falcon was right—and given Antonio's well-known and well-documented taste in downmarket females, he probably was—the mother of his child would pretty soon recognise the commercial value of her child, and would want to take full advantage of that fact.

The Leopardi men might not publicly boast about their high social status or their wealth, but that did not alter the fact that both existed.

As a first step toward ascertaining if the child was Antonio's, it had been agreed that the mother would have to be persuaded to allow the child to undergo DNA tests, without being allowed access to either the press or a lawyer whilst they were awaiting the results.

All three brothers had agreed that until such time as the child had either been confirmed as Antonio's or proved not to be, the mother must be kept secluded from any contact with others—either voluntarily or, more feasibly, given the type of woman she would be, not voluntarily.

'You mean we shall have to bring this woman to Sicily and keep her here until we have ascertained whether or not Antonio was the father of her child?' Alessandro had asked Falcon, frowning disapprovingly as he did so.

Falcon had simply shrugged aside his brother's distaste, stating coolly, 'Unless you have a better idea?'

None of them had, but Rocco had had another issue with which he was not happy.

'Our father has stated that it is the child he wants, but not the mother, so that it can be raised as a Leopardi. Apart from the damage it could do to a child to be deprived of any contact with its mother, given the way Antonio turned out—'

'You are worrying unnecessarily, Rocco,' Falcon had told him. 'Our father's life expectancy is limited. It is true that he is not quite as close to death's door as he would have us think—he could have another year—but ultimately it is us who will decide the future of this child, if it should be Antonio's. I assure you that I share your feelings with regard to the child's mother. Whatever decision is made about the child's future, that future will include its mother. You have my word on that and so will she. No child should grow up without its mother.'

They had all looked at one another. Rocco knew how badly the death of their mother had affected both his brothers. However, it wasn't true that he himself had no knowledge of her. She had after all carried him close to her heart for nine months, and he had been born knowing that—knowing too that he had lost her.

'And if this child is not Antonio's?' Alessandro had asked.

'Then she will be recompensed for her co-operation—and her future silence regarding this debacle,' Falcon had answered.

'It is damnable that our father should impose this duty on us,' Alessandro had said angrily.

'Damnable, indeed. But we shall be damned if we do not accept the duty imposed on us by our father. The duty to accept such a charge—father to son—came to us with our conception. It is encoded in our genes. We cannot change that any more than we can change our inherited bone structure or the blood that runs through our veins. Antonio's child, if he or she exists, is of those genes and therefore of us. We have a duty and a responsibility towards it that goes beyond any promise we have made our father.'

Who could argue with that? Not him, Rocco admitted now, although he *had* argued—and very passionately— with Falcon's announcement that since he had commitments overseas he could not escape, and because Alessandro was in the middle of negotiating tricky new contracts for his airline business it would fall to Rocco to go to London and persuade this Julie Simmonds to return to Sicily with him, bringing her child with her.

'Now, the first thing we need to do is persuade the woman to come to Sicily with her child, and…'

Rocco grimaced now, remembering how Falcon had paused and then looked at him.

'Me? Why me?' Rocco had objected, with a lifetime's worth of a youngest sibling's indignation and resentment.

'I have just explained,' Falcon had pointed out, adding firmly, 'In performing this task you are carrying a heavy responsibility for all of us, Rocco.'

Trust Falcon to make it sound as though he had been awarded a prize instead of being dumped on, Rocco thought grimly now. He wasn't liking the 'duty' which, according to Falcon, his genes imposed on him any more than he had expected. Perhaps the streak of rebelliousness within him that pulled against the iron grip of the Leopardi family code was something that had come down to him from his mother? She had, after all, been only part-Sicilian. *Her* father's family had come from Florence—the city that Falcon loved so much.

Rocco glanced at his watch.

They had been in the air for close on an hour. He was hungry and ready for his dinner. The steward had assured him that he had told Julie Simmonds when he would be serving their meal. If she was one of those women who believed that good time keeping was an unnecessary nuisance that need not apply to her, she needed to have the error of her ways pointed out to her.

Rocco stood up and strode towards the bedroom door.

CHAPTER THREE

THE shower area of the bathroom was designed as a wet room, without any protective screen, and the water was blissfully hot and there was plenty of it. Such a treat after the miserable trickle of never more than lukewarm water that came from her own shower.

Julie acknowledged that she had stayed under its wonderful spray longer than perhaps she should, but even so it was still a shock when the bathroom door—which she hadn't thought to lock—was suddenly pulled open, and she saw Rocco Leopardi standing there, fully dressed, his gaze travelling slowly and deliberately the full length of her naked body. Such a shock, in fact, that Julie didn't even think to cover either her sex or her breasts until it was far too late and that gaze had swept all the way back up over her and come to rest on her flushed face.

'Well, well—a natural blonde. Now, that *is* a surprise,' Rocco drawled mockingly.

What was also a surprise, although he had no intention of feeding her vanity by saying so, was just how erotic he found the sight of the naturally neat rather than sleekly waxed tousle of damp blonde curls that clung to the gentle rise of her flesh, just above the sensually shaped and softly closed lips that concealed the inner intimacy of her sex.

Already, and against his own wishes, he could feel himself responding to what he could see.

She might be a natural blonde, but she was every bit as thin as he had suspected, he told himself, hoping to channel his thoughts into rejection of her rather than desire. Then, yes—but her breasts were far fuller than he had imagined, and natural too, perfectly shaped, with a full lower curve and nipples that tilted erotically upwards. A party girl's breasts, not a nursing mother's. In focusing on her sexuality she was depriving her child. But then a woman like her would do that, wouldn't she?

It had been her total abandonment to the sensual pleasure he had seen in every line of her body as she had stood naked beneath the shower, her face tilted up towards the water, her eyes closed and every inch of her flesh showing its joy, that was responsible for the hardening of his own flesh right now, Rocco acknowledged. Something about that abandonment made him want to walk into the shower and share it with her. It made him want to take her swiftly and hotly, his flesh sinking deep into hers, whilst her muscles closed around him, in a primitive shared physical orgy of greedy pleasure and hedonistic satisfaction. Like rough wine on a hot day after hard physical activity—the base, thoughtless satisfaction of a momentary fierce need.

If he did feel like that then he was a fool, Rocco told himself cynically. She was a piece of flesh that had no doubt been handed out to any number of other men before his brother, and would be handed out to others. That was her choice, and he certainly wasn't moralizing, but her type did nothing for him. Right now the only hunger he wanted to recognise was the hunger that was driving him, which came from his stomach and not from his loins, he told himself determinedly.

Reaching for a towel, he threw it towards her, telling her coolly, 'Russell is waiting to serve dinner. You've got five minutes. And let me warn you that my temper doesn't improve with hunger.'

Five minutes. Julie didn't even bother looking at the clothes which Russell the steward had said he'd hung in the wardrobe. She simply dried her body, plaited her wet hair, and then pulled on one of the thick white towelling robes she found hanging on the bathroom door.

She was out of breath and her heart was pounding when she slid into the chair that Rocco Leopardi pulled out for her.

'Four minutes and fifty-five seconds,' he commented as he went round to the other side of the elegantly set table and sat down.

If Rocco Leopardi found anything odd in the fact that she had chosen to eat wearing a bathrobe, he obviously wasn't going to say so. Which was just as well, Julie thought fiercely, because if he did she would tell him that it wasn't *her* choice that she was here on board his private jet, without a clean top to replace the one on which Josh had been sick.

It was, in fact, almost impossible to believe that they were actually on a plane and flying, Julie acknowledged, as she looked towards the bedroom door, which she had left propped open so that she could hear Josh if he woke up and started to cry.

Russell arrived with soup, putting Julie's down in front of her and then placing a linen napkin on her lap before she could do so herself.

The soup—lobster bisque—smelled heavenly. Julie couldn't remember the last time she had sat down to eat any kind of meal, never mind one like this, with beautiful napery and china, silver cutlery and Michelin-star-type food.

Russell was pouring them both a glass of wine. Julie looked at hers a little uncertainly. She wasn't a big drinker and, given that she hadn't eaten all day, alcohol on an empty stomach might not be a good idea.

'I dare say your tastes run more to Cristal?' Rocco said, seeing her expression and mistaking its cause.

Julie didn't bother to respond. She doubted he would believe her if she were to tell him that she had never even tasted Cristal champagne.

The soup was delicious, but very rich—too rich, Julie suspected, for her digestive system, which was more accustomed to baked beans on toast and porridge: cheap, filling food that somehow she never seemed to get the time to finish eating.

She took a quick sip of her wine and then wished she hadn't, when the alcohol went straight to her head.

If she was trying to impress him with her make-up-free face, and by wearing something that enveloped her from the neck virtually down to her ankles, she was wasting her time, Rocco thought grimly.

For one thing the bathrobe was gaping, so that every time she lifted her soup spoon he could see a bit more of the vulnerable curve of her throat and the soft pale skin below it, where her breasts lifted against the thick toweling, and for another he already had a perfectly recorded image of her standing naked beneath the shower imprinted on his memory.

The soup was good. Julie lifted another spoonful to her mouth and then paused, listening as she turned her head in the direction of the open bedroom door.

'Josh is awake,' she told Rocco, putting her spoon down. 'I'd better go to him. He might be hungry.'

'You've only just fed him,' Rocco pointed out as he too heard the thin, fretful cry from the bedroom.

'He's had a digestive problem which means that he needs small, regular feeds,' Julie told him.

Rocco frowned as he listened to her. 'Perhaps,' he pointed out, 'if you were less concerned about preserving your admittedly exceptionally well-shaped breasts and were feeding him as nature intended babies should be fed, he'd be more satisfied?'

Clearly her argument that she needed to work hadn't registered. Julie longed to tell him that his criticism was unfounded, but how could she without revealing the fact that she was not Josh's mother?

An unfamiliar feeling gathered inside her in a tense ball. A mixture of self-consciousness—she wasn't used to men commenting on the shape of her breasts—anxiety— she could hardly tell him *why* she wasn't breastfeeding— and something that had nothing to do with either of those feelings but instead had rather a lot to do with the knowledge that he had seen her naked, had her body responding to that fact. She hurried into the bedroom, glad of an excuse to escape from the table and the unwanted proximity of Rocco Leopardi.

Josh's fretful cry increased in volume the minute he saw her. At least now he recognised her and knew that she was the source of his food, Julie acknowledged, as she lifted him out of the travel cot. She'd have to ask Russell if she could use the galley to make Josh up a fresh bottle. She felt his nappy. He was dry and clean. She knew from experience that if she put him down he would get more upset and start to scream. Because Judy had often picked him up and then put him back down when he was hungry without feeding him? Her late sister had been the first to admit that she wasn't maternal, and that she had found the responsibilities of motherhood an onerous and unwanted burden.

Holding him against her shoulder, Julie popped a dummy in his mouth and carried him back to the main cabin, where Russell was clearing away their soup bowls.

'I need to make Josh a fresh bottle,' Julie told him.

'No problem,' he assured her. 'Everything is ready in the galley. I can't hold back the lamb cutlets much longer, though.'

'I don't want to interrupt your meal,' Julie told Rocco immediately. 'Josh can wait until it's been served, then I'll go and feed him in the other cabin.'

Her comment about the baby was made so naturally that it was impossible to accuse her of trying to score points, but at the same time it so directly opposed the selfish, non-maternal character he'd assigned her it made Rocco frown. He didn't like having his judgements challenged— especially when the person doing the challenging was himself.

'I rather think that Russell was thinking about your dinner as much as mine,' he told Julie succinctly, shaking his head as the steward reached for the wine bottle to refill his glass.

'Oh.' Julie smiled at the steward. A warm, natural smile that lit up her pale and thin face, illuminating it with the illusion—or was it the past shadow?—of a delicate, piquant beauty. 'That's kind of you, but I'm not really hungry.'

Russell nodded and headed back towards the galley.

He had just disappeared inside it when Josh spat out his dummy, his face creasing up as he started to cry.

'You'd better sort his food out,' Rocco announced. He had to raise his voice slightly over the sound of Josh's cries, and he wasn't looking very pleased.

Josh was probably getting on Rocco Leopardi's nerves, Julie thought, hugging the baby even more protectively. He was the kind of man—rich, powerful and no doubt spoiled—who wasn't used to having his wishes or himself taking second place to anything or anyone. No doubt when he had children they would be presented to their father only when he wished them to be. It would be someone else who would be there for the sleepless nights, the colic, and all the other exhausting aspects of parenthood.

He was the kind of man who would enjoy creating his children, though.

The thought slipped past the gates that should have barred it. Then, like a serpent, once it was there on the fertile ground from which it had been banished it luxuriated in its freedom and soon found a willing accomplice to listen to its dangerous story in the shape of a female instinct Julie hadn't even known she possessed until now.

It struck too swiftly for her to escape its deadly venom. One minute she was picturing Rocco Leopardi as a selfish father—the next she was imagining him as an arrogantly sensual lover, wanting to impregnate his woman, wanting to make his mark on the future via the creation of a child that would carry his genes into that future with it.

Inside her head she could see the face of the woman, and in it her intense pleasure—*her* face.

Shock gripped her body in a violent tremor.

'I'll go through to the galley and sort out Josh's bottle,' Julie said, desperate to get away from Rocco even whilst she calmed her frantic thoughts. They ricocheted around inside her head in every direction in their flight to escape from what she had 'seen'.

Turning on her heel, she bolted for the galley, her heart jumping inside her chest in a panicky, unsteady rhythm that made her feel slightly sick.

'I'm really sorry about this,' she apologised to the steward as he looked up at her, 'but I think Josh is getting on Rocco's nerves. I thought I'd better come and do his bottle.' As she spoke she was measuring out the formula with practised ease, whilst holding Josh.

'No worries,' Russell reassured her calmly.

The lamb cutlets he was just sliding onto a serving dish decorated with wilted radicchio and mint leaves, before ornamenting them with white frilled 'caps', looked and smelled delicious, but Julie's anxiety about Josh had killed her appetite. She just hoped he would take his feed this time, and not have another attack of colic.

Josh was still crying when she carried him back to the bedroom, where she settled herself down in a chair with him and offered him his bottle.

Surely there was no sound more satisfying than the hungry sucking and assorted snuffling sounds made by a baby who was enjoying his feed? Julie thought, smiling when Josh gripped her finger tightly as she held the bottle and he held on to her. She stifled a small yawn, and then a much larger one. Josh released the teat of the bottle, and looked up at her, but then reached for it again when she made to take it away.

Five minutes later Julie could see that his eyelids looked as heavy with the desire to sleep as hers felt. He was only sucking drowsily now, his eyes tightly closed. Gently she eased the teat away, and then winded him gently before carrying him back to the cot.

Predictably, the minute she put him down his eyes opened wide and his face crumpled. 'It's all right. I'm not going anywhere,' she told him softly.

As though he understood what she was saying he started to relax, and then smiled at her, making her heart turn over with love.

She'd have to stay with him until he'd fallen asleep. She lifted her hand to her mouth to cover another yawn. She might as well lie down for a few minutes. She could see him from the bed, after all, and he could see her...

Rocco had finished his lamb cutlets, drunk his wine, shaken his head in refusal of pudding, and still Julie Simmonds had not re-emerged from the bedroom.

Rocco supposed irritably that he had better go and find out what was going on. He signalled to Russell to clear the table and strode over to the bedroom door, opening it and stepping inside the room, closing the door behind him.

A single lamp illuminated the room. Julie Simmonds was lying fast asleep on top of the bed, still wearing the bathrobe. If anything she looked even more fragile asleep than she did awake. She was lying with one arm out-stretched, so that her hand was touching the side of the travel cot, as though even in her sleep her first concern was for her child. The towelling robe had fallen off her shoulder to reveal the fragility of her shoulder blade and its contrast with the soft fullness of her almost exposed breast.

An unfamiliar feeling shadowed Rocco's thoughts like the melancholic darkness of a deserted and lonely home. He had been born into one of the most patrician and wealthy of Sicilian families, but he had never known the kind of tender maternal love that this child was receiving.

From a mother who was little better than an unpaid whore and who was more concerned about preserving the sexuality of her future than feeding her child?

Was he really trying to tell himself that he was envious of that? So his mother had died within hours of his birth. He had at least been brought up with every material comfort and luxury, and his loss had taught him the value of emotional independence.

Rocco was about to turn away, when a movement from the cot caught his attention. The baby was awake, but quiet—and watching him, Rocco realised. It was impossible to see his features clearly in the shadowy room, but Rocco knew that the boy had dark curly hair, and that his eyes were still blue. He had felt no sense of looking at a child of his own blood. How could he, when as yet it was not known whether or not he was Leopardi? And yet somehow there was something—some feeling within himself, some deep awareness of a child's need to have a strong male protector and a man's need to honour his duty to be the guardian of a child's vulnerability—that called out to him as clearly as though the child himself had reminded him of that duty. Generation to generation, the responsibility was passed down, male to male, and when that golden chain of responsibility for the life of another was broken a small heart was left to bear the pain that was branded on it for ever: an imprint of what it was to be male, neither given nor received.

Someone had fathered this child; someone had to take responsibility for him.

Someone—but not him—not unless it turned out to be Antonio's child, and then he would share the responsibility with his brothers.

The baby wriggled and smiled a wide gummy smile. Rocco started to move closer to the cot and then stepped back, shaking off the primeval feelings that had no place in his logical mind and his busy life.

'We'll be landing in half an hour. Rocco said to warn you that it will be cold and possibly raining.'

'In Sicily?' Somehow Julie had assumed that the island would have warm weather all year round.

'The island faces three different seas, and its winters can be harsh. By the end of this month, though, the tempera-ture will be rising and the weather will be much warmer.'

The steward's entrance had brought Julie out of her un-planned sleep.

He'd brought her a tray of tea when he'd come to wake her, and to warn her that they would soon be landing, but after he'd left her Julie was too busy to have time to pour and drink it.

For one thing Josh had to be changed, and fastened into clean clothes and a padded outdoor all-in-one suit before she could even think about getting ready herself. She doubted somehow that Rocco would have much patience if they delayed him.

To her dismay there was no sign of her wet jumper in

the bathroom, or in fact of any of her own clothes, and there was certainly no time to go and find Russell and ask what had happened to them. Trying not to panic, Julie pulled open the wardrobe door, remembering that the steward had said he had hung her clothes there. Thankfully Josh was content to lie quietly as she stood staring at the things hanging inside the wardrobe, whilst her heart sank.

Designer jeans   she recognised the label as one that Judy had coveted—a silk shirt, a cashmere sweater, and a beautiful trench coat with a thick, warm removable lining swung invitingly in front of her. Timelessly elegant clothes, every single one of them way beyond her budget, never mind all of them together—and paid for by a man who had already shown his contempt for her. Wearing them would be a form of accepting his contempt, accepting his patronage, becoming a Leopardi possession—a woman who could be bought as easily as Antonio Leopardi had bought Judy—but what choice did she have? Her own clothes had vanished. She could hardly leave the plane wearing a towelling bathrobe—which in any case also belonged to Rocco Leopardi.

Almost fiercely she reached for the clothes and pulled them on, her angry movements softening the moment she touched the cashmere and the luxurious silk. It was a crime to treat such beautiful fabrics so harshly and uncaringly. The cashmere clung to the pads of her fingertips, slightly rough from all the domestic work she had to do without the luxury of protective gloves.

She had told herself that she wouldn't wear the expensive leather boots, but in the end she had to, when she found that her shoes had vanished along with everything else.

She was just folding the bathrobe when Russell knocked briefly on the door, and then came in carrying a butter soft suede bag of the type that Julie had seen A-list celebrity mothers toting.

'I've packed all the babe's things in it, and filled a fresh bottle. I'll make sure that everything else is sent on to Villa Rosa for you,' he told Julie with a smile. 'Oh, and you'll need the raincoat.' He pulled a wry face. 'When it rains in Sicily in the winter, it really rains.'

She had her own nappy bag. Designer bags were an affectation and a waste of money, Julie told herself. But the butter-soft suede was already packed full. What was more important— her pride or Josh's comfort? There was no contest, really, was there?

When Julie emerged from the sleeping compartment carrying Josh, Rocco had to admit that the change in their appearance momentarily caught him off guard.

Julie still had her hair in a plait, and her face free of make-up, but somehow that simplicity only served to accentuate how perfectly suited she was to the stylish elegance of what she was wearing. Even the way she was carrying herself had altered, Rocco noted. She was standing taller, her shoulders straighter.

The concierge service had done an excellent job and he must remember to thank them. He had simply instructed them to make sure that enough clothes to last a young mother and her child for a fortnight, including both indoor and outdoor things, were sent to his private jet in time for their flight, along with adequate supplies of baby formula and other necessities.

If he said one word about the clothes he had bought, which she had been forced to wear, she would rip them off and refuse to leave the plane until she had her own clothes back, Julie decided defiantly, lifting her chin. She certainly wasn't going to thank him for them, was she? But somehow she heard herself saying huskily, 'Thank you for…for providing everything for Josh and me. You shouldn't have gone to so much trouble.'

Her voice made it plain that she was more resentful of his generosity than grateful, Rocco acknowledged grimly, and he told her, 'One phone call to a concierge service is hardly going to any trouble.'

He'd put his suit jacket back on, and over it he was wearing a raincoat with the collar turned up—with that special kind of aplomb and style that Italian men were so very good at.

A flashing light warned that their descent was about to begin, and broke the tension. Julie let Russell help her into her seat and fasten Josh into his, glad of the fact that their descent allowed her to escape from further conversation.

CHAPTER FOUR

IT WAS raining—hard. The rain bounced noisily off the umbrella that the steward was struggling to keep open over her against the fierce force of the wind as he escorted her to a waiting car, making sure she was safely inside it and settled comfortably in the rear with Josh in the baby seat before returning to the plane for Rocco.

The bright lights of the landing strip and the airfield illuminated a landscape that could have been anywhere: scrubby vegetation just visible beyond the perimeter fence under the flare of the lights, vanishing into an ink-black darkness that could have been land, sky or sea.

The cream leather upholstery of the car was so luxurious Julie was almost afraid of touching it. She looked at Josh, mentally praying that he would not be sick.

They were soon leaving the airfield and its lights behind them, to be sucked into the rain-lashed darkness. Despite the warmth of the interior of the car, Julie shivered. The darkness was so intense it almost felt as though it was pressing in on the car, driven by the same wind that was forcing the rain against the car windows with a buffeting roar.

She didn't really know very much about Sicily, but she had never imagined it would be subject to this kind of violent weather.

Like a tightly wound spring, abruptly released to

unravel too quickly, thoughts as wild as the night spun frantically through Julie's head. What if Rocco Leopardi's intentions towards Josh were not benign? What if Josh was an obstacle to him in some way? Why hadn't she thought of this before? Who would know—or care—if tonight she and Josh were driven away into the darkness never to return?

Reaction not just to the extraordinary events of the last few hours but also to everything else that had happened over the last few months and which she had refused to allow herself to react to—first for James's sake and then later for Josh's sake—hit her, smashing her self-control and thrusting her headlong into the grip of an attack of panic and self-blame so strong that it seized her breath and made her heart thump so heavily and with such speed that she thought it was going to burst out of her chest.

Rocco knew every centimetre of the single-track road that led from his private airstrip to Villa Rosa, one of the Leopardi country houses, but as always, as he drove round the final sharp curve in the road to reveal the villa up ahead, he felt the familiar surge of pride and pleasure at the sight of it, rising from the fertile plain to dominate the landscape with its elegance.

The sight of the villa materialising virtually out of the darkness, its honey-coloured walls illuminated by the large wrought-iron flambeaux that threw a soft flickering light not just over the building but also over the setting that housed it, brought Julie a merciful release from her anxiety.

Who could not look at something so stunningly architecturally beautiful and not be entranced by the sight of it?

'It's almost too perfect to be real.' Julie couldn't keep the awe from her voice as she stared up at the high portal, where what she assumed must be the Leopardi coat of arms was illuminated by the light of the flambeaux.

'It is real, I assure you,' Rocco drawled. 'It was built in the eighteenth century, originally as a summer retreat from the heat of the city. Caspar Leopardi designed it himself, and brought the very best craftsmen of the day here to work on it. He wanted to combine in the architecture all those things that were Leopardi—thus the front of the villa you see here is built on the classical lines of the eighteenth century, with reference to Greek and Roman architecture and thus the Greek and Roman influence on Sicily, whilst the enclosed courtyard around which the villa is built echoes the Arab influence on the island and on the Leopardi family.

'The flambeaux you can see here on the walls were especially commissioned on the island. Each one embraces a different part of our history via an heraldic design, and the gardens are of the Italianate style that was so popular amongst the English who travelled to Italy in the eighteenth century.'

As he spoke Rocco was driving them through the portal to a formal courtyard dominated by an imposing marble stairway.

'The marble was quarried in Carrera,' Rocco told Julie, 'and the stairs lead up to the *piano nobile*—that is to say the main floor into the formal reception rooms of the villa.'

Julie's face burned with angry pride.

'I do know what *piano nobile* means,' she informed him sharply, but even if he realised he had offended her he certainly wasn't going to apologise, she recognised.

The emotional switchback she had been riding since he had stopped her in the street outside her flat, culminating as it just had with a surge of terror followed by an equally powerful release of that tension, was beginning to take effect on her body, Julie recognised muzzily. She had gone through too much, climbed too far too fast and fallen back too quickly, to maintain any equilibrium. She felt distinctly odd—weak, breathless, trembling inside, whilst her heart raced and thudded.

Rocco had brought the car to a halt in front of the double flight of stone stairs. His arrogant, 'I will take the child,' as he got out of the driver's seat, had Julie rushing feverishly to remove Josh from the baby seat, determined not to let him do so. She held her nephew tightly.

Instead of calming her, the sensation of the night air on her face made her feel slightly sick and dizzy. Holding on to Josh, she looked towards the flight of steps. So many of them, and she felt so very odd and weak—not like herself at all. Way above the porticoed entrance up at the top of the villa the carved stone heads of gargoyles and mystical animals stared down at her. All her growing doubts rushed in on her.

Why had she allowed him to persuade her to come here? Just as soon as she could she was going to demand some proper reassurances and explanations—and a lawyer to hear them, she told herself fiercely as she started to climb the stone steps.

She was halfway up them when it happened—her foot somehow slipping on the wet stone so that she half stumbled forward, with Josh in her arms.

Before she had time to cry out strong arms were gripping them, holding them both safe. She could smell male flesh—alien, and yet at the same time recognised by senses already attuned to him. She could feel male warmth, and had to fight to stop herself from simply wanting to relax into it, to give in to the weakness that had invaded her. She wanted to lie here against him, protected by him, never to have to leave that protection. She wanted his arms to close round her and stay closed round her. She ached almost desperately for a man like this one—a totally male, totally strong man—to lift the burdens she was carrying from her heart and heal the hurt inside her.

What was she thinking? The only man she had ever wanted—the only man she *would* ever want—was dead.

How long had passed? How many minutes had she been lying against him, her heart thumping sickly, too weak to move, whilst shocked tears of reaction and remorse blurred her vision? Too long.

If he hadn't been close enough and quick enough—if she had dropped Josh on the steps—if he had been hurt because of *her*...

'Give me the child. Unless, of course, you *want* to risk hurting him.'

He knew how to hurt her, she recognised. How to sense her weaknesses and use them against her.

Numbly, Julie handed the still-sleeping baby over to him.

It was Josh he wanted—just as it was for Josh's sake that he had saved her, not her own. And now that he had Josh he was striding up the stairs away from her, leaving her to follow on her own.

Out of nowhere a terrible lethargy rolled over her, accompanied by a bizarre longing to lie down and close her eyes. She looked up to the portico, her heart thumping ever harder. She could not climb the steps. She could not climb even one of them. But she must. Somehow, leaning against the stair wall for support, she managed to drag herself up one step and then another, closing her mind against the ache of pain in her legs.

Rocco took the steps two at a time, driven by the savage bite of his anger. Of all the stupid, irresponsible things to do.

She was a woman with pride.

What if he hadn't caught her in time?

She had defied him.

She had lain against him like a trapped fawn, too exhausted to flee its hunter, her heartbeat shaking her whole body.

She had risked the child's safety.

She had looked at the child with such anguish in her eyes that it was as though she had bared her whole heart.

She was a good-time girl—an easy lay who had no appeal for him.

She was a devoted mother who touched some chord deep within him that overran the settings of his moral criteria of what he found desirable in a woman.

Something frightening was overwhelming her. Everything seemed to be happening in slow motion. The ache in her legs that had become so familiar to her over the last couple of weeks had intensified to such a pitch that it made her want to cry out.

Her heart was thudding so much it frightened her. She desperately wanted to sit—no, to lie down, Julie corrected herself tiredly, even as her fingers curled round the metal handrail, so that she could pull herself up the final few stairs and follow Rocco into the villa.

Normally she would have been entranced by the hallway, with its frescoes and its magnificent return staircase to the upper floors, its walls filled with paintings which Julie suspected were each worth a prince's ransom. Normally she would have been thrilled by the opportunity to enjoy such a feast of artworks. But right now she longed so much to lie down that she couldn't think of anything else. She was actually grateful that Rocco was holding Josh.

Rocco was talking to a plump woman whose dark hair was streaked with grey, and who Julie assumed from her demeanour must be the housekeeper. He was handing Josh over to her and she was beaming down at him.

Rocco was turning back to her.

'A room has been prepared for you,' he told Julie. 'Maria will show you to it.'

Julie nodded her head and made to follow Maria, who was already walking up the stairs.

Rocco frowned as he watched Julie. Her face was bone-white and she was staring at the stairs as though she was terrified of them. She took a step towards them—and then stopped moving, suddenly crumpling to the floor.

Rocco covered the distance between them in three easy strides, catching Julie as she collapsed. She wasn't, as he had first thought, unconscious. Her eyes were open and dark with confusion.

'I'm all right. Just a bit tired, that's all.'

Her face looked as bloodless as the marble steps, and he could feel the frantic tolling thud of her heartbeat through the silk blouse where her trenchcoat had fallen open. She was so slight that carrying her felt like carrying a child—except no child had such magnificent breasts. The sensation of them pressed against his own body as he carried her up the stairs stirred his body as well as his senses.

Rocco headed for the stairs still carrying her, ignoring her frantic demands to be put down, simply telling her tersely, 'Keep still.'

Through her embarrassment and her exhaustion Julie had a dizzy impression of white marble stairs, ancestral portraits, a long corridor with white walls, and very dark polished and carved wooden doors—one of which was open.

It was heaven to be lying down, even if her heart was pounding so uncomfortably that it was making her feel sick and anxious.

The bed on which she was lying was large and canopied, in a room that looked as though it had come out of an eighteenth-century film set. A fire burned in the marble fireplace beyond the bed, and Maria was placing Josh in what looked like a brand-new cot at the bottom of the bed, fussing over him. Julie wanted to go to him, but she simply felt too weak.

Rocco frowned as he watched her, folding his arms across his chest and leaning back against the wall. Something was wrong—and, given her lifestyle, it could be drugs. He knew the signs; after all they were easy enough to recognise in these modern times. But, no—this was something other than substance abuse. She was very thin—dieting, then? She hadn't eaten during the flight, and if celebrities were anything to go by it was the fashion to be skeletally thin—skeletally thin but with such large surgically enhanced breasts that women turned themselves into something close to physical freakery.

Maria spoke to him, telling him that the baby was asleep.

Nodding his head, he turned back to the bed and demanded curtly, 'When was the last time you ate a proper meal?'

Julie tried to think, but even that was too much for her. What was the truth? Did she even know? Could she remember? Did she care?

These last weeks had been a nightmare jumble of trying to look after Josh whilst worrying about Judy's debts. Making a meal for herself had been the last thing on her mind, even if she had had the money to buy proper food. And she hadn't really felt like eating. She had lost James. Not just once, but a second time. Losing him to Judy had hurt dreadfully, but losing him to death had brought another kind of pain—this time not just for herself but for Josh, and for James himself as well. Just the thought of the physical effort it would take to eat had made her feel even worse. She simply had not had the energy.

Her tormentor was still looking at her. Waiting for her to reply. He wouldn't leave her in peace to sleep as she so longed to do until she had answered him. She knew that.

She struggled to sit up.

'I would have had a meal at home in my own flat this evening if I hadn't been virtually hijacked,' she told him, trying to inject a note of scathing contempt into her voice and wondering if it sounded as thin and frail to him as it did to her.

'And before that—at lunchtime, for instance? You ate then? What?'

He was asking her too many questions andtoo fast.

'There wasn't time. The shop was busy, and Jenny the other girl didn't come in.'

'No lunch, then—breakfast?'

'I had coffee and toast.'

It was a lie. She had *made* coffee and toast, but all she had had time for was a few sips of the coffee before she'd had to take Josh to nursery.

'And every day is like that, is it? You deliberately starve yourself, out of some pathetic belief that being thin makes you more desirable to men like my late brother?'

'No!'

There was real denial as well as outrage in her voice.

'You say no, but it is obvious that you do not eat.'

Spirit flashed in her eyes as she told him fiercely, 'We aren't all rich enough to own private jets and have staff to cook for us, you know.'

Ignoring her attack, Rocco said flatly, 'If you are not starving yourself out of some self-destructive desire to attract the attention of men who can only be aroused by women who look like children and behave like whores, then why are you not more aware of your responsibility to your child? He is wholly dependent on you. After all he has no one else.'

'Do you think I don't know that?' Julie demanded, goaded beyond endurance. 'Do you think I don't think about that every waking hour?' Her eyes were burning with the emotion spilling through her. 'Do you think I don't wish more than anything else that his father were still alive? That he was here to care for and protect his son as I know he would?'

'Antonio?' Rocco eased his shoulders away from the wall on which he had been leaning. He didn't want to admit her championing of his half-brother had hit a nerve that was more sensitive than he had known, causing pain to strike searingly into him. His dead half-brother didn't deserve such loyalty, and she was a fool for giving it to a man who was so unworthy of it.

'The only person my half-brother would ever protect is himself—and if you don't know that then you didn't know him very well.' His voice was harsh and unkind, its contempt making Julie wince as he added, 'But then of course you did *not* know him, did you? How long does it take, after all, to perform the act that created your child? Five minutes? He couldn't even remember your—'

Just in time Rocco caught himself back. It went against his own pride to tell her that Antonio hadn't even been able to remember her name.

Thank goodness he had interrupted her when he had, Julie thought sickly. Otherwise she would have said James's name. She had been so caught up in her grief, but she couldn't do that—not until she had some kind of as-surance from Rocco that they would be returned safely to London.

'Dr Vittorio, our family doctor, is coming tomorrow morning to take swabs from the child for DNA testing. Whilst he is here I shall ask him to take a look at you.'

'There is nothing wrong with me.'

The dark eyebrows slanted in ironic query. 'You cannot climb a dozen stone steps without collapsing and you say there is nothing wrong with you? I beg to differ. Did you stay in touch with Antonio when you returned to England?'

The question was casual enough, but it made Julie's heart bound in fear.

What exactly had Judy said about Antonio? Julie wondered frantically, trying to remember. Her sister had implied that she had told Antonio she was expecting Josh and he had not wanted to know. That was when she had decided to tell James that the baby she was carrying was his.

'I informed him that I was carrying Josh, yes,' Julie lied. 'But he didn't want to know.' That at least was the truth.

'And yet you have just claimed to me that he would have wanted to love and protect his child?'

'As its father, I would hope he would have wanted to do that,' she felt forced to say—even though the truth was that she had been talking about James, who had loved Josh so much, not Antonio.

'As I have already told you, if the child turns out not to be my brother's then you will be compensated for your time and the disruption caused to your life. You will be asked to sign a confidentially agreement never to discuss the matter with anyone—for which you will be paid.'

Julie nodded her head, fighting back her natural instinct to say that she did not want any money. The appropriate time to announce that would be once the DNA results were known.

'And that is all?' she pressed him. 'There is nothing else? No further conditions?'

Rocco walked over to the bed and looked down at her.

'If by that you are daring to imply that I or my brothers would want some kind of sexual payment from you, then let me tell you—'

A sudden wail from the cot had them both looking over to it.

'Now look what you've done,' Julie protested tiredly. 'You've woken Josh.'

'Stay where you are. Maria will attend to him.'

'No. He's my child.'

She was sliding her feet onto the floor, but Rocco was standing in front of her.

'You are in no condition to look after him. Do you really want to risk dropping him again?'

It was a low blow, and it hurt, but to her relief Josh stopped crying and seemed to have gone back off to sleep.

Sleep. How she craved it herself right now.

'It's four o'clock. I suggest you try and get some sleep. Dr Vittorio will be here at ten to do the DNA tests. And, in answer to your question, no—there are no other conditions. All my brothers and I wish to do is fulfil our promise to our father to find Antonio's child—if indeed such a child exists, and was not merely a figment of Antonio's imagination. He was always very good at telling our father what he wanted to hear.'

Long after Rocco had gone Julie lay awake, staring up at the tented silk ceiling of her vast bed, her head aching with too many conflicting thoughts.

Family. What an emotive concept that was. She had always known that their parents preferred Judy, their first-born, the clever, pretty and bright one, and that she had come a poor second in their affections. Not that they had ever been unkind to her. They hadn't been like that. It was just that they had never been able to hide their joy and delight in Judy, or their mere tolerance of her.

She had craved the closeness of a loving family all through her childhood and her teenage years. She had thought she had found it with James, whom she had met during her time at university.

She had fallen in love with him, and she had loved his parents too, when he had taken her home with him to Newcastle to meet them. But then James had met Judy, and she had known immediately what was happening. Though the man Judy had stolen so easily had clearly not been dear to her, as she had cheated on James early into their relationship.

Judy had betrayed them both, but at least Julie still had Josh.

Had Judy and James and their parents lived Josh would have had a family—parents and grandparents, and a loving auntie in her—but they had not, and now all he had was her.

If he should prove to be Antonio Leopardi's child then he would still have a large extended family, with uncles, aunts and cousins, and of course his grandfather.

Lying sleepless in the dark, Julie acknowledged that for Josh's sake she should hope that he *was* a Leopardi.

CHAPTER FIVE

'WELL, although it can't be confirmed, of course, until I have the results of the blood tests, I am reasonably confident from what you have told me that the cause of your current symptoms is a shortage of iron.'

Dr Vittorio's diagnosis was delivered as he deftly released Julie's arm from the pressure of the cuff he had put round it whilst he took blood samples from her. It left Julie feeling extremely relieved, but even more of a fraud than she had done before.

Her intention to be up early to prove to Rocco how competent and capable she was had been well and truly sabotaged when she overslept, waking only when Maria had arrived carrying a tray containing a formidably hearty breakfast and wearing an equally formidable expression. What was worse was that she had made it clear that she intended to stand over Julie until every last scrap of food had been eaten.

Julie could sense that Maria did not approve of her—and who could blame her, given what she must believe about her? To Maria she was a young woman who slept around and who didn't even know who the father of her child really was.

However much Maria might disapprove of her, though, Julie could not fault her care of Josh.

Julie had been halfway through the poached eggs when Josh had woken up and started to cry, but before she had even had the chance to put down her knife and fork Maria had swung into action.

By the time Julie had finished her breakfast Maria had, under Julie's anxiously protective watch, changed, fed, bathed and dressed Josh, whilst explaining in her hesitant English that she was a mother of five children, a grandmother of twelve and a great-grandmother of three. Julie was a convert to the efficacy of her maternal skills, and ready to do virtually anything to acquire Maria's ability to soothe a fractious baby. Even more importantly and impressively, Maria had also managed to get Josh to feed steadily and happily.

'It is because the little one know that *I* know what is right,' Maria had told Julie firmly, when honesty had obliged Julie to confess how much she worried about Josh's refusal to take all his feed.

'He puts up the fuss because he is scared—because he knows that you are scared,' Maria had unbent enough to tell her.

'I just want to do what's best for him,' Julie had responded emotionally, so relieved to see Josh take all his bottle that she forgot that Maria's loyalties would lie with Rocco Leopardi. 'I love him so much.'

Maria's watchful expression had softened a little then, and she had shaken her head, telling Julie calmly, 'He knows that you love him. And he loves you. He watches for you all the time.'

They had exchanged tentative and cautious smiles, their relationship now on a shared footing of wanting to do their best for Josh.

What with wanting to make the most of the unexpected opportunity to get some valuable baby-raising tips from an expert, and the pleasure of watching Josh lying kicking and gurgling happily on his changing mat—a totally different baby from the fretful child she was used to—Julie hadn't realised what time it was until Maria had reminded her, pointing out that the doctor would soon be arriving.

Realising that she only had half an hour to shower and dress, Julie had nodded her head gratefully when Maria had offered to take charge of Josh and take him downstairs with her so that Julie could get ready speedily.

Dr Vittorio had been shown up to her room at ten on the dot by Rocco, who had introduced them and then said that Maria would bring Josh back upstairs for his DNA test once the doctor had let Rocco know that he was ready.

When Rocco had described Dr Vittorio as their family doctor Julie had anticipated that he would be an older man, not someone who at the most was only in his very early thirties, a similar age to Rocco himself, although thankfully with a very different and kinder personality.

His kindness and his excellent English had put her completely at her ease.

So much so, in fact, that now that he had given her his early diagnosis of the cause of her symptoms she was able to shake her head and marvel in relief, 'Is that all? I felt so dreadful that I was beginning to worry it could be something serious.'

'Anaemia *is* serious,' Dr Vittorio told her firmly. 'Rocco tells me that you have not been eating?'

'He has only known me a matter of hours, so how he can think he has the right to make that kind of assumption about me?' Julie began heatedly—only to stop self-consciously when she remembered that Dr Vittorio was the Leopardi family's doctor, and that meant his allegiance would be to them, and with it his sympathy.

'You are a single mother with a young child. For Rocco that alone would be enough to bring to the fore his most protective instincts.'

The doctor was speaking as easily and openly as though what he had just said was the most acceptable comment in the world—so much so that Julie wondered if she might have misheard him.

But, as though he sensed her confusion, the doctor continued, 'The death of the Princess shortly after Rocco's birth affected all three of her sons, naturally, but especially Rocco. I can understand that you will feel that his concern is overly protective, and perhaps even an unwarranted interference,' he acknowledged, 'but the death of their mother has left its mark on all her sons.'

'Yes, of course,' Julie was forced to agree, swallowing against her own unwanted sympathy as she added, 'I hadn't realised that that was the case.'

The doctor gave a small, dismissive shrug.

'There was perhaps no reason for Antonio to tell you. He was not, after all, close to his older brothers.'

In those few short words the doctor's contempt and dislike of the dead man was made quite plain.

'As for your anaemia, it is not unusual for a new mother to suffer from such a condition. The child was delivered several weeks short of full term, I understand?'

'Yes,' Julie agreed. 'He was. He was delivered by Caesarean section.'

James had pleaded with Judy not to go ahead with the early Caesarean she had insisted she wanted, having claimed that 'everyone' had their baby a month early to avoid putting on too much weight, but she had refused to change her mind.

'There were complications?'

Julie was getting into deep and dangerous waters now.

'No, not really,' Julie made herself admit.

'So it was more a matter of convenience?' The doctor made it clear that he disapproved with his small frown. 'Such a major operation can affect the health of both mother and child, but I shall know more once I have the results of the blood tests.'

Dr Vittorio had been thorough; Julie had to give him that. He had taken enough blood from her to fill several small phials, taking swabs from inside her mouth as well—presumably because she had told him that she had had a heavy cold.

He had been professional and courteous, apart from that brief lapse when she had admitted that Josh had been delivered in a non-medically necessary pre-full-term Caesarean. He had to know, of course, that she was not sure if Antonio was the father or not, and that must colour his view of her even if he hadn't shown it.

Unlike Rocco Leopardi, who *had* made it very plain what he thought of her morals—or rather what he assumed was the lack of them.

Was she being selfish in hoping that Josh would *not* turn out to be Antonio Leopardi's child? No matter who had fathered Josh, she would still love him every bit as much as she did now, but for James's sake she so much hoped that he was Josh's father, and that in that way a little of him would live on in Josh. James had been such a kind, loving person, with so much to give. Even though he had fallen so desperately in love with Judy he had always been kind and caring towards her, Julie, never wanting to hurt her. But he *had* hurt her.

Julie didn't want to think about that. It was easier and safer to focus on the anger Rocco aroused in her rather than the pain James had caused her. She could never imagine someone like Rocco Leopardi being so gentle with an unwanted ex-lover. He would have no compassion for a woman he no longer wanted in his bed or in his life, and yet when he did desire a woman Julie sensed that his desire would burn white-hot, driven by the kind of sensual sexuality that was still a mystery to her. But then she wasn't really the kind of woman who ignited that kind of desire in a man, was she? She and James had been friends—good pals, who had enjoyed one another's company, whose friendship had grown into love. With James Julie had felt safe from the awkwardness and the dread of mockery and rejection she had experienced so much growing up in Judy's shadow.

During their teens she had had to learn to accept that boys wanted Judy and found her desirable, and that she paled in comparison—just as she had had to learn to put a brave smile on her face when Judy had mocked her publicly in front of those boys for her lack of allure and sexual experience.

When she had gone to university and Judy had gone to train as a beautician Julie had carried with her the hang-ups of her teens. Julie had met James when she'd started a postgraduate course. He had been doing the same course, but had been a year ahead of her—twenty-four to her twenty-two. He had laughed gently at her when she had explained self-consciously and uncomfortably to him that she was still a virgin and why.

Their lovemaking had been tender and caring, but somehow Julie had always felt conscious of trying not to overwhelm James with her own passionate need. She wondered now if that might have been because she had sensed deep down inside herself that, despite the fact that he had said that he loved her, his love had been more the feelings of a friend than a lover? Because she had feared even whilst she was in his arms that somehow she was not good enough, not worthy of a man's real passion?

If James hadn't felt passionate about her then a man like Rocco certainly wasn't going to be, was he?

Julie was aghast at the speed with which her mind had summoned up such an inappropriate question. Why on earth should she want Rocco to desire her? She didn't. Not at all—not even one tiny little bit. The very thought of being in his arms and his bed made her feel… Julie could feel her face starting to burn as she fought to reject exactly what it did make her feel.

She couldn't imagine Judy feeling humiliated because a stunningly handsome and obviously sensual and sexually experienced man had seen her naked. Far from it. Her late sister would have been the first to take advantage of that kind of situation—she'd have been posing and preening and generally making sure that Rocco was so turned on by her body that he couldn't resist her. Judy had been wholly confident about her own sexuality. Her attitude had been that men found her irresistible. They always had and they always would.

Sometimes Julie wished she could have a little of her sister's self-confidence, although she shrank from the thought of sleeping around in the way that Judy had done. It would have been good, though, to be able to put Rocco in his place by knowing that she had the power to ensure that if she wanted to do so she could make him want her.

Not that she would have wanted that, of course. The mere thought of being in bed with a man like him, who could probably do things to a woman's senses with just the touch of his hands on her naked flesh that she couldn't even imagine, was enough to have her heart thudding in wary warning.

To her shock, Julie realised how far her thoughts had strayed from thinking how much she hoped that Josh was James's son.

One thing she was determined on, though, no matter who had fathered Josh. She was his legal guardian and she was not going to give him up—to anyone.

'What will I have to do, if I am anaemic?' she asked the doctor, seeing that he had finished putting everything back in his bag.

'That will depend on how severe your anaemia is. You will certainly need iron tablets, and I think perhaps some of our good warm Sicilian sunshine might do you some good—although you will have to wait a week or so longer for that. Shall I tell Rocco that I am ready to test the little one now, with your agreement?'

Julie nodded her head, watching him as he walked over to the door and then opened it, disappearing through it only to return within a matter of minutes, accompanied by Maria, who was carrying Josh, and Rocco.

Josh was wide awake, his face breaking into a wide smile the minute he saw her.

Julie's heart melted with love.

'He is still a bit underweight,' she told the doctor defensively as she thanked Maria and took Josh from her.

She'd already told him about Josh's post-birth health problems.

The doctor nodded his head, but he was concentrating on checking Josh over.

'He is a little small for his age,' he agreed, before asking Julie to hold Josh whilst he did the DNA test.

A few seconds later, watching as he swabbed the inside of the baby's mouth, Julie's heart gave an uncomfortable little thud.

That was how you took a sample for a DNA test? Had the reason he had swabbed the inside of her mouth been because he intended to test *her* DNA? That he might do so had never occurred to her. What did it matter if he did? she asked herself. She and Josh were related, after all.

Related, yes, but she was not Josh's mother. How accurate would the DNA test be? She didn't dare ask. But Rocco, it seemed, did.

'How accurate an indication of the child's paternity will this test be, and when will we have the results of it?' he asked the doctor.

'It will be accurate enough to make it clear whether or not Antonio is the little one's father,' Dr Vittorio answered him, smiling at Julie and thanking her for holding Josh steady for him. 'And I should have the results through within a week.'

Julie couldn't, of course, ask if he was testing her, and if it was possible to establish her relationship to Josh from the swabs he had taken. They would be suspicious if she did. And besides it didn't matter anyway, did it? She was Josh's legal guardian. But Rocco thought that she was Josh's mother, and she wasn't.

So what? It wasn't her fault that Rocco had got things wrong, was it?

She could have and perhaps should have told him the truth in London.

The Leopardi family were obviously used to getting their own way and making their own rules. If Josh *was* Antonio Leopardi's son then it might suit the Leopardis merely to have Josh's legal guardian to deal with and not his birth mother. Instinctively Julie knew that if Josh was Antonio's son then the Leopardis would do everything in their power to bring him up as one of their own, despite Rocco's assurance to her that he and his brothers considered the mother and baby bond sacrosanct. After all, she was not Josh's mother.

The doctor, Rocco and Maria had all gone, and Julie was free to put Josh down on the beautiful baby mat she had found, along with all the other expensive baby equipment, in the room off her own bedroom which had been fitted out as a nursery.

Josh loved lying on his back, and having the freedom to kick and wave his arms in a room warm enough to allow him to do so in comfort. Julie kissed his bare tummy, and laughed when he tightened his fingers in her hair, gently releasing them. He was smiling up at her so happily. Emotional tears filled her eyes. He *was* James's child. She was sure of it.

'You re so precious—do you know that?' she told him, adding softly, 'And your daddy would have loved you so very much.'

'Whoever his daddy actually was.'

Julie's heart lurched and rolled into her chest wall with a crash that seized her breath.

She hadn't realised that Rocco had come back, and that he was now standing in the doorway between the nursery and her bedroom. His voice was as hard as diamonds on glass, and able to penetrate her defences just as easily.

'You may think that I want your half-brother to be Josh's father because your family is rich, but the truth is that I hope he isn't,' she retaliated fiercely, as soon as she could speak.

'Liar. If that was the truth then you wouldn't have made contact with Antonio to tell him that you were pregnant, and you certainly wouldn't have accepted £25,000 from him to buy you off. There's no point in denying it. The cheque went through Antonio's bank account.'

Judy had taken money from Antonio Leopardi? She had never said anything about that to Julie. But then that was typical of Judy, and she would have known how much Julie would have disapproved. All Judy had told her was that Antonio Leopardi didn't want to know that she was pregnant, and that she intended to tell James that the baby was his, having broken off their engagement just before she had gone to Cannes, but knowing that James adored her and would take her back. Which of course he had.

'Strange and extremely clever, the way you've reinvented yourself as such an adoring mother—ready to go without herself in order to benefit her precious child.'

'There's more to being a good mother than buying expensive baby clothes,' Julie defended herself.

'Yes, and the first of those things is knowing who your baby's father is. Unless, of course, you do know but you are keeping quiet about it in the hope of getting more money. If that's the case let me warn you that you're wasting your time. I've already told you what the terms of any deal will be for any child proved not to be Antonio's.'

'How typical of a man like you that you think of everything in terms of money. What I want for Josh can't be bought.'

'A man like me?'

He had left the doorway now and was striding towards her like some dark avenging Lucifer, intent on her destruction. Julie scrambled to her feet to stand protectively in front of Josh.

'You, of course, are an expert on the male sex, aren't you? So tell me. What exactly *is* a man like me?'

He was standing too close to her. Far too close to her.

'You're arrogant and…and selfish. You think that all that matters is what you want, and that just because you want—'

'Just because I want what? You? Is that what you think?'

Julie was horrified. How on earth had the situation got so out of control so quickly?

'No, of course not,' she denied. The way he was looking at her and the silence he was maintaining unnerved her, and so fatally she rushed into it, adding frantically, 'Why should you want me? I—'

'You what? You want me to want you? You want me to tell you that every centimetre of you is now committed to my memory and engraved on my sexual responses? That in future I shall never be able to look at or touch any woman without comparing her to you? That from now on the pattern of woman carved on my desire is your image? Is that what you want?'

Without waiting for her response—which was just as well, Julie acknowledged inwardly, because she was in no state to think or say anything after hearing what he had just said—he continued dryly, 'Of course such things come at a price, don't they? And for that price I am sure that you would be very willing to assuage my longings and help me expunge those images. We are not, after all, talking of anything here other than a very basic form of lust.'

His voice was soft and mocking, and yet underscored with something age-old, man to woman, that was recognised deep within her. Recognised and responded to, Julie admitted apprehensively. She wanted to run from him, from the unwanted senses deep within her that he had aroused. But—dangerously—even more she wanted to stay. She abhorred what he was saying, and yet a wild, wilful *something* deep inside her wanted, if only for once, to be the kind of woman who would respond easily to such a challenge and enjoy arousing and sharing his lust—who would feel triumph in having aroused it and who would satisfy it and then walk away from it and from him without a single second of guilt or regret.

Very few women walked away from a man like this one, Julie suspected. It would be very empowering to be a woman who could do so. Judy could have done so, of course—but would she have? Would any woman if she thought— If she thought what? That she could tame Rocco and keep him?

What kind of foolish thoughts were those? In Rocco's eyes wasn't she already that woman she had just been describing mentally to herself, since he believed that she was her sister? What would it be like for once in her life to live that role? To know the power of being a woman who gloried in her sexuality and who used it to get whatever she wanted. What would it be like to walk that other road, live that other life, and know her sexuality?

Was she mad? She had other far more important things to think about than finding her own sad, repressed sensuality. She had Josh to think about and to protect.

Rocco gave her a heavy-lidded look of slanting sensuality that heated her blood, spreading arousal through her body unstoppably, like a swift floodtide flowing swiftly under the drag of a full moon. Inescapable and undeniable, it took her and possessed her, running wild and free within her.

'Nothing to say?' he challenged her.

It would be his fault if she took up his challenge. And he owed her something, didn't he, after the way he had behaved towards her? Why didn't she just take what she wanted? Her heart thumped unsteadily with the enormity of her own unfamiliar thoughts. What she wanted? She didn't want him, did she? No, of course not. But there *was* a temptation there—a fierce, yearning surge as volcanic as Etna itself, demanding expression. Maybe so. But it could not be allowed that expression, Julie warned herself sternly.

What she was thinking was far too dangerous, and a form of madness. Perhaps it was a symptom of her anaemia, she thought shakily, like the weakness in her legs and the pounding in her heart.

'No, I have nothing to say,' she answered him. 'You are not Antonio, after all.'

What on earth had she said *that* for?

'No, I damned well am not.'

The quietly savage words told her all she needed to know about the extent of her folly—and her danger.

She tried to sidestep it—and him—but it was too late. He caught her as easily as he had lifted and carried her the previous night, his hands curling round her upper arms, making it impossible for her to escape.

'You might think you are being very clever, taunting me,

but I promise you that I shall extract full payment.' His voice was harsh against her skin, grazing its sensitivity with needle-sharp darts of warning.

'Fine—but you'll have to extract it via your insults, because you won't be getting it any other way,' Julie responded promptly, trying to make her voice sound far more determined and self-confident than she felt.

'No?' The heavy golden leopard's eyes focused on their prey—her.

This had gone too far. What had started out simply as an intention to underline his contempt for Julie had somehow or other twisted and then turned itself around, so that his own weapon was now hurtling back towards him, Rocco admitted grimly. The words he had intended to use to distance himself from her had actually rebounded on him, conjuring up images of her inside his head that were now making him ache with an extremely inconvenient and an even more unacceptable desire.

How could he want a woman like this one? It should have been impossible, based on her sexual morals alone, and doubly so given the fact that he knew she had been one of Antonio's playthings. It should have been impossible, but it wasn't. The sight of her crouched on the floor, her face alight with love as she kissed her baby, had pierced the defences he had thought impenetrable, forcing him into direct contact with his own feelings about the loss of his mother. That in turn had filled him with anger—against himself for being vulnerable, and against her for causing that vulnerability—and now that anger had burned itself into a fierce male desire that was raging out of control inside him.

For his own emotional safety he needed to separate her

inside his head from that unwanted image he now had of her as a devoted mother. And the best way to do that was to let his body fill his head with some very different images of her. That was the only reason he wanted her. Out of self-protection. Nothing more.

When he kissed her and she responded to him as he knew she would his brain would register *exactly* what she was. He looked at her mouth and felt her tremble in sensual awareness of his intent. Beneath the silk blouse she was wearing—the blouse he had paid for, like all the other expensive clothes now hanging up in the room's wardrobes—he could see quite clearly not just the tight thrust of her nipples but also the faint raised edge that marked the place where the areolae of her breasts rose from the surrounding flesh. Almost absently he removed his right hand from her arm and slowly traced the raised line.

Julie shuddered violently, and closed her eyes in shocked awareness of how deep the abyss of her own sexuality actually was—and how dangerous. If a simple touch like this one could have such an effect on her, then what would his kiss do to her? How far would it take her down into the hot velvet darkness of that place she had never been? She felt dizzy and light-headed—with longing? With lust? Because she was anaemic? Did it matter why? Wasn't it only important that somehow she didn't want to resist what she was feeling, that she wanted to bring it and the man who was the cause of it closer instead of pushing them away?

His touch on her nipple, stroking it between his thumb and forefinger, shot pangs of erotic sensation deep into her. She looked up at his mouth, so beautifully carved that it could have been painted by a Renaissance artist, indenting at the corners, his bottom lip sensually full. Once against her own mouth it was both a possession and a caress, drawing her deeper under the spell of her own sexuality. She could feel his breath—warm, scented with maleness—as he urged her closer, and the hand that had been holding her arm pressed flat into the arch of her spine, so that her body fitted itself to his. Weakly she leaned into him, savouring the sensation of his hand on her breast, her own weight against his thighs, soft flesh against hard muscle, the one accommodating the other, her softness excited by that accommodation of his hardness and wanting to take things further.

Here in this unknown place where she now was there was no need for her to watch or regulate her reactions, no need for her to care how she might be judged, or to feel humbled as she had done with James—grateful for his love, knowing that his passion did not match her own, and desperate not to do anything that would tip the balance of his acceptance into male revulsion of too much female sexual need.

Here she could step away from the image her life had moulded her into and find out what it was like to be free to truly be herself. Softly the siren song of her own desire whispered its addictive message of persuasion to her.

His mouth was skilled and knowing. This was sexuality stripped bare, raw and urgent, binding her to its will and her own need. His tongue probed the seal of her closed lips, his hand kneading her breast, so that the twin assault on her senses made her body ache in time to his rhythm. She could hear the sound of her own breathing in all its ragged and charged betrayal of her need. She melted into him—and then tensed as she heard Josh cry.

Immediately she snapped back to reality, ignoring Rocco as he released her to let her go to Josh.

If there had been a moment when they had looked at one another, sharing regret, then she did not want to think about it.

'I have some business matters to attend to. If there is anything you need for the child, please inform Maria.'

Julie kept her back to Rocco, nodding her head to signify that she had heard him, not daring to so much as breathe properly, never mind turn round, until she was sure he had left the room.

Her hands trembled as she held Josh. She was icy-cold with reaction to her own behaviour. What on earth had possessed her? The emotions and feelings she had experienced had been so frighteningly alien to everything that she felt about herself.

Or had they? Had they instead been a reflection of the anger that had been locked inside her for so long? Because the reality Julie admitted was that she had been angry for a very long time: angry with Judy, angry with herself, even angry with James. So much so that the anger Rocco Leopardi had made her feel had been the burning spark that had ignited a positive volcano of emotion.

Well, she had certainly confirmed his opinion of her as someone little better than a call girl, Julie acknowledged shakily as she dressed Josh. A wanton hussy who had offered herself to him. A wanton hussy who didn't have the first idea of what it was like to truly experience sexual passion—who had, in fact, subdued her longing to do so with the only lover she had known.

It was just as well Rocco didn't really want her. If he had made love to her he might just have fired her passion to the

Penny Jordan

extent that her desire for him would have burned out of control.

What would it be like to really be wanted by a man like Rocco? To be desired by him, to be taken to his bed and kept there until he had aroused and then slaked their mutual passion past the point where either of them was in control of themselves or their destinies? How dangerous it would be to crave that kind of intimate possession from a man like him. How much safer she had been walking the path she had, where her desires and her emotions had been closeted and controlled.

CHAPTER SIX

IT WAS three days now since she had arrived on Sicily, and finally the wind had dropped and it had stopped raining.

This morning for the first time Julie had woken up to blue skies, with the dazzling beauty of a snow-capped Etna visible for once without its veil of mist and rain.

Sicily's weather like Sicily's history, was turbulent and demanding, Julie had learned, and now its passion was softened in the aftermath of its own excess, as if sated by the demands it had made at the height of its need to prove itself.

Whilst Josh had napped she had walked slowly through the formal salons of the *piano nobile*, gazing with awe at their magnificence. The most homely—if such a word could be used to describe such wonderful rooms—was the Sala degli Arazzi, with its priceless tapestries, from which a set of double doors opened out into the library, with row upon row of leather-bound volumes and silk curtains woven, so Maria had told her, in Lyons, to a design that had later been destroyed so that no one else could ever use it.

The rooms led one into the other in the classic *enfilade* style of the eighteenth century—the library giving way to the Chinese Salon, with its lacquered furniture, and then the Egyptian hallway, rectangular and galleried, with niches housing marble busts. Beyond that was a large square room with late eighteenth-century allegorical frescoes and elegant gilt wood furniture, its chairs and sofas covered in a blue silk that had also been specially woven in Lyons.

The last room overlooked an inner courtyard garden dominated by a large baroque fountain ornamented with mythical creatures spouting water into the stone pool beneath it. And yet for all its magnificence the house still had the definite air of being a home. Fresh flowers in ornate priceless bowls set on equally priceless furniture, filled the air with their scent, and Maria orchestrated her own army of skilled workers to keep the house clean.

Now, Julie made her way downstairs to the kitchen.

Through the open door she could smell the scent of citrus for the first time, wafting into the courtyard on the soft caress of a breeze from the orange and lemon groves that lay beyond the villa.

'You have taken your medicine?' Maria demanded.

Julie smiled and nodded her head. She had been taking iron tablets twice a day for the last two days, on the instructions of Dr Vittorio, who had said he wanted her to take them pending the results of her blood tests. She had to admit that already she was feeling more like her old self.

Julie had grown used to the older woman's sharpness now, and even if Maria disapproved of her, Julie had to admit that when it came to Josh, Maria was as dotingly protective as though he were a part of her own family.

'It is just as well that Rocco is a strong man as well as a good one. It will be hard for him to watch the little one.'

'Because he could be Antonio's son?' Julie queried.

'No. It is seeing you with the child that will be hard for him,' Maria corrected her firmly.

'Why?' Julie asked, her attention more on Josh, who she

was feeding, than on Maria who, Julie had learned, enjoyed a good gossip.

'Because he will have to witness the little one enjoying something that he never had. The love and attention of a mother,' Maria announced, looking up from the dough she was kneading.

Julie frowned—it was easy and tempting, if unrealistic, to imagine that Rocco had sprung fully formed and armed into adult male maturity without ever going through any process that involved him being dependent on anyone, much less a mere female.

'The Princess—his mother—died with Rocco's birth,' Maria told Julie dramatically. 'Poor woman. Many said that she did not want to live because of the cruelty of her husband. It was always known that the Prince only married her for her family's land, and the fact that her blood lines went back as far as his. That is the way with the nobility. She was much younger than him—only seventeen when they married—and convent-reared. Poor girl, she fell in love with him at first sight. But he was not the kind of man to be satisfied with a young, innocent wife. Not when there was already another in possession of his heart.'

Maria was certainly relishing the telling of her story, Julie acknowledged ruefully, although it sounded more like a fictitious drama than any kind of reality. She smiled down at Josh, who was sucking strongly on his bottle, feeding so much better than he had been.

'I dare say she might have borne it better if there had been many mistresses and not just the one,' Maria continued. 'And such a one, who refused to know her place,' she added darkly. 'The poor little Princess didn't stand a chance against one such as her, experienced in the ways of keeping a man within her power. She boasted openly to anyone who would listen to her that the Prince loved her and not his wife. There were no tears shed by either of them when the Princess died, I can tell you that, and I dare say if she could Isabella would have seen her children in Princess Lucia's grave with her.

'But the Prince, of course, knew what was due to his blood. The Princess had given him three fine sons, but now she was dead and he was free to marry Isabella. Five years later she had her own son, and the Prince doted on him in the same way that he did on her. No other man could have got away with such shameful behaviour but the Prince answers to no higher authority. The Leopardis are born into pride—they wear it like their skin and cannot be separated from it,' Maria informed her with obvious relish.

Julie frowned. Rocco had not made any mention of Josh having a grandmother, but maybe that was understandable in the circumstances.

'Where is Isabella now?' she asked Maria. Josh had finished his bottle and she lifted him against her shoulder to wind him.

'Ha! She is where she deserves to be—in her grave. She fell on the top steps of the castle tower and broke her neck. Some say that the ghost of the Princess pushed her, and certainly no one apart from the Prince and her son mourned her death. She had no understanding of the way things are, or of what it means to be a Leopardi wife and the mother of Leopardi sons. She was not worthy.'

Maria might gossip about the Leopardi family, but she was at the same time steadfastly loyal to them, and ready to defend them against anyone who might dare to criticise them, Julie knew.

'It must have been hard for Rocco, growing up without his mother,' she agreed.

'It was hard for all three of them,' Maria told her. 'Their father had no time for them, and Isabella made sure they knew that she held the whip hand—sometimes literally, I can tell you. I worked up at the castle then, and there was more than one occasion when someone would come down from the nursery asking for some of Cook's special salve for Falcon's wounds. Him being the eldest, he always took the punishment for the other two, you see.'

Poor little boys, Julie thought sympathetically. But Rocco wasn't a boy now. He was a man. In an attempt to ignore the ache tightening her lower body, she paced the length of the kitchen, holding Josh against her shoulder.

'I'd like to take Josh outside,' she told Maria. 'Perhaps go for a walk. There's a baby buggy in the nursery.'

'It is too cold,' Maria told her immediately.

'The sun's out,' Julie protested.

'We have a wind here that slices into the flesh like a knife,' she warned Julie. 'On one side of the island even the vines and lemon trees have to be cut close to the ground to protect them from it. Here we might be on the most favoured part of the coast, where the nobility built their fine summer villas so that they could enjoy the summer breeze away from the heat of their estates, but it is still not warm enough for any walking. Besides, you would have to ask Rocco for his permission, and he is not here.'

Immediately Julie could feel herself stiffening in angry resentment at the thought of having to ask Rocco Leopardi's permission for anything. It was bad enough that she had to accept his charity by living under his roof, eating his food, and worst of all wearing the clothes that he had paid for. She was not going to let him control her by forcing her to ask him for permission to do something as ordinary as go for a walk, Julie told herself firmly, instantly and rebelliously making up her mind that taking Josh for a walk was exactly what she was going to do.

It might not have been quite as easy as she had imagined to get the buggy—a solid affair, which was heavier than she had expected—down all the stairs, but Julie possessed an obstinacy that would not allow her to give up. Even though virtually all the good work done by the iron tablets had been undone by the time she had got the buggy down to the ground floor. Her heart was racing and thumping, and the horrible sense of needing to lie down was back, but she wasn't going to give in. She still had to go back upstairs to get Josh after all.

Ten minutes later, as she pushed the buggy along a dirt road towards the grove of citrus trees up ahead of her, Julie admitted that the wind *was* colder than she had expected. Josh, though, at least was securely protected from it, carefully wrapped up in several layers of warm clothes and tucked up securely in the buggy. She was not so fortunate, having come out in one of the fine wool skirts that filled the wardrobes of her bedroom. It was off white, and worn with a beautiful grey Italian knitted top and a pair of butter-soft steel-grey leather shoes with a small heel, but she was without a coat, having been deceived by the sunshine and by the warmth generated from her exertions with the buggy into thinking it was a lot warmer than it actually was. The sun was warm, but the wind, once she had left the protection of the courtyard, cut into her like a knife—just as Maria had predicted that it would.

Only her stubborn determination not to be dictated to any more than she had to be kept her from turning back—that and the fact that Josh was smiling happily, so obviously enjoying the outing that she didn't have the heart to take him back.

She'd only intended to go as far as the citrus grove, but what she hadn't bargained for was the fact that the land sloped down to it, so that once she turned round to come back she had to walk uphill, buffeted by the wind that had now blown clouds up out of nowhere to fill the sky and blot out the sun.

The effort she was having to make to push the heavy buggy along the muddy track should have warmed her up, but strangely it seemed to be having the opposite effect of making her shiver.

She felt the first spot of rain at the same time as she realised she had walked a lot farther than she had thought and was still a good half an hour away from the villa, judging from her current frustratingly slow rate of progress. By the time she had pulled up the hood of the buggy and fastened on the protective waterproof cover it was raining quite hard, and the buggy, which might have travelled at speed on tarmac or proper pavements, was difficult to push on a dirt track that was rapidly turning into muddy puddles.

How could it have gone so cold in such a short space of time? The rain felt like ice, reminding her of London and the cold winter they had just endured, especially now that the storm clouds had grown so heavy that it almost seemed dark. Mount Etna, whose snow-capped summit she had admired only that morning through the windows of the villa, was now wreathed in a mist of ominously grey cloud.

It was too late now to wish that she hadn't given in to that foolish surge of rebellious defiance.

Her head was bent into the wind as she pushed the buggy, whilst her body shivered and her heart pounded with the sick exhaustion that was draining her of energy. And Julie didn't even know that she wasn't alone anymore until she saw the dark male hands on the buggy's handles next to her own.

'Rocco!'

Did Rocco hear the relief in her voice beneath the angry guilt? If he did he wasn't saying so. The look in his eyes as she turned her head to glance uncertainly up at him was one of incensed biting disapproval.

She was trapped between him and the buggy, but the warmth coming off his body felt so blissful that she didn't feel inclined to object.

'Here—put this on,' he told her, thrusting a thick leather jacket over her shoulders. His own jacket, Julie recognized, as she caught the scent of him on it. He didn't wait for her to obey him, but instead pulled the jacket round her and removed one of her hands from the buggy to push it into the sleeve, whilst holding securely on to the buggy himself with his free hand.

'You need this yourself,' Julie protested, realising now that he had turned her to face him that he hadn't brought the jacket with him, but had removed it from his own body.

He shook his head, ignoring her protest. The rain was coming down so heavily now that it had already plastered the fabric of his shirt to his body, revealing the outline of the solidly muscled torso beneath it.

'What is it with you?' he demanded furiously, raising his voice so that it would carry above the increasing noise of the fiercely buffeting wind. 'You claim to love your child, and yet you do something like this—bringing him out here when you were warned that the weather isn't suitable.'

Maria had obviously told him what she had said to her, Julie realised. 'I wanted him to have some fresh air.'

'Did you? He could have had that in the courtyard— in safety.'

'He *is* safe.'

'No thanks to you.'

That was too much.

'I would never put Josh at risk. He's wrapped up and warm.'

'And in your care. And you are suffering from a debilitating illness that doesn't allow you enough strength to climb a flight of stairs without the risk of passing out, never mind go for a walk in these conditions.'

'That's not fair,' Julie protested. 'I've been a lot better since I've been taking the iron tablets.'

'A lot better?' She could hear the derision in his voice. 'I watched you just now—you were so exhausted that you could hardly put one foot in front of the other, never mind anything else. What is it with you British that you have this need to trudge over every landscape even when common sense must tell you that it is inhospitable?'

'I don't know—probably the same level of gene that makes Leopardi men so bossy and arrogant,' Julie was stung into retorting.

All the time he had been hectoring her they had been walking back towards the villa, with Rocco pushing the buggy and making much better progress than she had done as she struggled to keep up with him.

'You claim that you are better,' Rocco told her, ignoring her comment about his arrogance and returning instead to a subject that obviously suited him much better since it involved criticising her, Julie thought darkly as he continued, 'Look at you now. You are struggling to cover a few yards. Don't bother denying it. And what the hell were you about, coming out without a coat?'

'What's wrong?' Julie yelled at him, her self-control snapping. 'Are you worried that I might have ruined the expensive clothes you paid for?'

'Don't be ridiculous. You should know perfectly well that my concern isn't for a few pieces of cloth. Your child is my concern—just as he should be yours. Didn't you stop to think what might happen if you collapsed, or how long the pair of you might be out here? You've seen how the weather has turned. You must be able to feel the force of the wind.'

Julie could only nod her head in grudging admission of the truth of his words.

'If this wind had caught the buggy it could quite easily have turned it over. The pair of you would have been lucky to get away with pneumonia—if fate had been less kind you could have died.'

Rocco wasn't going to tell her just how he had felt when he had come back from a site meeting earlier than he had planned to discover that she and Josh were missing—only to learn from Maria that Julie had been talking about going out for a walk.

Rocco had no idea what had made him check the track that led to the lemon grove first, but she was damned lucky that he had.

He was furiously angry with her for putting at risk all

the effort he had gone to to get her and Josh here and thus start to fulfil his part of the responsibility he and his brothers had taken on. A prize fool he would have looked if something had happened to her and the child whilst they were in his care. And if Josh did turn out to be Antonio's child then there was no doubt that his father would have accused him—totally without any foundation or truth—of being only too glad that Josh had not survived.

Rocco could feel his heart thudding with a mixture of anger and relief. Relief that he had found them and anger because he had had to come and do so.

'What the hell did you want to go out for anyway? No, let me guess—you were bored and missing your normal way of life. Well, you won't find the kind of party scene that you like so much, nor the men that go with it, here.'

'I wasn't looking for any party scene or any man,' Julie denied. 'In fact a man is the last thing I want.'

They were back, and she was exhausted. Exhausted and sick with the fear instilled in her by Rocco's far too graphic descriptions of what might have happened to Josh. Despite accepting that she was at fault, somehow she was still so angry at him that her anger was virtually all that was keeping her on her feet.

It was Rocco who now removed Josh, who had miraculously fallen fast asleep and stayed that way, from his buggy, and Rocco who carried him upstairs to the nursery—whilst Julie trailed behind him, willing herself to find the strength to make it to the bedroom. Josh looked so small clasped against Rocco's shoulder—and so safe.

'You'd better take this,' Julie told Rocco ungraciously, removing his jacket and holding it out to him at arm's length as she informed him, 'I'll take Josh.'

'I may as well put him in his cot, since he's asleep.'

He was refusing to give Josh to her? Why? What did he think she was going to do? Drop him?

'He can't go in his cot like that. He's wearing an outdoor all-in-one suit.'

'Yes, but presumably it comes off?'

Rocco wasn't even bothering to wait for her response, or to give her demand even a second's proper considera- tion. He was ignoring her, just as though she had no say at all in what was best for Josh.

Julie fumed as Rocco carried Josh through into the nursery, leaving her to drop his leather coat onto her bed and hurry after him, protesting, 'There's no need for you to do that. You might wake him up.'

He was still ignoring her, laying Josh on his changing table with unexpected expertise and then efficiently removing his outdoor suit. Josh slept on obliviously.

'Perhaps you'd like to check his nappy and change him as well?' Julie suggested sarcastically.

'What I'd like is to feel that he's got someone in his life who takes a responsible attitude towards his care. But right now, much as I'd like to think that, I can't,' Rocco told her pointedly.

Guilt and pride warred with one another inside Julie's heart. She hated having her care of Josh questioned, but at the same time she was guiltily aware that she *had* allowed herself to be blinded by her own stubborn determination not to let Rocco dictate to her what she could and could not do.

'If anything had happened to Josh I'd never have forgiven myself,' she admitted in a low, tortured voice, her guilt and honesty winning the battle.

Rocco hid his surprise at her admission. Somehow it was out of character for the kind of woman he knew her to be—and yet, if he was honest, this wasn't the first time in their short acquaintanceship when she had surprised him and challenged his perceptions of her. Nor the first time either that she had driven him to the point where she had tested his self-control way beyond its normal limits, he admitted—and not just the self-control that governed his temper. He was still battling to deny the extent to which she aroused him sexually—and failing, as his body was telling him very clearly right now.

How was it possible for him to want a woman he could only despise? A drowned rat of a woman who ricocheted between stubborn folly, aggressive antagonism and the kind of passionately intense sexual response to him that his head told him had to be manufactured, given her history, but that this body swore was the adult version of being a child let loose in a sweet shop.

Deftly, Rocco slid Josh into his cot and covered him up.

'Maria said to tell you that she's making you a special dish of liver cooked to her special recipe for dinner, along with a good helping of spinach. Or perhaps I should have said *warn* you,' he told Julie dryly.

Maria had taken the doctor's dietary suggestions for Julie to heart, with the result that iron-rich meat and greens had been served to her at every meal since the doctor's visit apart from at breakfast, when she was served her iron in the form of eggs.

Julie managed a wan smile. 'I was hoping to persuade Maria that cannelloni filled with spinach and ricotta cheese would be just as beneficial.'

'You need to get out of those wet clothes.'

'Yes.' Rocco was walking past her and heading for the bedroom door. Julie took a deep breath and told him reluctantly, 'Thank you for…for coming to find us.'

Her head was bowed, so she didn't see the way his gaze rested on her before he said coolly, 'There's no need to thank me. After all, I have a vested interest in protecting Josh.'

He'd gone before Julie had time to raise her head and look at him—much to her relief. The last thing she needed right now was to endure the discomfort of having him realise that his pointed reminder that it was Josh who mattered to him and not her had hurt her. Hurt her? How crazy was that? How could a man she had only known four days possibly be able to hurt her emotionally?

It was possible for one heart to recognise another in the space of a single heartbeat, with all that that meant, she reminded herself. But she and Rocco didn't have hearts that recognised each other, did they? In fact Rocco probably didn't have a heart at all.

No heart? Then what was pumping the blood round that magnificent body?

And it *was* magnificent. The way in which his damp shirt had clung to his flesh had shown her that. Julie rubbed her eyes. She was cold and wet, and in need of a hot shower and probably a rest. A sudden gust of wind drove the rain against her bedroom window, making her shiver as she contemplated what might have so easily happened if Rocco hadn't come to look for them. He might not have said it in so many words, but she knew he thought that she wasn't fit to have charge of Josh, and perhaps he was right. She hadn't done a very good job so far of looking after her little nephew, had she? It was only since he had been here that Josh had finally started to thrive and put on weight.

What was going to happen if he *did* turn out to be Antonio's child?

Did she really need to ask herself that? Rocco and his brothers would take Josh from her. They would find him a proper, suitable substitute mother; they would surround him with all the care that Leopardi money could buy; they would cherish and protect him.

But she would love him, Julie told herself fiercely. And surely that meant something?

CHAPTER SEVEN

THE sight of the buggy, its wheels solid with mud and grit, abandoned in the hallway, acted on Rocco's temper like a match to a highly flammable substance, representing as it did everything about the current state of his life—both professional and private—that infuriated and irked him.

He was in the middle of a building project on which every day of work lost cost money and which the heavy rain of Sicily's always unpredictable pre-spring weather was already threatening to delay; his site manager—a passionate Lombardese whose personal life was more dramatic than anything that had ever been put on at La Scala—had just informed him that he was taking a week's leave because his wife was threatening to leave him over an affair he had been having with an underwear model and he needed to go home to sort things out; somehow his grandfather had got wind of Josh's presence at the villa, and according to Maria there had been five telephone calls from the castle since the morning, commanding Rocco's presence at his father's bedside, and on top of all that a woman who should have meant nothing whatsoever to him at all was disturbing and disrupting his thoughts and emotions as well as his desires, in a way that made him feel furious at his own inability to control what he was experiencing.

And as if all of that wasn't enough, that same woman

had had the idiocy to put both herself and her child at risk because she had felt that the baby needed some fresh air. Had she no sense of her own vulnerability? Had she really thought she was well enough to push a buggy up a steep incline over thick mud, when only days ago she had hardly been able to climb a flight of steps? If her child *was* Antonio's son then she would soon learn that his father wouldn't tolerate or make allowances for her stubborn foolishness in the way that Rocco had.

Rocco looked at his watch. He had better drive over to the castle before his father brought on his own end with a self-induced heart attack, he acknowledged grimly.

Julie looked longingly towards her bed. Josh—fed, bathed and content—was clearly not suffering any setback from their walk, but she was exhausted, she admitted, and still cold inside right through to her bones, despite her shower and the warm, dry clothes she was now wearing.

It was only half past three—plenty of time for her to have a rest before dinner.

At least she was over her latest bout of whatever alien weirdness it was that was taking her over and somehow convincing her that she needed to experience the full intimacy of raw, passionate sex and with Rocco Leopardi, Julie thought with relief as she lay down on top of the bed, too exhausted to even think of getting undressed. It shocked her not just that she could even feel like that, but also because of the unwanted and upsetting anger she had discovered within herself—especially against James. After all, it wasn't his fault that he had not wanted her as passionately as she had done him. It would be far safer and make far more sense for her to simply accept that she was not the sort of woman to inspire intense sexual passion in the kind of man she could love.

And that other kind of man? The kind like Rocco Leopardi? That kind of man she did not *want* to love—the kind of man to whom intense sexual passion came as naturally as breathing and meant nothing other than an appetite to satisfy. It simply wasn't possible for her to want to have sex with a man she knew despised her. Her pride and her self-respect would not allow it. And anyway, that had all been a silly mistake brought on by the fact that she hadn't been feeling well. She didn't really want him at all, Julie told herself firmly, before finally allowing herself the luxury of sliding into sleep.

His interview with his father over, Rocco felt the familiar surge of relief that always accompanied his departure from the castle. His father had tried to pressure him into taking Josh to the castle for him to inspect, claiming that he 'would know Antonio's child immediately,' but Rocco had remained steadfast, pointing out that in law it was the DNA test result that would be accepted as prove of parentage, not his grandfather's recognition. Naturally the older man hadn't liked that, and the kind of argument familiar to Rocco from his youth had ensued, during which the Prince had accused all three of his sons from his first marriage of having their own agenda, claiming that they had always resented his second wife and their half-brother.

This had led on to the Prince stating that Rocco and his brothers were deliberately trying to keep his grandson from him, despite having given him their word that they would find him—all of which Rocco had refuted, refusing to allow his father to bully him or, when that failed, use emotional blackmail to force Rocco to bring Josh to the castle.

'I am not yet the powerless old man you think me,' the Prince had told Rocco. 'I still have my friends, and I warn you, Rocco, that no one will keep my Antonio's child from me.'

'No one wants to keep him from you, Father,' Rocco had pointed out. 'But first we have to ascertain if the child is in fact Antonio's.'

'You should let me, his father, be the judge of that. What man does not know his own flesh? No man who dares to call himself a true man,' the Prince had countered theatrically.

It was a pity that his father had found out about Josh's presence on the island, Rocco admitted, because it could only complicate matters.

The sudden, unplanned surge of power that came from his foot pressing hard on the accelerator of his car warned him of the danger of his antagonistic feelings over the fact that Julie had been Antonio's lover. His *lover*? Rocco's mouth twisted. Since when had the kind of shallow, meaningless sex Antonio had indulged in ever had anything to do with love? He pitied Josh, knowing as he did himself what it did to the soul to know that your life had been created by an act divorced from any kind of emotional communion.

Given her obvious determination to do exactly the opposite of whatever he said to her, even when that meant risking Josh's life, Rocco suspected that he would be wasting his time, having decided he ought to warn Julie that his father might seek to trick her into taking Josh to see him. Nevertheless, his own conscience was insisting that it was something he must do, he acknowledged, as he tapped on her half-open bedroom door before pushing it fully open and going in.

The sight of Julie lying fast asleep and fully dressed on top of the bed checked him, causing him to frown in a renewal of the fury he had felt when he had first seen her pushing the buggy uphill along the muddy track, looking so frail that she'd seemed almost on the point of collapse.

He had used the Leopardi authority he rarely needed to resort to with Dr Vittorio after the doctor had examined Julie, to find out if hegenuinely thought that Julie was merely suffering from a lack of iron or if he suspected that something more serious might be wrong.

At first Luca Vittorio had refused to answer him. But Luca and Rocco had played together as boys. When Rocco had pointed out that he simply wanted to know so that he could ensure Julie received the treatment she needed, Luca had relented and shaken his head, saying that he was fairly sure her symptoms were caused by an iron deficiency, but that that did not mean that it wasn't serious—dependent upon the extent of the deficiency and its cause. The iron tablets Luca had prescribed were a stop-gap solution, designed only to boost her energy levels pending the results of the tests.

Julie knew the situation as well as Rocco did, and yet she had still risked potentially causing more damage to her health. She infuriated him in ways he had not known existed until she came into his life, Rocco admitted grimly. Just as she— Just as she what? Aroused him in exactly the same intense and extraordinarily all-encompassing way?

She did not arouse him. He was a man. A man who had been living the life of a monk for the better part of a year. And since that was more by accident than design, because of the amount of work he had taken on, it was only natural that when a woman threw herself at him as she had done he was going to respond. The fact that he had even momentarily been tempted by her filled him with self-derision.

The door between the bedroom and the nursery was open, drawing Rocco towards it. How could his father expect anyone to believe that it was possible to 'know' an unknown child's bloodlines? Rocco looked down into the cot, where Josh lay fast asleep. Being here was doing Josh good. He had put on weight, and his skin looked less sallow, warmer.

Rocco leaned closer and studied the sleeping baby. His fluff of dark hair had a slight curl to it. All the Leopardi men had thick dark hair with a curl, even if in adulthood Rocco had chosen to have his own hair cut so short that its curl couldn't be seen. Josh's eyelashes fanned out across his cheeks. His eyes were growing darker in colour. But what, after all, did that mean? Rocco could see nothing in Josh that reminded him of Antonio, but that would not stop his father from doing so if he was so minded. His father might now be bedridden, and living in the shadow of his own death, but he was still a very powerful and autocratic man—a man who was used to making sure that his will prevailed, no matter what the cost to others.

Rocco could see a difficult future ahead for this child lying so peacefully asleep in his cot if he did turn out to be Antonio's son—and an even harder one for his mother. For all that he would welcome Josh into the family, Rocco knew his father would feel very differently about Josh's mother. The Prince had indulged and spoiled Antonio from the moment he had been born, turning a blind eye to all his excesses as he grew to adulthood. How much had that indulgence been responsible for Antonio's lifestyle and ultimately for his death?

Rocco smoothed the cover over Josh's sleeping body, smiling at the small star-shaped little hand and watching Josh's fingers curl round his own index finger, as though even in sleep the baby instinctively reached for the security of an adult touch.

The first thing Julie saw when she woke up was Rocco, bending over Josh's cot, with one hand on the side of the cot and the other inside it. Her heart lurched into her chest wall. Rocco might deny it, but neither he nor his brothers had any reason to love Josh. They certainly hadn't loved their own half-brother. Maria had gossiped to her, saying that all three brothers were independently wealthy, and there was certainly no question of any child of Antonio's usurping their right to inherit their father's titles. But if their father chose to leave his grandson money they had assumed would be theirs...

Immediately her protective instincts had her on her feet and hurrying into the nursery, demanding sharply, 'What are you doing?'

Rocco turned his head to look at her, but didn't remove his hand.

Protectively, Julie went round to the other side of the cot to look anxiously at Josh, only able to relax when she recognised that he was breathing safely and easily. That should have been enough to steady her, but the sight of

Josh's small hand curled tightly round Rocco's finger caused a fresh lurch of her heart—this time from angry pain rather than fear for the little boy.

Rocco had no right to enter the nursery and watch over the child in a way that should have belonged only to Josh's father. Julie had to fight not to snatch Josh up and hold him tightly, but she had to satisfy herself with demanding, 'Why are you in here?'

'Because I choose to be. This is after all my home, and Josh could be my nephew. It's only natural that I should want to check that he hasn't taken any harm from the reckless behaviour of his mother.'

His suave response, with its reminder of things she'd rather forget, increased Julie's anxiety—but that was nothing to the sudden downward plunge of her heart when Rocco gently eased his finger free of Josh's grip and urged Julie back into her own room with a calm, 'I have news.

'Unfortunately my father is aware that you and Josh are on the island,' he began, 'and even more unfortunately he has decided that he will know Antonio's son, without recourse to a DNA test, the minute he sets eyes on him. I realize, of course, that you will probably be delighted by the thought that my father in his desperation to find his grandson may well decide that Josh *is* Antonio's child.'

'Well, that is where you are wrong,' Julie denied immediately. 'Surprising though you might find it, the truth is that I do *not* want Josh to be Antonio's son. I'd much rather that James is his father—after all, James was prepared to marry…me, and bring Josh up as his own.'

The minute the hot words were out Julie wished desperately that she had not said them. But it was too late for those regrets now. Rocco was giving her a very grim look indeed, and as she watched he strode over to her bedroom door and closed it, turning round to confront her.

'So there *is* another man whom you know could be Josh's father?' he demanded coldly.

'Not is—was,' Julie was forced to admit. 'He's dead now. Killed in a rail accident.'

'Why have you not said anything of this before?'

'You hardly gave me the chance. All you cared about was proving whether or not your half-brother was Josh's father.'

'You say you do not want Josh to be Antonio's, and yet you contacted Antonio to tell him that you were having his child. He gave you money to buy you off.'

Rocco was angry—furiously, savagely angry—at the thought of all the time that had been wasted when with a few simple words she could have said right from the start that Antonio was not Josh's father.

'Was there ever any chance that Josh might be Antonio's? Or was it all a scam cooked up between you and your lover to get money out of Antonio for a child that you knew all along was not his? Answer me,' he demanded harshly, 'unless you want me to shake the answer out of you.'

'I don't know,' Julie admitted.

CHAPTER EIGHT

ROCCO stared at her.

'You don't know what?' he demanded caustically.

'I don't know who Josh's father was,' she told him truthfully. 'But I do know that I want it to be James and not Antonio.'

'You loved him? This James?'

What was he doing? What possible difference did it make what she had felt, and why should he care?

'Yes.' The tears Julie didn't want to shed blurred her vision and her voice.

'But you still had sex with my brother.'

His voice might be flat, but there was no mistaking the contempt it held.

'James and I had quarrelled. I thought it was over. I went on holiday and…and it just happened…'

'It just happened?' Rocco mimicked her. 'Just like that? A moment of weakness when you were missing the man you really loved. Is that what you mean?'

Julie swallowed. That was what had happened to her when she had for those awful, dreadful minutes actually wanted him, Rocco, wasn't it? The betrayal of her long-standing love for James had merely been a shameful moment of madness and weakness.

'Yes,' she agreed woodenly.

Rocco strode towards her, his hands gripping her shoulders so tightly that his fingers dug painfully into her tender flesh. He half shook her as he told her bitingly, 'Liar. What "just happened", as you call it, was that Antonio hired you—along with another girl—to indulge him in his sexual fantasies. We know that because we found the receipt amongst his papers—although of course you and the other girl who put on that shabby little show for him weren't the only entertainment he paid for during his visit to Cannes. At least the madam he used ensured that her girls had regular health checks—the cost of those was on the bill as well. I must say, though, that I'm surprised you used your real name instead of a fictional name of some kind.'

Rocco made a sound of disgust, and released her with so much force that Julie fell back against the bed. She was trembling so much that she had to sit down. This was awful—dreadful—worse than anything she had ever imagined having to face. She had known that Judy was sexually promiscuous, of course, but not this. Poor James. He had loved her so very much. Thank goodness he had never known what she was really like. It also answered the riddle of why Rocco had never questioned the discrepancy in their names. Judy had used Julie's name while in Cannes, betraying her yet again. Hot tears seared the backs of Julie's eyes.

'Did you tell James how you spent your time in Cannes?' Rocco demanded, as though he had somehow guessed the direction of her own thoughts.

'That's none of your business,' Julie told him, almost spitting the words at him in her determination to protect the man she had loved.

'That's where you're wrong. You've made it my business by being here. Did you plan the whole thing between you? You and this James? Did he procure you for Antonio, setting him up so that the pair of you could blackmail him with the threat of a child? That would certainly make you two of a kind.'

Julie sprang up off the bed, her face burning with the heat of her anger.

'James was a decent, kind and gentle man. He was worth a thousand men like you and your half-brother— arrogant, selfish, emotionally barren men, who think they can buy whatever they want.'

'What? You *dare* to put me in the same category as Antonio?'

'Why not?' Julie shot back. 'You both carry the same blood in your veins, after all.'

'Why, you—'

He was bending over her, dragging her to her feet. Frantically Julie fought to break free of his manacling grip on her wrists.

'I loved James,' she told him. 'But someone like you could never understand that.' Her voice caught and then broke.

Stifling an oath, Rocco released one of her wrists to cup her chin and lift it, so that he could look into her eyes. She looked like a martyr, all trampled pride and virtue, defending a lost love.

'You say that now,' he told her savagely, 'but you were still prepared to give yourself to me.'

'No. I loathe the thought of you touching me.'

'Like this, you mean?'

He was going to regret this when he had calmed down,

Rocco knew, but right now his pride was asserting its need to be assuaged in a way that was driving out everything else.

Whilst she protested, he bent his head and silenced her with the pressure of his mouth on hers.

Julie told herself that she didn't want him, that she truly did loathe him, but some irresistible form of alchemy was taking place, transforming those feelings into their exact opposite. Her free hand lifted to his jaw—rough with nearly a full day's growth of beard, prickling the tender pads of her fingertips—to keep his mouth on her own.

Her heart was jerking in hot, tight spasms that echoed the speed with which the dull, heavy weight of the ache in her lower body was growing.

Rocco had released her other wrist to tangle his hand in her hair. He spread it flat against the back of her head, holding her beneath his kiss whilst his tongue prised open her lips.

Her heart shuddered, and burst into a flurry of heavy beats. The dull ache low down in her body spread to her thighs. Her tongue found his and she explored it with delicate little touches of her own tongue. She and James had never kissed like this. She had wanted to, but James had never initiated the intimacy.

Her heart slalomed as Rocco curled his tongue round her own, stroking it rhythmically, making her whole body move against his in an answering rhythm.

When had he last found this kind of sensuality in a kiss? Rocco wondered, already knowing the answer to his own question. Her response to him was sending rivers of molten desire speeding through him, destroying every obstacle in their way. Wasn't it more a matter of admitting that he had *never* found it—had never known that it could be found or that he wanted to find it—until now?

Rocco cupped the side of Julie's face with his free hand and kissed the tender spot just behind her ear, stroking it with his tongue tip.

Violent shudders of pleasure rocked through Julie's body. She turned her face into Rocco's hand, caressing his fingers with her tongue, feeling the need inside her building to a hot, tight pulse.

Frantically she pushed Rocco away, catching him off guard.

'What is it?' His voice was raw and thick with arousal, and his hands returned to her body, shaping her waist, moving upward towards her breasts.

'I can't bear it,' Julie told him desperately, too caught up in the intensity of what she was feeling to hold back the truth. 'I don't want to feel likc this. I don't want to want you so much. It's too much.' She trembled visibly.

The heaviness of her longing lay within her like an alien life form, possessing and controlling her. She looked at his hand, wondering what he would do if she reached for it and placed it against her sex, where the pulse of her desire had gone from a small flutter to a fierce, almost painful clamour. She felt lost, afraid, and terribly alone, in a place that was totally alien to all her previous experience, taken there by her desire for a man she didn't want to want.

How the hell did she expect him to back off after saying something like that to him? Never mind when she was looking at him in the way that she was—as though all she wanted was to be possessed by him? Rocco wondered grimly. He felt his self-control give way beneath the combined weight of her words and his own desire.

'*You* are too much,' he told her thickly. 'Too much for me to resist.'

His hold encircled her, his hands sweeping up over her ribcage beneath the silky-fine knit of her top, pushing aside the decorative rather than practical barrier of her bra. His heat invaded her skin, branding his touch upon it. Her breasts, turgid now with desire, welcomed the cupped pressure of his hands, whilst the kisses he skimmed along the length of her neck and into her shoulder set off a reaction that burned its way through every sensory nerve ending her body possessed, so that her whole body vibrated visibly in mute shudders to the music of his touch, like an instrument played by a master musician.

Here on this island, with its buried veins of molten lava that ran so deep and possessed such danger, she was, Julie recognised distantly, finally discovering the hidden depths of her own passion. Like someone standing on its edge, looking down into the sleeping heart of the volcano, oblivious to its true nature, she had stood for so long on the edge of her own passions that she had overlooked how powerful they were.

Now, like lava running hot from deep down inside the earth, this man—a man whose blood and history had made him part of this island of volcanic uncertainty—was deliberately inciting her own fevered desire to the point where she could no longer control it. She could feel the need building up inside her—overpowering, commanding, demanding that she give herself over to it and to the man who had aroused it.

What was it about this woman that enabled her to transform herself into this living, breathing embodiment of such erotic and intense sensual responsiveness? He asked himself. It was as though she knew his every need, and could answer it in a way that took him deeper than he had ever previously gone into the molten heart of his own desire.

What her touch, her flesh, her self were drawing from him could never have been conjured up by mere sexual experience or tired, over-used mechanical responses of the 'you touch me like this and I respond like this' variety.

Somehow she was able to imbue even something as simple as the unsteady breath of her heartbeat against his flesh with such passion that her pleasure seemed new and tumultuous—an acknowledgement of a gift from him that took her into sensual realms she had never known before. Just the heavy-lidded and helplessly liquid look of longing that seemed to be dragged from her as though her need for him completely overwhelmed her was a form of arousal, and it took him in turn to a pitch that promised—and threatened—a degree of pleasure that challenged his own self-control.

When his touch had brought her to a state of semi-collapse, to lie boneless and mutely imploring against him, Rocco removed her top and then her bra, before sliding off her linen trousers.

Below the twin concave dips on either side of the minute swell of her stomach, he could see quite clearly, through the sheer fabric of her knickers and the more intimate covering of silky blonde hair that covered her sex, the frantic fast pulse of her need.

Rocco closed his eyes protectively and took a deep breath that lifted his torso, exhaling slowly as he fought for the command of himself that he could feel slipping away. But it was no good. The minute his eyelids lifted his gaze and returned it to that pulse, his whole body reacted to it.

He started to undress, unfastening just a few buttons on his shirt before he stopped, driven by his own need to lean forward and place his palms flat on the bed on either side of her hips, so that he could lower his head and feel that pulse, with its message of sensual untrammelled heat, against his mouth, so that he could take it deep inside himself to where his own body ached in exactly the same way.

Julie heard herself cry out—a sharp, keening sound somewhere between uncontrollable longing and helpless recognition that she was lost now to any kind of self-restraint.

The heat of Rocco's mouth penetrated the fine fabric covering her sex, making her feel as though she was melting inside, turning wet and soft, her flesh yearning.

When Rocco straightened up she wanted to protest, to beg him to continue. A wild, feverish and driving clamour of physical urgency was possessing her, causing her to move restlessly on the bed. The small out-of-control movements of her body reflected her impatience and her need, but then she realised that Rocco was removing his clothes, and her movements stilled. Her concentration was focused on watching as he shrugged off his shirt. The late afternoon sunlight breaking through the clouds strobed golden bars of light against his naked torso—honey against amber, sleeked with silk and velvet darkness where his body hair arrowed down beneath the waistband of the trousers he was now unfastening.

At some point he had removed his shoes, and for some reason the sight of his feet, bare, tanned and masculine, caused her heart to flip over. It was laughable, really, that such a small intimacy should possess such an intense charge. Was it because when James had made love to her he had never properly undressed, claiming that his shared student digs made it unwise? Did the sight of Rocco's bare feet somehow signal to her senses that now at last they would be able to experience what true sexual passion and the possession that went with it really meant?

Was it true after all that one did not need to be in love to enjoy passionate sex? Did she care?

Rocco stepped out of his trousers. Julie's heart took a high dive into shuddering delight. She had seen adverts for men's underwear, featuring what she had always suspected must surely be digitally honed and enhanced male models, but now she realised they had come nowhere even close to reflecting anything like the degree of male sexual perfection that was Rocco Leopardi. And how well that name suited him. Like the leopard, his flesh clung to sensuously strong muscles that moved sinuously and gracefully: a hunter's body, dangerously sleek with strength and purpose, its flesh satin-smooth, making her ache to reach out and stroke her hand against it.

When he removed his sleek-fitting white boxer shorts Julie sucked in her breath.

Had she actually ever seen James naked? If so, suddenly she not only couldn't remember but didn't really care. This—Rocco's body—was surely physically male sexual perfection? She had never given any thought to wondering if one day she might look at a naked man and want to feast her gaze on his sexuality. She simply hadn't thought in those kind of terms. She had loved James as a person, not for sex, and she was not the kind of woman who had ever been interested in going on a girls' night out to watch male strippers. She had believed that desiring a man came from loving him, but now, shockingly, she realised that just looking at Rocco was making her feel positively faint with lust.

Rocco watched Julie looking at him with a slanting half-hidden glance. Her lips were parted, her tongue pushing between them to dampen them, and her heart was thudding visibly and unevenly against her ribs. Her nipples were gathered and hard, but it was the look of open and awed delight he could see in her eyes that his own flesh registered first and responded to.

It was a look that said she was paying him the greatest compliment a woman could pay a man who had not yet been her lover. A look that aroused him even as it honoured and welcomed him.

He lay down on the bed beside her, kissing her slowly and with deliberately erotic intensity, using his tongue to tease and enflame her until she was reaching for him, her hands curling into the hard muscles of his arms, her mouth opening beneath his and her body arching up against him in open abandonment.

He cupped her breast and rubbed the pad of his thumb against her nipple as he kissed her neck, and then her shoulder, feeling her whole body jerk up against him in hot pleasure. He took her hand, lacing his fingers with her own and kissing the inside of her wrist as he played sensually with her nipple, before drawing her hand down to place it against his erection.

She made a semi-mute sound, her eyes widening as though with confusion and uncertainty. Her fingers trembled as they brushed against him, and then closed round him whilst she released her breath in a ragged exhalation.

His flesh felt hot and slick and heavy, moving almost of its own volition within her hold, causing her hand to tighten around it in possessive female delight. She released him to touch and stroke the full length of him, from the hard and shiny tip to the thick hair growing round the base that prickled against her fingers and then back again, until the sensation of his mouth against her breasts pierced her with such unbearable pleasure that her hand automatically gripped him. She was unable to enclose him fully, but still she tightened her fingers around him as the movement of her hand mirrored the slow, deep tug of his mouth against her nipple.

Rocco reached down and slid his hand into the open silk organza leg of her knickers, probing the already swollen and unfolding protective outer lips of her sex. Just as her tongue-tip had tempted him earlier, so the hard arousal of her clitoris tempted him now.

What was Rocco doing? James had never... But of course she knew what he was doing, Julie realized, and as she lay back, panting softly under the intensity her own pleasure. She wasn't that naïve, even if she had not experienced such a pleasure before. It gripped her and took her, softening some muscles and tightening others, opening her legs, lifting her hips, making her tremble violently, ready to throw herself into the heart of the volcano if necessary, rather than be denied pleasure.

Pleasure that Rocco's touch was promising her with a long, lazy caress that went the full length of her eager wetness in a way that made her ache and long feverishly for the thrust of his flesh within her own. She opened to his touch and cried out beneath the onslaught of sensation, her senses overloaded by the movement of his fingers against her clitoris.

Impatiently Rocco tugged off Julie's silky knickers, and then tensed as he realised what he was doing. She was lying naked and ready for him, her hips arched to allow him to remove her underwear, exposed intimately to his gaze. He tracked the frantic and unsteady pulse he could see beating beneath her skin. He didn't have a condom, and he didn't trust her. She had been his half-brother's plaything, and that of heaven alone knew how many other men. It was unthinkable that he could want her—and even if he did it was more unthinkable that he should take the risk involved in having sex with her. He started to move away from her, and then checked when she made a small agonised sound.

She was looking at him with helpless need and longing, pleading silently with him, pain and pride mingling with her shock at the extent of her wanting. She wasn't making any attempt to hide from him what was happening to her. The look on her face could have been that of a virgin who had never known such pleasures before, who was still half-afraid of them. But of course she was no such thing.

Rocco sighed and placed his hand on her thigh to push it closed against its twin, so that he could reject her without having to say the words he knew would humiliate her. Where had it come from, this extraordinary feeling he had of wanting to be gentle, of not wanting to hurt her? And more importantly why?

Her eyes closed, tears seeping from their corners, and a deep shudder racked through her.

She was in his hands—literally as well as figuratively. His to take or leave; his to pleasure or leave unfulfilled; his…

Something about her need for him, and the manner in which she was so helplessly vulnerable to it and to him reached out to him, touching his heart and making it impossible for him to deny her.

Rocco leaned over her, kissing her closed eyelids, tasting the salt of her tears, stroking her until her flesh quickened to his touch beyond the point of no recall.

It should have ended there, with the sound of her ragged breathing soft in his ear and the frantic pump of her heart easing back under the post-orgasm tremors seizing her body. He had, after all, given her what she had wanted, but in doing so he had unleashed his own passion, and now it was his turn to ache and burn for her beyond sanity or safety.

Her arms held him, wrapping around him. Her body was sweat-slick against his own. He lifted her hips and gave in to his need to sink into her, slowly, deeply, letting the mind-destroying pleasure take him as her flesh caressed him, her muscles holding him tighter than he had imagined possible.

How was it possible for a woman of her experience to show so little artifice? To be so held in the grip of her desire that her awe of it shone in her eyes and echoed in her soft cries of pleasure? How was it possible for her to be so sweetly shocked by the way he filled her, murmuring incoherent words of admiration and delight into his ear whilst her lips pressed eager kisses against his flesh? How was it possible—?

But anything and everything was possible when a woman aroused a man the way she had aroused him, Rocco acknowledged as he let the fire take him and burn him, commanding his thrusts and his rhythm in the same way that he was commanding her response to them, possessing them both and driving them through urgency and need to the heart of their shared desire. The volcanic explosion that brought his climax a second ahead of hers let him feel the pressure of her flesh gripping him and releasing him in swift convulsive movements.

It was over, leaving her boneless, mindless…and heartless? Julie closed her eyes. Her body was too sated by the extraordinarily intense power of her orgasm for her to have the energy to think. She reached out and let her fingers drift down Rocco's back, damp with the sweat she could still taste on her own lips. She felt humbled and awed, almost unable to believe she had known so much pleasure, and she was hugely grateful to fate for giving her both the opportunity to do so and the man who could arouse it as she lay in a post-coital state of euphoric bliss.

Rocco had given her something that James never had, and she would always be grateful to him, and to life, for that.

The post-orgasm scent of their bodies surrounded her, soothing and relaxing. Julie closed her eyes and moved closer to Rocco, burrowing against him, wanting to be close to him…

She was nothing like he had imagined, he thought. She was a voluptuous innocent who had somehow undermined his defences and taken him to a place he had never previously been.

A voluptuous innocent? She was practically a whore, Rocco reminded himself grimly, and if she seemed innocent it was probably because she was experienced enough to know that men who should know better were turned into helpless fools by her toxic masquerade.

And yet still he couldn't bring himself to leave her…

CHAPTER NINE

JULIE'S hands trembled as she fastened Josh's nappy and paused to blow a kiss at him as he looked back at her and smiled. Today was the day they would learn the results of the DNA tests, and in fact the doctor was due in less than half an hour, according to the message Maria had given her from Rocco at breakfast time.

Rocco. Julie hadn't been alone with him since she had gone to sleep in his arms two days ago. It was quite clear what message he wanted to send to her. She had known that the moment she had woken up in the dark alone.

Perhaps she should feel ashamed of what she had done? Rocco probably thought so, but Julie wasn't ashamed. She wasn't ashamed of anything—not a single, wonderful second of it. She had wanted to know the depth and breadth of her own sensuality and now she did. And if Rocco Leopardi thought that that meant she was going to pursue him for more of the same then he couldn't be more wrong.

One day maybe she would meet someone with whom she could fall in love in the same way that she had fallen in love with James, but this time she would know her own sexual nature, and its needs.

Poor James. He had hated hurting people so very much, and she suspected now that he had probably allowed her to believe that he loved her rather than hurt her with the truth that he merely liked her as a person rather than desired her as a woman. His love for her, she was sure, had been that of a friend, not a lover. That made her feel sad and regretful—more for her lack of understanding and awareness than anything else. But the anger she had felt was gone—swept away in the torrent of passion she had known beneath Rocco's hands and in his arms.

She picked Josh up and cuddled him, in part to distract herself from the direction of her thoughts and to conceal her faint blush, although she never needed an excuse to show her love for her precious nephew. He was growing bigger by the day now, putting on weight and responding to the attention she gave him with smiles and joy that turned her heart over, until it felt as though it was melting with her love for him.

There was nothing she wouldn't do for him to keep him safe and well.

She wished the ordeal ahead of her was already over, and that she knew one way or the other where Josh's future lay: here in Sicily or at home in London. But wherever it was she intended to be with him.

'You're my baby,' she whispered lovingly to him. 'My adorable, gorgeous, wonderful baby.'

His chuckle made her laugh and Rocco, who had heard both her words and her soft loving laughter, paused on the landing outside her bedroom on his way past, immediately rejecting the sensation that tightened round his heart.

She meant nothing to him. How could she? He just hoped that her child would *not* turn out to be Antonio's son. That way he could have her on the first flight back to London so that he could get on with his life and forget that he had ever met her, his duty to his family done.

And if the boy *was* Antonio's?

The same thing applied. He had his own life. She and the boy would become his father's responsibility, not his, and the castle her home—if his father allowed her to stay.

It was almost eleven o'clock. He'd been out at the development since seven o'clock, and he needed a shower before Luca arrived. Rocco rubbed his hand over his jaw. He hadn't been sleeping well, waking up in the night with an ache in his body and a sense of loss and aloneness.

He cursed himself under his breath. Wasn't it bad enough that he'd had unprotected sex with a party girl, without developing some maudlin sense of thinking that his bed felt empty without her in it?

Julie tried to smile naturally as she walked into the salon which she had previously considered to be the most 'homely' of all the villa's formal reception rooms, but which now felt formidably grand.

Dr Vittorio and Rocco were already there. The doctor was formally dressed in a dark suit, in contrast to Rocco, who was wearing a soft, white, short-sleeved cotton top and a pair of clean but slightly faded chinos. His hair looked damp, as though he had recently been in the shower. Her belly cramped, her muscles compressing against the now-familiar ache that accompanied his presence in her thoughts.

Whilst the doctor smiled at her Rocco came forward, taking Josh out of her arms before she could protest.

Apprehension surged through her, leaching the blood from under her skin and leaving it milk-white.

Had the doctor already given Rocco the results of the tests? Had he taken Josh from her because—?

Maria's entrance with coffee and some of her home-made almond biscuits, plus—thoughtfully—a bottle for Josh, cranked up Julie's tension.

Maria had poured their coffee and left them before Dr Vittorio reached for his leather case and opened it, saying calmly, 'Since I know you will both be anxious to hear the results of the tests, I will not delay any longer.'

He looked at Julie, giving her a look that made her heart turn over. It contained compassion and, she thought, regret. She watched him remove some papers from his case and hand them each a set.

'You will both see for yourselves that the tests show quite clearly that Antonio is not Josh's father.'

Not his father! Julie's hand trembled, her whole body going weak with relief. The papers she was holding slipped from her grasp. She had to sit down. Only now could she admit how much she had wanted this result—and not just because she'd wanted to believe that James was Josh's father. It was for Josh's own sake that she did not want him to have been fathered by Antonio Leopardi.

And for her own? Because she didn't think she could trust herself if she had to remain in close proximity to Rocco Leopardi?

Rocco frowned as he saw Julie's reaction, his frown deepening when Luca helped her to one of the hard-backed satin-covered sofas, urging her to sit down.

Still holding Josh, Rocco went towards them, bending down to pick up the papers she had dropped as he did so. He registered both how much thicker the set she had was, compared with his own, and then the look of concern on Luca's face as he stepped forward to say, 'Let me take that for you, Rocco.' He reached not for Josh, but for the DNA document.

Julie leaned back against the sofa. It was over. Josh was hers and only hers. The relief was making her feel slightly sick, as though it was almost too rich for her to digest.

Ignoring Luca's words, Rocco flipped over the printed sheets of data. The first one was an exact copy of his own, but the second was different.

He had to read what it said twice before he could rationalise it, then his mouth thinned as he looked first at Luca and then across to where Julie was leaning back against the sofa with her eyes closed.

Luca placed a restraining hand on Rocco's arm, his expression one of concern and disquiet, but Rocco ignored his silent message, shaking off his hand and striding over to the sofa.

She had nothing to fear from Rocco now, Julie reassured herself, reaching up to take Josh from him, assuming that that was the only reason he had come over to her despite the look of compressed anger he was giving her. But instead of handing Josh to her he sat down beside her, still holding him in the crook of his arm whilst with the other hand he waved the papers he was gripping in front of her.

'What the hell does this mean?' he demanded.

Julie looked at him blankly, and Dr Vittorio interceded warningly. 'Rocco, Julie hasn't seen the results herself yet.'

'She doesn't need to see them, does she? After all, she knows perfectly well already that she isn't Josh's mother.'

Julie gasped and looked helplessly at the doctor, who shrugged in apology and told her, 'I'm sorry—I should have warned you. But I didn't give Rocco a set of your results. Since I was going to talk to you later about your own health, I had planned to mention it to you then.'

'So if you aren't Josh's mother then who the hell are you?' Rocco demanded, barely waiting for the doctor to finish speaking before he fired his furious question at her.

Rocco still had Josh cradled in the crook of his arm. Julie wanted very badly to take her nephew from him, but to do so she would have to reach across Rocco himself.

It was easier to say huskily instead, 'Please give Josh to me.'

'Why? He isn't your child.'

It was as though he wanted to hurt her—his words a deliberate blow, a rejection of her place in Josh's life. But why? Josh meant nothing to him. He wasn't Antonio's child after all. The DNA tests had proved that as conclusively as they had obviously also proved that she wasn't his mother.

'Not my child, no,' Julie agreed, her chin firming with determination as she confronted him. 'But he is related to me—I am his aunt.'

'His aunt?'

'Yes.'

'So where's his real mother? Or can I guess? Living it up with the man she found to take Antonio's place—if indeed it is only one man. What do the pair of you do? Take it in turns to live the good life?'

Julie had had enough—more than enough, in fact.

'You have no right to say that. You don't know anything about me or the way I live my life.'

Colour stained her skin as she saw the manner in which he was looking at her. She knew he wanted to remind her of what had happened between them, and how she had abandoned herself to his lovemaking. It had been a lie to say that he knew nothing about her. Of course he knew something about her—he knew a great deal about her in one sense. Certainly more than any other man did. Maybe more than any other man ever would. There wouldn't be many men prepared to take on a young woman with a child—especially when they learned the story of Josh's conception and she was obliged to admit that she had no idea who had fathered him. It was too late now to wish, as she had so passionately on many occasions these last few days, that she had thought to ask for DNA tests to be done herself to see if James was Josh's father. Unfortunately at the time of his death the issue of Josh's paternity had been the last thing on her mind.

Julie exhaled shakily. 'My sister is not partying.' Her voice twisted. 'And before you ask me how I can be so sure about that, the reason I know is that she is dead.'

Julie bent her head, concentrating on watching the way her fingers pleated the silky fabric of her long cardigan as carefully as though her life depended upon it.

'Judy—my sister—our parents, James—her fiancé— and his parents were all killed in a rail accident earlier this year. They were going to Scotland to look at a castle Judy had read about as a possible venue for their wedding. They'd left Josh with me because—'

'Because your sister didn't want to be bothered with him.'

The ugly brutality of Rocco's statement fell painfully across her heart.

'It is difficult, when you've got something as important as a wedding to plan, to look after a small baby, and Josh hadn't been very well. Our parents agreed that for his own sake he should be left with me.'

'So it was your sister who was Josh's mother, and presumably Antonio's bed-mate?'

'Yes. She told me about him. And…and about the fact that she was pregnant.'

'Did she tell you he was the father?'

'She thought he might be,' Julie replied carefully. Thanks to Rocco, she now knew just what her sister had been doing whilst she had been in Cannes, and so could understand why Judy hadn't been sure who'd fathered Josh, telling her that she only *thought* that Antonio could be the father of the child she was carrying.

'You mentioned a fiancé?'

'James? Yes.'

'James.'

The way Rocco said James's name told Julie that he had recognised it—and why.

'Tell me something. When you referred to James in our discussions were you referring to him in your assumed role as your sister or on your own behalf?'

Julie frowned.

'I'm sorry—I don't quite understand.'

'Was he your lover or your sister's?' he demanded bluntly.

Julie could feel the raw burn of her own humiliation.

Lifting her head, she faced him squarely and told him quietly, 'He was my lover first and then Judy's. Not that it is really any of your business.'

She wasn't going to explain or attempt to defend herself. Let him believe what he wanted to believe.

Dr Vittorio, who had moved over to the window, must have moved back, because Julie heard him saying firmly, 'Rocco, that's enough, I think. All you really have a right or a need to know is that Julie here is the little one's blood relative.'

'And his legal guardian,' Julie put in determinedly.

'I need to speak with Julie about her own health, but first I'm afraid there's something else I should tell you. Your father rang me this morning, insisting that I tell him the results of the DNA tests.'

'And did you?'

'Yes—since he was working himself up into a bit of a state, and it had in fact been proved that Josh is not his grandson. He is naturally disappointed.'

He certainly would be, Rocco reflected, but if he was honest he felt relieved for little Josh's sake. At least now the child would be spared over-indulgence coupled with emotional manipulation—which, Rocco and his brothers believed, had led to Antonio turning into the adult he had become.

Julie was grateful to the doctor for having taken Rocco's attention from her, and even more grateful when he asked quietly if he could talk to her in private about the results of her blood tests.

She was just about to nod her head when Rocco shocked her, by confronting the doctor and telling him crisply, 'Patient confidentiality is all very well, Luca, but since I have a vested interest in Julie's health, I should warn you that I intend to be made fully aware of her results *and* your diagnosis.'

In saying that he had a 'vested interest' in her health, was he reminding her that he had paid Dr Vittorio's fees? Julie wondered uncomfortably. It was humiliating to know that she simply could not afford to stand up and tell him that she would pay her own bills and buy Josh's and her own clothes.

'Julie must give her permission.'

They were both looking at her.

He knew the secret she had been keeping from him now, so what was the point in refusing? Except, of course, for the boost it would give her pride. Until he pointed out that she had no money to pay the doctor's bill.

'I don't know why you should be interested in my health,' she told Rocco, before turning away to look up at the doctor and say quietly, 'But, since obviously you are, then, yes, Dr Vittorio—I give my permission.'

The doctor opened his bag again and withdrew a file of papers, giving Julie a brief, reassuring smile as he saw the anxious look she gave it.

'You are, as I thought, suffering from anaemia,' he told her. 'But as the blood tests I ordered have not shown cause for concern in the form of any kind of serious medical complaint which could have led to problems with your blood cell count, I think we must put your condition down to other influences. You are a young woman in sole charge of a small child, with no partner or family to support you. You told me yourself that Josh had health problems of his own, and I can guess that the deaths of so many people close to you must have had a traumatic effect. If in addition to that you have perhaps had financial problems...' He paused tactfully, whilst the colour came and went in Julie's face.

'I... The nature of the deaths of my sister and our parents has meant that there will be delays in sorting things out. Josh and I are, of course, the sole beneficiaries of my parents' estate, but my parents' will did not cover this kind of eventuality. My solicitor is doing his best, but he doesn't know how long it will be before we are able to receive anything. I did have some savings—not much,

and when Josh was ill I had to take time off work. Then…'
She bit her lip, not wanting to betray Judy. 'There were
certain monies owing that had to be paid.'

'You mean that your sister left you her debts?' Rocco
challenged her.

'Not deliberately. Judy didn't know what was going to
happen.'

'She knew she had a child to support, and that she was
shortly to get married.'

'Things *have* been difficult,' Julie admitted to the doctor,
ignoring Rocco.

'There is no real serious problem with your health, but
I do not wish to minimise the danger of your anaemia. You
really do need to eat properly and rest. Some warm
sunshine and freedom from the burden of the worries you
have been carrying would do a great deal to improve
things.'

Julie managed a small smile.

'I shall do my best to follow your advice,' she told him,
turning back to Rocco to say coolly, 'Now that Josh has
been ruled out as a potential Leopardi, I'd like to return to
London as soon as possible. There's no need for us to
remain here now.'

It was Rocco's turn not to answer. She was right. There
was no reason for her to remain here now. His duty to his
brothers and the Leopardi name was done; it only
remained for him to inform Falcon of the results of the
DNA tests.

There was, of course, the matter of their financially recompensing Julie for the disruption to her life—as Falcon
had said they must if her child should prove not to be
Antonio's.

Rocco started to frown. That should surely be his responsibility, since he was in the best position to judge what adequate recompense might be. Swiftly he mentally surveyed his memories of the area in which Julie and Josh lived, and their circumstances when he had found them, adding them to the information about her health that the doctor had just given them. He came to an immediate decision.

'On the contrary,' he corrected Julie tersely. 'There are two very good reasons why you should remain here, and I am surprised that you have not thought of them for yourself.'

Julie looked at him uncertainly and waited.

'I am sure that Dr Vittorio will agree with me that, given your own poor health—'

'My health is not poor. I am anaemic, that is all.'

Ignoring her outburst, Rocco continued, 'And given the fact that Josh is making such good progress here, it not only makes sense but in many ways I consider it essential that you should stay here until your health has improved.'

'I can't do that,' Julie protested. But even though she was saying the words, she knew perfectly well that there was nothing she really wanted more than to stay.

'Rocco is right.' Dr Vittorio joined the conversation, nodding his head. 'In fact, I cannot think of a better prescription for both you *and* Josh.'

'I have a job, and a flat, and...'

'You have a serious health problem which will surely deteriorate if you return too quickly to the life you were living. No, my mind is made up,' Rocco said firmly. 'You and Josh will remain here in Sicily until Dr Vittorio pronounces you well enough to leave.'

Julie gasped. Well, honestly—of all the arrogant, high-handed things to do! But what could she say? She knew Rocco well enough now to know that there was no point in arguing with him. And he was right about her health and about Josh. She would never forgive herself if she insisted on returning to London only to find that Josh's health started to deteriorate. How could she provide the kind of environment for him that he had here? And besides, if she stayed, then perhaps...

Perhaps what? Perhaps because Rocco had had sex with her it meant something? She would be foolish in the extreme to start believing that, Julie warned herself. He didn't care about her at all. And what was more she didn't care about him either. What they had shared had just been sex, and she had better not forget that.

Just? How could the word 'just' be applied to the wondrous life-changing experience she had had in his arms? But she must not admit to that. Not even to herself. In fact, she must not think about it at all.

It had been a tumultuously difficult morning, and Julie was relieved to finally be on her own with Josh, enjoying the sunshine in a sheltered part of the courtyard garden.

At least she *had* been enjoying it on her own. She grimaced, her heart sinking as she looked up and saw Rocco striding purposefully towards them. His shadow cast a long silhouette in front of him that touched her before he himself reached her, reminding her, if she had been in need of any reminder, that there was no part of her he himself had not touched—physically and emotionally.

'This James,' he demanded abruptly. 'You were in love with him?'

Julie looked away from him. Now what did he want?

'Yes,' she acknowledged.

'He was your first lover?'

Immediately she turned to look at him, the startled shock in her expression betraying her ahead of her reluctant, 'Yes.'

Josh, lying on his rug on top of a comfortably padded throw Maria had found for them, crowed in triumph as he found his own toes, momentarily distracting them both.

'Before you say anything, I've put sunscreen on him.' Julie rushed into the silence to defend herself from the question she suspected might be coming—only to stop, torn between discomfort and an unwanted feeling of sharp grief as she realised that there was no reason for Rocco to care what happened to her nephew anymore.

Perhaps, though, he was as slow to recognise that fact as she had been, because he answered coolly, 'Maria said that you had. It's just as well that you are keeping him out of the direct sunlight, though. His skin won't be used to it.'

He turned back to her, resting one foot on a stone tortoise close to where she was sitting so that he could lean closer to her and demand, 'And he has been your only lover?'

Her heart jumped so much that it felt as though it had lodged in her throat.

'I can't see what relevance that could have to anything we might need to discuss.'

She'd been proud of the calm levelness of her voice, convinced that it hadn't given anything away, until he stood upright and said, in a voice that seemed oddly to hold satisfaction, 'So he has. And what happened? Obviously it wasn't anything to do with your lack of willingness in bed.'

Julie was torn between chagrin and indignation.

'What James and I felt for one other didn't have anything to do with sex,' she told him, only realising when it was too late, and one dark eyebrow had risen in a mocking gesture of cynicism, just how her defence could be interpreted. 'What I meant was that we loved one another and…and our relationship wasn't based merely on sex,' she corrected herself.

'You loved him but he didn't turn you on?'

'No! I mean, yes—I loved him and of course he turned me on.'

'So what happened?'

When she looked uncertainly at him he sat down on the stone bench next to her chair. 'What do you mean what happened?' she asked.

'You said that he was potentially Josh's father, and that he had been your sister's lover—which begs the question why? According to what you've just said, you loved one another and were already lovers.'

Julie looked at Josh. Watching him gave her a valid reason for not looking at Rocco.

'My sister was extremely beautiful. She liked to boast that she could have any man she wanted, and she wanted James.'

'Your sister was a tart, who traded sex for material possessions and a taste of the kind of life she lusted after more than she did the men foolish enough to find her attractive.'

'James fell in love with her,' Julie continued, refusing to argue with him. 'I was dreadfully hurt at the time. Poor

James—it must have been so difficult for him. He knew how much I loved him, and he didn't want to hurt me, so...'

'So he continued to have sex with you as well as with her?'

'No!' Julie was too shocked to lie. 'No, of course not. There was no question of anything like that.'

Enlightenment dawned, and she gave him a bitter smile.

'If it's your health you're worrying about, and the reason for all these questions, I can assure you are quite safe from any contamination from me. I had a full check-up when I fell ill with a virus that I caught from Josh. My local surgery is involved in a government-sponsored drive to do that kind of thing.'

'You must have found it difficult to go without sex once he'd left you for your sister,' said Rocco, ignoring her bitter outburst.

His blunt comment made her feel defensive. 'Why do you say that?'

'Because you were so hungry for it with me,' he told her, even more bluntly. 'More hungry than I've ever known any other woman to be.'

'I'm sorry if you found my...me offensive.' Her voice was stiff with pride now.

'I didn't say that,' Rocco told her laconically. 'I simply said that you were desperately hungry for a man's touch and the satisfaction that goes with it.'

'I'd really rather we didn't discuss this subject anymore.' How prim she sounded. But what he was saying reminded her far too intimately of just how abandoned she had been.

Julie moved uncomfortably in her chair, the small movement watched thoughtfully by Rocco.

It had shocked him at first to discover that she wasn't the woman he had thought. But he couldn't deny that the discovery had made sense of several things about her that had puzzled him. Talking to her now had added a certain piquancy to what he already knew—like a delicate sauce added to a dish that was already tempting the appetite.

'Why didn't you tell me right from the start that you were not Josh's mother? It would certainly have saved us both a great deal of aggravation.'

'You didn't exactly give me the chance, did you? How could I, when you'd already made up your mind about me? Besides, I was afraid that if Josh did turn out to be your half-brother's child your family would take him away from me straight away if they knew I wasn't his mother.'

'I gave you my word that that would not happen,' Rocco pointed out.

'Well, I won't have to worry about it now, will I? Because Josh isn't Antonio's son, thank goodness. I always hoped that James would be his father.'

'Because you loved him?'

He was too astute.

'Yes,' she admitted. 'Not that I don't love Josh for his own sake. I do.'

She meant what she said, Rocco thought, watching her. Josh was very lucky to have a mother figure in his life who was so protective of him.

'There is still the matter of our recompensing you for coming here,' Rocco continued. 'I cannot say how much the sum will be until I have spoken with my eldest brother.'

'I don't want any money.' Julie could feel her heart thudding with angry pride.

'It has already been agreed that you will be recompensed. It is our duty to do so.'

How arrogant he sounded and looked. Julie's throat ached with her own painful emotions. It was so easy for her to see how he viewed her. To him she was someone of no account, whose feelings did not matter—someone he could simply pay to disappear from his life.

'No. I will not take it.'

The ferocity and passion in her voice surprised Rocco.

'Why not? After all, you were quick enough to agree to come with me when I told you in London that there would be a financial advantage in your agreeing to come to Sicily with me.'

That was different, Julie wanted to tell him. That was before you touched me and I knew... But she must not admit even to herself what she knew.

'I thought you meant that Antonio had made some kind of financial provision for his child,' Julie said stiffly. It was in part the truth.

Rocco shrugged dismissively. 'So the money will come from us, Antonio's half-brothers, there is no difference.'

'Yes, there is,' Julie insisted. 'You talk of your own pride—the Leopardi pride—well, you are not the only person to have pride. I have it too, and I will not accept money. Josh is not a Leopardi. My pride is every bit as important to me as yours is to you, and I do not want your money.'

To his shock Rocco realised that something—a combination of emotions that gripped his heart in some unfathomable way—was making him want to take hold of her and go on holding her. Determinedly, he pushed the feeling away.

'Maybe not, but you have Josh to think of.'

'It is because I am thinking of him. I don't want him growing up thinking that it is acceptable to live off other people. I want you to give me an account of everything you have spent on us so that I can repay you once my parents' estate is settled.'

'Absolutely not,' Rocco told her arrogantly. 'Your request is offensive, and an insult to me as a Leopardi.'

Julie's eyes widened. What about his offensiveness to her? she wanted to say, but she knew there was no point. Rocco might describe his father as arrogant but he himself was no better. Arrogant, high-handed, incredibly and over-poweringly sexy—

Julie clamped down on the unwanted thought that had somehow or other managed to slip past her defences.

Her defences? Why would she need to defend herself against acknowledging that Rocco was a very sexually attractive male?

Did she really need to ask herself that, when she didn't even have to see him or be with him to ache for a repeat of the pleasure he had already shown her?

CHAPTER TEN

IT HAD been Maria's idea, and her determined lobbying of Rocco on Julie and Josh's behalf, that had finally led to Rocco giving in and agreeing to take them both to watch the annual ceremonial parade in a small town ten miles away from the villa. Traditionally, to mark the start of spring and to bring luck for a good harvest to the town's surrounding citrus groves, the townspeople paraded through the town on floats and in costumes. The event was one of the highlights of the year in the area.

As though the weather was determined to be in accord with the date—and very auspiciously, according to Maria—they had woken up to brilliant sunshine and a warmth in the air which, combined with the scent of citrus, couldn't help but lift anyone's spirits, Julie admitted.

Julie had dressed Josh for the event in one of his new outfits—a pair of neutral-coloured baby chinos, and a checked shirt in blue-greys and yellow, over which she had slipped a small matching pullover in blue-grey with a knitted yellow border. He looked absolutely adorable, Julie decided, and as though he knew that himself—or had picked up on her own excitement at the thought of having a day out—he was all beaming smiles.

But was her happy mood occasioned by the thought of a day out because she would be spending the day in

Rocco's company? Julie asked herself sternly as she finished getting ready.

What if she *did* want to spend the day with Rocco? There was nothing wrong in that, was there? Julie's eyes widened slightly at her own naïveté. Of course there was something wrong with it. And what was wrong with it was the fact that she wanted to be with Rocco at all. She would soon be going home. Once she was back in London she would never see him again.

All the more reason to make any most of the opportunity to spend time with him now, the reckless voice inside her urged. Whilst that other voice, the one that knew her better, warned her that if she listened to its opponent she would end up being badly hurt.

It was foolish and dangerous to build fantasies inside her head that could never be anything *but* fantasy. So Rocco had made love to her and it had been a life-changing experience for her? That did not mean he felt the same way. For him it had simply been sex, and she must accept that and move on from it. Yes, now she knew what it was to be sexually fulfilled, and she could dream if she wished of how wonderful it would be one day to meet a man whom she could love sexually and emotionally, but she must accept that that man would not be Rocco.

By repeating that warning to herself when Rocco came to take Josh downstairs for her she was almost able to behave naturally, and as though the sensation of his hand brushing against her bare arm as he took the baby from her had absolutely no effect on her at all.

Although Maria had assured her that the parade had no religious significance, Julie had decided that it might be as well to cover up rather than risk causing any offence. She was wearing a pair of off-white linen trousers teamed with a cobalt-blue silky strappy top in case it got warm, with a matching prettily shaped knitted jacket over the top.

When she saw the way Rocco was looking at her she laughed and told him, 'Whoever selected these clothes obviously didn't realise they'd be worn by someone who spends her time with a small child. They are impractical, I know, but it's such a sunny day that I couldn't resist wearing them.'

'You've put on weight,' Rocco told her, ignoring her comment. 'Good. You needed to.'

'I suppose I *had* begun to look slightly scrawny,' she agreed.

'Not scrawny. That is an ugly word, and you could never look ugly.' Before she had time to register the fact that he was actually paying her a compliment he continued, 'Fragile is the word I would have used. Maria has told you, I expect, that she is joining her own family for the celebrations?'

Julie nodded her head.

'I should warn you that it will be very crowded; it is best, I think, that we stick together.'

The minute the local lotharios saw Julie on her own they would home in on her like locusts, Rocco thought grimly. Had he ever actually thought of her as plain and dull? It wasn't just the little bit of much-needed weight she had put on that was responsible for the glow that now seemed to illuminate her face, Rocco suspected. The fact that she was now free from the pressure of having to struggle to support herself and Josh as well as pay off her late sister's debts must also have played its part.

* * *

They were in the car, Josh strapped into his baby seat and cooing happily to himself, and Julie couldn't help smiling herself.

How could he possibly not have recognised her beauty right from the start? Rocco asked himself. When she smiled, as she was doing now, she had such a serene look of joy about her that it caught at his heart and stopped his breath. Any man would be proud to call such a woman his own.

Now what was he thinking? Hadn't he always sworn that he would never marry or make a commitment to any woman?

It didn't take them long to reach their destination, and Julie gave a small exclamation of pleasure as she saw the ancient walls of the town rising from the rocks on which it was built, the grilled windows of the houses which had obviously been built into the walls over the years looking down at them.

'The present-day town was built on the site of an Arab fort,' Rocco explained, deciding that it would be wiser and safer for him to talk about the history of the town than to let his thoughts travel in the direction in which they seemed rebelliously determined to travel.

'As one of the conquering Normans who fought for and won the island, our ancestor was given land and this town—which he in turn fortified. It was only later that our family moved out of their fortified home here in the town to the castle—although of course we still retain strong links with the town. In fact, you will see signs of that everywhere—in the names of streets, in the Leopardi coat of arms on walls here and there, and some say in the faces of some of the townspeople as well, from the days when it was considered a matter of honour for the daughter of a family to be selected by her lord to warm his bed for a season.'

Julie winced. Small wonder, with a family history such as the one Rocco was so casually outlining, that he should think nothing of taking her to bed.

Rocco parked the car on a piece of flat ground which was obviously serving as a temporary car park. 'The streets of the town are very narrow, and whilst traffic is not prohibited it is not encouraged. In the summer as well as now, during the festival, it attracts a good many visitors—all the more so since Falcon persuaded our father to allow work to begin on the restoration of the ancient steam and mud baths. Legend has it that the Greek architect Daedalus designed the building which surrounds them after he fled here from Crete. The restoration work is due to be completed this year.'

'It sounds fascinating,' Julie told him truthfully, holding Josh whilst Rocco dealt with the buggy.

As they joined the stream of people walking towards the main gated entrance to the town, Julie reflected that they could have been any small family on a day out—except for the fact that it was plain to her from the looks Rocco was attracting that most people knew who he was and were slightly in awe of him. And of course she was nothing to him other than someone who might have been the mother of his half-brother's illegitimate child.

What was it, she wondered, about a certain kind of man that automatically set him apart and elevated him from other men, causing his own sex to view him with respect and her own with animated delight? Whatever it was,

Rocco certainly had that quality in spades. The Leopardis might be lords of all they could survey here in this part of Sicily, but Rocco had no need of the Leopardi name to attract female interest or to prove that he was an alpha male, Julie thought ruefully. Even the way he pushed the buggy somehow reinforced and emphasised his maleness.

The place to watch the parade was in the *piazza* in front of the town's main church, according to Maria, and it was there that Julie and Rocco headed, to rendezvous with the housekeeper and her family.

Their progress was held up by the number of people who came forward to pay their respects to Rocco, but finally they reached the square, guided through the crowd by two young men who had introduced themselves as Maria's grandsons, with the information that Maria and her family had saved them a grandstand view.

A grandstand view would have been found for Rocco in any case, Julie guessed—which made it all the more touching to see the way in which he courteously thanked Maria for her trouble.

Josh had to be admired by Maria's female relatives and passed round amongst them in a way that slightly alarmed Julie at first—until she reminded herself that this would be the custom in a large family clan, and it would be churlish to make a fuss.

By the time the parade started Josh was back in her arms, wide awake and gazing around—although of course he was far too young to be aware of what was happening.

For sheer pageantry the parade took one's breath away, Julie admitted, wincing slightly at the noise from the trumpets of the brightly clothed heralds in their scarlet and gold tabards, followed by 'men at arms' dragging 'prisoners', and then floats filled with people in all manner of costumes.

On the other side of the square, during a small gap in the parade, Julie watched as a young couple embraced, the girl turning her face for her partner's kiss. Their happiness, so very evident and joyous, made her feel very alone.

Someone wanting to get closer to the parade pushed past her, causing her to half stumble into Rocco. As he steadied her Julie started to apologise, but Rocco shook his head, telling her calmly as he put his arm round her waist and drew her closer to him, 'Whilst we're in this crowd I think it would be safer if you stood close to me.'

Since Rocco had already reached for the buggy with his free hand, whilst keeping his arm around her, Julie had no option but to stay where she was.

She would be safer, Rocco had said. Safe from being accidentally pushed by the crowd, perhaps, but certainly not safe from an even greater danger. The scent of his cologne, so barely and yet so tantalisingly discernible against all the stronger smells of hot food and sunshine, made her want to turn her head so that she could seek it out and breathe it in. But would she be able to stop at that? Wouldn't she then be tempted to nuzzle the warm column of his throat, exploring it with her kisses and all the time moving closer to his mouth? Her heart slammed into her ribs, desire curling insidiously through her body as light as smoke and as dangerous as fire.

'You are enjoying the parade?' Rocco asked, his lips close to her ear so that she could hear him above the noise of the crowd.

Of course it was to hear him that she half turned into his body. His hand was a warm heavy weight against her hip, and Julie was thankful that he didn't know that the ache in her breasts and the ache in her lower body were in competition over which was most intensely in need of the touch of his hand.

When it was time for them to go and have some lunch Julie didn't know whether to be relieved or disappointed that there was no longer any need for them to share such physical intimacy.

It had been a wonderful day—a special, magical day out of time—and she would treasure its memory for ever, Julie decided happily later on in the afternoon, as she and Rocco made their way back to the car. Rocco was pushing the buggy, and when he reached for her hand to help her over a patch of rocky ground, then kept on holding it, Julie felt her heart somersault with delight.

They were back at the villa when Julie's happiness was suddenly changed to shocked fear and disbelief.

The bleep of her mobile phone warning her of a voice-mail message was unusual enough to have her immediately removing the phone from her handbag, and she excused herself to Rocco when she saw that the message was from her solicitor.

It was long and complex, and the news it contained was dreadful. It drove the happy pink flush of colour from her face, and she had to hear it again to make sure she had not misunderstood it.

Her solicitor reported that, due to the fact that her parents had remortgaged their house a year before their deaths and given a very large sum of money to Judy, and also the fact that for some reason her father had omitted to pay the premiums on his life insurance, there would be very little value in their estate for Julie and Josh to inherit.

And, if that was not bad enough, he added that he also had to inform Julie that a solicitor for James's sister and her husband had been in touch, advising that they intended to ask the courts to revoke Julie's status as Josh's legal guardian in their favour because they did not think that as a single young woman she could provide the same quality of care and financial security for Josh as they could.

The fact that they were a couple and were far more comfortably circumstanced than she was herself, thus better able to provide Josh with a stable and secure home, meant that in his view their challenge had to be taken very seriously indeed, her solicitor warned her, adding that the process would be a long and very expensive one, and that in the circumstances Julie might want to think seriously about where Josh's best long-term interests lay.

In other words, her solicitor thought that she should give Josh up.

'No!' The mobile slipped through her fingers to fall on the floor whilst Julie sat down on the stairs and covered her face with her hands.

Rocco scooped up the mobile, checking that Josh was still safely asleep in his buggy. When Julie failed to respond he autocratically listened to the message himself, and strode towards her.

Somehow she had managed to get herself under control and stand up, even though she felt sick with shock and despair. What was she going to do?

'I don't understand,' she told Rocco. 'Annette doesn't even like children. She's always refused to have a family, even though her husband desperately wants one. She wouldn't even look at Josh, never mind hold him. She told me to keep him away from her in case he dirtied her expensive coat. I can't let her take him. She won't love him properly. I know she won't.'

Her shocked distress aroused all Rocco's protective instincts. He had grown up without his own mother and he knew the pain that caused. Josh had already bonded with Julie, and the truth was that he had grown attached to the child himself. Why should Josh be handed over to strangers just because they were a couple, when he could provide him not only with financial security but also with a father?

'There is a solution,' he told Julie, his mind made up.

'What?'

'Marriage.'

CHAPTER ELEVEN

'MARRIAGE,' Julie repeated uncomprehendingly.

'Yes,' Rocco confirmed, telling her coolly, 'If you and I were to marry, then there would be no question of anyone trying to take Josh from you.'

'What? That's…that's not possible.'

Rocco frowned, his resolution, like his pride, hardened by her rejection and denial.

'Why not?'

You don't love me. How easily those words might have slipped from her lips—and how illuminatingly, shining an unwanted and far too bright light into the most private recesses of her own heart.

'It doesn't make sense,' Julie told him weakly.

'On the contrary—it makes perfect sense.' Rocco over-ruled her. 'I know what the lack of parental love and the loss of a mother can do to a child, and since it is within my power to ensure that that does not happen to Josh, then—'

'But to marry me? Josh is not your responsibility after all.'

'I cannot agree with that. Whilst you and Josh are living beneath my roof you are both as much my responsibility as my father's people are his. That is what it means to be a Leopardi. I cannot abdicate that responsibility any more than I can deny my name and my blood. It is my duty to honour my responsibility to my blood and to you.'

'That's…that's feudal—' Julie began, only to have Rocco stop her.

'You believe, do you not, that you have a responsibility towards Josh, and that you must put his needs first and above your own and do what is right for him?' he said.

Julie nodded her head, her heart sinking as she realised where this conversation might be leading.

'Then you must understand that I too have my own sense of responsibility.'

He meant what he was saying, Julie recognized, but she still shook her head and said, 'But we are nothing to you…'

'You are here beneath my roof. Therefore you are my responsibility,' Rocco repeated, before continuing. 'On the other hand, if I have misunderstood your feelings and you do not feel you have to put your nephew's best interests first—'

'Of course I do.'

'Then you will agree that in marrying me you will be doing exactly that and providing him not just with the security of two parents but also with financial security.'

What could she say? It was impossible to deny the logic of Rocco's argument.

Every word he said reinforced for Julie what she had already come to know about him—namely that he was a man whose sense of responsibility was incredibly deep.

Her emotions see-sawed wildly between hope and dread, longing and revulsion, need and pride. Rocco was offering her a way to secure Josh's future. But it was a permanent place in his heart that she longed and ached for, and that was never going to be on offer. Did she really want to submit herself to the emotional anguish of living with

Rocco as his wife when he did not love her? Wouldn't it be better for her own safety to reject his proposal? But what about Josh? Wasn't it her duty to put his needs first? Hadn't she been worrying about raising Josh on her own, all too aware of how important it was going to be for Josh to have the right kind of man in his life to model himself on? Josh had no male relatives of his own blood; he only had her. If she married Rocco he would not only provide Josh with material security, he would also be there for him as a father. No matter what her own personal feelings, didn't she owe it to Josh to recognise how important a role Rocco could play in his life?

As though he had picked up on her own thoughts, Rocco continued firmly, 'It is Josh we must both think of first here. He is a child who has already lost his parents and his grandparents. He loves you and depends on you. You have said yourself that this woman who wishes to claim him is not a fit mother for him.'

'But marriage...' Julie protested weakly.

Rocco shrugged. 'You may think of it as a temporary business arrangement, if you wish.'

A business arrangement. How those words hurt her. But it was not her own feelings that mattered here, Julie reminded herself sternly.

'As Josh's stepfather I shall do everything within my power to ensure that he is happy and well cared for. And before you ask, no, I do not have any particular desire for children of my own. I am not my father's eldest son, after all, with a duty to provide an heir.'

And of course any marriage to her would not stop him from finding whatever sexual pleasure he wanted outside that marriage. Pain ripped through her, tearing away the pitiful attempt she had made to conceal her real feelings about him. She wanted to be the only woman he sought for pleasure; she wanted to be totally and completely his; she wanted his desire and his love.

Julie could taste the sour bitterness of her awareness of the bleakness of her future. But if she refused Rocco's proposal, and James's sister did try to get custody of Josh, how was she going to feel? She did not have the money to fight a lengthy court case, and neither did she have the emotional and physical reserves to cope with months and maybe years of not knowing whether she would have to give Josh up. She couldn't ignore the effect that kind of pressure was likely to have on Josh. And then there were the final implications of her solicitor's message…

Why was she hesitating? Logically, what Rocco was proposing was the ideal solution—and if she wasn't careful he might start probing to find out why she was holding back, what personal emotions she might be hiding.

The thought of her humiliation were he to discover that she had fallen in love with him galvanised her into saying unsteadily, 'Marriage just seems such a big step to take.'

'Too big? And yet you have told me over and over again how committed you are to Josh—and were to the man who fathered him. He can never share your life, but Josh can.'

'I understand what you're saying, and I'm grateful to you for suggesting it,' Julie felt bound to say. 'But…well, it seems so huge…I mean, for you to marry me to protect Josh. You are being very generous to…to both of us, but I have my pride too, and the thought of taking advantage of your generosity worries me.'

'Does it? Or is it in reality the thought of me taking advantage of our marital status that is actually worrying you?' Rocco asked her silkily.

Immediately Julie's face flamed with guilt and longing.

'That never crossed my mind,' she protested untruthfully. Such a scenario had indeed crossed her mind, but she was afraid not of any advances on his part, but of her own reactions to him, and what they would betray. She could hardly admit that, though, could she?

'We have no time to lose,' Rocco told her, dropping the subject of her fears, much to her relief. 'The sooner we are married the sooner Josh will be safe. Then you can reply to your solicitor that there is no question of you giving Josh up, since your circumstances have changed and you are no longer a single mother but have a husband. But of course the decision must be yours.'

Helplessly, Julie admitted to herself that there was only one decision she could make.

She nodded her head, and told him huskily, 'Yes. I mean, yes—thank you. I would like to marry you.'

When Rocco had said that things needed to be done swiftly, that was exactly what he'd meant, Julie recognised two days later, her head spinning at the speed with which events were progressing.

Naturally as a Leopardi Rocco knew all the right people to talk to both in Sicily and in London in order to make sure that the practical legalities were dealt with, but Julie was still astounded to learn that they were to be married the next morning in the small private chapel attached to the villa.

All the paperwork in preparation for their marriage had been completed, and once dinner was over Julie excused herself. The events of the last few days had exhausted her—if anything, even more emotionally than physically. Her medication was helping her to overcome her anaemia, but Julie doubted that the doctor would have anything to prescribe for the heartache that she suspected lay ahead of her.

She had brought Josh downstairs and put him in his buggy whilst they were having dinner, because Maria had gone to see her family and Julie hadn't wanted to leave Josh on his own in his bedroom.

Now, as she excused herself, Rocco got up to pull out her chair for her, saying something in Italian to his lawyer, who had joined them for dinner, before turning to her and stating firmly, 'I shall see you both to your room.' He wheeled the buggy towards the door.

Josh woke up when Rocco lifted him out of the buggy, and the look of recognition in her nephew's eyes, and the happy smile that followed it as he looked up at Rocco, were all the proof that Julie needed that she had made the right decision for Josh.

The right decision for Josh, but what about for her?

She was marrying a man who aroused her sexually and with whom she had fallen passionately in love—a man whose conversation stimulated her and whose personality intrigued her and challenged her. A man with whom she would never be bored and within whom she suspected there was a strong streak of compassion for others that with the right kind of encouragement could be harnessed to do so much good for others less happily circumstanced. There was nothing she wanted more than to be the true partner of such a man, to be loved by him as his one true soul mate. But that, of course, was a foolish fantasy.

They had reached her bedroom. Rocco opened the door for her and stepped back so that she could precede him into the room.

Three cream full-length dress bags had been placed on her bed.

'Wedding gowns,' Rocco told her. 'Unfortunately there isn't time for you to choose your own, so I arranged for a fashion house in Milan to send these out with Ricardo.'

Ricardo was the lawyer, and Julie wondered how he had felt about escorting three wedding gowns from Milan to Sicily.

Josh had gone back to sleep, so Rocco put him down in the middle of the bed, and then reached into his pocket, producing a small turquoise jeweller's box.

Mutely, Julie watched as he came towards her. There was a horrible hard lump of misery in her throat, and an aching sense of loss and despair in her heart.

No doubt the ring she was about to receive would be as tasteful and expensive as the wedding gowns lying on the bed. And just as devoid of any of the real feelings they should have signified as their marriage itself would be.

Rocco had flipped open the lid of the box, and just as she had guessed the glittering dazzle from the rings inside it made her blink.

The solitaire diamond surrounded by a circle of smaller diamonds and set on a diamond and white gold band perfectly matched the diamond and white gold wedding ring that went with it. They were rings that caught at the heart with their beauty and exclusively expensive allure, but diamonds were a poor substitute for love, Julie thought painfully.

Somehow she wasn't surprised that the rings should be

so very much to her taste—nor that the engagement ring which Rocco insisted on sliding onto her finger fitted it perfectly.

He was still holding her hand. Without thinking Julie looked up at him, her eyes widening slightly in a mixture of panic and longing as she saw the way he was looking back at her, his eyes darkening as he shifted his gaze from her eyes to her mouth and then began to lower his head. His intention of kissing her was quite plain.

Ridiculously, Julie panicked, shaking her head and pulling back from him as she told him quickly, 'There's no need for that. We both know that it doesn't mean anything.'

Why was he frowning at her? She would have thought that he'd be pleased that she was being so sensible and businesslike, that she was not expecting him to behave as though he was a real bridegroom-to-be and she his bride. If that had been the case then…

Then what? Then right now she would be in his arms, her love for him spilling emotionally from her heart as she told him how much his love meant to her?

A small noise indicated that Josh had woken up, and, glad of the opportunity to do so, Julie turned away from Rocco to go to her nephew.

Having picked Josh up, it was safe to turn round and look at him. She was holding Josh like a barrier between them.

There was something she had to say to him. She took a deep breath, and said huskily, 'Thank you.' She swallowed, and then added, 'For…for everything. I know this can't be something that you really want. It's different for me, of course. I have to put Josh first. But…what I'm trying to say is…I'm very grateful to you for what you're doing.'

Rocco nodded his head, but the grim look he was giving her suggested that her gratitude didn't really mean very much to him. Was he having second thoughts? Wishing that he hadn't behaved so gallantly and taken on such a heavy responsibility?

When he left without saying anything more, Julie didn't know whether to be relieved or disappointed.

In the corridor outside Julie's room, Rocco stared unseeingly into the shadows. His reaction when Julie had recoiled from him as he'd bent his head to kiss her had stunned him, catching him off guard. But it was irritation he felt, nothing else. Irritation because she was clinging so naïvely and stubbornly to her adolescent crush, elevating it to a status it didn't deserve. She had rejected his kiss out of some misguided loyalty to a man who had never taken the time to show her pleasure. Well, let her deny herself the pleasure they could have shared if she wished. Why should he care?

But he did care, Rocco recognised as he headed for the stairs. He cared very much. Abruptly he stopped in mid-step. He cared? For her? Was that his real motivation for marrying her? No! He was marrying her because it was his responsibility to do so and for no other reason.

Daylight was creeping into the room through the uncurtained windows as the night's shadows lifted. Julie didn't know whether to be alarmed or relieved. She had barely slept—how could she, knowing what the morning would bring?—and now that the day was here she could feel the enormity of what lay ahead flooding her senses.

Removed from their protective covers, the gowns fluttered like fragile ghosts in the breeze from the open windows. Julie had already made up her mind which one she would wear—the simplest of the three, in matt cream silk satin and cut on the bias, its seams sewn with tiny pearls. Pearls for tears? No, she mustn't think of that. It had a high neckline and long sleeves, and a small bustle at the back, falling into a demi-train. She had chosen it because she felt that its plainness and its high neckline and long sleeves were more suited to the occasion than the more flamboyant styles of the other two gowns.

There was no time for her to linger over her preparations.

Maria, who had brought her the breakfast she had not been able to eat, had returned to help her dress and take charge of Josh for her.

Julie leaned over the cot to look at the sleeping baby. She could see for herself the way in which their time here had already benefited him. He looked so much healthier, and he was happier too. It had startled her at first to see the way Josh looked towards Rocco whenever he was in the same room. His delight when Rocco smiled at him or picked him up was plain to see. If he were never to see Rocco again he would miss him, but he was barely two months old—he would forget him.

It was all very well her telling herself that it would be wrong to deprive Josh of Rocco's presence in his life, but wasn't she only doing so to mask the fact that she wanted to marry Rocco? Rocco was not connected by blood in any way to Josh, after all. But that did not mean they could not form a deep emotional bond. Just as it had surprised her to see how Josh responded to Rocco, so too it had amazed her to see the genuine warmth and tenderness in Rocco whenever he was with Josh. Was she doing the right thing? Or was she rushing into something that she would later regret?

It was too late. Maria was holding out her dress for her.

Giving Josh a light kiss, Julie went back to stand submissive whilst Maria fussed round her, her manner and her expression filled with the delight and excitement that Julie knew she should be sharing.

It felt so unreal, stepping into her wedding dress. In the past when she had dreamed of this moment she had imagined herself in her childhood home with her parents—not here, in this feudal land of powerful, arrogant men who lived by their word, their honour and their pride. She had dreamed of marrying James and of a quiet, steadfast love. Not Rocco and the fierce, dangerous passion he aroused in her.

Maria was sobbing emotionally, praising the beauty of her gown and her good luck in securing such a wonderful man—a Leopardi—for her husband.

All too soon it was time for her to go downstairs to where Rocco's lawyer was waiting to escort her to the private chapel. He told her Rocco was already waiting for her.

The chapel was small but magnificent, its ceiling and walls brilliantly frescoed with biblical images and its pews beautifully carved. Julie could feel the weight of its years of devotion, and panic started to fill her at the thought of the awesome nature of the commitment she was about to make here in this holy place.

She hesitated in mid-step and felt the quick look the

lawyer gave her. She was doing this for Josh, Julie reminded herself shakily, and she focused on Rocco's ramrod-straight back. Somehow just looking at him calmed her, and filled her with a deep spiritual awareness of the purpose of the commitment she and Rocco were making, so that her body stopped trembling. The lawyer, who was holding her arm, paused to give her an approving smile, as though he sensed her determination to do what she felt so deeply to be right.

But it was only when Rocco turned to look at her that she felt truly able to take the final steps that brought her level with him, as though somehow he himself was drawing her to him and giving her strength.

The service was simple, its words timeless and beautiful and the priest compassionate and yet stern as he underlined the gravity of the commitment they were making, joining their hands and commanding them to repeat after him their vows to one another.

This time she did not evade Rocco's kiss. In fact she desperately wanted to cling to it and to him, needing reality in a world that seemed all too unreal.

In the small room off the chapel there were papers to sign, and then Rocco was guiding her back into the chapel and down the aisle to the font, where Maria and Josh, awake and dressed and lying happily in his buggy, were waiting for them.

It was done. Josh was safe. But at what cost to her? Only time would tell if she had the strength to endure her love for Rocco and his lack of love for her. It wasn't as though she hadn't already had practice, she reminded herself, remembering James. But her feelings for James couldn't in any way compare with what she felt for Rocco.

Rocco looked at Julie's pale, set face. She was his now. His wife. A feeling he couldn't analyse seized him: primitive, male, and very possessive. The satin gown caressed her body so lovingly that he almost felt jealous of its intimate contact with her, wanting to replace its touch with his own. He could see the admiring looks his lawyer was giving her, and he wanted to draw her away from him, to keep her from the desiring looks of all other men and for himself alone. She and the child were both now beneath his protection. His. He was now a husband and a father, and his duty was to keep them both safe. Their future was his responsibility.

A husband, but not a lover—nor loved.

Did he want to be?

That he should even need to ask himself that question was a warning that rubbed against Rocco's pride like wet sandpaper against tender flesh.

It astonished Julie just how much attention to detail Rocco had given to the outward form of their marriage— there was a photographer to capture their images, and a small, hastily arranged but nonetheless elegant champagne reception to which a variety of local dignitaries had been invited. Rocco informed Julie, as they stood side by side whilst Rocco introduced her to their guests, that it was expected and would give rise to comment if he did not show public pride in their marriage and in her as his wife.

'Oh, and by the way,' he added, 'I've told Maria that rather than disrupt Josh, since his nursery is off your bedroom, it makes sense for you to continue to sleep in your own room rather than move into the master bedroom.'

Simple enough words, and there had been a time when

she would have received them with gratitude, but now they felt like a mortal blow to her heart, Julie admitted.

'I wouldn't want things any other way,' she managed to answer, but she didn't dare risk looking at him as she spoke, just in case he could see her real feelings in her eyes.

But what else could she reasonably have expected? She knew he didn't love her, that he had only married her for Josh's sake, and logically she ought to be pleased he had found such a tactful way of pointing out to her that he didn't want her sharing his bed, given his almost arrogantly alpha maleness.

Their 'guests' had left, Rocco was escorting his lawyer to a car waiting to take him to the private plane that would fly him back to the mainland, and Josh, who had been awake to be admired during the champagne breakfast, was now a soft, sleeping weight in her arms. The silk satin dress, for all its elegance, somehow felt tawdry, given the real reason for her marriage, and Julie longed to take it off and put on clothes that she had bought for herself, no matter how cheap and unstylish they might be compared with the things Rocco had bought for her. Like the champagne that had soured her palette and left her longing for clean, fresh water, those designer clothes were part of a lifestyle that was not really hers, and they reinforced the fact that she had in one sense been bought by Rocco just as easily as Antonio had bought her sister.

But for very different reasons. Everything she had agreed to and had done was for Josh's sake.

That wasn't true. Hadn't at least part of the reason she had agreed to marry Rocco been the fact that she had fallen in love with him, and had snatched eagerly at the opportunity to share his life?

Share his life? She was indeed a fool if she really thought there was any chance of that. If Rocco wouldn't let her share his bed then there was precious little hope that he would allow her to share anything else, was there? A single tear splashed down onto Josh's face, causing him to open his eyes and then yawn sleepily before closing them again. His trust in her touched Julie's heart, and she curved her mouth in a softly tender smile as she bent to wipe away the tear.

Watching her unobserved from the doorway, Rocco frowned. There could be only one reason for a bride to cry tears of sorrow on her wedding day, and that was because she had married the wrong man, her love having been given to someone else. Anyone observing her with Josh could see how much he meant to her—the child of the man she loved.

With the curves of her body hidden by the sleeping baby she looked more like a Madonna than a bride, untouchable and aloof. But he wanted to touch her, he wanted to hold her, he wanted to hear her cry out to him in her need as she had done before. He wanted her, Rocco admitted, stepping back from the doorway before Julie could see him mooning over her like some yearning lovesick adolescent. For a moment he wondered if that was why he had deliberately left it too late for his brothers to make it in time for the wedding.

No, he had done his duty by Julie and Josh, that was all. Now he had a duty to his business, to the construction site where he had had to postpone several important meetings in order to make time for today's hurried marriage.

There was no need for him to hang around the villa as though he was waiting around to beg for what few spare crumbs of attention Julie might throw his way. He had better things to do with his time.

It was Maria who informed Julie that Rocco had gone out and that she didn't know when he would be back.

Was that sympathy or pity she could see in Maria's eyes? Julie wondered as she asked Maria to help her unfasten her wedding dress—a duty and a pleasure that should surely have been Rocco's. Only there was no pleasure for him in touching her, was there? Not for him. But for her that pleasure was the sweetest and the most dangerous she had ever known or would ever know.

CHAPTER TWELVE

IT WAS gone ten o'clock in the evening and Rocco had still not returned. There was nothing to keep her downstairs. The last thing she wanted was for Rocco to come in and find her hanging around as though she was waiting for him, desperate for his company. Maria had already locked up, and she might as well go up to her room as stay downstairs Julie acknowledged.

In the nursery Josh lay fast asleep, his eyelashes fanning across his healthily pink cheeks. For his sake if not for her own she knew beyond any doubt that she had done the right thing. She had no idea just why James's sister had decided that she wanted Josh, but what Julie did know was that she would never have been a good mother to him.

Her wedding dress had been carefully packed away in its dress bag, and there was no sign anywhere in the room that today had been her wedding day unless it was in the new shine of her rings. There was certainly no husband— no Rocco here with her, to make the vows they had exchanged real in the only way a marriage could be made real.

Julie undressed and headed for the shower before changing her mind, tempted instead by the thought of a luxurious soak in the large deep bath.

Pinning up her hair, she started to run the bath. On impulse she closed the nursery door so that she wouldn't disturb Josh and switched on the bathroom's state-of-the-art music system, which was loaded with a wide selection of different kinds of music.

Tonight the haunting sound of female blues singers crooning about their lost love best suited her mood.

The bathroom was its own private oasis of blissful self-indulgence, and the music and the bittersweet scent of the bath oil she had chosen perfectly matched her mood of melancholy and longing. The blues music whispered its knowledge of what it meant to be a woman hungering for a man who did not hunger back for her.

The bath was deep enough for her to slide her body beneath the water and let it lap at her throat, caressing her like warm scented silk. Her flesh was so aware of the pleasure it had known with Rocco and was now denied that every small movement of the water was almost a physical touch. If she closed her eyes it would be so easy to remember, to imagine, to transfer her memories of Rocco's possession from the past to the present, to pretend that she was in truth his bride, lying here waiting for him and for his caress…

Rocco heard the muted strains of music the minute he opened the door and walked into the bedroom. He had spent longer at the site than he had planned, and even though he'd known that Julie wouldn't have waited up for him there had been something about entering the darkened villa on this, his wedding night, that had touched a newly exposed nerve deep within his sense of self, where he felt most vulnerable. He had thought himself safe from the pain that came from emotional loss through the death of his mother, as though the intensity of that had seared and sealed away his vulnerability, but now he recognised that he had been wrong. Rocco didn't like being wrong—about anything—and he liked even less the driving need that had brought him here to this night-shadowed bedroom that smelled of the rose scent Julie had worn when they exchanged their vows.

The bedroom was empty, and when he opened the door to the nursery Josh, its only occupant, lay sleeping peacefully in his cot. Closing the nursery door as he exited, Rocco looked towards the bathroom. A blues singer was sobbing out her tale of angry, passionate grief, her song drowning out the sound of his entrance. Julie was lying in the bath, her eyes closed, damp tendrils of hair escaping from her topknot to cling to her face. She was lost, oblivious to his presence, her parted lips and accelerated breathing telling his senses that she had given herself over to some private, sensual daydream. But not of him! Her left hand rested on the side of the bath, devoid of the ring he had placed there earlier.

A feeling Rocco didn't want to analyse ripped through him in a tidal wave, sucking away reason and replacing it with the powerful rip curl of emotions it had dredged up from deep within him.

Julie was his wife, and this was their wedding night. No way was he going to have her fantasising about some other man. Without stopping to analyse his own reactions, he strode over to the bath, reaching down to take hold of her hand.

Julie opened her eyes and struggled to sit up, shocked into a panicky reaction by the unexpectedness of Rocco's touch. The violence of her movements sent the bathwater splashing over the side of the bath, soaking Rocco's shirt and jeans.

'Where is your wedding ring? Why have you taken it off?'

Why was he looking at her as though she had committed some heinous crime? 'It's a bit loose and I didn't want to lose it.'

'Liar. You took it off because you didn't want to be reminded of me whilst you lay there imagining your precious James pleasuring you.'

They stared at one another, as though neither of them could quite believe what Rocco had said.

'That's not true,' Julie denied.

'Isn't it? I'm not a fool. It was obvious when I came in here where your thoughts were—as obvious as the sensuality of their nature. Your body can't lie about that even if you want to do so.'

Before she could stop him Rocco had drawn his fingertip swiftly down her wet skin to the curve of her breast, unintentionally exposed when she had sat up in surprise. He moved along it to the flushed peak of her nipple, eagerly flaunting its erotic arousal.

'*Now* tell me that you weren't thinking about your lover,' Rocco challenged her angrily.

Julie tilted her chin. Her heart was thudding—with anger, she assured herself, even though she knew perfectly well that those jerky, fast-paced unsteady thuds within her ribcage were born more of excitement than anger, and that the sharp thrill of sensation shooting through her was pure, desire-driven heat.

'Very well, then,' she told him dangerously. 'Yes, I was thinking about my lover.' It was true, after all, even if he had mistaken the identity of that lover, not realising that it was Rocco himself she had been longing for and not James. 'And why shouldn't I if I want to?'

Now she really had shocked herself. And yet there was a thrilling sense of wanton delight in having said those words.

'Why shouldn't you?' Rocco's lips thinned, his eyes almost black as he stared down at her. 'Do you really need to ask me that? It's less than twenty-four hours since I took you as my wife.'

Fiery, illicit pleasure poured through her at the sound of those words, reinforcing for her everything she already knew about her own feelings.

She wasn't really actually trying to egg Rocco on to physically possess her, was she? And if she was? He was her husband, after all, so she had the right...

The right? To what? To torment a man into making love to her when he didn't really want to? Hot shame burned her conscience.

'I think you should leave,' she told Rocco unsteadily. The bathwater had gone cold and she was starting to shiver, chilled as much by her self-disgust as the cooling water.

'Really?'

Rocco's voice was as soft as silk, wrapped around the wicked danger of a sharp stiletto blade—like whispers from the shadows that held a Pandora's box of enticing delight laced with unknown dangers.

'Well, I think I should do this.'

His iron grip already held her shackled, but it was her own desire for him that really held her imprisoned and was her greatest enemy, Julie recognised as he lifted her from the bath with one easy movement that barely moved his chest, ignoring the water cascading from her as easily as he ignored her feebly voiced protests. In the background the music rose to a crescendo of pleading, but Julie no longer needed to plead for her lover.

'Your clothes are wet.' What an inane comment to make.

'Then, like a good wife, you'd better take them off for me.' Rocco mocked her.

Undress him? Julie felt boneless with the melting heat of her own longing.

The signs of her desire were clearly evident, but that desire was not for him, Rocco warned himself. Her thoughts had been with another man when she had lain there beneath the water, thinking of his touch.

He wanted her. He was her husband.

He took her hands and placed them on the wet fabric that covered his chest. 'Undress me,' he commanded.

If she did as he was demanding she would be lost.

'No,' she refused, shaking her head. 'I don't want to.'

It was a lie, but he couldn't know that. For a minute, when he released her hands, she thought he was going to let her go and walk away. But then he cupped her face and started to kiss her—oh, so slowly and deliberately—in such an intensely focused way that she knew exactly what the punishment for refusing him was going to be.

She tried to resist, keeping her lips tightly locked together, keeping her eyes wide open and refusing to look at him, tensing her whole body against his slow, sensual seduction of her.

It had to be someone else who was making that small husky sound of pleasure. Another Julie who was tipping back her head and closing her eyes as she willingly offered herself up for his caress, who trembled wildly in a paroxysm of fevered arousal when his fingertips gently brushed her throat and then her breasts, whilst his mouth coaxed and tormented her own into eager participation in the kind of kiss that ravished her senses and laid bare her longing for him.

She wanted him so badly. She wanted him body to body with her, flesh to flesh, touch to touch. Her hunger for him was fed by the thrust of his tongue against her own and the touch of his hands on her naked body, caressing her naked breasts, shaping the indentation of her waist and the curve of her hip. His fingers dipped into her own secret wetness, sending showers of fireworks of liquid pleasure exploding through her.

She had to touch him as he was touching her. Impatiently she started to tug buttons through buttonholes in the urgency of her need, meeting and matching the passion of his kisses as the sensation of his skin beneath her fingertips accelerated her arousal.

Her lips followed the eager, explorative journey of her fingertips, tracing the strong column of his throat and the broad sweep of his chest. His body hair was soft against her mouth; her fingers were clumsy on the belt that barred her way to the intimacy she longed for.

Her protest when Rocco suddenly seized her hands to stay them was a raw sound of female deprivation.

'Hush. Wait,' Rocco told her, sweeping her up in his arms to carry her from the bathroom into the bedroom, where he placed her on the large bed.

Looking up at him through the shadows, Julie felt as though her heart was so filled with love for him that it couldn't contain the intensity of her emotions, that it was spilling from her like tears of acute pleasure. She lifted her hand to his face, tracing its shape wonderingly. If he left her now— But he was removing the rest of his clothes, and her heart lifted on the surging tide of her own desire as she looked at him, visually absorbing and recording every precious detail of his physical presence before finally giving in to her need to reach out and stroke her fingertips along the hard, erect length of him.

Her intimate touch tipped Rocco over the edge of his self-control. He took hold of her, kissing her mouth and then her breasts, tugging gently on her nipples, and then less gently when he felt the immediate surge of her response and heard her cry out to him. Her hands reached down to hold his head against her body. His hands found her and caressed her, pleasured her to the point where her pleasure was almost more than she could endure.

'My love,' Julie whispered emotionally, moving feverishly against his touch, commanded by it and yet driven to push past that command to a place where she could command him. 'My only love.'

Thought and feeling melded together, burning away the old Julie, setting their mark on her for ever. She didn't even see the look of dark bitterness shadowing Rocco's eyes as he listened to her, much less register the moment of tension in his body as he swung between pride and desire, wanting her so desperately and yet filled with a need to reject that wanting, having heard her proclaim her love for another man.

In the end his desire won. The pleasure his touch gave her was his mark of possession as he waited for her to come down from that place where he had taken her with the knowing stroke of his fingers to the plateau where his own desire waited impatiently for her.

How well they fitted together—as though she had been made only for him, Julie thought dizzily as he stroked into her, filling her, re-sensitising her still-responsive flesh. Her muscles closed possessively around him, wanting him, rocking with sweet erotic pleasure at each movement within her, until the sweetness was stripped away and there was only a dark, raw passion that had her clinging to him as they swung above the chasm. She cried out to him in the darkness, feeling him sweep them both upwards to brilliance so surely that she was both laughing and crying with joy when he held her through the powerful spasms of their shared orgasm.

It was over. She felt so weak, so lost—and so afraid. Rocco was lying on his back, apart from her instead of holding her as she longed for him to do.

She had called him her love, but of course he was no such thing, Rocco acknowledged. She had meant those words for another man; the man she had exchanged inside her head for him.

What a fool he had been not to recognise until he had her exactly what had happened to him. He didn't just want her. He loved her.

Rocco was regretting what had happened. Julie could tell. That was why he was lying so far away from her. How was it possible to have known so much happiness and yet now feel such dreadful pain? She longed for him to hold her and to whisper to her that he wanted her love. What a fool she was.

CHAPTER THIRTEEN

THEY had been married ten days. Maria had informed her again that Rocco had left the villa early to attend a site meeting. Every night Rocco came to her bed and made love to her, and every morning she woke up alone. Painful though it was for her to admit it, Julie acknowledged that she couldn't avoid knowing that the physical intimacy they now shared had, instead of bringing them closer together, actually destroyed the bond she had felt they were beginning to build. Rocco no longer sought her out to talk with her. He no longer smiled at her, or seemed to want to be with her, and even in bed there was a repressed tension about him that was almost tinged with anger— because he regretted his generosity in marrying her?

It was Julie's nature to give generously to those she loved, without counting the cost to herself, and never more so than when it came to Rocco. She hated the thought that she could be blighting his life and shadowing his enjoyment of it. She wanted him to be happy, to see him smile, hear him laugh. But even if that meant it was someone else, another woman, whose presence gave him those things?

She loved him, and that meant putting his happiness first, Julie insisted to herself as she reached out to unclamp Josh's too exploratory fingers from the edge of the rug on which he was lying, which he was now trying desperately to tug from beneath himself.

The patio where Julie was sitting was warm from the morning sun; her body still had that lethargic ache that came from intense sexual pleasure. Julie looked up lazily when Maria suddenly appeared, her laziness disappearing when Maria told her importantly, 'Il Principe is here to see you.'

The Prince? Rocco's father? She had understood from Rocco that his father was suffering from a terminal heart condition and was virtually bedridden. Why on earth would he want to see *her*?

'Are you sure it is me he wishes to see and not Rocco?' she asked Maria uncertainly.

'It is you he wishes to see,' Maria confirmed, adding, 'Quick—you must hurry and not keep him waiting.'

Against her better judgement Julie found that she was allowing herself to be coaxed and bullied into hurrying back into the house, Josh clasped tightly in her arms.

Maria had shown Rocco's father into the grandest of all the formal salons, twenty metres long and fifteen metres wide, with heavy rococo décor and gilded furniture. Its rich blue embroidered silk drapes threw shadows that reached out to create dim pools of darkness, making it almost impossible to see anything clearly.

It was a shock to see Rocco's good looks stamped so clearly on the face of the man seated in a wheelchair behind which was standing a harassed-looking middle-aged man, whom Julie assumed must be his attendant. The Prince's mouth was etched with pride, and his eyes were colder than polished black marble.

He was, Julie recognised, everything that Rocco had

warned her he would be, and her heart ached for the three small boys left to this man's pitiless care by the death of the mother who had loved them.

'So!' His angry gaze raked Julie from top to toe. 'There is no need for me to ask why you married my son. There can only be one reason.'

Rocco, alerted to his father's arrival at the villa by a phone call from Maria, arrived just as his father and Julie were confronting one another. Both of them were oblivious to his presence, the hostility between them so powerful it was almost like a force field.

'Actually, there are two reasons,' Julie corrected the Prince determinedly. 'One is my love for my nephew, and the other is my love for Rocco himself.'

Pride and truth rang in the clear enunciation of her words, causing Rocco to remain where he was instead of alerting them to his presence.

'You love my son?' Rocco's father gave a contemptuous shrug. 'Of course you do. After all, he is a rich man.'

'I love Rocco for what he is himself, not for his wealth. I would love him just as much if he was poor. In fact I wish he was,' Julie told the Prince passionately.

Rocco's father gave her another cold look.

'Such words are the words of the ignorant and the foolish. How naïve you are. I suppose you believe that Rocco returns your feelings, do you? Your kind always do.'

Rocco had heard enough. He wasn't about to let his father verbally abuse and hurt Julie. He started to move forward, but once again the sound of Julie's emotionally charged voice stopped him.

'No. I don't,' Julie answered her inquisitor. 'I know that

Rocco married me for reasons of duty and of…of chivalry. Because he wants to protect Josh from being stolen from me to suffer as he himself did as a child.'

She could be accused of being cruel, Julie knew, but hadn't this man been cruel to his three eldest sons? Hadn't he denied them the love they had had every right to expect from him? Shouldn't she, out of her love for Rocco, redress the balance if only a little, and show him what an honourable and wonderful man his third son was—even if his father didn't have the wisdom to see it for himself?

'I don't love Rocco because he is your son, or because he has wealth and position. I love him because despite everything he has had to endure the love his mother bore him has touched his heart and made him something that money can never buy.'

'And what might that be?'

'Rocco may have his pride—the pride of his ancestors—but he also has magnanimity of spirit. He has compassion and wisdom; he understands the true meaning of love. He is a man who as a child never knew the true love of a father, and yet he has grown beyond that, instead of allowing it to cripple him emotionally, to take into his protection a child who has no claim whatsoever on him.

'You may be a Prince, but Rocco bears a higher and far more worthy title—and that is the title of a good and honest man, the best of men. The kind of man other men will always look up to because of what he is, not who he is, the kind of man who deserves to have a loving father who values him as he should be valued. I will never burden Rocco with my love. He already has enough to bear. But neither will I allow you to think that he needs anything to win a woman's love other than himself. I would be proud to follow him in rags to the end of the earth if he asked that of me.'

She almost threw her last words at Rocco's father, turning on her heel as she did so, unable to endure another second in his company. She was not going to allow Rocco's father to denigrate the man she loved, no matter how afraid he made her feel, Julie told herself fiercely—and then gasped with shock when she saw Rocco standing in front of her.

'Julie.'

He was angry with her. He had to be. Shaking her head, Julie evaded him, holding Josh tightly as she fled.

Rocco let her go. What he needed to say to her was best said in private—and besides, there were things he had to say to his father, issues that must now be dealt with.

Approaching the wheelchair, he stood looking down at the man seated in it. Falcon had taught him by example to give their father respect, as a matter of duty and as a gift of love and honour to their dead mother, but it was not a respect that came freely and lovingly from his heart, Rocco acknowledged.

'How could you, a Leopardi, marry this—this nobody?' the Prince demanded furiously. 'You are my son. You have a duty to me and to your name. Now you have shamed me and that name by marrying this *nothing*, who should have been sent back where she came from once you knew that her child was not Antonio's. It is no wonder that you married in secret to hide your shame.'

There was so much Rocco wanted to say to his father. But he could see where the swollen vein in his temple had started to throb and pulse under the force of his anger, and he could see, too, the anxious concern of the medical attendant Dr Vittorio had placed in charge of the Prince's day-to-day care.

How pitiful he was, this man who had dominated his childhood and who had filled Rocco with both the longing for approval and attention and the bitter realisation that he would never receive them.

Now, as a result of his treatment of them as children, at a time when a good father should at this stage of his life have commanded their love and care, his father could only command the cold emptiness of duty. Rocco thought of the way in which Josh was already recognising him, smiling up at him and holding out his arms to him. He made himself a promise that the baby's trust would never be abused, and that the small shoot of love was something he would protect and nurture for as long as Josh needed those things from him.

'What you mistake for secrecy, Father, was in fact speed. And the reason I married Julie with speed was because I was afraid she might realise how unworthy of her I am and that I would lose her.'

As he spoke Rocco recognised that there was a great deal of truth in what he was saying.

'Far from being ashamed of my wife, I am very proud of her, and there is nothing I would have liked more than to have my brothers witness our marriage.'

'Your brothers! Bah! The three of you cling together, speaking with one voice, when it is to me, your father, that you owe your loyalty.'

'It is not loyalty that binds the three of us together, Father. It is our mutual love for one another. And as for our loyalty, there we have followed your example. Our loyalty is given to the Leopardi name, not those who carry it.'

Rocco watched as something that might have been vulnerability flickered across his father's face, quickly replaced by anger.

'With every word you say you show how much you are the son of your mother,' the Prince told Rocco with contempt. 'I came here to see what could be salvaged from the folly of this marriage, and was fully prepared to pay this Englishwoman to leave. But now I shall leave you to suffer the consequences of your own making.'

'As all men must,' Rocco agreed calmly, then ignored his father to speak to his attendant. 'My father treats you very unfairly, Aldo. I know it is through no fault of yours that Dr Vittorio's instructions have been ignored. If you will take my father back to the castle, I shall speak to Dr Vittorio and ask him to call there and see my father as soon as he can. Father, Aldo will take you home now.'

Rocco could see expressions of fury, bafflement and confusion crossing his father's face at Rocco's refusal to engage in an acrimonious exchange of words with him.

'I know you will be disappointed that it has not been possible to find this child Antonio said existed, but maybe it is for the best,' Rocco told his father, exhaling before acknowledging that Julie had already had a very profound effect upon him, even if she herself didn't know it. Why else, after all, would he be standing here like this, considering his father's feelings, and actually feeling pity for him where once he would have only felt bitterness and loathing.

'Aldo, take me back to the car,' the Prince ordered his attendant.

Silently Rocco walked alongside the wheelchair as he escorted his father out to his waiting car.

Before Aldo activated the electric ramp that would lift the chair into place in the specially adapted car, Rocco placed his hands on his father's shoulders and bent to kiss him, first on one cheek and then the other. Not as a supplicant, or even as a survivor, but for the first time as a victor who knew that his victory was unchallengable and who could afford to be generous because of that knowledge.

It was Julie who had given him that gift.

Julie.

As the car pulled away Rocco looked up towards the second-floor windows.

Maria was waiting for him in the hall.

'I have something I need to discuss with my wife,' he told her crisply. 'And I do not wish to be disturbed by anyone for any reason.'

When he crossed the hallway a second time he was carrying an ice bucket containing a bottle of champagne and two glasses.

Maria smiled happily to herself. A house like the villa needed a big family to fill it—many *bambini*—and, unless she was very wrong, the first of them wouldn't be very long in the creating. She must have a word with her daughter. She was just the right age to train up as a nursery nurse…

'I think there's something you need to tell me.'

How calm Rocco sounded as he carefully placed the champagne bucket down on a small table next to the bedroom armchair along with two glasses.

Julie felt sick with despair. She had known that he was bound to demand an explanation for what he had obviously overheard.

'I'm sorry if I spoke out of turn and…and offended your father.' Her voice was stiff with the need to protect herself, and she wasn't going to risk looking at him.

'To hell with my father. He isn't what matters right now. Neither is he what I'm talking about, and you know it.'

'No, I don't.'

She was almost stammering now, her heart hammering as she wondered wildly just how much Rocco might have overheard.

Rocco counted inwardly to ten. They could play this game all day long, but right now it was the end result he needed and wanted, not the playing of it. He turned his back on Julie, busying himself with opening the bottle of champagne and pouring two glasses, handing her one as he sought an eloquent way to seek an answer to the question that burned in his heart.

Finally he asked baldly, 'You told my father that you love me, but you told me that you still love James. Which is the truth?'

Dared she tell him? Dared she not? Julie took a quick gulp of her champagne, half gasping under the influence of the bubbles. Rocco was looking at her in the most extraordinary way, with the most wonderful expression in his eyes. As though…as though his gaze was somehow caressing and reassuring her—or was that simply the effect of the champagne? If so… Recklessly Julie took another deep gulp. Now she felt positively light-headed, free of all her doubts and her inhibitions, suddenly overwhelmingly proud of her love for him.

'The truth is…'

'The truth is…?' Rocco prompted.

Julie looked wildly towards the nursery door. This was one occasion on which she would actually be grateful if Josh did wake up without finishing his nap. But her nephew seemed to be more inclined to support his new father than her, because he remained soundly asleep.

'The truth?' Rocco repeated.

'I love you,' Julie told him shakily. 'I didn't mean to, and I certainly didn't want to, but I do.'

The champagne glass was removed from her hand with such speed that she barely had time to blink before she was in Rocco's arms and he was demanding against her lips, 'Tell me that again.'

She tried to frame the words, but how could she when Rocco was licking and nibbling at her lips? He was teasing them with the stroke of his tongue, tormenting her to the point where the only sound she was capable of making was a long moan of hungry need followed by a soft sound of pleasure when Rocco answered the need and kissed her with all the passion and love she had so longed for.

Later, lying together naked in bed, their bodies sated and the air around them soft with the echo of their mutually given pledges of love for one anther, Julie traced the arrogant line of Rocco's jaw, laughing when he took hold of her hand and pressed a fiercely possessive kiss into her palm.

'There's still some champagne left,' he told her.

Julie laughed and went slightly pink. She had protested at first when he had poured some of the champagne onto her skin, kissing her and tasting her through it, but she hadn't protested for very long.

'If we have a daughter we are not going to call her Cristal,' Julie warned him.

Rocco grinned, the sensuality of the way he was looking at her making her heart turn over with joy and love.

'If we have a daughter I shall no doubt feel compelled to lock any man who offers her champagne in my father's dungeons.'

'I thought we might name her after your mother.'

They looked at one another.

'You really think…just now…we…?' Rocco asked tenderly.

Julie nodded her head. 'Yes,' she told him simply. 'After the way you loved me, it just isn't possible that we haven't created a new life. It was so magical, Rocco, so powerful and wonderful, and I love you so very much.'

'You tugged on my heartstrings the first time I saw you, do you know that?'

'What? Looking like a drowned rat?'

'A drowned rat with the heart of a lioness and the spirit of a dove. My one and only love, my heart,' Rocco told her softly, and he took her in his arms and kissed her.

* * * * *

ALESSANDRO

CHAPTER ONE

THE bed on which they both lay naked was high, draped with richly sensuous silk fabric. But its touch against her flesh was nowhere near as sensuously erotic as *his* touch, nor could the whisper of the fabric's kiss compare with the fierce passion of *his* kiss.

His face was in the shadows, but she knew its features by heart—from the burning intensity of his dark eyes through the arrogance of his profile to the explicit sensuality of his mouth. Excited pleasure curled and then kicked through her. Simply looking at him awoke and aroused the woman in her in a way and at a level that no other man ever could. Just as she was the only woman who was woman enough to truly complement him as a man. They were made for one another, a perfect match, and they both knew it. Only here, with him, could she truly be herself and let down her guard to share her longing and her love.

He made her ache for him in a thousand—no, a hundred thousand different ways, and the way his knowing smile lifted the corners of his mouth told her that he *knew* that her whole body shuddered in mute delight at the slow, deliberate stroke of his fingertips along the curve of her breast.

She sucked in her breath and closed her eyes. His stroking hand moved lower, over her quivering belly, and then lower…

Guiltily Leonora shook herself out of her daydream and

warned herself that if she didn't start getting ready and stop wasting time she was going to be late.

What a fool she was. Her brothers would certainly think so. She could just imagine the hoots of derision with which they would have greeted her fantasy—and the secret of her own deeply sensual nature.

That was the trouble with growing up a girl sandwiched in the middle of two brothers. The three of them had been born so close together that Piers was only eighteen months older than her, and Leo a year younger. The fact that they had lost their mother so early, killed by a speeding driver as she was on her way to meet them from junior school, had naturally affected them all—including their father, an ex-professional sportsman who had retired from his sport to manage and then take over a sportswear manufacturing company. Their father had believed in fostering competition between his children as a way of preparing them for the adult world. He was also very much a stiff-upper-lip kind of man. After their mother's death Leonora had felt she had to work even harder at being 'one of the boys' for her father's sake, so that she wouldn't let the side down by crying like a girl.

Her father loved them all very much, but he was an old-fashioned man's man, and he hadn't been very good at showing that love to a motherless daughter. Not that Leonora blamed him for anything. In fact she was fiercely defensive of both him and her brothers, and they were even as adults a close-knit family. But not so close knit that they hadn't welcomed their new stepmother when their father had remarried three years ago. But watching her father unbend and get in touch with his emotions under the gentle tutelage of his second wife had reinforced for Leonora how much she had lost with her mother.

It was only her pride that kept her going sometimes, as she struggled with her growing need to be the woman she instinctively knew she might have been against the often harsh reality of being the competitive tomboy girl her father had taught her to be. Sometimes she felt so helpless and lost that she was afraid that she would *never* find her real self. Sometimes when she was being true to her real self and one of her brothers laughed at her she felt so crushed that she retreated immediately into the combative sibling hostility of their childhood.

And sometimes, like now, she took refuge in private dreams.

The fact that she needed to fantasise about being with a man who loved and desired her, and with whom she could have wonderful sensual sex, instead of actually knowing what it felt like from first-hand experience was, of course, partly a result of the way she had grown up. Listening to her brothers discussing their own sexual experimentation had made her wary of being judged and found wanting, as they so often seemed to judge other girls.

Leonora didn't consider herself to be the cringing, over-sensitive type, but there was something about the way her brothers, as pubescent boys, had talked about girls—giving them scores for availability, looks and sexual skill—that had made her believe that she never, ever wanted to wonder if some boy was talking to his friends about her in the way that her brothers had about girls. Because of that she had fought against and denied the depth of her own passion-ate nature, concealing it instead with a jokey 'one of the boys' manner.

Whilst other girls had been learning to be confident

with their sexuality on their way to becoming women, somehow she had learned to fear hers.

It was different now, of course. Her brothers had grown up and, at twenty-seven and twenty-four, were well past the teenage stage of discussing their sex lives and their girl-friends with anyone.

She had grown up too, and at twenty-five felt uncom-fortably self-conscious about her still-virginal state, and very thankful that no one, most especially her brothers, knew about it. Not that she allowed herself to think about her lack of sexual experience very often, other than in that self-protective jokey way she had developed. She had more important things to worry about, such as getting a job. Or rather getting *the* job, she admitted, as she stepped into the shower and turned on the water.

As children, all three of them had been skinny and tall. Whilst Piers and Leo had broadened out, Leonora—whilst not skinny—was still very slender for her five-feet-nine-inch height. But her skin was still golden from a late October holiday in the Canary Islands the previous year, and her breasts were softly rounded, with dark pert nipples, and just that bit too full for her to go braless. In her tomboy days she had longed to be able to do so, hating the unwanted restriction of 'girls' clothes' as she struggled to compete with her elder brother and at the same time make sure that her younger brother knew his place.

The life-long fate of the poor middle child, she thought ruefully, and a struggle that was still ongoing now.

She was out of the shower as speedily as she had stepped into it, crossing her bedroom floor on long, slim legs and drying herself as she did so, her long dark hair a tangle of damp curls.

Her pilot's uniform lay on the bed, and her heart did a somersault as she looked at it. Leo had complained so much about the loss of his spare uniform over Christmas, when they had all gone home to Gloucestershire to spend Christmas, that she had felt sure that someone in the family would suspect her—especially as Leo had already promised to let her take his place. But luckily nothing had been said.

Poor Mavis, who worked at the dry cleaners two streets away from the tiny London flat Leonora rented, had protested that there was no way she could adjust the jacket to fit her, never mind the hat. But Leonora had told her that she had every faith in her, and ultimately that faith had been rewarded.

Leonora knew that many of her friends thought that she was very lucky to work freelance, giving private lessons in Mandarin, but it hadn't been with becoming a language coach in mind that Leonora had honed her gift for languages, adding Russian and Mandarin to her existing French and Italian.

Life just wasn't fair at times, and it seemed to treat a person even more unfairly when she was a girl with two brothers. *She* had been the one to say first that more than anything else she wanted to learn to fly and become an airline pilot, but it was her younger brother who was now on his way to having her dream job—piloting the privately owned jet of the billionaire owner of a private airline based near Florence—whilst she, with all her flying qualifications, was teaching Mandarin. But then, as her elder brother had commented on more than one occasion, it was her own fault for insisting on qualifying in a world in which it was always going to be difficult for a woman to make her mark.

There were women pilots, of course—any number of them, but a humdrum job flying in and out of one of Britain's regional airports wasn't what Leonora wanted. Nor was it what she had trained for. No—her aspirations went much higher than that.

As a middle child, and a girl sandwiched between two brothers, Leonora felt as though she'd had to fight all her life to make her voice heard and her presence felt. Well, today she was certainly going to be doing that, when she took her brother's place at the controls of the private jet belonging to the owner of Avanti Airlines.

Leo had tried to wriggle out of letting her do it, as she had known he would, but she had reminded him that he owed her a birthday present and a big, *big* favour for introducing him to Angelica, his stunningly beautiful Polish girlfriend.

'Be reasonable,' he had protested. 'I can't possibly let you take my place.'

But Leonora had no intention of being reasonable. *Reasonable* went with the kind of girls who were sexually self-assured, whom men adored and flirted with. Not someone like her, who had put up barriers around herself, acting the jokey tomboy, always ready for a dare. She had done it for so long that she didn't think she would ever be able to find her way back to the woman she might have been. Far easier now to simply carry on being outrageous, always ready to challenge either of her brothers—or indeed any man—at his own game and win, than to admit that sometimes she longed desperately to be a different kind of girl.

Alessandro had been frowning when he left the meeting he had come to London to attend, and he was still

frowning twenty minutes later, when he got out of the limousine at the Carlton Tower Hotel, despite the fact that
the meeting had gone very well.

A tall man, he carried himself with what other men
often tended to think was arrogance but which women
knew immediately was the confidence of a man who knew
what it was to experience the true give and take of sensual
pleasure. The facial features stamped onto the sun-warmed
Sicilian flesh might have been those of a warrior Roman
Emperor tempered by endurance into a fierce strength.
They signalled that pride, and a sense of being set apart
from or even above other men. His dark hair, with its
strong curl, was close-cropped to his head, and the eyes
set beneath dark brows and framed with thick dark lashes
were an extraordinary shade of dark grey. When he moved
there was a leanness about his movements, a hint of the
hunter intent on the swift capture of its prey. Men treated
him with wary respect. Women were intrigued by him and
desired him.

The doorman recognised him and greeted him by name,
and the pretty receptionist eyed him covertly as he strode
through the foyer, busy with designer-clad women and
their escorts, heading for the lift.

In his jacket pocket was the cause of his irritation—a
formal invitation, and with it a letter that was more a
command than a fraternal request, from his elder brother, reminding him that his presence would be expected at the
weekend of celebrations to mark the nine-hundredth anni-
versary of the granting to his family of their titles. They were
due to begin tomorrow evening, and were being held at the
family's main residence on Sicily. His absence was not an
option.

And of course whenever Falcon, the eldest of the three of them, made such a statement it was the duty of his younger siblings to support him—just as he had always supported them during the years of their shared childhood when they had suffered so much.

On this occasion, though, Rocco, their younger brother, had been granted a leave of absence from his family duty as he was on honeymoon, and Alessandro had thought that *he* was going to get away with not going in view of the buy-out negotiations he was involved in with another airline. But Falcon's ironic sending of the formal invitation together with a letter of reminder made it plain that he expected Alessandro to be there.

He and Falcon would be the only two of their father's sons to attend, with Rocco away. Antonio, their younger half-brother, would not be there. He was dead, killed in a car accident, as a result of which their father, who had loved his youngest son with far more emotion and intensity than he had felt for his eldest three all put together, had developed a terminal heart condition from which he was not expected to survive for more than a year at best.

Only his own brothers could know and understand why Alessandro felt so little sorrow at the thought of his father's demise, since they had all shared the same childhood. It was Antonio their father had loved, not them. No one had loved them. Not their mother, whose death after Rocco's birth had meant that she had not been there to love them, and certainly not their father.

Alessandro gazed towards the window, not seeing the view of Carlton Gardens that lay beyond it but seeing instead the dark shadows of Castello Leopardi, and the room where he had lain staring into the darkness after his father had mocked him for crying for his dead mother.

'Only a fool and a weakling fool cries for a woman. But then that is exactly what you are—a worthless second son who will never be anything other than second best. Remember that when you are a man, Alessandro. All you will ever be is second best.'

Second best. How those words had tortured and haunted him. And how they had driven him as well.

But it had not been his first-born, Falcon, whom their father had loved beyond reason. It had been Antonio, the only child of their father's second marriage to a woman who had been his mistress for years, who had humiliated and shamed their own mother with their father's help. Antonio—sly, manipulative, well aware of the power he'd had over their father's affections and how to make use of it to his own best advantage—had not been liked by *any* of his three half-brothers, but Alessandro acknowledged that he'd probably had more reason to dislike him than either of his siblings.

He might have distanced himself now from the boy he had been—the child who had grown up being told by his father that his only role in life was to play second fiddle to his elder brother, a spare heir in case anything should happen to Falcon—but the scars from having grown up always feeling that he had to justify his existence and prove that he was of value were still there.

On the day of his seventh birthday party, after some childish quarrel with his half-brother during which Antonio had started mimicking their father, taunting him by telling him their father loved him the best, he had retaliated by saying that he was the second eldest.

Their father had told spoken to him coldly. 'You are a second son—conceived so that if necessary you can take your elder brother's place. You as yourself have and are nothing. A second son is of no account whilst there is a first-born. Think about that in future, when you attempt to place yourself above your youngest brother, for God knows I wish with all my heart that he might have been my only son.'

Strange the powerful effect that words could have. His father had meant to humiliate and shame him for daring to stand against the favouritism he showed to his youngest son; he had wanted to cow him and make him feel inferior. But his cruelty had had exactly the opposite effect, burning into Alessandro a determination to forge a life for himself that had no reliance on the Leopardi name or his father's influence.

Instead of becoming a part of the old feudal world of his father and family history, Alessandro had turned towards the new, modern world, where a man was judged on his business acumen and his personal achievements. He had adopted his mother's family name instead of using his own, and that name was still proudly displayed on the fleet of aircraft that had earned him his billionaire status— even though these days he was secure enough in what and who he was to answer to both Leopardi and Avanti.

He had proved beyond any kind of doubt that he had no need of his father's help or his father's name, and in fact it now amused him to see the frustrated lack of understanding in his father's expression when he adapted so easily to being addressed as Leopardi, instead of reacting angrily and rejecting its usage as he had once done.

But then his father never had understood him and never

would. It was easy for Alessandro to accept the name now, because he no longer needed it to identify himself. In his estimation he was now a first amongst equals—more than an heir-in-waiting, and certainly more than any poor second son.

And yet, as Falcon had so succinctly reminded him when he had discussed the coming celebrations with him, he was still a Leopardi, and so far as Falcon was concerned that meant he still had a duty to the family.

Alessandro bore a grudging respect for his elder brother, but their relationship was shadowed by their childhood, by their father—and by the memory of Sofia.

But it was over a decade now since he had deliberately challenged Falcon in every way he could, engaging his elder brother in a power struggle, a battle to prove himself, which had ultimately resulted in them pitted against one another for the same woman—a struggle which Falcon had ultimately won.

Alessandro's frown deepened. He was not an insecure twenty-six-year-old desperate to prove himself any more. He was an adult, successful and confident, with no need to prove anything to his elder brother. Or to himself.

But wasn't it the truth that part of the reason he was so reluctant to attend tomorrow night's celebrations was because of those two words on the invitation: 'and guest'?

His pride insisted that he could not attend the celebratory ball without a partner, a fact his father would see as a sign of failure, and yet at the same time he knew that if there *had* been anyone in his life at the moment, sharing his bed, he would not have wanted to take her. Because he was afraid of a repeat of the humiliation he had experienced with Sofia. Alessandro knew that his reaction was irrational.

He knew too that by letting that irrationality take hold he was creating a self-perpetuating ogre within his own psyche. Perhaps his father had been right after all, he derided himself contemptuously. Perhaps he was a coward, and second rate.

At twenty-six he had been so proud to show Sofia, a model he'd met in Milan at a PR event—off to his elder brother, driven in those days by a single-minded determination to prove that far from being second best he could come first.

He had been flattered when Sofia had flirted with him. She had been older than him, twenty-eight to his twenty-six, and although he hadn't realised it then she had already been past the prime of her modelling career, and searching for a rich husband. Any rich husband, just so long as he was gullible.

It was easy for him to recognise now that what he had mistaken for love on his own part had merely been lust, and he knew too that he had much to be grateful to Falcon for. He had shown him just what Sofia had been—after all she was on her third husband now. Falcon had told him afterwards that the reason he had seduced Sofia away from him had been to show him exactly what she was, to protect him as it was his duty as the elder brother to do.

Without their father's love and protection it had been on Falcon's shoulders that the duty of protection for his younger siblings had fallen, and Falcon had taken that responsibility very seriously. Alessandro knew that. But the manner of his elder's brother's intervention had, in Alessandro's eyes, been humiliating—reinforcing the fact that he was second best—and it had left him with a cynical belief that all women would make themselves available to the most successful man they could find, no matter what kind of commitment they had already made to someone else, and could therefore not be trusted. Especially around his charismatic elder brother.

That belief had marked a changing point in his life, Alessandro acknowledged. Aside from the fact that he had taken care to ensure that his future mistresses did not get to meet his elder brother, he had also come to recognise that if he did not want to spend the rest of his life fighting to prove that he was worthy of more than being labelled a second son, and thus second best, then it was up to him to break free of the shackles that fastened him into that unwanted prison.

He had left Sicily for Milan, where he'd started up a small air freight business—ironically initially transporting the products of the city's designers to international shows. He had gone on from there to passenger flights and the separate luxury of first-class-only flights, so that now he had every aspect of the modern airline business covered.

He had even learned to use his second-son status to his own advantage. Membership of a titled family was something he used as cynically and deliberately as he used the powerful streak of sensuality he had discovered he possessed in the self-indulgent hedonistic months that had followed Sofia's defection.

The shell of the personality he had constructed for himself as Alessandro Leopardi was simply an image he projected for business purposes—an outer garment he could remove at will. Only he knew that somewhere deep inside himself there was still a vulnerable part of him that was the 'spare heir'—conceived only to fill that role, and of no value to anyone outside of that.

Alessandro could hardly remember their mother—she had died shortly after his younger brother Rocco's birth, when he had been only two years old himself. Everyone who had known her said that she had been a saint. Too saintly by far for her husband, who had spurned her and humiliated her publicly, turning instead to his mistress.

Did that same dark tide from his father's veins run within his own? Alessandro had no idea. He was merely thankful that, unlike his elder brother, he would never need to find out—because his own duty to the Leopardi name stopped well short of having to provide it with a future heir.

He removed a bottle of water from the suite's well-stocked bar and poured some into a glass. He could feel the stiff, unyielding thickness of the formal invitation jabbing his flesh in exactly the same way in which Falcon's stiff, unyielding determination that his brothers should pay their dues to their Leopardi blood jabbed his own conscience.

He and Rocco both owed Falcon a great deal. He had taught them and guided them, and he had protected them. Those were heavy duties for a young boy to have taken on, and it was perhaps no wonder that he had always imposed his own sense of duty on them—that he still did so now.

Alessandro didn't need to remove Falcon's letter from his pocket to remember what it said. Falcon never wasted words.

'Alessandro Leopardi,' he had written on the invitation, 'and guest'.

A challenge to him? Alessandro shrugged away the sharp pinprick of angry pride.

He would have to go, of course.

He was never comfortable when he had to return to the castle in Sicily where he had grown up. It held far too many unhappy memories. If he had to visit the island he preferred to stay in the family villa in town. Home for him now was wherever he happened to be—although he had an apartment in Milan and another in Florence, and a villa in a secluded and exclusive enclave close to Positano.

He looked at his watch, a one-off made especially for him. He would be leaving by helicopter from City Airport soon, for his own private jet and the onward flight to Florence, where he would stay at his apartment in the exclusive renovated *palazzo* that had originally belonged to his mother's family.

'Look, Leonora, I really don't think this is a good idea.'

Leonora gave her younger brother a scathing look.

'Well, I do—and you promised.'

Leo groaned. 'That was when I was halfway down one of Dad's best reds, and you'd tricked me.' He stood up, his brown hair tousled. He might be six foot three in his socks, but right now he still managed to have the frustrated look of a younger brother who had just been outwitted by his older and smarter sister, Leonora decided triumphantly.

'You agreed that the next time you flew your boss into London in the private jet I could fly him back.'

'Why? He hates women pilots.'

'I know. After all, he's turned my job applications down often enough.'

Leo's expression changed. 'Look, you aren't going to do anything silly, are you? Like barging into his office, telling him you flew the plane and asking him for a job?

You'd have as much chance of succeeding as you would have of getting into his bed,' Leo told her forthrightly.

Leonora knew all about the stunning beauties the Sicilian billionaire who owned the airline her younger brother worked for dated, and she certainly wasn't going to allow Leo to guess how much his comment hurt—as though somehow it was a given that she wasn't woman enough to attract the interest of a man like Alessandro Leopardi. Not, of course, that she *wanted* to be one of Alessandro Leopardi's women, but she certainly did want to be one of his pilots.

'No, of course I'm not going to ask him for a job.'

Leonora crossed her fingers behind her back. She was in full jokey can-do Leonora mode now—even in the privacy of her own thoughts. It just wasn't fair. She was every bit as good a pilot as her younger brother, if not better, and she just knew that if she proved that to Alessandro Leopardi he *would* offer her a job. His exclusive first-class service flew passengers all over the world, and she wanted to be one of that elite group even more than she had once wanted to work for someone like Alessandro himself as a private pilot.

'You can't possibly think you'll really get away with this,' Leo protested.

'No, I don't think it. I know it,' Leonora told him promptly, going on firmly, 'Since you let me fly the new jet when you were sent to collect it I've been having extra lessons in one, and I've probably racked up more flying hours than you have.' She didn't even want to think about how much it had cost her to get those flying miles in such an expensive craft, or how many lessons in Mandarin she had had to teach to earn the money.

'Okay, so you can fly the plane. But you haven't got a uniform.'

'Ta-dah!' Leonora said, opening her trench coat to reveal the uniform, and then producing her cap from the supermarket bag in which she had been carrying it.

Leo's face was a picture. 'You know if you get found out that *I'll* be the one losing my job.'

'Only wimps get found out,' Leonora replied as she slipped off her coat and swept up her hair before cramming it under the cap

'Captain Leo Thaxton at your service.'

Leo groaned again. 'Isn't it enough that you've stolen my uniform without stealing my name as well?'

'No,' Leonora told him. 'It's my name too. I've never had cause until now to be glad our parents thought it a good idea to give us practically the same name. Now, come on.'

'What about the co-pilot?'

'What about him? It's Paul Watson, isn't it? The one who breaks Alessandro Leopardi's rule about his pilots not partying with the stewardesses? I'm sure I shall be able to persuade him that it wouldn't be a good idea for him to say anything.'

'I knew I should never have told you about Paul. He's going to kill me.'

Ignoring him, Leonora demanded, 'Come on. I need you to drive me to the airport and get me through all the security stuff.'

'I do not know why you're doing this.' Leo groaned again, and then corrected himself. 'That's not true, of course. I do know why you're doing it. You are doing it because you are the most stubborn and determined female ever.'

'That's right,' Leonora agreed breezily. But inwardly she was thinking, *I'm doing it because I hate, hate, hate not getting what I want, and I want that job with Avanti Airlines more than I want anything else in the world.*

Yes, all of that was true—and when she was working full-pelt in her 'I'm up for anything' tomboy mode in front of an audience it was easy to pretend that the other Leonora—the one who longed for love and commitment, and to be allowed to be that other self she dreamed of—simply did not exist. At least for the length of her 'performance'.

She *did* want her dream job, of course, and she certainly wanted the opportunity to challenge Alessandro Leopardi, to demand that he explain to her just why her sex weighed so heavily against her when she had such excellent qualifications. It was, after all, against the law to disqualify an applicant for a job on the grounds of their sex. There was no point in telling Leo about her plans, though. He would only worry. Better to let him think she was trying to make a point to him rather than planning to make Alessandro Leopardi agree that she was a good pilot and worthy of being given the job she craved so much.

CHAPTER TWO

IT HAD been a good flight, but then Alessandro had not expected it would be anything other than good. He had, after all, flown the new jet himself shortly after they had first taken delivery of it six months earlier, and had been very impressed with the way it handled.

Alessandro did not have his own pilot. Instead he preferred to use one of the pilots who flew his executive jets for the first-class-only service, because that way he got to ensure that they were maintaining the high standard he set for all those who worked for him.

Leo Thaxton was his youngest pilot, and today's flight had shown how well he was maturing into the job. Alessandro had particularly liked the way he had handled the small amount of turbulent weather they had run into halfway through the flight, smoothing the plane through it by taking it a little higher. Thaxton had shown good judgement there.

Nodding to the steward who was holding out his coat and his laptop for him, Alessandro left the aircraft. His car was already waiting for him on the tarmac, and he didn't so much as give the plane a backwards glance as his chauffeur opened the passenger door for him.

She had done it! Alessandro Leopardi couldn't say now that she wasn't good enough to fly his planes any more.

Leonora felt almost ready to burst with triumph and excitement—only there was no one there for her to share her triumph with. Paul and the rest of the crew had left the minute Alessandro Leopardi had disappeared in his car.

She had booked herself into a small hotel in Florence and onto a returning commercial flight to London in a couple of days' time. Now that phase one of her plan had been completed she needed to move on to phase two, which was to confront Alessandro Leopardi in his office and persuade him to give her a job. It shouldn't be difficult now. She had the qualifications, and now she had proved that she had the skill as well. Plus, there was such a thing as legal equal opportunities, as she was perfectly willing to remind him should she need to do so.

They had only just reached the barrier to the private car park when Alessandro realised that he had left his mobile on the plane. Leaning forward, he instructed the driver to turn round and drive back.

Lost in her excited dreams, Leonora hadn't seen the car come back, or the door open, or Alessandro Leopardi get out as she left the plane, pulling off her cap as she did so to let her hair cascade down her back.

She saw him when she had reached the bottom of the gangway, though. Because he was standing there waiting for her, blocking her exit from it.

For a moment they looked at one another in silence. She was tall, but even standing on the steps she was still not quite at eye level with him and had to tilt her head back slightly to look up at him properly.

His question—'What is the meaning of this? Where is

the pilot?'—was so icily cold that for once Leonora struggled to manage her normal flip tone.

'You're looking at her,' she told him.

He knew who she was immediately. After all he had looked at her many job applications often enough, and the photographs accompanying them. She looked far more sensually attractive in the flesh, with her hair worn loose. To his own disbelief, given the situation and his own normally unbreakable control over every aspect of himself and most especially his sexuality, he could feel his body responding to her proximity and that sensuality. Had he somehow known that she would affect him like this? Was that why he was so resolutely opposed to employing her? Of course not. He did not employ female pilots on principle—equal opportunities rules or not. Besides, he was Sicilian—and generally speaking everyone knew that Sicilian men had their own code of contact.

His eyes were so dark it was impossible to see their colour, and they were unreadable. But the slight flaring of his nostrils had already given away his rage. Leonora tried to clamp down on her sudden feeling that just maybe she had flown higher than she had planned. Her lungs certainly felt that the air was short of oxygen—or was that just her own apprehension?

'If that's true then you are in one hell of a lot of trouble—and so is Leo Thaxton.'

Alessandro Leopardi's harsh words confirmed that he wasn't about to treat her behaviour lightly.

'You can't blame Leo.' She immediately defended her brother. 'I made him do it. I wanted to prove to you that I can fly just as well as any man, and that I deserve a job.'

'What you and your brother both deserve is a prison

sentence,' he told her mercilessly. 'And what you certainly will be doing is looking for a job together.'

Leonora's eyes rounded. This wasn't going the way she had planned at all.

'You can't sack Leo. It wasn't his fault.'

'Then whose fault was it?'

'Yours—for not giving me a chance to try out for a job,' she told him promptly.

Alessandro had never met anyone so infuriating or so reckless in ignoring the realities of the situation. By rights she ought to be treating him with kid gloves, not challenging him and arguing with him. He moved irritably from one foot to the other, reminded of the presence of the invitation in his pocket as its sharpness dug into his flesh.

The invitation. He looked at Leonora, and a plan began to form inside his head. She was attractive, if you liked her type—which he didn't. He liked groomed women, not girls with a mass of hair, too much attitude and too little sensuality.

'I most certainly can sack him, and I fully intend to do so,' he assured Leonora grimly.

He meant it, Leonora recognised. She could see that, and for the first time she realised that this wasn't a game she was playing. The consequences of what she had done were going to be very damaging—not just for her, but for Leo as well. Even worse was the mortifying recognition that, far from showing him that she could be the best, all she had done was prove that she was a failure.

Humiliation burned bright flags of red into her high sculpted cheekbones, highlighting the purity of her bone structure. She couldn't let him sack Leo. Apart from the fact that her brother loved his job, she could just imagine the comments that he and Piers—especially Piers—would make for the rest of her life, lording it over her as they so liked to do, because she was a girl and she had been born second.

Which would be worse? Swallowing her pride now and begging this man she would never see again to spare Leo, or facing her brothers as a failure?

She took a deep breath.

'I'm sorry. I shouldn't have done it. Please don't sack Leo.'

She sounded as though she was choking on every word, Alessandro recognised. Her brother obviously meant a great deal to her. *Good.*

'I will think about it. Provided you—'

Leonora's head jerked up immediately, her eyes shadowing with apprehension. Whatever it took to make sure Leo did not lose his job she would have to do—even if Alessandro Leopardi told her that she was never to apply for a job with him again. Even that, Leonora recognised bleakly.

'I'll do anything just so long as you don't sack Leo,' she interrupted fiercely. 'Anything! Whatever it is you want me to do, I'll do it.'

The moment her impetuous words were out, Leonora's mouth formed a self-conscious *O* whilst her face burned even more hotly as she realised just how her offer might be interpreted. However, before she had time to correct any possible misinterpretation, Alessandro Leopardi was speaking coolly.

'I won't sack your brother—little as he deserves to be kept on, in view of his stupidity and weakness in agreeing or allowing you to force him to agree to your illegal charade—provided you accompany me to a family function I am obliged to attend.'

Leonora stared at him, disbelief and distaste clearly visible in her expression. 'There are escort agencies who provide women for that kind of thing. Why don't you use one of them? After all, it isn't as though you can't afford to.'

She knew immediately that her blunt speaking had been a bad mistake. She could see the tinge of angry heat burning his face, moving into the high cheekbones and then flashing like a warning beacon in the darkness of his eyes.

'I would remind you that whilst I *could* afford to pay a woman to accompany me, *you* cannot afford to refuse me. Unless, of course, you are prepared to see your brother lose his job?'

To her chagrin his attitude caused Leonora to do something she hadn't done since she'd left her early teenage years behind her. She glowered at him and stuck out her bottom lip, with all the angry defiance of a rebellious teenager facing a resolute and immovable human obstacle to what they wanted to do. And then she compounded her regression to impotent resentment by saying crossly, 'Well, I can't think why you'd want to pick me to accompany you. After all, I'm not a model, or…or…a C-list starlet.'

Her face was burning again, but it wasn't her fault if his penchant for glamorous airheads was regularly recorded in celebrity gossip magazines—not that she ever bothered reading such things. It was Leo who was constantly pointing out yet another paparazzi photograph of his boss with some leggy, pouting beauty on his arm.

'The reason I've *picked* you, as you put it, has nothing

whatsoever to do with your looks—or lack of them,' Alessandro told her unkindly.

This time she wasn't going to overreact, Leonora told herself. She was a mature woman, after all. A professional and fully qualified pilot. Someone who was not going to be tricked into behaving like an immature teenager because she couldn't control her own emotions.

'You are such a girl!' her brothers had loved to tease her when they had been growing up, and she still hated being put in a position where her emotions might threaten to make her look vulnerable or betray her.

'But you obviously want me to accompany you badly enough to blackmail me?' Leonora couldn't resist pointing out.

'That's right,' Alessandro agreed, so pleasantly and with such an unexpectedly warm smile that for a handful of seconds Leonora was caught off guard. And she found that for some inexplicable reason she was curling her toes in her navy-blue loafers.

He exuded an air of male virility that aroused within her a raft of unfamiliar and complex emotions that undermined and weakened her. There was something about the way he turned his head, the look in the slate-grey eyes and the shape of his wholly male mouth that disrupted her ability to think logically and forced her to keep looking at him.

'You see, this way I shall have complete control over both the situation and you, without having to face any future comebacks—or indeed the kickbacks your sex has a less than lovable habit of demanding.'

'If you don't like the demands your girlfriends make on you then I would suggest that the fault lies with you and your judgement, and not my sex as a whole. There are any number of heterosexual women who don't ask for, or expect or even want anything from a man.'

'You're wrong about that. All women want something—either materially, emotionally or physically, and very often all three. Whereas all I want from you is your presence at my side in public as my partner, your recognition that in future there will be no relationship of any kind between us, and your complete silence on the whole subject—publicly and privately.'

'Not much, then,' Leonora muttered under her breath.

But he must have heard her, because he gave her a coldly arrogant look and told her, 'Set against your brother's future career, I would have said that it is not very much at all. Merely your absolute obedience to my will and to the instructions I shall give you for one single evening.'

'Like I said—that's blackmail,' Lenora was objecting, before she could stop herself.

'You may choose to see it as blackmail. I on the other hand see it as a justifiable claim for compensation from a person who has knowingly deprived me of something that is mine by right—in this case the skills of my employee, your brother.'

'I'm just as qualified as Leo—in fact I'm more qualified.'

'Maybe so, but you were not my choice of pilot. Now, as I was saying, if I am to refrain from sacking your brother then I shall require your complete obedience to my will.'

Her complete obedience to his will? Leonora opened her mouth in a furious hiss of disagreement, and then closed it again as she remembered Leo.

There was one thing she had to say, though—one stand she had to make.

Holding his gaze, she told him bluntly, 'If this complete obedience to your instructions has anything to do with any kind of sexual activity then I'm afraid that Leo will have to lose his job.'

Alessandro looked at her in disbelief.

'Are you seriously suggesting that you think I am sexually propositioning you?' he demanded haughtily.

Leonora stood her ground.

'Not necessarily. I'm simply letting you know what I won't do.'

She had surprised him, Alessandro admitted. He was so used to women throwing themselves at him, practically begging him to take what they were offering, that it had simply never occurred to him that a woman like this one—so desperate to get a job with his airline that she was prepared to risk doing something that was both illegal and dangerous—would baulk at the thought of offering him sex. But patently that was exactly what she was doing, and he could see from the tension gripping her body that she meant what she had said.

Something—curiosity, male pride, his deep-rooted inherited Leopardi arrogance—Alessandro did not know which—spiked into life inside him, hard-edged and determined to make its presence felt. He shrugged it aside. Some ancient macho instinct had been aroused by her challenge—so what? He was mature enough, sophisticated enough, well supplied enough with all the sexual companionship he needed not to have to take any notice of it.

'Good. And now I shall let you know that you will never

be asked. My standards in that regard, as in everything else in my life, are very high. You do not come anywhere near meeting them.' His smile was cruel and mocking as he went on coldly, 'I may be a second son, but I never, ever accept second best, much less third-rate. Now, since we have both made our position clear, maybe we can discuss what I shall require of you rather than what I most certainly do not?'

He had insulted her, but he could not hurt her, Leonora assured herself as she glared dry-eyed at him. She didn't care how third-rate he considered her to be sexually. In fact she was glad that he wasn't interested in her.

Alessandro pushed back the cuff of his shirt and looked at his watch. Why had he made that comment to her about his position as a second son? He didn't have to justify or explain himself in any way to anyone, never mind this irritatingly challenging woman who was the very last person he would have chosen to accompany him to the *castello* had he actually had any choice.

He could, of course, always go on his own, but that stubborn stiff pride that had driven him all his life insisted he had to prove to his elder brother that he could produce a woman who would not under any circumstances look at any other man—and that included Falcon himself. In that respect Leonora Thaxton was perfect, since he possessed the power to ensure that she would not do so.

He gave her a mercilessly assessing look, his mouth compressing. The raw material might be there, in the tumbled hair and the well-shaped face with its clear skin, but that raw material was in need of a good deal of polishing if his elder brother was not to take one look at her and, with a lift of that famously derogatory eyebrow of his, burst out laughing.

'Come,' he announced. 'My chauffeur's wife will be wondering where he is, and Pietro himself will be wanting his supper. My car is this way.'

Did he really expect her to believe that he was in the least bit concerned about his chauffeur or his chauffeur's wife? Leonora thought indignantly, as she was forced to run to catch up with him as he strode away from her, plainly expecting her to follow him to where she could now see a large limousine waiting in the shadows.

The chauffeur had the doors open for them as they reached the car, and Leonora's heart sank as she realised that she was going to have to share the admittedly generously proportioned back seat of the car with Alessandro.

As she sat down beside him on the tan leather seat he instructed her, 'You will need to give Pietro your passport so that he can show it at the customs office at the gate.' And then opened his laptop and ignored her, leaving her to seethe.

She handed over her passport, which was duly presented to the customs officer, but it was into Alessandro's outstretched hand that the chauffeur placed the returned passport once they were through the gate, not her own. Alessandro did not return it to her, despite the demanding look she gave him, choosing instead to slip it into the inside pocket of his jacket without so much as lifting his eyes from his laptop to meet her angry look.

CHAPTER THREE

'CATERINA will show you to the guest suite, and once you have refreshed yourself I will explain to you over supper the role I wish you to play. Since we shall have to leave Florence by mid-afternoon tomorrow we will not have much time, so immediately after breakfast we will address the matter of providing you with a suitable wardrobe for the weekend.'

'I have a change of clothes with me,' Leonora said, pointedly looking down at the small case which Pietro had placed on the marble-tiled floor of the elegant hallway in the two-storey apartment inside this eighteenth-century *palazzo* to which Alessandro had brought her.

Alessandro followed her gaze, and then swept his eyes from the case to the full length of her body and her face, with a comprehensive thoroughness that lifted the hairs on the back of her neck.

'And that change will be what? A pair of jeans and a shirt?'

'What if it is?' Leonora demanded

'The events to which I wish you to accompany me have been organised by my elder brother to celebrate and com-memorate the granting to our family of its titles. They are not the kind of events at which guests will appear wearing jeans, which is why I am about to organise the services of a personal shopper who will ensure that you have the correct clothes.'

He began ticking the items off on his fingers, their lean, strong length somehow managing to distract Leonora to such an extent that she couldn't drag her gaze away from them. They were such very male hands, she thought, leaner and longer-fingered than the broader hands of her father and her brothers, tanned and with well-groomed nails, and yet here and there she could see small telltale white scars, as though the artistic streak revealed by the elegant length of his hands had manifested itself in a creative skill, but that of master sculptor rather than a painter.

'Tomorrow evening we shall be attending a cocktail party. And then on Saturday there will be an official luncheon party at the *castello*, with various civic guests of honour. In the evening there is to be a grand costume ball, and the celebrations are concluding with a special church service on Sunday.'

A cocktail party, a formal lunch, a costume ball and a church service. Leonora's heart sank further with every item Alessandro added to the list. She didn't have to search very far back in her memory to produce an unhappy image of the horrors of her one and only attempt at 'glamour' dressing, and the howls of laughter with which her brothers had greeted her appearance in the prom dress she had been persuaded into buying by a university friend for their finals ball. She just wasn't the pretty dress type—never mind the glam cocktail dress type. Whenever she did have to attend any kind of formal event she always stuck to a plain tuxedo trouser suit, with the jacket worn over a simple silk camisole top.

'I really think it would be much easier if you chose someone else to accompany you,' she felt obliged to say, her face burning when he looked at her in a way that made her feel as though she was piloting a plane that had just dropped ten thousand feet through the sky without any warning.

'I'm sure you do,' he agreed dryly.

'You must know dozens of women who would be more suitable.'

'That depends on how you define suitability,' he told her. 'Certainly I know many women who possess the sophistication and the beauty to carry off such a role, but, as I've already said, their compliance with my requirements would lead to them making demands for payment that I am not prepared to make. Whereas, whilst you may lack what they possess, I have the advantage of knowing that you will follow my wishes to the letter or risk costing your brother his job.'

'I can't see what can possibly be so important about accompanying you to a few social events that it necessitates a vow of absolute obedience and my agreement to your total control over that obedience.' Leonora chafed against his warning.

'I have my reasons for wishing to ensure that the woman who accompanies me to these events conducts herself in such a way that there can be no doubt in anyone's mind that she is wholly and absolutely committed to me and only to me, and at the same time also conducts herself with dignity and elegance—of manner and mind.'

'So a stunning Z-list glamour puss whose *modus operandi* involves going commando and drinking cocktails isn't high on your list of potential arm candy for this weekend, then?' Leonora guessed mischievously.

The manner in which he drew himself up to his full

height and gave her a look that would have set Mount Etna alight if they'd been anywhere near it was certainly impressive, Leonora admitted. Her comment had certainly got under his skin.

'That kind of vulgarity is exactly what I do *not* want,' he agreed coldly, adding warningly, 'And that extends to the vulgarity of mind that gives rise to such comments.' He stared at her. 'Fortunately you are well educated enough to be able to converse intelligently with my brother's guests, and if you are asked about our relationship you will say simply that we met through your brother, who is one of my pilots. Falcon in particular will try to question you. My younger brother and I have good cause to be grateful to our elder brother for the care he gave us whilst we were growing up, and I must warn you that he will attempt to test you to see if you are worthy of me.'

When Leonora's eyes glittered with angry resentment, Alessandro shook his head.

'You are jumping to conclusions which are not valid. My brother's anxiety as to your worthiness has nothing to do with your social status. His concern will be to see that you will not hurt me, and it is on that issue that he will seek to test you, by hinting that he can offer you far more than I.' He frowned as his mobile purred, telling Leonora briskly before he answered it, 'We shall discuss all of this in more detail over supper.'

He turned away from her to take his call, leaving Leonora to look helplessly towards the magnificent wrought-iron staircase that soared up from the hallway to the upper floor. She was a reluctant eavesdropper on his conversation as he said coolly, 'Yes, I shall be bringing someone with me, Don Falcon. Her name?' He paused and looked at Leonora. 'Her name is Leonora Thaxton.'

Leonora's heart thundered with half a dozen heavy and dizzying beats. Hunger, she told herself pragmatically. That was all it was.

She focused on the cream marble of the staircase, which should have been so cold but somehow, in this Florentine setting, was a thing of beauty and sensuality that made her long to reach out and stroke the beautiful stone. Wanting to stroke the marble was fine, but she'd better not allow that longing to spread to wanting to reach out and stroke its owner, she warned herself—and then was thoroughly shocked that she should feel it necessary to give herself such a warning.

After all, why on earth would she want to touch Alessandro Leopardi, when she could barely tolerate being in the same room with him?

The only piece of furniture in the hallway was a large and ornate gilded table with a dark onyx top, on which sat a large alabaster urn filled with greenery and white lilies, their scent perfuming the air like a caress. Everything about the hallway made Leonora feel out of place and awkward, somehow underlining her own lack of sensuality whilst subtly highlighting its own. But was it the hallway that was making her so aware of her own lack of sensuality or Alessandro himself?

What if it *was* him? He could think what he liked about her—she didn't care, Leonora told herself stoutly, reverting to the defensive mechanisms she had learned as a girl. She didn't care one little bit as he finished his call and turned back to her.

A woman—Caterina, Leonora presumed—emerged

from a door set at the back of the hallway. She gave Leonora a sharp look that whilst not exactly welcoming wasn't hostile either.

Alessandro addressed her in Italian, instructing her to take Leonora to the guest suite. Leonora, whose own Italian was excellent, was just thinking to herself that it might be a good idea not to reveal that she spoke Italian when Alessandro turned to her and said in that language, 'I seem to recall that your many job applications made mention of the fact that you are proficient in several languages, one of which is Italian.'

He had read her applications himself, and had still rejected her—despite the excellence of her qualifications? Rejected her as her brothers had so often done because she was female? Immediately and instinctively Leonora reverted to another of the habits of her childhood: wanting to get her own back. Without stopping to think she answered him in Mandarin, but the rush of triumph she felt was quickly destroyed when he spoke to her in the same language.

'Since Caterina does not speak Mandarin, I have to assume that your decision to do so is an exhibition of showing off more suited to a foolish child than an adult woman, and as such it reinforces my belief that you are not the kind of candidate who is suited to work for me,' he said coldly.

'Really? And to think I thought that it was my sex and my hormones that barred me,' Leonora retaliated sweetly.

'You've just underlined the reason for yourself—your immaturity,' Alessandro told her crushingly.

Why, why, *why* had she let that stupid childish desire to show she was not just as good as but better than any male goad her? Leonora asked herself grimly. She turned away from him and spoke directly to Caterina in fluent Italian, earning the reward of a delighted smile from the older woman as she explained that she was Alessandro's house-keeper.

Five minutes later Leonora was earning herself another approving smile from Caterina as she gazed round the guest suite to which Caterina had taken her with awed delight.

The *palazzo* had obviously undergone a very sympa-thetic restoration and refurbishment process in the recent past, Leonora guessed as she admired the strong clean lines of the large, high-ceilinged rooms connected by a magnifi-cent pair of open double doors. Whilst the elegance of its original plasterwork and ceiling cornicing and the beauti-fully panelled and carved doors had been retained, the walls had obviously been replastered, and were painted in an ivory that seemed to change colour with the light pouring in from the glass doors that led onto an ironwork girded balcony overlooking an internal courtyard garden. Silver-grey floor-boards reflected more light, and the room's mix of an antique bed with pieces of far more modern furniture gave the suite an air of being lived in rather than being a museum set-piece.

At the touch of a remote control Caterina proudly revealed not just a flatscreen TV but a computer, a pull-out desk and a sound system discreetly hidden away behind a folding wall.

'Is good, *sì*?' she asked Leonora in English, inviting praise of something of which she was obviously proud.

'It is wonderful,' Leonora agreed, telling her in Italian, 'It is a perfect blend of past and present—a very *simpatico* restoration.'

Caterina beamed. 'This building and many others

belonged to the family of Signor Alessandro's *mamma*, and so came to him and his brothers. Together they have worked to keep the family history but also to make it comfortable to live in now. Don Falcon, he sits on the council that takes care of those buildings that are owned by many of the old Florentine families, and he makes Signor Alessandro pay much money from his airline to help with the restoration work. Signor Alessandro knows that he cannot refuse his elder brother. Don Falcon has the most power because he is the eldest.'

'How many brothers and sisters are there?' Leonora asked her curiously.

'No sister. They are all three boys. Signor Alessandro is the second brother.'

The second brother—the second child, just like her. Leonora frowned. She didn't want to find any kind of connection between them, but as a second child he must have experienced, as she had, all that it meant to be a middle child, sandwiched between the lordly eldest and the favoured baby of the family, constantly having to fight for his position and for adult attention and love, never quite as good or grown-up as his elder sibling nor allowed to get away with as much as his indulged younger sibling. She wanted instead to continue to dislike and resent him. And besides, her situation had been worse—because she had been a girl sandwiched between two brothers. As same-sex siblings Alessandro and his siblings would have been able to bond together.

Or would he have had to compete even harder than she had done? Not that it mattered. She refused to start feeling sympathetic towards him. Look at the way he was treating her—threatening and blackmailing her…

Caterina had gone, giving her some time to freshen up before going back downstairs to have supper with Alessandro and receive her instructions.

In addition to the sitting room and bedroom, the guest suite also possessed a dressing room and a huge bathroom, with a sunken rectangular bath so large it could have easily accommodated a whole family and a state-of-the-art wet-room-style shower area.

Since it wasn't going to take her very long to get changed, Leonora allowed herself to be tempted out onto the balcony. Florence… Right now she should have been enjoying the magic of the city, making plans to visit all those treasures she wanted to see, instead of standing here, the captive of a man who was ruthlessly using her for his own ends.

It was dark outside, and all she could see of the courtyard garden beneath her balcony were various small areas illuminated by strategically placed floodlights that revealed a long, narrow canal-style water feature, gravel walkways and various plants. There was a staircase from her balcony down to the garden, and as she stood on the balcony she could smell the scents of the night air and—so she told herself—of Florence itself.

Half an hour later, having showered and changed into her jeans and a top, she had just finished answering Leo's anxious text asking if all had gone well. She had given an airy and untrue response to the effect that there was nothing for him to worry about and that she was looking forward to her short break in Florence.

Caterina tapped on her sitting room door and then came in, announcing that she had come to escort Leonora back downstairs.

Several doors led off the hallway, and the one through which Caterina took her opened onto a wide corridor hung with a variety of modern paintings mingled with framed pieces of what Leonora thought must be medieval fabric and parchment. The whole somehow worked together in a way that once again made her feel acutely aware of the harmony of their shared composition.

At the end of the corridor a wide doorway opened onto a semi-enclosed loggia-type terrace, overlooking the court-yard garden, where Alessandro was waiting for her.

Like her, he had changed. What was it about him that enabled him to look so effortlessly stylish and yet at the same time so intimidatingly arrogant and sexually male? Leonora wondered on a small shiver. In profile his features reminded her of the profiles of ancient Roman heroes. She could quite easily imagine that close-cropped head wearing a laurel wreath. Her heart jolted into her ribs as though his compelling aura had reached out and somehow claimed her. She must not let him get to her like this. So he possessed both extraordinary male good looks and extraordinary male power? She was impervious to both. She had to be. That pumice-stone-grey gaze could not really penetrate her defences and see into her most private thoughts.

'*Grazie*, Caterina.'

He thanked his housekeeper with a smile so warm that it had Leonora's eyes widening with surprise. This was the first time she had seen him showing any kind of human warmth, but she had no idea why it should have caused her such a sharply acute pang of melancholy. There was no reason why she should feel upset because he didn't smile like that at *her*.

'Since what I wish to say to you is confidential, and

needs to be said in privacy, I thought it best that we eat here and serve ourselves,' he told her, as soon as Caterina had left, moving towards a buffet placed on a table against one wall, in which she could see an assortment of salads and *antipasti.* 'There are various hot dishes inside the cabinet. Are you familiar with Florentine dishes? Because if you wish me to explain any of them to you then please say so.'

Going to join him, Leonora marvelled. 'Has Caterina prepared all this?'

Alessandro shook his head.

'No. Normally when I am here in Florence I either eat out with friends or cook for myself, but on this occasion I ordered the food in from a nearby restaurant.'

'You can cook?' The gauche words were out before she could silence them, causing him to arch an eyebrow and give her a look that made her feel even more self-conscious.

'My elder brother insisted that we learn when we were growing up.'

Alessandro spoke of his elder brother as though he had parented them, and yet Leonora knew that Alessandro's father was still alive.

Ten minutes later, with her main course of *bistecca alla fiorentina*, a salad dish of sundried tomatoes, olives and green leaves, and a glass of Sassicaia red wine in front of her—which Alessandro had explained to her was made from the French Cabernet Sauvignon grape—Leonora could feel her mouth starting to water with anticipation. Her appetite, though, was somewhat spoiled when Alessandro began to outline what he expected from her in return for not firing Leo.

'As I have already said, the celebrations and ceremonies

of the weekend will be of a formal nature, during which, as my father's second son, I shall be expected to play my part in representing the Leopardi family. Family is important to all Italians, but to be Sicilian means that the honour of the family and the respect accorded to it are particularly sacred. If Falcon allowed him to do so my father would still rule those who live on Leopardi land as though he owned them body and soul.'

Because she could hear the angry loathing and frustration in his voice, Leonora fought not to speak her mind.

'Falcon, when the time comes, will guide our people towards a more enlightened way of life, as our father should have done. But all his life our father has controlled others through fear and oppression, none more so than his sons. Now in the last months of his life, he expects us to give him the love and respect he delighted in withholding from us as the children of his first marriage, while he lavished everything within him on the woman who supplanted our mother and the son he never let us forget he wished might have supplanted us. Some might think it a fitting punishment that he has had to live through the death of both of them.'

Leonora was too shocked by Alessandro's revelations to hide her feelings. The delicious food she had been eating had suddenly lost its flavour.

'He must have hurt you all very badly.' That was all she could manage to say.

'One cannot be hurt when one does not care.'

But he *had* cared. Leonora could tell.

'It is important that you know a little of our recent family history so that you will understand the importance of the role I wish you to play. During his lifetime our halfbrother,

Antonio, was our father's favourite and most favoured child. In fact he loved him so much that when, on his deathbed, Antonio told our father that he believed he had an illegitimate son, he insisted that the child must be found. Not for its own sake, you understand, but so that he could use it as a substitute for the son he had lost. Falcon was able to trace the young woman who might have conceived Antonio's child.'

'And the baby?' Leonora pressed, immediately fearful and hardly daring to ask.

'The child was not Antonio's. Although as it happens he will be brought up as a member of the Leopardi family, since my youngest brother is now married to the child's aunt. My father is so obsessed with Antonio that initially he refused to accept that the child was not his, but, as Falcon has said, it is just as well that there *was* no child. If there had been our father would no doubt have repeated the mistakes he made with Antonio and ruined another young life. Had there been a child I would certainly have done my utmost to ensure that it remained with its mother, and that both of them were kept safe from my father's interference in their lives.'

He meant what he was saying, and Leonora was forced to admit that she could only admire him for his stance.

He moved slightly, reminding her of a dangerous animal of prey, dragging her thoughts away from the child whose potential fate he had described so compellingly and to her own unwanted vulnerability—to him. But then she saw the expression in his eyes as he gazed beyond her, as though looking back into his own past, and she recognised that he had his own vulnerabilities. He too had once been a small child—lonely, afraid, needing to be loved and protected.

She saw his mouth and then his whole expression harden, all his past vulnerability overridden by sheer will as he told her, 'These days I consider myself fortunate that I was our father's least favourite. The one he liked to humiliate the most by reminding me of the fact that I had been given life merely to be a second son whose usefulness would come to an end the day Falcon produced his own first-born son.'

As a second-born child herself, Leonora had thought she knew what it meant not to come first, but the cruelty Alessandro had just revealed so unemotionally was horrific. So much so that she had started to reach across the table towards him, in an instinctive gesture of comfort, before she realised what she was doing, quickly curling her fingers into her palm and withdrawing her hand, her face burning when she saw the frowning, dismissive way his gaze had followed her betraying movement.

'To his credit, Falcon did his best to protect both us and himself. I have a great deal of respect and admiration for my elder brother, and all three of us share a bond that is there because, young as he was, he took it upon himself to ensure that we stood together and supported one another. My father thought to continue to control us all into adulthood through the loyalty we bear to our family name and of course through his wealth. But, whilst Falcon insists that the Leopardi name is accorded loyalty and respect, we have all three of us in our different ways made ourselves financially independent and successful as ourselves, rather than as his sons. Even me—the son he labelled second-born and second-rate.'

Leonora took a deep gulp of her wine in an effort to suppress her unwanted surge of aching sympathy for him.

'Of course in my father's eyes no man can consider himself to be a true man unless he has succeeded beyond all other men in every aspect of his life. My younger brother is married. But since Falcon is the heir, there is no woman alive that he could not, if he wishes to do so, command and demand as his wife. Were I to attend the weekend's celebrations without an appropriate female partner then my father would no doubt publicly and repeatedly claim that for all my financial success I am a failure as a man. I cannot and will not allow that to happen.'

How well she understood that need to prove oneself, Leonora admitted to herself.

'Your father is hardly likely to be impressed by *me*,' she felt obliged to point out.

'You underestimate yourself.'

She stared at Alessandro in astonishment, whilst something warm and sweet and wholly unexpected unfurled tentatively inside her heart—only to wither like life in an oxygen-deprived stratosphere as he continued.

'It is not, after all, your looks that matter. Any fool can buy the company of someone who currently passes for a beautiful woman, and most fools do. You, on the other hand, have a certain authenticity that comes from your lack of plastic prettiness which, allied to your qualifications, make it more rather than less likely that we could share a relationship. My father sees and understands only what he wants to see and understand. Falcon, however, is not so easily deceived—which is why you will remain at my side at all times and not allow yourself to be drawn into any kind of private conversation with my eldest brother.'

'If you want me to act the doting adoring girlfriend and cling to you like a limpet, then I'm sorry but—'

'What I want you to do is behave as any intelligent, sophisticated and self-confident woman would—with dignity and grace to which you will add total and absolute loyalty of a type that speaks discreetly rather than loudly of your devotion to me.'

He reached for the bottle of wine and held it out to her, but Leonora shook her head, afraid that if she drank any more wine she might be tempted to tell him just what she thought of the prospect of having to pretend to be devoted to him—either discreetly or loud. Even so, she couldn't resist saying sweetly, 'You won't want me displaying this loyalty by saying that it would be a good idea to skip the socialising and go and have sex instead, then, I take it?'

The look he gave her was hard-edged, with a mixture of warning and contempt.

'Only the immature believe that sexual vulgarity is attractive. And besides, no woman of mine has ever needed to *ask* me to take her to bed. You will not speak with, flirt with, dance with or disappear with anyone else. If asked, you will say that we met through your brother, and you will remain charmingly and discreetly vague about the length of time we have known one another, and the nature of our relationship and its past and future, referring anyone who asks about it to me. You will behave towards me as though you are proud to be with me and as though you love me. As an example you will, for instance, place your hand on my arm and look intimately at me, making clear to others that there is no man on this earth you would rather be with who could take my place in your heart and your life.'

'So I don't have to do much, then?' Leonora couldn't resist saying.

'You are the one who put your brother's career at risk.'

'But you are the one who is blackmailing me into playing a role that is totally abhorrent to me,' Leonora retaliated. 'If I did love anyone then it would be a love born of mutual respect and commitment. Not some…simpering, adoring, dutiful hero-worship thing. And if I wanted to give the man I loved a look in public that said I wanted to go to bed with him, then he would be pleased and proud to drop everything to do just that.'

'That may have been your experience with previous lovers.'

'My experience is nothing whatsoever to do with you.' And nor was her lack of it, thank goodness, Leonora acknowledged, recognising that the conversation was beginning to move into a potentially hazardous area.

Somehow she doubted that Alessandro Leopardi was a man who would understand why a woman of her age was as lacking in sexual experience as she was other than to say that such a lack reinforced his already low opinion of her. It couldn't be easy for him, she decided, having to depend on her to play what was obviously an important role so far as he was concerned when he disliked and despised her so much.

'If you really want my acting as your besotted but *über*-discreet love interest to work then you're going to have to behave publicly as though you *want* me in that role,' Leonora pointed out to Alessandro.

'It will be enough that I have asked you to accompany me.'

For sheer arrogance he really took the prize, thought Leonora in disbelief.

She could hear a bird singing in the courtyard, and she turned to look towards it, commenting, 'Your garden looks lovely.'

'But I must warn you it is out of bounds,' Alessandro informed her. 'And I must ask you not to go into it. Now, I shall run through everything with you again, just to be sure that everything is understood. Tomorrow morning, after breakfast, you will be taken to acquire a suitable wardrobe for the weekend. Your measurements will be taken and sent to a theatrical costume agency in Milan, which will supply a costume for you to match my own and fly it direct to Sicily. Immediately after lunch we shall leave for Sicily. I shall fly us myself on this occasion. My brother will greet us on our arrival at the *castello*, and you will be welcomed formally as my current lover.'

'How are you going to explain my disappearance so immediately after the weekend is over?' Leonora asked him curiously.

'Easy. I shall have discovered during the course of the weekend that you were beginning to bore me.'

'I'm not surprised,' Leonora couldn't resist saying. 'I'd be in danger of expiring from boredom myself if I was really anything like the dull creature you seem to think so perfect.'

CHAPTER FOUR

IT MIGHT be midnight but she was still wide awake—and the forbidden garden below her balcony was really too tempting to resist. All the more so because it was forbidden. What harm could it really do for her to go down the stairs and just take a look? None at all. Alessandro was obviously the kind of man who liked making rules for the sake of it, in order to flaunt his power.

The matching strapless top and three-quarter-length bottoms of the leisure suit-cum-sleepwear combo she was wearing were practical and respectable enough for her to go down into the garden, and if Alessandro should happen to see her then so what? He was hardly going to do anything, was he? He needed her compliance over the weekend too much to lock her up in a dungeon, or whatever it was his ancestors had done to those who annoyed or opposed them in any way.

As she negotiated the narrow flight of wrought-iron stairs Leonora mused that it was puzzling that, whilst Alessandro so evidently admired his elder brother and felt grateful to him, at the same time he did not trust him enough to confide in him about his planned deceit—which ostensibly he was carrying out because of his father.

Since they were both middle children, Leonora tried to imagine herself in his position. Piers had never been her protector in quite the same way that Falcon Leopardi appeared to have been Alessandro's, so that wasn't quite the same. She did love her brother, though. But she had felt sharply aware of being the only non-partnered one of the three of them the last time they had all been at home together, she reminded herself.

She had reached the garden, but she didn't move into it, stopping instead to digest the reality of her own admission to herself. That was not the same as what Alessandro was planning to do, though—and anyway, his elder brother did not have a partner. She didn't know why she was bothering to try to understand what was motivating him, anyway. He didn't deserve her sympathy.

She wandered into the garden, intrigued by the formality of the long, narrow canal.

'Arrgghh—'

The sudden shock of spurts of icy-cold water hitting her from every direction had Leonora screeching in shock, trying to dodge out of the way of the jets that were soaking her clothes and her hair with ever-increasing force.

'I warned you not to come down here.'

A firm hand closed round her wet arm, ruthlessly yanking her away from the canal and through the darkness of the garden to another set of stairs.

Soaking wet, her teeth chattering, Leonora complained, 'But you didn't warn me that you'd set up a booby trap for me in case I did.'

'Don't be ridiculous. The water jets are the reason I told you not to use the garden. They were at one time a traditional feature of Renaissance Italian gardens, installed to amuse their owners and soak unsuspecting guests. These are undergoing some restoration work, which has resulted in an inability to turn off the jets whilst new parts are awaited.'

'If you'd told me all of that in the first place then I'd never have come into the garden.'

'My warning should have been enough. To anyone other than a woman who insists on behaving like a rebellious child it would have been.'

He was still holding on to her, and Leonora pulled away from him. Her movement activated a security light, which burst into life, illuminating the marble paved area on which they were standing, a statue clinging lovingly to a basket of grapes—and the fact that the shirt which Alessandro had been wearing during dinner was now plastered to his torso and that her own drenching had resulted in her leisurewear turning completely see-through.

Leonora's panicky squeak combined with her frantic attempt to move back into the shadows brought an audibly impatient exhalation from Alessandro's grim, downturned mouth.

'Your modesty is risibly unnecessary,' he told her bluntly. 'Even if you were the most desirable woman I had ever met, and I had spent the entire evening anticipating taking you to bed, the sight of you right now would have dampened my ardour even more thoroughly than the water jets have done your clothes. What on earth *are* you wearing, by the way?'

'It's leisure and sleepwear,' Leonora answered.

'Appalling. The only thing a woman should ever sleep in is her lover's arms or her own skin.'

Right now the unpleasantly clammy embrace she was enduring was beginning to make her shiver and long for one of the huge, thick, fluffy towels she had found in her *en suite* bathroom, Leonora decided.

'Well, now that we've both agreed that we don't turn one another on, and that a bit of unplanned alfresco sex is out of the question, would you mind telling me the fastest and driest route back to my bedroom?'

By the time she had finished speaking she was shivering so much her teeth had started to chatter.

He, on the other hand, looked predictably arrogantly handsome—the victor surveying the spoils of war with a contemptuous downward glance at her from beneath deliberately dropped eyelids. The light fell cleanly on the pride-honed sculpted flesh of his cheekbones and the hard masculinity of his jaw. A shudder of something she could neither control nor understand jolted through her.

'This way,' Alessandro told her, gesturing towards the stairs. 'It's a bit of a long way round, but it will be dry.'

The steps went up to a balcony much wider than her own, complete with a table and chairs, and to an open door through which she could see a starkly and magnificently male bedroom, illuminated by a modern chandelier of driftwood and silver.

Leonora looked at Alessandro, and then at the room, and then back at him, resisting the firm pressure of his hand in the small of her back as she hung back a little, and said foolishly, 'But that's your bedroom.'

'Correct. It is also the only way you can get to your own room without going back through the garden.'

He sounded exasperated and irritated, but Leonora had now become distracted by the delicious warmth spreading out through her body from his hand against her back. If she leaned into it the warmth would increase and spread further, reaching right down to her toes, for instance, and up to her…

'This is all your fault,' she accused him. And it certainly was—because no one else had ever made her feel that she wanted to soak up the warmth of their touch in such a blatantly sensual way.

'You were the one who initiated it.'

Stung by his claim, Leonora whipped round and defended herself indignantly.

'No, I wasn't. You were the one who touched me. *Oh!*'

Oh, indeed. It was obvious from Alessandro's expression that they were at cross purposes, and Leonora's face flamed as his gaze, which had been fixed grimly on her face, slid down over her body, resting deliberately on the full thrust of her breasts against the wet fabric of her top. Its intensity was somehow, and quite shockingly, causing her nipples to tighten into aching peaks, making her want to wrap her arms protectively around her body to conceal their betrayal.

This really wasn't a good idea, Alessandro warned himself. She wasn't his type—and anyway, her temporary role in his life was better remaining strictly business. But her ridiculous comment had caught his sense of humour, and her breasts *were* absolutely delicious—would be even more so without the top that was clinging to them, covered instead by his hands, their hard, flaunting nipples caressed by his lips and his tongue… What harm could it really do? In fact it could only add authenticity to their roles.

Alessandro was going to touch her, kiss her—do something more than that, perhaps. Leonora panicked and backed into the bedroom.

Alessandro followed her, his hunting instincts aroused.

'You said you didn't want me,' Leonora reminded him as he reached for her and drew her towards him with one lazy movement of his arm.

'*You* said you didn't want *me*,' he taunted her, rubbing his nose erotically against her own in a way that sent a jolt with the power of a dozen jet engines surging though her body. His words were a whisper as soft as morning clouds against her lips, as he added meaningfully, 'And you lied.'

Leonora sucked in her breath, a dozen furious objections on the tip of her tongue. But Alessandro's tongue was tracing the shape of her mouth, and its intimacy shocked her into a heart-thudding silence. Any thought of doing verbal battle with him had been vanquished. Any thought of doing anything at all was an impossibility, she admitted helplessly as the soft, teasing stroke of the experienced male tongue suddenly became a determined thrust that took advantage of her weakness. She clung on to Alessandro's shoulders for dear life as the dizzyingly swift ascent of her response to the sensual possession of his kiss took her so high that she felt as though she was suffering from oxygen deprivation.

How could such an argumentative, awkward, irritating woman cling to him as though helpless beneath the sensuality they had ignited? How could she melt into his arms and into his kiss as though they were what she had been born for? And how could he be stupid enough to respond to her reactions like some raw, crass boy who had never known a woman's arousal before?

Alessandro didn't know. What he did know, though, was that her response was inciting him to push aside her wet top and then span her narrow ribcage with his hands, deliberately tormenting himself by delaying the moment when he slid them upwards to hold the soft weight of her breasts, splaying his fingers against them, rubbing her nipples with the pads of his thumbs, feeling the jolt of pleasure that rocked through her body and hearing the sharp, almost shocked moan she sobbed against his kiss.

At the sound of her arousal pleasure ricocheted through him. He wanted more—her naked body in his arms, beneath his hands and his lips, her cries of need filling his ears in the hot, secret darkness of his bed. He wanted to know her and enjoy her and fill her with a pleasure and a satisfaction that would be unique within her sexual experience. She had challenged him, and now, having done so, she had totally undermined the hostility he had felt, with the sheer sensuality of her abandoned response to him, like honey after vinegar, stealing from him his resistance to her.

And he must resist, Alessandro recognised. He must resist or face the consequences. There was no place in the purpose for which he was allowing her into his life for any kind of intimacy between them—least of all this kind.

Alessandro could feel the resistance of his body to his thoughts, but he was not a man who allowed physical needs—of any kind—to dominate his actions.

Alessandro had stopped kissing her, Leonora recognised. He had stopped touching her too, and was stepping back from her, leaving her to shiver, bereft of his body heat. The night air touched her damp clothes and naked skin.

'So,' Alessandro announced calmly, 'now that I have indulged your sexual curiosity, perhaps I should remind you of my warning to you earlier about the role I expect you to play? It is a role that does not and will not—ever—require your presence in my bed.'

He had indulged her sexual curiosity? Leonora's face burned. She wasn't the one who had kissed him or pushed up his top and touched him. No, but she was the one who had responded to his kiss and quivered with open longing beneath the experienced touch of his hands on her breasts.

'You were the one who brought me here,' she told him fiercely.

'And you were the one who was curious.'

Leonora opened her mouth to deny his accusation, and then closed it again. Could she honestly put her hand on her heart and say that she had *not* been curious about what it would be like to be kissed by him, a man so far outside her own circles and way, way outside her personal experience? But surely it was only natural that she should have wondered? Wondering, though, did not mean that she had actually wanted him to kiss her. Had she? Not beforehand, perhaps, but once she had felt the warmth of his breath on her lips and the touch of his hands on her body, hadn't she wanted more?

'I'd like to go back to my room, if you could point me in the right direction?' she told Alessandro, desperate to escape from her own thoughts as well as from him and his too-knowing questions.

Nodding his head, he answered her. 'This way.' Striding across the bedroom and then into a large open-plan sitting-room-cum-office, he turned to look at her, frowning before telling her briskly, 'Wait here.'

What else could she do? She had no idea how to find her way back to her room, and she certainly didn't fancy wandering all over the apartment dressed as she was, in a still very damp leisure suit.

He wasn't gone long, returning carrying a large taupe-coloured bath towel, which he tossed towards her saying, 'You'd better wrap this around you,' before going to open the door and waiting for her to join him. 'Follow this corridor until you reach the stairs, then go past them and continue down the next corridor. You room is the first door on your right.'

Thanking him, Leonora hugged the towel around herself and made her escape.

That was the trouble with women, Alessandro told himself as he returned to the work he had been doing before he had seen Leonora in the garden. They just could not resist giving themselves the ego boost of getting some man—any man, more often than not—hot for them.

He sat at his desk, frowning as he re-read the e-mail he had found in his in-box earlier. His concierge service apologised, but the stylist they had found for him had cancelled, and they weren't able to replace her with a substitute of equally high calibre. That left him with two options: to trust Leonora, or accompany her himself.

No man of his wealth and position could get to the age Alessandro had without the experience of being coaxed, coerced, sweet-talked and seduced into accompanying beautiful women to expensive and exclusive designer shops—especially if they were Italian. And besides, sometimes it was easier and speedier to end a relationship that had served its purpose with a goodbye gift of a few designer outfits as a sweetener.

Not that there had been anyone sharing his bed for the last year—or longer. Which was no doubt why Leonora Thaxton had had such an unexpected and powerful effect on his libido. His pride might not like the fact that she had aroused him but, looking at things from a more practical point of view, the fact that they had shared a handful of minutes of pre-coital sexual intimacy at least meant that there was a familiarity between them now, which could only work to his advantage in public. In private there would not be a repeat of that intimacy—that went without saying.

But back to the matter of providing her with a suitable wardrobe—and quickly… His frown deepened, and then eased as he searched though his e-mail addresses until he found the one he wanted. Cristina Rosetti was one of a certain top-flight designer's right-hand women, and she owed him a favour, having had to ask him once or twice to arrange for models to be flown to New York when their original travel arrangements had fallen through at the last minute. Several designers used his airline to freight their priceless one-off pieces of clothing around the world to private and public showings, but he had known and liked Cristina for several years—on a strictly business basis.

CHAPTER FIVE

LEONORA woke up slowly and reluctantly, trying to hang on to the protective ignorance of sleep whilst she fought against the growing feeling of panic and apprehension that waking up was bringing.

By the time she had opened her eyes she had total recall of the events of the previous day, and her heart had sunk to the depths of the hollowed-out, aching space that was her chest. She looked at her watch. Half past eight? She sat bolt-upright, pushing her tangled curls out of her eyes. How could it be that late? She was always up early. It must have been her dread at what lay ahead of her today that had kept her protectively asleep and oblivious.

She wasn't either of those things any more, though. She wondered what time she was being collected to be taken shopping for clothes suitable for the weekend's events—and, of course, suitable to meet the high sartorial standard he no doubt required of his female companions. Leonora pulled a face at herself. She hated the restrictions of 'result' clothes. She was strictly a casual-clothes woman.

She heard the outer door to the suite opening and tensed—but it was only Caterina, bringing in her breakfast.

'*Buon giorno*, Caterina,' Leonora offered with a warm smile, getting out of bed and looking appreciatively at the selection of food on the tray, which included what looked like home-made muesli as well as the ingredients of a more traditional continental breakfast and—most important of all—a jug of fragrant-smelling coffee.

Leonora contemplated the personal shopper who would be accompanying her as she tucked into her muesli. Stick-thin, probably, and dressed like someone out of *Sex and the City*—either that or one of those fearsomely elegant women who populated the designer outlets of the more upmarket parts of London. Leonora had seen them from outside the shops, on her way to give private Mandarin lessons to her wealthy clients.

Oh, yes, she was quite happy to think about what lay ahead of her—but what she was not happy to think about was what had happened last night. How could she have responded to Alessandro Leopardi in the way that she had? Wildly, passionately, and as though she had actually *wanted* him to kiss her. When the reality was that he was the kind of man—sexually experienced, predatory, too macho, too much of all things male—that she would normally have taken one look and fled.

When it came to sex they were not even in the same league table, never mind sexually matched. When she thought of how she had lived for so long with a dread of being publicly exposed and then ridiculed as an inexperienced virgin, neither wanted enough by a man to be swept off her feet and into his bed, nor having ever wanted any man enough to encourage him, she felt positively ill at the memory of what she had done last night. Just imagining the humiliation she would have suffered if Alessandro hadn't stopped when he had, and had gone on to discover her shameful secret, was enough to make it impossible for her to eat another mouthful of food because of the sick churning in her stomach.

Why, why, *why* hadn't she done what virtually every other girl she knew had done and unburdened herself of her wretched virginity at university? Because she had been too busy fighting to out-do her brothers, that was why. How much simpler her life would be now if she had focused instead on losing her virginity. Taking a rest between lovers because one was focused on forging one's career was understood and accepted by others. But never ever having had sex was a social embarrassment of huge proportions, and something that rubbed painfully against Leonora's always easily stung pride.

She had thought that the person she most dreaded finding out was probably Leo, but now she recognised that Alessandro had replaced Leo as the man she would least like to know of her embarrassing virginity. If Alessandro had continued to make love to her last night how long would it have been before he had guessed? Would something in her response have given her away, or would he have only realised later?

Whatever the answer to that was, she had no difficulty at all in imagining what his reaction would have been. Leonora guessed that as a middle child, a second son who had obviously been emotionally scarred by his father's cruelty to him, his pride would have objected to the idea of bedding a woman no other man had wanted to bed. He would have seen her as a reject—even an oddity, perhaps—and he would have recoiled from her because of that. A man like Alessandro would always be driven to acquire and possess that which other alpha men either craved or already possessed. That went with the territory of having been the child he had and having become the man he was.

Just as she was trapped in her tomboy image, so he was equally trapped in his drive to be first, and to have the best. The difference between them, she suspected, was that whilst she as an adult very often disliked the persona she had created to protect the child she had been, finding it wearisome and immature, Alessandro *liked* his alter ego.

Leonora rarely allowed herself to dwell on such profound and personal thoughts. They cut too deep and exposed too much—especially at times like this. She didn't want to be marooned in the tomboy girl she had taught herself to be in order to compete with and excel against her brothers. Her brothers had unwittingly reinforced that role, keeping her in it within their family makeup. Out of pride and stubbornness she had remained the eternal tomboy rather than admit to those who knew her best that she longed to be recognised as a woman; she was afraid to ask them for the help and acceptance she needed to retrace her steps to the point where the tomboy should have slipped naturally away and the woman should have taken her place in a natural girl-to-woman transformation.

There was no point in her wondering what she should wear, she acknowledged now, putting aside her unproductive and uncomfortable soul-searching, since it would have to be her jeans. Somehow she didn't think that the stylist was going to be impressed by them.

Alessandro watched from the shadows of the hallway as Leonora came down the stairs, his body disobeying his head with its unwanted and irritatingly juvenile immediate response to her. Despite her ill-fitting jeans and loose top he was sharply aware that beneath them she possessed lushly sensual breasts and a waist so narrow that any red-blooded man would instinctively want to span it with his hands. She was long-legged too—something that no doubt Falcon, whose women were always tall and leggy, would immediately notice.

This morning the tangled curls were constrained in a thick plait, which showed off her cheekbones and the fullness of her mouth. He hadn't thought of her initially as a beauty, much less as a woman possessed of alluring sensuality with the power to arouse a man against his better judgement, but now his body was reacting to her as though she were all of those things, and in doing so it was forcing Alessandro to acknowledge a potential and very unwanted complication to his plans.

When he had blackmailed her into agreeing to his plans the thought that he might find her sexually attractive had been the last thing on his mind. Alessandro was scrupulous about not mixing business with pleasure. He had seen what happened to others when they did and he had no intention of allowing his own life to become inconvenienced by the toxic effect of extricating himself from a sexual relationship he no longer wanted with a woman with whom he was involved in another area of his life.

Not, of course, that he was saying he was in danger of becoming sexually involved with Leonora Thaxton. He was, after all, a man who prided himself on his control over himself. He was simply annoyed with himself for initially letting the fact that she had managed to win his approval for her flying whilst deceiving him as to her identity blind him to her sexuality.

Leonora came to a wary halt at the bottom of the stairs. When Caterina had informed her that she was to go down to the main entrance to the apartment once she had finished her breakfast, she had hoped that the only person she would meet there would be the stylist—not Alessandro Leopardi.

Stepping out of the shadows, Alessandro announced coolly, 'There has been a change of plan. I shall now accompany you myself.'

Leonora knew that her indrawn breath was both audible and a betrayal of her feelings. An indignant flush of colour stained her face. She also knew that Alessandro wouldn't care how much she objected to his change of plan. But maybe after he'd told the stylist about her she'd refused point-blank to take on such an unrewarding challenge, Leonora thought with black humour.

'As most of the better-known designer stores are here on Tournabouni Street, we may as well walk rather than risk being stuck in the city's traffic.'

Leonora was feeling too dispirited to respond as she compared the way she was going to be spending her precious time in Florence with the way she had planned to spend it—visiting museums, exploring the streets and enjoying the timeless ambience of the Medici city.

Even though it was only just gone nine o' clock in the morning there was already a warning strength in the sun, where it fell in slats of gold from the side streets. Tournabouni Street was a busy thoroughfare, bordered by imposing buildings, many of which had been converted into designer stores. Their doors were closed to shoppers at this early hour of the day—but not, apparently, to Alessandro, as Leonora discovered when he stopped outside one exclusive shop and then removed his cell phone from the inside pocket of the elegantly cut linen jacket he was wearing over a striped shirt and a pair of jeans far better cut than her own.

He texted something swiftly, speaking to her without looking up. 'I have told Cristina, who will be here to take charge of you in a minute, that you are to accompany me to Sicily and that you have lost your luggage in transit—'

He broke off as the door opened and a stunningly elegant woman stepped out to embrace him with a warm, '*Ciao*, Alessandro.'

As he kissed her on both cheeks, he told her, 'I shall forever be indebted to you, Tina.'

How many women must he have brought here in order to merit the store being opened early for him? What did it matter to her how many there had been—and what was the cause of that sudden fierce flash of painful anger? Not jealousy, Leonora assured herself.

'Well, we owe you several favours, Sandro, for getting the models to New York for us in time for the last collection's show.'

So perhaps it wasn't because he bought clothes for his lovers here that the store had been opened. If that was relief Leonora was feeling it was only because she didn't want anyone thinking that she was one of his women.

'Here is Leonora, Tina,' Alessandro was saying, 'I shall leave her in your capable hands.'

After another very Italian embrace between them he was gone, striding down the street, leaving her feeling curiously bereft when she ought to have felt relief, Leonora admitted, as Cristina beckoned her inside, and then relocked the door.

'It is every woman's dread that her clothes disappear,

no?' she sympathised with a swift shrug. 'Before we started to use Alessandro's cargo service every time we pack for one of the international clothes shows, I am—what do you say in England?—on needles until I see that all is well and everything has arrived.'

'On pins,' Leonora told her, with a smile that Cristina returned. She was older than Leonora, in her late thirties or maybe her early forties, Leonora guessed, but so elegant that it was hard to put an exact age on her.

'I have brought with me some of the stock from Milan, as we have things there that we do not have here in Florence, and also a hairdresser and a make-up artist, since Alessandro tells me your work has meant that you have not been able to visit a proper hairdresser for some months.'

If by a 'proper hairdresser' Cristina meant the kind of hairdresser who charged a fortune and with whom it was impossible to get an appointment, then her 'some months' should have been 'ever,' Leonora admitted ruefully. It would take more than designer clothes and an expensive haircut to transform her into the kind of woman Alessandro normally dated.

But then he wasn't dating her, was he? she reminded herself as she followed Cristina down a long white-walled corridor that curved and then straightened before opening out into a white space furnished with low black chairs and a black table.

As though by magic two black-suited young women suddenly appeared, folding back a section of the white 'wall' to reveal neatly hanging and folded clothes.

'We will start, I think, with the basics. Jeans—which you will need for Sicily, especially if you plan to do any sightseeing around the Etna area—worn with perhaps a blazer and a silk shirt, and some fine knits as an alternative.'

As Cristina spoke the two girls were removing clothes from the rails and placing them on one of the chairs.

'You will, of course, want to create the right impression when you arrive—you are tall, and so can get away with trousers. I think this pair in neutral cream will be perfect. Here is this cardigan to go with them, and this silver necklace with the matching cuff—very smart. And for the cocktail party I have brought this from Milan.'

Leonora's eyes widened as she gazed at the lilac and grey layers of silk chiffon that made up a short dress with a bubble hem and a fitted strapless bodice, and at the neat fitted jacket that was worn over it. It was beautiful—but not for her. She never wore clothes like that. She didn't have what it took to carry it off.

Shaking her head, she told Cristina regretfully, 'It's lovely, but I don't think it's really me.'

'We will try it and see,' Cristina said, overruling her.

Two hours later, exhausted and bemused, Leonora stood in front of a mirror and caught her breath in disbelief at her own reflection. Her hair was newly cut, in a style that seemed to consist of a mass of shiny sensual layers where once had been a tangle of too-thick curls, and it seemed somehow to emphasise her cheekbones and make her eyes look bigger. Her bare shoulders rose from the silk chiffon cocktail dress, whilst her eyes—thanks to the clever application of make-up—seemed to glow a smoky violet colour. The dress made her look fragile and feminine in a way she had never imagined she could look.

'It is perfect for you,' Cristina pronounced, looking pleased. 'I knew it would be when Alessandro described to me your colouring. This gown, and the cream silk satin full-length gown you must also have—you have the perfect figure for them. The jeans also, and the trousers. You have the long legs that look so good in them.'

Leonora wasn't going to argue with her. She had never imagined that she could look so good. She even felt confident about wearing the bright acid-yellow cotton sundress that Cristina had insisted was a 'must' for sight-seeing daywear, along with the pair of skinny-legged jeans which could be rolled up to Capri length. There were also a couple of outrageously expensive T-shirts, along with a gorgeous silk parka in pewter-grey, to tone in with the whites, silvers and greys of her other new 'casual' clothes.

Both evening dresses had their own matching shoes and clutch bags, and she'd been given a make-up lesson to go with the designer cosmetics that were to replace those she had 'lost in transit.' She also had a large, soft and squishy 'daytime' bag, that worked with both the trousers and the jeans.

After instructing one of the girls to unzip the cocktail dress for Leonora, Christina had left her alone in the fitting room. Leonora couldn't help delaying the moment when she removed the dress, as she stood in front of the mirror and marvelled again at the transformation it had effected. For the first time she saw an image of what she could be— all that she had secretly longed to be since she had left her university years behind. Now she saw in the mirror a woman who was hardly daring to hope, as yet not entirely comfortable with her new image, looking back at her. The beginning of the woman that she could become—a woman at ease with herself, confident about her ability and her right to be both vulnerable and strong, to be both feminine and capable of holding down a demanding job in what was still in many ways a man's world without having to compromise herself.

It was one of the pretty black-suited young salesgirls who told Alessandro where he could find Leonora. Having assumed that he and Leonora were lovers, she omitted to mention that Leonora was alone in the private changing suite, so that when he walked in, his arrival masked by the thickness of the dove-grey pile carpet, Leonora was oblivious to his presence.

Alessandro, because of the angle of a long pier glass mirror in the lounge area off the changing room, and because Cristina had fastened back the curtain, was perfectly able to see and study her. Anyone witnessing his reaction could have been forgiven for thinking that he was not pleased with what he saw, since he had started to frown.

The reflection in the mirror showed him a stunningly beautiful young woman, wearing an elegant dress that suited her to perfection. But it was the look in Leonora's unexpectedly violet-tinged eyes that was responsible for his frown, not her appearance. Alone, and unaware that she was being watched, she wore an expression so open and revealing that it was an intimacy he didn't want to have—one that rolled his heart over inside his chest, seizing it in a tight fist of compassion streaked with an angry awareness of the knowledge of what he could see so plainly in her face. She looked like a little girl, scarcely able to believe in her own luck, delighted and yet at the same time struggling to balance between something she desperately wanted and some long-held inability to believe she was worthy of such joy.

Leonora could feel her eyes burning with very private tears. She tried to blink them away, and then felt laughter bubbling in her throat as she realised she couldn't wipe them away without ruining her new make-up or risking getting it on her beautiful dress, since she didn't have a tissue to hand... Holding the dress to her, she turned round, remembering that there was a box of tissues on the coffee table in the lounge area—and then froze as she saw Alessandro.

Even if he hadn't already been able to see that her emotions had nothing whatsoever to do with the acquisition of an expensive gown and everything to do with something very private within herself, Alessandro suspected that the intensity of her shocked reaction to his presence would have convinced him on that point.

How long had he been there? He couldn't have—must not have seen her looking at herself in the way that she had. She could not have borne for anyone to see that, but most of all not him. Her face began to burn, her old tomboy-style defences springing into action.

Not a man who was used to putting the emotional needs of others first, Alessandro surprised himself when he heard himself saying calmly, as he backed out of the room, 'Sorry—I didn't realise that you weren't ready.'

Leonora's relief was so intense that it dizzied her. He had not seen her. If he had he would not have been able to resist saying something. She knew that from what she had experienced at his hands—and, of course, from her experience of growing up with brothers. She knew other girls who had brothers, of course—some of those girls were eldest sisters and some of them youngest, and their experience did not mirror hers. The elder sisters often mothered their men, and the youngest ones always seemed to attract men who were protective of them and indulgent towards them.

Just as Leonora was nodding her head, not trusting herself to speak, Cristina reappeared, clicking her tongue when she saw that Leonora was on her own and still wearing the cocktail dress.

CHAPTER SIX

So MUCH had happened that it was hard to accept that it was less than twenty-four hours since she had come down these steps, Leonora admitted as Alessandro stood to one side to allow her to precede him up the steps to his private jet.

This time, instead of wearing her pilot's uniform, she was dressed in her new clothes: designer jeans encasing the slender length of her legs, stiletto heels on her feet and a plain white T-shirt that had cost the earth. Personally she thought it clung far too neatly to her breasts, which was why she was wearing a butter-soft leather jacket over it, despite the heat of the Italian afternoon. Expensive designer sunglasses and the new soft leather bag completed her outfit; the whole look was one that was almost a uniform for well-bred and well-to-do women—one that could be found from Fifth Avenue to Knightsbridge, taking in Paris and Milan on the way.

Below her she could see her new matching leather luggage—white with tan straps, and a logo so small and discreet that it could only be found by the *cognoscenti*—being loaded, along with two more masculine and rather more travelled versions.

She had been taken off guard when Alessandro had announced that he would be flying them himself to Sicily, and even more surprised when he had informed her that she would be in the cockpit with him, as his co-pilot.

'Not that you will be doing anything other than acting as a non-flying co-pilot,' he had told her emphatically.

'You didn't have any complaints about my handling of the jet when I flew you out from London,' Leonora had felt defensive enough to point out. 'And I *am* a fully qualified pilot.'

'For the moment. Had anything happened, the fact that you were illegally flying the plane would have made the insurance null and void, and that alone would have been enough to ensure that you were stripped of your licence for a very long time.'

His warning had sent a cold chill of apprehension icing down Lenora's spine—and not just because of the threat it had contained. He had made a legitimate point that she, in her determination to prove herself, had overlooked— and it stung her pride that he should have spotted her error and pointed it out to her.

Ascending the steps into the jet behind Leonora gave Alessandro ample opportunity to take in the neat curve of her bottom in the new jeans, as well as the length of her legs. Even with heels on she was still several inches shorter than him and, unlike her bulky borrowed and adapted uniform, her jeans showed off her curves and her femininity.

Although he wasn't going to say so to Leonora, the main reason he had decided to fly the jet himself, with her in the co-pilot's seat, was that he didn't want to arouse the curiosity of his pilots over how or why he was suddenly squiring around the sister of one of their number. For another thing, he wouldn't put it past Falcon to start asking some typically awkward questions as to why, since Alessandro and Leonora shared a passion for flying, they had not shared the intimacy of that passion coming out to Sicily. Falcon knew how much he hated handing over control of anything he could do himself to anyone else, and it was part and parcel of his elder brother's analytical and protective nature to ask far too astute questions when he suspected that something was being withheld from him.

Had someone told her twenty-four hours ago that she would be seated in the co-pilot's seat of Alessandro Leopardi's private jet, with Alessandro himself at the controls, Leonora would have been so filled with excitement and triumph at the thought of getting to show him the excellence and capability of her skills that she would have been overjoyed. But twenty-four hours ago she hadn't known what she knew now, having met Alessandro Leopardi.

Now she had. Leonora risked a quick, brief look at his profile whilst his attention was focused on the pre-flight checks, her heartbeat suddenly speeding up to a heavy drumroll. Her heart itself did a series of back flips that threatened to leave her severely deprived of oxygen. Speedily Leonora transferred her gaze to his hands, but far from being a safer option this too resulted in her heart doing a spectacular loop the loop as for her eyes only, her memory ran an inner video of those hands on her breasts.

It was all very well telling herself that a bit of role playing would not go amiss, given what lay ahead, but there was certainly no need for her to take things that far, Leonora told herself, hastily reaching for her own headset, ejecting the seriously disruptive images from her head so that she too could concentrate of the pre-flight checks.

He had been right to make it a rule never to employ female pilots, Alessandro decided, as the scent of

Leonora's skin mingling with the perfume she was wearing intruded between him and his focus on the familiar pre-take-off routine. And the distraction of her smell was second only to the soft thrust of her breasts beneath the white T-shirt now that she had removed the leather jacket she had been wearing. There was no need to ask him just why it was that the visual impact of natural breasts was so much more effective than the solid unmoving thrust of pumped-up silicon.

If she had removed her jacket in some kind of attempt to soften him up for a fresh attempt to persuade him to give her a job she had made a very big mistake. No way, having felt the impact the sight of that soft jiggle was having on his own body, was he going to risk exposing his pilots to it.

Flying a plane demanded total concentration. Not the distraction of the sight and scent of a sexually alluring woman.

It was warm inside the cockpit, and Alessandro had removed the linen jacket he had been wearing when they boarded the plane. His shirt, short-sleeved and casually open at the throat, pulled against the breadth of his back when he leaned forward, making Leonora foolishly catch her breath and fight to suppress a soft squirm of pleasure at the memory of how it had felt to have the breadth of his shoulders and the heat of his flesh beneath her hands. Today his torso might be covered by the cotton of his shirt, but last night the dampness had moulded cloth to flesh, allowing her to see quite clearly the structure of his muscles and the darkness of his body hair, somehow dangerously erotic in comparison to the waxed torsos of the male models favoured by advertising campaigns.

Guiltily Leonora looked away and felt her face and then her whole body overheat as she realised that in her haste to avoid looking at his torso she had inadvertently allowed her gaze to drop down to the open spread of his legs. Not that she could actually see anything—well, only that he was a man, of course. But it just wasn't the done thing to stare at the male crotch. Or at least it wasn't *her* done thing, but now...

Her mouth had gone dry, and her heart was pounding too fast and too unevenly. Somehow she managed to drag her gaze away, her guilt sending her lurching into a frantically fast burst of speech as she asked, 'How long is the flight?'

Too long for the kind of intimacy the flight deck was imposing on him, Alessandro admitted to himself, as he shifted slightly in his seat to ease the ache he could already feel pulsing in his groin.

'An hour—less if we get a tail wind.'

Leonora nodded her head vigorously, to mask the horrified embarrassment she felt at the way in which Alessandro was moving his body as though in warning against her intrusive visual attention.

A voice crackling in the headphones from air traffic control brought her back to reality, and years of training enabled her to focus on what she should be doing.

They had been in the air for less than fifteen minutes when Leonora had been forced to admit to herself that Alessandro was a first-rate pilot—superbly skilled technically, and in absolute control of both himself and the aircraft. But now, with Sicily spread out below them, offering herself and her beauty up to them, Alessandro's flying skills were taking second place to Sicily's beauty. The sight of Mount Etna, so dangerous and yet so compelling, made her reflect on how well suited Alessandro was to the land of his birth.

'If you look to the east now you will see the *castello*.'

His unexpected advice had her eyes widening and her breath catching with dismay as well as awe when she saw the size of the castellated fortress on a rocky outcrop, separated from an equally medieval walled town by several acres of olive trees. Beyond the town the land rose towards the mountains, and here and there a small cluster of buildings clung to their steep sides.

Alessandro frowned as he looked down at the mountain villages below them. His father ruled his lands and those who lived on them with a feudal mindset he refused to relinquish. He might like to think of himself as a patriarch revered by his people, but the truth was that he was more of a despot. There were children living in the remote mountain villages on Leopardi land whose families were so poor that they were still forced to leave school to work on land for which they still had to pay Alessandro's father a tithe.

Falcon had sworn to abandon the practice once he inherited, but in the meantime there was unrest in one of the villages in particular. Alessandro's sympathies lay entirely with the villagers, but at the moment it was the absorbed, marvelling look on Leonora's face that caused him to circle round so that she could have a better view.

Their shared role on the flight deck had been unexpectedly harmonious—a good omen for the weekend and for his determination to ensure that everyone, but most of all his father, would be forced to recognise that there was nothing and no one he could not have exclusively to himself if he chose to do so.

After a textbook-perfect descent onto what Alessandro told Leonora was his own private airfield, the jet hummed gently to a halt. Sharp bright sunshine burned down onto the runway, turning it blindingly white under a pure blue sky.

The first thing Leonora noticed, as she stepped out onto the steps rolled into place by immaculately turned-out ground staff in overalls bearing the Avanti Airlines logo, was the scent of citrus mingling with the hot, acrid smell of aircraft fuel, exhaust fumes and hot metal. The heat of the sun, so much stronger here than it had been in Florence, had her reaching immediately for her sunglasses and mentally thanking Cristina for warning her that she would need a hat to protect her head if she went out in the heat of the day.

Some men were unloading their luggage, and Alessandro had joined her on the metal platform at the top of the steps. As they stood together in silence, an immaculately polished limousine, with a small pennant fluttering on its bonnet, slid through the dusty afternoon to come to a halt with its passenger door exactly in line with the steps. A uniformed chauffeur emerged from the driver's seat and went to open the rear passenger door, facing them. The man uncoiling himself from inside the car was tall and dark-haired, and his physical resemblance to Alessandro was unmistakable as his air of authority, Leonora recognised.

Uncertainly, but automatically, she turned to look at Alessandro. She could see his chest expand as he breathed in and then exhaled with perfect control, and his mouth was chiselled and hard as he told her in a clipped voice, 'It seems that Falcon has come to welcome us in person.'

Falcon. The name suited him, Leonora acknowledged. Every bit of him exuded an aura that spoke of total power allied to total self-control, underscored with something that suggested that he could be very dangerous if provoked. And yet for all his power and good looks he did not send her heart into freefall, or force the muscles of her lower body to clench in agonised denial of the intimate sensual ache he had caused in them, in the way that Alessandro could and did.

Leonora found herself reluctant to descend the steps. Because she didn't want to be here and was being forced to do so? Or because she feared that the man standing impassively waiting for them might see through their deceit and Alessandro would punish her for that by sacking Leo?

Without realising what she was doing she backed into Alessandro, trembling slightly as she did so. Automatically he reached out to steady her, placing his arm round her waist and turning her into his own body, holding her so that she was practically leaning against him, the hard muscles of his thigh pressed between her own jean-clad legs.

Leonora felt shock seize her breath, causing her to tremble even more at the unexpectedly sensual intimacy of his hold. She was torn between pulling back and—shockingly—wanting to lean closer, to be closer, to bury her face against his shoulder so that she wouldn't have to face the scrutiny of the man waiting for them.

Panic filled her. She gave in to it, turning her face towards him as she whispered shakily, 'I can't do it. He—your brother will know. I…'

Alessandro's arm tightened round her.

He should be used by now to the effect his elder brother had on women. There was no real reason why he should feel such a fierce, primeval surge of male possessiveness. He felt nothing for Leonora, after all, and she would be a fool to risk her brother's dismissal by flirting with Falcon.

'Falcon is merely a man, not a magician. He cannot read minds or hearts, no matter how much he sometimes wants others to believe that he can. Like any other man he will believe what he sees—and this is what he will see.'

He pulled her closer and bent his head, and her eyes betrayed her as she looked up at him, offering him free access to her lips as though she wanted his kiss. His hand cupped the side of her face. To protect her from the sun and his brother's gaze or to hold her captive? Alessandro didn't know—and as soon as his mouth covered hers he discovered that he didn't really care.

Why was it with this woman that where there should have been suspicion, the belief that she was putting on an act to entice him, instead the sensation of her mouth trembling with excitement beneath his own made him believe in her, made him feel both powerful and vulnerable? And so aroused that he was drawing her in close against his body and holding her tighter, deepening the kiss, probing that soft, trembling mouth mindlessly and seamlessly, for all the world as though he had her to himself and they were alone in a place where nothing mattered other than the way she was making him feel.

This wasn't real. It was a role Alessandro was playing—that was all. Leonora tried to remind herself, but her body wasn't listening to her mind. Instead it was reacting to the fact that she was in the arms of a man who was kissing her with fierce, compulsive desire. But Alessandro did not desire her, and she must not let her mouth soften under his or her body melt into his. She must not put herself in a position where she could and would be humiliated and hurt.

Hurt?

It was the frantic trembling of Leonora's body and the agitated pressure of the hand she lifted to his chest to push him away that wrenched Alessandro back to reality.

As soon as he released her Leonora started to descend the steps, panicked by the shock of recognition that Alessandro could hurt her. How had that happened? How on earth had she managed to become emotionally involved in any kind of way with a man she had known less than twenty-four hours? But it wasn't the quantity of time she had spent with him so much as its quality. Their intimacy, both cerebral and sensual, had brought her closer to him than she had ever been with any other man. From the moment he had stopped her as she left the plane he had occupied every single one of her thoughts, full-time.

Gripped by her unwanted discovery Leonora forgot about her high heels and gave a startled gasp as she caught one of them on the steps and started to fall forward.

Strong arms caught her and held her safe—but they were not Alessandro's arms. Her body knew that immediately, and thus she was able to relax into them without fearing what it might betray.

Falcon Leopardi was as tall as Alessandro, and as broad, but where Alessandro possessed a fierce, sensual intensity that strobed danger into her senses, Falcon had an unmistakable air of right and of acceptance of that right, in a way that reminded her of her own elder brother. He was plainly at ease with himself and his position. His magnetic dark-eyed gaze sweeping her from head to foot—not merely in a man's assessment of her but also that of an elder brother checking her out to see if she was good enough for Alessandro.

She felt safe with him, Leonora recognised. But she would only be safe as long as he believed that his brother was her first priority.

'I'm sorry. So silly of me. I forgot that I was wearing high heels,' she apologised as she eased back. He immediately released her.

'Well, well—and what have I done to deserve the reception, Falcon?'

Alessandro's voice, sarcastic and cynical, came from immediately behind her, sending her heart jerking against her ribs as though he was holding it on a string.

'Is there any reason why I should not be the first to welcome you home? And, of course, Miss Thaxton with you.' Falcon's smile for Leonora was brief but warm as he turned to her and said, 'You must have impressed Alessandro if he allowed you to co-pilot the plane.'

'Leonora doesn't need to impress me with her flying skills. It is her absolute loyalty to me for which I value her,' Alessandro told his brother, slipping his arm round Leonora's waist and drawing her close to him. He looked down at her and reached with his free hand to brush a stray hair off her face, then rubbed his thumb across her lower lip, caressing the curve of her waist as he did so, as though he was totally unable to stop himself from touching her.

He was giving such a good performance of a man besotted with her that even Leonora herself was impressed. But what was the purpose of the deliberate challenge he had thrown down to his brother with his comment about her loyalty? It hinted at a rivalry between them that at some point had gone deep and still festered—at least on Alessandro's part. Was that the reason for his demand that she show him absolute loyalty and devotion as 'his woman' over the course of the weekend?

Somehow, without even having to make a deliberate decision to do so, she was automatically trying to imagine how *she* would have reacted had she had an older sister and there had been a contest between them over a boy. The rush of emotions that gripped her told their own story— anger, fierce anger, against both the boy and her sister. But the real scalding heat of that anger would have been directed at her sibling, along with a ferocious need not just to show her that she could find another boy who would not be tempted by her but find one who would be far, far better than the one she had lost.

Was that why Alessandro had blackmailed her into being here?

'I hope my brother has managed to be practical enough to explain what this weekend is about, Leonora, and what is going to take place?'

Falcon's calm voice broke into her inner speculations and forced her to put them to one side.

'Oh, yes,' she was able to assure him truthfully. 'Alessandro has been through everything with me.' Well, that much was true...

'It was kind of you to come down and welcome us, Falcon, but rather a waste of time. I prefer to drive us back to the *castello* myself, since I'll need my car whilst I'm here. I've promised Leonora that I'll make time to show her something of the island.'

That was news to her, but Leonora managed not to betray her surprise.

'I've already arranged for your car to be driven home for you,' Falcon assured Alessandro smoothly.

An elder, superior sibling, reminding a younger and inferior one that he was ahead of him in every way and always would be? Or was she reading too much into their exchange? It wasn't like her to allow herself to become so involved in the dynamics of another person's family relationships—she was normally far too busy being defensive about her own—but somewhere deep inside her a tiny seed of fellow feeling for Alessandro had taken root, and much as she wanted to be able to do so she couldn't ignore it.

'The shared drive back together will enable me to get to know Leonora a little better,' Falcon was saying smoothly, turning to Leonora herself as he added, 'Your brother is one of Alessandro's pilots, I believe, Leonora?'

'My younger brother—yes,' Leonora agreed, adding, 'Like Alessandro, I'm a middle child. Something else we share—like our love of flying.'

Now, why had she said that? As though she was making a point and taking a stance, declaring not just her loyalty to Alessandro but the fact that she felt they shared a special bond. She could see the frowning reception Alessandro was giving her statement, and wished she had not been so impulsive and spoken out so forcefully. It wasn't as though Alessandro needed her to make a stand on his behalf. They weren't a proper couple, after all—one for all and all for one, facing the world together utterly united. And now Falcon was looking at her very thoughtfully indeed, and Alessandro's frown had grown deeper.

It was Falcon who ushered her towards the chauffeur, who was waiting for them to get into the car. Although he had initially got out of the back seat, now Falcon got into the front passenger seat, leaving Alessandro to sit behind him whilst Leonora sat behind the chauffeur.

'Alessandro will, I am sure, have informed you that since he is the only one of the family attending the weekend's events to have a partner, you will be looked upon by many of our guests as their hostess.'

Leonora gave Alessandro a frantic look. He had certainly *not* told her that.

Ignoring the look she was giving him, but reaching for her hand and holding it in what looked like a lover's clasp but which was in effect, Leonora suspected, a warning grip, he told his brother, 'Leonora is more than capable of playing her part, Falcon.'

Leonora suspected that both his words and his grip on her hand were intended as a reminder to her of the control he had over her and the obedience he expected from her.

The drive to the *castello* didn't take very long—barely long enough for Leonora to take in the olive groves through which they were being driven, which gave way to a more barren landscape as the road climbed upwards, with the sea to one side of them and the mountains to the other.

Finally, after the road curved round one of the mountains, she could see the *castello* up ahead of them—not so much clinging to the sheer rocks on which it was built as gripping them in its talons like a bird of prey. Despite the sunlight warming the steep escarpments and the crenellated walls, Leonora shivered slightly. The sight of the *castello* filled her with the sense that it was designed to intimidate and overwhelm, to entrap and imprison. It was, she decided, a true fortress—hard, unyielding and hostile. Like Alessandro himself.

When they drove through a stone archway into a large flagged courtyard that contained an ornate fountain, Leonora saw not the medieval castle building she had been expecting but the elegant façade of a magnificent eighteenth-century palace. She could not stop herself from gasping in surprise.

It wasn't Alessandro who responded to her astonishment but Falcon, turning round in his seat to smile at her and tell her, 'One of our ancestors had the good sense to replace the original buildings. All that is actually left of the original *castello* are the outer walls and a couple of towers. Which reminds me, Sandro, I've told Maria to put you both in the West Tower Suite, to give you a bit of privacy. As you can imagine, the house is going to be packed to the rafters with guests, so I thought you'd be more comfortable there than in your old room.'

What did he mean, he'd put 'them' in the West Tower Suite? Leonora wondered in an apprehensive silence. She looked at Alessandro, but he wasn't looking back in her direction, and now wasn't the time to start asking Alessandro exactly what their sleeping arrangements were going to be, Leonora acknowledged.

As they climbed the steep marble steps leading to impressive double doors, Leonora realised that she was going to struggle to climb them elegantly in her unfamiliar high heels. Unexpectedly, as Alessandro hadn't seemed to notice the anxious look she had given him in the car, he did seem to notice she was having trouble with the steps, because without saying anything he placed his hand beneath her elbow to steady and support her.

For a second the tomboy in her wanted to insist she could manage, but tomboys didn't wear stilettos, and the truth was that she was glad of his help. The last thing she wanted to do was make a fool of herself by falling flat on her face. But climbing the steps so close together brought her thigh into contact with his, sending a frisson of something that quite definitely did *not* belong to her tomboy days sizzling through her body.

'You're the first to arrive,' Falcon was saying. 'Officially the cocktail party begins at seven, with dinner for the house guests at ten, but Father is planning to hold court at around six, although I want to keep that as low-key as possible, given his poor health.'

'Is his heart as weak as we've all been told? Or is it just another of his ploys to make us all jump through hoops of his making?'

When Leonora heard the bitterness in Alessandro's voice she instinctively started to move closer to him, in a mute gesture of comfort and support—and then abruptly stopped. Why on earth would Alessandro want comfort or support from her? And, even more to the point, why should she want to offer them?

To her relief he appeared not to have noticed her instinctive movement towards him, although his hand had slipped from her elbow along her back, and was now resting on her hip, which had brought her closer to him. But he had not so much as looked at her, his focus entirely on his brother.

'His heart condition is real enough,' Falcon was saying. 'I would have preferred not to have risked worsening it with all this fuss, but he insisted, threatening that if I did not organise something then he would do so himself.'

'And his word, of course, is law,' Alessandro said cynically.

'He is the head of our family and our name, and it is—

as it has always been—our duty to respect the traditions
and the responsibilities that go with being a Leopardi.'

'You may respect him if you wish to do so, Falcon, but
I never shall.'

'I did not say that I respected him. What I said was that
it is our duty to respect our responsibilities to our name.
Not for our own sake, and certainly not for the sake of our
father, but for the sake of our people. It is their traditions
that we are honouring this weekend, not our father's.'

They had reached the top of the steps now. Both men
were standing still, facing one another, and Alessandro still
had his arm around her waist, securing her to him. It was
just because of the role she was forced to play that she was
not objecting to that imprisonment, Leonora assured herself.

'You sound as feudal as he is, Falcon, and you know
my views on that,' Alessandro told his brother.

'Yes. You say you are a modern man, who does not bow
his head to anyone or expect them to bow to him. That is
all very well for you, Alessandro, but many of our people
do not think as you do. And if we ignore and insult our
heritage then in effect we ignore and insult them as well.'

'It is thanks to our father that they have been kept in the
Dark Ages and treated like serfs—exactly as he tried to
treat us when we were young. I can never and will never
accept that. You know that. In my opinion our true duty and
responsibility is to free our people from the feudal yoke
our father has no right to continue to impose on them.'

'I agree. But for some of them—the older ones—that
freedom is feared because it means change.'

'I am glad I am not in your shoes, Falcon, and that as
our father's heir the responsibility for righting his wrongs
is yours and not mine.'

'A fitting punishment for being born first, Sandro? We are all born to our given roles in life and we have no power over that. What we do have power over is how we choose to deal with that role. You have chosen to show the world that you do not and will not accept any limitations imposed on you by others in any way. But you are still a Leopardi. We still share the same blood—'

'Our father's blood,' Alessandro interrupted him bitterly.

'The blood of many generations of our name.' Falcon overrode him. 'Your example will show our people that they need not accept any limitations, whilst the duty I have shown our father will, I hope, enable the younger ones to make the transition to a more modern way of life without riding roughshod over the older generation. It is my wish that we use this weekend to set an example of all that is good and just and honourable about being a Leopardi.'

Falcon Leopardi spoke less assertively than Alessandro, but there was no mistaking the determination of his purpose, Leonora recognised. He was very much the eldest sibling, very much making it plain that his will would prevail, and yet at the same time he was also showing true respect and brotherly love for Alessandro. But would that ever be enough for a man like Alessandro, who was so obviously driven by a need to come first? Would he ever be content with what he had achieved? Or would he always feel that it was not enough because he had not been born first?

The huge double doors had been opened whilst the brothers had been talking, and now they were walking through them together. Alessandro was keeping her close to his side.

The hallway beyond the doors had obviously been

designed to impress and awe, with its richly painted and frescoed ceiling, its ornate gilded rococo decor and the huge glittering chandelier that dominated the curving stairway. The whole area breathed power and wealth.

Another set of double doors stood open, giving visual access to not just the room beyond them but to an entire series of rooms, their doors also flung open, with sunlight illuminating intricately inlaid wooden floors. This wasn't a home, Leonora decided, it was a statement of intent—a kingdom in its own right.

Falcon looked at his watch.

'It's four o'clock now. I dare say you'll want to take advantage of the chance to relax and settle in while you can, so I'll leave you to take Leonora up to your suite, Sandro, and then we can meet in the library at five-thirty, just in case there are any last-minute changes to any of the arrangements that we need to discuss.'

'This way.' Alessandro turned her round so that they were facing the main doors, guiding her through them and across the courtyard to a narrow door in the wall. 'It's quicker than going through the main house,' he explained, as Leonora looked uncertainly at the spiral of stone steps leading upwards in the half-light coming in through the narrow slits in the bare stone walls.

On impulse she removed her shoes, answering the look Alessandro gave her with a firm, 'I'd rather have dirty feet than a broken ankle.'

In fact the stone steps were immaculately clean and dust-free, although climbing them ahead of Alessandro, as they were only wide enough for one person, was causing her heart to pound erratically. Not because she was so very aware of him behind her, of course. No, it was because there were so many of them, winding upwards in the narrow tower, and the climb was dizzying her and leaving her short of breath.

At last the top was reached—an empty round space with whitewashed walls and a wooden floor, dark with age. One door was set into the curved wall, and Alessandro opened it for her.

Leonora wasn't sure what she had expected. The plain bareness of the tower and its stone steps were such a contrast to the almost overpowering extravagance of the main entrance and the hallway of the *castello*. The hallway that lay beyond this door, though, was surprisingly modern, reminding her of the skilled renovation of Alessandro's apartment. A niche in one of the walls held a piece of abstract sculpture, and the chandelier looked similarly modern. The floorboards pale and smooth, simple linen curtains were at the window, and the window seat was covered in a matt black fabric with a fine grey and white stripe, creating a classically understated look.

A pair of carved double doors opened into a large room in much the same style as the hallway, but Leonora wasn't paying any attention to its décor. Instead she was staring with horror at the enormous bed dominating the room.

'This isn't the only bedroom, is it?' she asked Alessandro.

'If you mean is this the only bedroom in the *castello*, then it is not. If you mean is it the only bedroom here in this suite—then, yes, it is,' he answered her promptly.

Leonora badly wanted to sit down. 'But we can't share a bedroom,' she protested.

The look he gave her was icy with disdain and sharp with impatience. 'We don't have any other option.'

'But there's only one bed.'

'Which is at least six feet wide. And I assure you that even if it were not, I do not have any intention of turning our public relationship as supposed lovers into a private reality. I thought I had already made that much clear to you? Unless, of course, what you fear is that you yourself may be so overcome with lust for me that you—'

'No!' Leonora stopped him hurriedly. 'Of course not.'

'Then there is nothing for you to fear,' he told her with a dismissive shrug. 'I agree that there will be a certain amount of inconvenience, but we are both adults, and I am sure that we are perfectly capable between us of working out a means of not intruding on one another's need for privacy.'

Not trusting herself to say anything, Leonora walked over to the windows and looked out, startled to discover that all she could see was the sea.

'This tower is built into the original walls,' Alessandro told her. 'It is one of only three that our ancestor left standing when he started his rebuilding programme. It is linked to the main house by a corridor through the doors opposite the windows, whilst the doors on either side of the bed lead respectively to a dressing room and the bathroom. I dare say that our cases will already have been brought up and unpacked.'

'I can't share a room with you,' Leonora insisted as the full recognition of exactly what that was going to mean burst in on her.

It wasn't just a matter of them having to share a bed. They would be sharing a bathroom. She would have to dress and undress in the same room as him. She would have to be there when he dressed and undressed. The fierce kick of excitement with which her body greeted that knowledge was not the reaction she wanted to admit to having.

'You have no choice,' Alessandro told her.

CHAPTER SEVEN

IN THE end it wasn't as bad as she had been dreading.
Alessandro disappeared into the hallway with his laptop,
whilst she showered in the enormous state-of-the-art
bathroom, with its wet room and its huge roll-top bath. He
left her the privacy of the dressing room in which to dress,
whilst he showered and then dressed in the bedroom, in
clothes he had removed from the dressing room beforehand.

Her new hairstyle was surprisingly easy to manage, and
so too were the make-up tricks of the trade she had been
taught. But what she was *not* able to do was zip her dress all
the way up the back. No matter how hard she tried it remained
stubbornly a few millimetres from the top—and nor could
she fasten the tiny hook and eye at the very top of the zip.

She could, of course, always ask Alessandro to do it for
her, but she wasn't going to admit to him that she needed
his help with anything. Besides, given what he had already
said about her being overcome with lust for him, he might
think that she was using some kind of deliberate ploy, pretending that she couldn't fasten her zip. She certainly
wasn't going to have him accuse her of that. Anyway, the
zip was secure enough, and the dress's slender shoulder
straps were holding it in place.

She heard him rap briefly on the door and call out, 'Are
you ready?'

Calling back, 'Yes,' she opened the door. Dressed in jeans and a shirt Alessandro had been impressive, but dressed in a dinner suit he was more than impressive. He was… Leonora gulped and swallowed, and willed her heartbeat to resume a more normal rhythm as she went to join him.

The cocktail dress stroked silkily against her skin, sensitising her nerve-endings—or was it Alessandro's presence that was doing that?

When he went to open the door for her the thin plain gold cufflinks gleamed discreetly in the light, and Leonora's heart gave a series of small skipping beats. Had she met a man like Alessandro when she was younger, would she still be a virgin? A man like Alessandro? No, there could not possibly be another. He was unique, a one-off—and besides, she suspected that a man of his sexual experience and expertise would be contemptuous of if not outright repelled by a woman like her.

Hadn't he already said as much, when he had told her that, having kissed her once, he had no desire to do so again? But he *had* kissed her again. For show—as part of the role he had decided they must both play—not for any other reason. What mattered most now was that she didn't give in to her own weakness, and that she didn't allow Alessandro to see or guess that she might be vulnerable to allowing him to win in any kind of contest between them. He had defeated her once by blackmailing her. Her pride would not allow her to acknowledge him as the victor a second time.

They were in a corridor, bare-walled and obviously old, which then opened up into a wider gallery panelled in dark wood and hung with heavily framed portraits.

'This corridor is just short of a quarter of a mile long. My brothers and I used to ride our bikes along here in wet weather,' Alessandro informed her, breaking the silence between them. 'There are no rooms off it, just two sets of stairs—one that goes down to the kitchens and up to what originally were the servants' quarters and the nursery, and another to my father's private apartments. It was one of his rules that we were not allowed to use the gallery in case we disturbed him whilst he was "working"—that being his euphemism for being with his mistress. He didn't spare the rod when any of us were caught transgressing.'

Leonora was appalled. 'My father never hit any of us. He wasn't that kind of man. In fact he would have encouraged us to use a gallery, and would probably have made us race against one another. Dad loves competitive sports, but most of all he loves winners.'

Alessandro frowned as he listened, his anger at himself for telling Leonora something so personal about his childhood vanquished by his reaction to her comment about her father. Maybe he had not physically abused his children, as Alessandro's own father had done, but there were other ways of inflicting pain on the young and vulnerable. Alessandro could see quite plainly that Leonora felt inferior to her brothers, although he knew that she would fiercely deny feeling any such thing were he to suggest it. The very fact that she had gone to such reckless lengths to prove that she could fly not just as well as but better than Leo proved that. It wasn't merely a matter of doing better, though. It was more than that. It was a need to be accepted and valued in a family situation where only the first was valued.

If he were to say as much to her she would reject his

assessment, of course, just as he would have done himself if their positions had been reversed. But she could not hide the truth from him. He could see and understand her motivation as clearly as though it had been his own. Because her reaction was so close to what his own would have been? Alessandro's frown deepened. This was the first time he had recognised in someone else the emotions that had so often driven him, and it wasn't a welcome or pleasant discovery.

He didn't want to recognise in Leonora his own vulnerabilities, and he most certainly did not want to accept that the two of them shared something as personal as the same kind of emotional triggers, resulting from their childhoods. Besides, their circumstances were not the same. He was the middle one in a trio of same-sex siblings; she was a girl in between two brothers. Which meant what? That she felt driven to compete with the male sex as a whole as well as to do better than her brothers? Potentially that would make her a woman who saw sex as yet another means of beating her male partner, since men traditionally were seen as the sexual instigators and the victors. She would feel a need to usurp that role. So why hadn't she made any attempt to challenge him sexually?

Alessandro had a keenly analytical brain, and he didn't like problems that did not add up. Right now—irritatingly—the problem that was Leonora Thaxton most definitely did not add up.

Just as Leonora was beginning to think it might have been a good idea for her to wear a pair of flat shoes for this hike, Alessandro turned towards a pair of double doors that opened up into a vaulted-ceilinged salon filled with dark furniture. They had to weave their way through it to reach another set of doors. The atmosphere of the room felt heavy with disapproval, and Leonora was glad to leave it behind even though the library they were now in felt just as unwelcoming.

Eventually, after traversing two more darkly formal rooms, they emerged onto another corridor—much shorter this time—which in turn brought them to an imposing flight of stairs that led down into the hallway Leonora recognised from their arrival.

Now for the first time—although as far as she could see there was no one below them in the hallway—Alessandro offered her his arm, so that they could descend the stairs together as a couple. Just as she had done before, Leonora noted how even with four-inch heels she was still several inches shorter than Alessandro. How odd it was that along with additional height had come the feeling of being unfamiliarly fragile and feminine. And, even more disconcertingly, the absurd impulse to move closer to Alessandro, tucking herself against him so that their shared descent of the stairs brought her hip into brief contact with his body.

When he felt Leonora moving closer to him Alessandro told himself that the only reason he was allowing her to do so was because their physical closeness would help to convince onlookers of her total commitment to him. That there were not as yet any onlookers to observe them as he adjusted his grasp on her elbow to keep her close was, he decided, immaterial. Before long there would be, and it was important that their intimacy came across as natural and second nature.

Once they were down in the hallway Alessandro guided Leonora towards the open double doors she had noticed before, and through them into an elegant salon littered with gilded furniture. Some of it was decorated with Egyptian motifs and some was covered in faded powder-blue silk, patterned with what Leonora guessed must be the family arms in gold thread. The room was illuminated by two chandeliers, their light thrown back by several pairs of gilded wall mirrors. Several low tables were crammed with small ornaments.

'Some of the decor in these rooms dates from the time of Napoleon, shortly after his victorious campaign in Egypt,' Alessandro informed Leonora. 'The blue silk was specially woven to incorporate the family's arms. It's rumoured that at one time our ancestor had ambitions to marry his eldest son off to Napoleon's sister Pauline. It was perhaps just as well that he didn't succeed.'

As they went through another room, decorated in faded yellow this time, Leonora could hear the hum of conversation coming from the next room. An imposingly liveried footman complete with a powdered wig emerged from the room, carrying an empty tray, and was quickly followed by another. Nervous apprehension bubbled in Leonora's stomach, for all the world as though she were in reality a young woman about to meet the father of the man she loved for the first time.

However, as she held back, Falcon suddenly came through the door saying easily, 'There you are,' and then she was stepping into the room on Alessandro's arm, whilst Falcon shepherded them through the small throng of guests, many of them members of the older generation, with the men wearing rows of medals and decorations that matched their wives' jewellery for magnificence.

The old Prince was seated in what Leonora suspected was a chair made to support an invalid, although it was plain that Alessandro's father considered it to be more of a throne. His silver hair glinted in the light, and his features were as proudly arrogant as those of his second son. One hand, its knuckles swollen with age, was gripping the silver head of a walking stick. He was a very regal figure indeed, Leonora thought, and then checked that thought as he turned his head to look at her. In place of Alessandro's proud gaze she saw that his father's eyes were small and his gaze spiteful, with a lifetime's worth of self-indulgence and conceit evident in his expression. Her first thought was that he was not worthy of being Alessandro's father—and her second was that she had no right to be thinking such thoughts.

As though a silent order had been given, a pathway to the old Prince had been cleared for them by the other guests, and the room was gripped by a watchful silence. Plainly the hostility that existed between father and son was common knowledge, Leonora recognised.

'So, Alessandro—you are taking a dangerous risk, aren't you? Bringing your friend here? How many times do I need to warn you that a mere second son must always run the risk of being supplanted—in all things—by the first-born? A woman will always look for the best possible father for her children—which is why first-born sons get the pick of the crop, and second-born sons have to make do with what is left or rejected.'

The Prince wasn't just cruel, he was wicked as well, Leonora thought angrily. What a dreadful thing to say to his own son—and in public. He had just implied that Alessandro could never hope to keep the woman he loved if his brother should want her. The Prince wasn't just insulting Alessandro, he was insulting her as well.

Before she could stop herself, Leonora drew herself up proudly and announced firmly, 'Alessandro knows that no one could ever take his place in my life or in my heart.' Leonora could almost feel the concerted indrawn breath of her audience. 'And as for him being a second son—that adds to my love for him instead of detracting from it.'

'Only a fool would believe that. There is no woman alive who would not wish to see her own son succeeding to the family's titles rather than the child of her husband's older brother. Your sex has lied, cheated and killed to claim such a birthright,' the Prince told her coldly.

'Maybe centuries ago, but in these modern times what a mother wants for her child is a loving father and the chance for that child to grow up free of the restrictions imposed on it by family expectation. Alessandro's gifts to his children will be far, far greater than an empty and meaningless title.'

Leonora could feel the wave of astonishment surging round her, and the euphoria she felt at having stepped in to defend Alessandro quickly retreated when she turned to look at him and saw that, far from looking pleased with her, Alessandro was looking at her very grimly indeed.

The Prince hadn't finished.

'Pah!' he exclaimed. 'You may believe that now, but no woman wants a man who stands silent whilst she has to defend him. But then you were always one to run for protection behind a woman's skirts, weren't you, Alessandro? You haven't changed.'

'And neither have you, Father,' Alessandro told him contemptuously. 'However, I have no wish to become involved in an exchange of verbal insults with a sick old man whose life has not much longer to run—much as I dare say you would like to force me to do.'

Without giving his father a chance to say any more, Alessandro gripped Leonora's arm and turned round, immediately introducing her to the middle-aged couple standing behind them. They were a local dignitary and his wife, whom Alessandro engaged in conversation about a restoration project on some civic buildings, the cost of which Leonora learned he was contributing to. The local dignitary obviously had a high opinion of Alessandro, and Leonora guessed that his sympathy lay with him— although he did not allude to the sharp exchange of words that had just taken place between father and son.

The Prince seemed to be a law unto himself, with no regard for the feelings of others—especially those of his second son. Growing up with such a father must have been hard—far, far harder than her own childhood. Her father might have encouraged rivalry and competition between them, and not been aware of the emotional needs of a teenage girl, but he did love them all. The Prince, on the other hand, did not appear to have any love for any of his sons.

Alessandro excused them both to the local dignitary and his wife, saying that he wanted to introduce Leonora to as many people as possible, but he pulled her into an alcove and stood in front of her, blocking both her escape and the curious looks of anyone else.

'If my father had paid you to humiliate me, you could not have done a better job for him,' he said, quietly and savagely.

Immediately Leonora snapped back, 'I was just trying to defend you, that's all.'

'Defend me?' Her protest seemed to increase his anger rather than lessen it. 'That's my role—not yours. A man defends *himself* and those who depend on him. A woman defends her child. But of course you couldn't resist seizing control, could you? Even though it meant humiliating me—the man, I might remind you, you are supposed to love.'

'You're accusing *me* of seizing control? That's rich, coming from you! And you'd be able to see that for yourself if you weren't so obsessed with proving to your father that being second born doesn't stop you from being a success.'

'I have nothing to prove to anyone, least of all my father. The only opinion and approval that matters to me is my own.'

They glared at one another as they exchanged increasingly furious whispers.

'Rubbish,' Leonora told him. 'If that was the truth you'd never have blackmailed me and brought me here. You know your trouble—'

'I certainly know *yours*,' Alessandro interrupted her. 'You just can't allow a man to be a man because you have to compete with him. In fact you are so obsessed with competing with my sex that you've turned yourself into a sexless mutation of a woman who thinks that men are turned on by an Amazonian intent on fighting their battles for them.'

'That's not true.' Leonora's voice trembled slightly, but deep down inside herself she knew that his unkind words had struck a painful chord.

How often had her brothers teased her that she frightened off their sex? Their teasing had hurt, but she had hidden that from them, not knowing how to change what she had become. It wasn't true, though, that she'd always wanted to compete with men and beat them. Deep down inside she longed for a man she could trust so implicitly that she could let down her guard with him—someone who would understand her and not laugh at her, but instead help her regain her womanhood. But how could she ever trust any man to that extent when she already feared rejection so much?

Alessandro knew he was overreacting, but listening to Leonora defending him had awakened painful memories of his childhood, of both his mother's and later Falcon's attempts to protect him from his father. He hated the memory of his vulnerability and inability to protect himself. It was his job to protect Leonora, not the other way around, but she had not allowed him to do so. Instead she had helped his father to humiliate him.

'Remember why you are here,' Alessandro warned Leonora as he stepped back from her. 'And if you want to defend a member of my sex, think about your brother.'

The room they were in had gradually filled up with new arrivals, and Leonora became separated from Alessandro, who had been appropriated by a stunning-looking woman who had put her arm through his and given Leonora an openly false smile as she had claimed that she promised to take Alessandro over to talk to her husband. There hadn't been any husband anywhere at hand five minutes later, when she had seen them standing close together, the brunette gazing up hungrily into Alessandro's face.

Not that she cared, of course. In fact she was glad to be relieved of his company after the way he had spoken to her. And yet for some reason she could feel a lump of misery forming in her throat, even though she was doing her best to circulate and speak to people. A strangely persistent man had just penned her into a corner and kept on asking her when an official announcement was going to be made. In the end she had escaped by telling him that he would have to ask Alessandro himself.

A passing waiter offered her a fresh drink but she shook her head. She wasn't used to eating so late, and she had gone beyond hunger now to the point where she actually felt slightly sick and dizzy from a mixture of unrequited hunger, misery and tiredness. A discreet glance at her watch told her that it was only just nine o'clock—another hour to go before they would be eating.

Her feet ached in the high heels, and she eased her foot out of one of them, sighing as it fell over. Unable to slip it back on while standing, she reached down to replace the shoe—and then realised to her horror that her movement had caused her zip to slide down. Straightening up, she hugged the now loose top of her dress to her body and tried at the same time to walk backwards towards the wall, wondering what on earth she was going to do. She had no idea where the nearest loo might be, and it was impossible for her to re-zip her dress discreetly. It would need two hands and a good deal of effort—and even then she would not be able to fasten it completely, as she already knew.

Standing frozen with apprehension, her arms folded beneath her breasts, she longed to simply magically disappear. Alessandro would be furious if she showed him up, and she wasn't exactly keen herself on the thought of her dress falling off—especially as all she was wearing underneath it was a pair of nude-coloured briefs.

'Cold?'

Falcon. Leonora gulped and shook her head, and then

felt her heart sink even further as one of her shoulder straps fell down.

'That was a very passionate defence you made of Sandro,' Falcon commented with a smile.

'I feel very passionately about him,' Leonora told him. That much was true, after all. She didn't have to say that the passion she felt was of the angry rather than the sensual variety.

'He's angry with me now. He said that I humiliated him.' Leonora didn't know why she had made the admission, except that there was something about Falcon's quiet demeanour that invited confessions like a magnet.

'He's a very proud man.'

'Yes.'

'Are you sure you aren't cold?'

Once again Leonora shook her head. And then, deciding that Falcon might well be her only chance of escaping from the room without losing both her dignity and her dress, she admitted, 'It's my dress. The zip wasn't fastened properly and now it's come down. I daren't move in case it comes down even more.'

'Ah, I see. Well, in that case—since Alessandro isn't here to do the chivalrous thing and rescue you, perhaps as I am his brother you will allow me to do so for you?'

Where normally she would have felt uncomfortable and embarrassed, instead she actually felt strangely relieved— and very safe. Just as though she and Alessandro actually were an item, and Falcon was a sort of extra brother.

'If you could,' she said gratefully. 'Only I don't know how you can help me without anyone seeing.'

'Easy. I shall just do this,' Falcon told her with another smile, and he reached out and pulled her firmly towards him, so that she was half at right angles to his body, with her shoulder tucked into his chest.

He screened her from the other guests and then reached behind her to ease up the zip with the kind of skill that told her Alessandro's brother was perfectly familiar with the complexities of fastening zips on female clothes. He even managed the hook and eye for her. Leonora gave him a smile of relieved gratitude.

On the other side of the room Alessandro watched Leonora and his brother with mounting fury. He had told her expressly not to flirt with Falcon, and yet that was exactly what she was doing—looking up at him with that doe-eyed look, smiling at him, laughing with him—whilst Falcon stood far too close to her. Fury—and it was fury, not jealousy, Alessandro assured himself—shot through him, every bit as potent and dangerous as Mount Etna erupting. It spewed rage through him like hot ashes and lava, burning its caustic path inside his head. She was doing it deliberately—she had to be. Well, she'd soon learn that that no one, least of all her, played him for a fool.

CHAPTER EIGHT

'I HOPE you enjoyed flirting with my brother, because it has cost *your* brother his job.'

They were on their way in for the buffet dinner for the house guests, but Alessandro's words had Leonora stopping in her tracks.

'I wasn't flirting with anyone.'

'Liar,' he contradicted her flatly. 'I saw you with my own eyes. And don't think I don't know why you went expressly against my orders. You just *had* to try to make your point, didn't you? But you'll never compete with me and win, Leonora. I'm not that kind of man.'

'No. It wasn't like that at all,' she protested immediately. 'The trouble with you is that you're so obsessed with proving that being a second son doesn't make you second rate that you think that everyone's out to challenge you, even when they aren't.'

Her accusation infuriated Alessandro. He grabbed hold of her arm and almost dragged her into a small empty anteroom, closing the door and then telling her, 'Falcon might flirt with you and allow you to think that he wants you, but I can tell you now that he doesn't. The only reason he would show any interest in you would be out of some misguided belief that he needs to protect me. But I never make the same mistake twice. Once I might have been foolish enough to allow a woman to convince me that she wanted me, when all she really wanted was to use me as a stepping stone to get to Falcon, and everything that marrying him would have given her. But the speed with which she transferred her affections from me to Falcon taught me a lesson I haven't forgotten.'

And what a painful lesson that would have been for him, Leonora recognised, given his pride and the cruelty with which his father reinforced his second-son status.

'Do you still love her?'

The words were out before she could stop herself, and she wasn't surprised when she saw a look of grim disbelief that she should ask such a personal question darkening his eyes.

'I never loved her,' he told her flatly. 'But I swore that I'd never allow myself to be publicly humiliated again by a woman transferring her affections from me to someone else—especially not to Falcon, however well-meaning his intentions. Which is why—'

'Why you blackmailed me into coming here with you.'

'Which is why your behaviour has just cost your brother his job,' Alessandro repeated.

'But I wasn't flirting with Falcon. You can ask him, if you like.'

'I don't need to ask him. I have eyes, and I could see what was going on.'

'No, you couldn't. Because what was "going on", as you call it, was that my zip had come down because I hadn't been able to fasten it properly. Falcon was zipping it up again for me.'

There was a ring of truth in her voice that forced Alessandro to listen.

'If that's true then why didn't you ask *me* to fasten it for you before we left our room?'

Good question. Leonora weighed up the consequences of telling the truth or trying to bluff her way out with a fabrication. She'd never been a good liar, so she took a deep breath and told him honestly, 'I didn't want you to think I was trying to…'

'To what?' Alessandro pressed impatiently.

Leonora tilted her chin and told him defensively, 'I didn't want you thinking that I was trying to…well, come on to you.'

Her statement was too ridiculous not to be the truth, Alessandro decided.

'And you have the gall to accuse *me* of being paranoid?' he said in disbelief, reaching for the door to open it as he added, 'Very well, I'll accept your explanation—on this occasion.'

'That's big of you,' Leonora muttered to herself as he held the door open for her.

She didn't realise that Alessandro had heard her until he agreed coldly, 'Yes, it is. And there'd better not be any more similar errors of judgement on your part, because I certainly shan't be as lenient a second time.'

Much as she was tempted to challenge his arrogant attitude, Leonora decided against it. Not whilst he was holding over her the power to hurt her brother.

The evening was drawing to a close, and as Leonora fought to suppress her yawns Alessandro leaned towards her and said quietly, 'You're tired. You may as well go up to the room. I'll follow you later.'

His apparent consideration for her now, contrasted with

his attitude towards her earlier, caught her off guard, and touched her emotions in a way she didn't want. Quickly she nodded her head, accepting his discreet hint that he was offering her the chance to get ready for bed in privacy.

As she stood up, Falcon, who had been engaged in conversation with someone seated further down the table, pushed his own chair back and came over to say, 'You are going to bed? Then I shall say goodnight.'

Leonora began to smile politely, but to her shock Falcon placed his hands on her arms and kissed her, first on one cheek and then the other.

He was Sicilian, of course. And there had been nothing in the least bit sensual or sexual about his embrace. He did, after all, think that she and Alessandro were a couple. Still, she felt rather self-conscious, turning away from him as soon as he had released her, only to find that Alessandro had also stood up and was now standing in front of her. As she made to sidestep him he stopped her, taking hold of her hand and drawing her towards him, then bending his head.

By the time she realised that he was going to kiss her it was too late to do anything to try to stop him. His mouth was on hers, his arm around her, her own lips softening into mute obedience at the command of his. A swift glance upwards revealed the glint of his eyes between the dark frame of his lashes. Mesmerised and helpless, she felt the aftershock of her own response to him, swiftly pulling back from him, her face on fire.

It was a relief to get away and follow the footman who had been summoned to escort her back to the tower suite.

As they left the salon behind she acknowledged that, to her own surprise, she had actually enjoyed some parts of the evening. She had met some fascinating people, and had learned a great deal about the lives of Alessandro and his brothers as young boys. Everyone had mentioned how sad it had been for them to lose their mother, and there had even been discreet and not so discreet references to their father's second marriage to his mistress, and his preference for the son he had with her over his sons by his first wife. She had learned too how unpopular Antonio had been and how many people thought that his death at the wheel of his sports car had removed a very unpleasant character from their lives. Alessandro himself had been spoken of with both admiration and respect for all that he had achieved.

When they reached the door to the tower suite the footman made a small half-bow to her, indicating that he was about to depart, and Leonora thanked him before opening the door and letting herself into the suite.

Her feet ached from her high-heeled shoes, and it was a relief to take them off. She'd have loved to soak in a long bath, but she wasn't sure how much time she would have before Alessandro arrived. Luckily she was able to unfasten the hook and eye on her dress and then the zip. After stepping out of it in the dressing room she hung it up and padded barefoot, wearing only her briefs, through the bedroom in which the bed had been turned down, averting her gaze from its intimacy and hurrying into the bathroom.

Alessandro frowned as he watched Falcon, who was seated several feet away from him, deep in conversation with one of the guests. The feeling of acute and immediate male possessiveness he had experienced when Falcon had kissed Leonora goodnight hadn't entirely subsided. Not that Leonora really meant anything to him, of course. No? Then why had he felt it so necessary to reinforce the fact that she was his? No reason. It had simply been a gut reaction, that was all. Impatiently he pushed back his chair, bidding those around him goodnight.

Removing her underwear, Leonora stepped into the glass-sided wet-room-style shower and turned on the water. The sensation of the powerful spray against her skin felt wonderful, and the heat of the water released the scent of the shower gel she'd found waiting for her in a basket of bathroom necessities.

She was so tired she'd be asleep the minute her head touched the pillow, Leonora decided thankfully, and she certainly had no fears that Alessandro would try to take advantage of the situation, despite the way he had kissed her downstairs in the salon. That had just been for show.

She reached out and turned off the water. She was about to step out of the shower when she saw it.

It was the most enormous spider she had ever seen, and it was crouching right in front of her exit from the shower. The only way she could get past it would be to step over it. A sick shudder ripped through her. She was terrified of spiders, always had been. Her brothers, of course, had been delighted to discover that their sister could be terrorised by creatures they were quite happy to pick up, and had teased her dreadfully with them until the day she had fainted when Leo had tried to put one down the back of her T-shirt.

What would it do? Would it come into the shower?

She started to shake, the blood leaving her face. She

dared not take her gaze off it in case it moved. It was staring back at her. She was sure it was. Her stomach churned. She was a quivering mass of total terror. She knew that her fear was irrational, but knowing it didn't help. Nothing had ever helped.

The spider lifted one leg—and then another. A petrified scream bubbled in her throat, but her throat muscles were too stiff with terror to let it escape. Her whole body was now rigid, her heart thundering into her chest wall so hard and so fast that it was making her feel dizzy. But she mustn't faint, because then it might run all over her. A deep shudder broke her rigidity.

Alessandro opened the bedroom door, removing his dinner jacket as he closed it. All the lights were on but there was no sign of Leonora. He had expected that she would be in bed by now. He unfastened his bow tie and opened the top buttons of his dress shirt. Formal occasions and formal clothes were not his favourite things. Removing the cuff-links from his cuffs, he walked towards the dressing room. The door was open, and there was no sign of Leonora inside it, which meant that she must be in the bathroom.

He walked towards the half-open door, rapping on it warningly before calling out, 'Leonora?'

Alessandro. Relief bubbled in Leonora's throat, and her gaze immediately went to the door—only to return swiftly to the spider. It had moved. It was coming into the shower.

Alessandro heard her scream and thrust open the bathroom door. She was huddled in a corner of the shower, naked and white-faced, one hand against her breasts, the other covering her sex, her eyes dark with terror.

'What is it?' Alessandro demanded, perplexed.

Leonora removed her hand from her breasts, every bit as softly full as he had imagined, with peach tip-tilted nipples, hard now, presumably from the cold, since he could see goosebumps on her arms. Between the fingers of her other splayed hand he could see the soft feathery curls of the hair covering her sex, and her modesty was somehow more erotic and tantalising than if she had been standing there naked. Her body had a lushness he hadn't expected, and his own was responding to it.

'It's a spider.' Her voice was thin with fear, and her body was shuddering as she looked at him, and then looked down again at the limestone floor, her breath catching in a terrified gasp as she cowered against the back of the shower. 'It's moving. Oh, please…no…'

Alessandro had never thought of himself as a potential hero—he was too cynical—but something about her obvious terror had him reacting as swiftly as any would-be James Bond. He reached for a towel, which he dropped over the spider, and then speedily lifted Leonora bodily from the shower, to hold her tightly as she shuddered convulsively in his arms in between sobs.

Grabbing another larger towel, he carried her into the bedroom and then put her down, wrapping the towel round her before heading back to the bathroom. He was just about to remove the towel from the trapped spider when he heard Leonora calling out shakily.

'Please don't kill it. It isn't its fault that I'm terrified of it.'

A woman who hated spiders and yet who wouldn't allow one to be despatched? She really was a one of a kind, he reflected as he scooped up the spider and very gently tipped it from his hand out of the bathroom window, and then closed the window.

Wrapped in her towel, but still shivering slightly with reaction, Leonora looked anxiously at Alessandro when he came back into the bedroom.

'What did you do with it?'

'Don't worry, it's quite safe and in one piece, with all its legs intact. I put it out of the window.'

'You must think I'm a total idiot.'

'You're a woman,' he told her. 'You're allowed to be—'

'An idiot?' she challenged him.

'Afraid of spiders,' he corrected her.

'Thanks for…for what you did. My brothers would have laughed.'

She looked up at him. Now that the spider had been removed and her terror had eased, she was beginning to feel acutely self-conscious. She had been naked in the shower, after all, and he had picked her up and…

'Your shirt's all wet now.' Her voice had gone husky, and her gaze was fastened on his torso, her heart thudding in a primitive beat that her body recognised and her mind shied away from in shock.

Alessandro shrugged. Wrapped in a towel, her hair tousled and her lips still trembling slightly from shock, she looked far too enticing. He watched as she touched the tip of her tongue to her lips, her gaze still concentrated on his body. Immediately he felt his own banked-down desire kick into fierce life as it recognised the subtle message she was giving him. He might have told himself that there must not be any intimacy between them, but that had been before he had seen her in Falcon's embrace and known that the only male arms he was prepared to tolerate seeing wrapped around her were his own.

'Then perhaps I'd better take it off. Or, even better, why don't you take it off for me?'

Leonora exhaled on an unsteady breath of intense longing. She didn't know how she had got to this point, but now that she was here she knew that she didn't want to turn back.

'I'm not very good at this kind of thing,' she warned him.

Alessandro looked at her.

'Liar,' he told her softly as he went to her. 'My body says that you are very good at it indeed.'

He was lifting her bodily out of the chair in which he had placed her when he had rescued her from the shower, only this time without the towel. He had pushed it aside, his hands warm and firm on her bare skin, his confidence putting to flight her own untutored hesitancy, compelling her body to recognise in his touch his right of possession.

As he carried her over to the bed she put one arm around his neck, her hand resting against his nape whilst the other instinctively slid inside his open shirt. His chest felt warm and hard, the sensation of muscle packed tight beneath male flesh causing the anticipation already curling through her belly to intensify into a low-lying persistent ache of need. She could feel that need burning, spreading through her, swelling her breasts and tightening her nipples. The fingers of the hand resting against his nape slid into the thick darkness of Alessandro's hair as she looked up at his mouth, her lips parting breathlessly. All her senses seemed to be intensified, her sensual awareness heightened, the mere smell of his skin an aphrodisiac so powerful that it made her weak with longing.

Just the way Leonora was looking at him was having a similar effect to raw spirit taken on a battle-hardened empty stomach, Alessandro recognised, filling him with a surge of primitive testosterone-fuelled male energy far too powerful and all-consuming to be contained by any barriers. Like Mount Etna at its most dangerous, it defied and mocked the frailty of a mere man's attempt to suppress it.

He had reached the bed, but instead of placing Leonora on it he continued to hold her, sitting down on the edge of the bed with her in his arms whilst he accepted the offering of her parted lips, his tongue thrusting deeply and fiercely into the hot, wild intimacy of her kiss, his free hand going to her breast to savour the erotic pleasure of the contrast between the globe's full softness and the tight, hard demand of her swollen nipple.

A wild shudder ripped through Leonora's body, arching her upwards in a mute appeal that begged for more, and she was answered by a thick groan of male enjoyment from Alessandro as he responded to her need, continuing to kiss her whilst he brought her flesh to helpless surrender with the skilled touch of his fingers against her eager nipple.

Just when his hand had left her breast to cover her sex with an immediacy that matched perfectly her own desire she had no idea. All she did know was that—blissfully—its weight against the mound of flesh within which an increasingly frantic longing pulsed brought her a momentary relief that was quickly replaced by an even more intense desire.

Breaking their kiss to look down at Leonora's naked

body, Alessandro felt his being gripped with urgency. Her nipples demanded the servitude of his lips. The sensual relaxation of her thighs into her own desire invited the probe of his thumb against the top of the sweetly closed outer lips to her sex, into the liquid heat they enclosed.

Leonora moaned—a long, slow, sweet sound of female pleasure rising from deep within her, mirroring the crescendo of pleasure to which she was being brought by the skilled movement of Alessandro's touch against her clitoris. She wanted both to move with it and hold that pleasure to her, and at the same time she wanted to escape its dominance, fearing that it would overwhelm her. Her body had become an alien, sweetly tormented instrument that responded only to Alessandro's command.

Deep down inside herself she could feel an ache of yearning that could only be satisfied by the shared possession of their flesh, by the feel of him deep within her, the feel of her flesh enclosing him and holding him. A surge of dizzying joy burst through her. At last it was over. Soon she would be the woman she had secretly longed to be for so long—complete, fulfilled, with ownership of the knowledge of her own sexuality and all its secrets given to her by Alessandro in exchange for her unwanted, soon-to-be cast off burden of virginity.

Leonora tensed in the midst of her lyrical pre-celebration, cold truth shadowing her joy. She couldn't let Alessandro find out that she was still a virgin. It would be the ultimate humiliation. And he would find out if she didn't stop him soon.

Leonora was pushing him away, retreating from him, struggling to sit up—rejecting him, Alessandro recognised. Swiftly he released her, his pride immediately reacting to her recoil from his touch.

'You said that…that this wouldn't happen,' Leonora reminded him. The ache of her body deprived of his touch was so strong that she could hardly bear it. It set all her nerve-endings jangling against the low dragging weight of her unsatisfied desire.

Alessandro got up and strode over to the chair, picking up the towel they had left there, tossing it over to her, keeping his back towards her whilst Leonora wrapped it clumsily around herself. Leonora's accusation stung. He *had* said he wouldn't touch her—but that had been before. Before what? Before he had seen Falcon looking at her? Before he had walked into the bathroom and felt that surge of arousal that had obliterated everything else?

'I'm a man,' he told Leonora with a dismissive shrug, once he had got his emotions and the fierce urgency of his still-aching need for her under control and was able to turn round and look at her. 'You offered yourself to me, so I responded.'

'I was frightened because of the spider,' Leonora defended herself.

The look Alessandro was giving her burned though her fragile defences.

'It was not in fear that you arched beneath my touch, offering yourself to me in all the ways that a sexually aroused woman offers herself to a man, begging for his touch and his possession. If I wished to do so I could show you all over again just how you responded to me. *If* I wished to do so. But I do not.'

His words shamed and scorched her. Leonora wanted to

deny them, but how could she? She *had* responded to him. But that had only been because in Alessandro's arms and beneath his touch her secret fantasy of how her imaginary perfect lover would be had come physically and overpoweringly to life. *That* was the reason she had responded to Alessandro as passionately as she had, not because she had wanted Alessandro himself. She could not and must not do that. It was far too risky to let herself want the real man, because then she might— She might what? Fall in love with him and want him for life? Fall in love with Alessandro? How ridiculous—and how very, very fatally dangerous.

He was being ungallant, Alessandro knew, saying things he would normally never have dreamed of saying to a woman, no matter how sexually frustrated he might have felt. But there was something about Leonora that drove him beyond the boundaries of his own rules— something that brought out an emotional passion that infuriated him every bit as much as she did. Neither of those things could be brought within his control, and both of them challenged and taunted him, driving him to want to stamp his possession and his superiority on them, even whilst they remained outside his grasp. Together, Leonora and his passion for her took him to a place he had thought he had conquered a long time ago, a place in which the supposedly cold ashes of his youthful need to prove himself were suddenly glowing dangerously hot.

Was he really so little in control of himself? So little of a man that a woman's rejection could unleash such a compulsive need to show her that he could make her want him above and beyond all other men? And why *this* woman?

* * *

Alessandro was in the bathroom, giving Leonora an opportunity to slip on the silky nightdress that had been part of the new wardrobe she had been supplied with, before getting into the enormous bed and lying as close as she could to its edge.

Alessandro had been right to accuse her of wanting him. She had. She still did. But, as shaming as that accusation had been, it was nothing to the shame she would have experienced had she not stopped him and he had discovered the truth. She had heard her brothers joking about 'ancient' virgins and the horror of accidentally finding one in one's bed. Modern men wanted sexual partners who were accomplished lovers—polished, sophisticated women who were informed and entertaining in bed as well as out of it. She, on the other hand, had felt like a raw novice in Alessandro's arms, giddy with excitement at the thought of the pleasures in store and yet at the same time too overwhelmed by her own excitement to know how to harness it properly.

She had felt like pulling off his shirt and exploring every bit of his torso with her hands as well as smothering it with kisses, when a more knowing woman would probably have aroused him with just one single touch. Alessandro would be a connoisseur of sensuality and all its many pleasures, she suspected, and likely to have nothing but disdain for her inexperienced attempts to show her desire for him.

As he stood under the lash of the shower, waiting for his desire to subside, Alessandro cursed himself. Why had he allowed himself to touch Leonora in the first place? And, having done so, why was he now unable to subdue and dismiss the physical ache for her that was gripping him? She was just a woman, and he never, *ever* allowed any woman to matter so much to him that he could not stop wanting her—much less have that wanting bringing him to the point he was at now.

It was because she had rejected him, that was all. Because she had rejected him here in his childhood home, where the memories of so many other rejections whipped his spirit and his emotions raw of their usual protection.

Why had she changed her mind? She had wanted him. What was she hoping to gain? Did she imagine that by withholding herself from him she could make him want her more—to the point where she was the one controlling him through his desire for her?

Everything that life had taught him to be in order to protect himself burned into life, fiercely repudiating the thought. *He* was the only who controlled his own desires. There never had been and there never would be a woman— any woman—who had the power to make him want her against his will, either physically or emotionally. If Leonora wanted to enter into a competition to see which of them had the most control over their sexuality then he was more than prepared to do so—and to win. And he *would* win. He had to do so. His pride demanded that he did.

Because a small part of him feared that he was not as well defended against her ability to arouse him as he would have liked? Defensive pride held his muscles rigid. He would not and could not tolerate allowing himself to admit that he might want her more than she wanted him. He didn't. And he would prove that to himself before the weekend was over.

Alessandro reached for the tap and turned it to cold, his body tensing as much under the pressure of his thoughts as against the icy blast that shocked it.

CHAPTER NINE

LEONORA woke up abruptly in the darkness. A dull, heavy ache was pressing down on her womb, a sense of emptiness and unsatisfied need. Somehow or other she must have rolled over in her sleep—and not once but at least a couple of times, given the width of the bed, because now, instead of lying on its edge, she was much further over, towards Alessandro's side. She knew that because she was lying facing him, and could see the curve of his naked shoulder where the bedclothes had slipped away. If she were to roll over again she could almost lie curled up against his back…

Resolutely she made herself turn away from him and inch her way back to her own side of the bed. Once there she looked at the luminous face of her watch, which she'd left on the beside table. Just gone half past two. The room was still and silent, the only movement coming from the curtain. Leonora's heart jumped. Was the window open? If it was then the spider would be able to get back in.

Instantly she was imagining it clambering through the window, dropping down onto the floor, and then making its way towards the bed. Beneath the bedclothes her toes twitched, and apprehension slithered down her spine. She wanted to get up and check the window, to put her mind at rest, but she was too afraid to do so. She tried to think of something else, but the only 'something else' she could think about was how much she wished that things could have been different earlier on in the evening.

What she meant, of course, was how much she wished that *she* could have been different. That she could have been the kind of woman who had the confidence to enjoy the sensual pleasure of being in Alessandro's arms instead of having to remind herself of the reason why she could not allow things to reach their natural conclusion. If she had been then right now she would probably be sleeping safely in his arms, her body replete with the satisfaction of their lovemaking, instead of lying here alone, still aching for him, terrified that the spider might return and miserably aware of how angry she had made him.

She should have brought things to a halt before they had got as far as they had, she admitted, but she had been caught off guard by the intensity of her own response to him. Because she had never allowed herself to be in such a situation before. And because he was, after all, a very, very attractive and sensually powerful man—no woman worthy of the name could fail to be aroused by a man like Alessandro. And she *was* a woman—very much a woman as far as her newly discovered sensual needs went. Even if she hadn't realised that before.

How much she wished now that she had lived her life differently and gained the experience that would have made it easy and natural for her to respond fully to Alessandro in the way she had wanted to. How wonderful it would have been in the future to look back on this time and know that she had lived it to the fullest extent. She had started out resenting Alessandro and everything she believed he stood for, her resentment springing originally from his refusal even to consider employing her.

But, having learned what she had about him and his childhood, now knowing that they were both middle children, she felt as though there was a special private bond between them—even though Alessandro himself wasn't aware of it.

A rustle from the curtain jolted her back to her original fear, making her cry out in panic.

Alessandro woke up immediately, automatically sitting up to switch on his bedside light. Its warm glow illuminated the bed, and Leonora's fear-tensed face.

'Is the window open, do you think?' she asked. 'Only if it is the spider might get back in.'

She had bruised his pride earlier, and would certainly have to be punished for that—but not by his making use of her very real fear, Alessandro decided grimly. He would never allow himself to descend to that level, no matter what other people might choose to do. He might feel angrily sure that a combination of her competitive nature and the fact that he had refused to employ her had led to her seizing the opportunity he had accidentally given her to prove that she could best him, but that did not mean he could now allow himself to use her fear against her.

Alessandro had witnessed his father using those kind of underhand tactics too often to want to use them himself. Besides, a victory based on another person's weakness rather than his own strength was no victory at all to Alessandro. No, when she admitted in his arms that she wanted him so much that nothing else mattered it would be because she *did* want to be in his arms, not because fear had driven here there for protection. His father would have called him a fool, no doubt, deriding him as he had done so often when he had been growing up, but his father's opinion of him no longer mattered. He had grown beyond that, and it was now his own moral estimation of himself that was the yardstick by which he measured himself as a man.

Which was why he was putting aside his earlier anger to offer calmly, 'Would you like me to check the window?'

'Would you?' Hope and disbelief mingled in her voice in equal measure. It was an unfamiliar and very fragile feeling to know that a man—especially a man like Alessandro—was willing to do something brave on her behalf. But then during the short time they had spent together she had already experienced more than one unfamiliar feeling with regard to Alessandro.

He was being very generous, given what had happened earlier, and through her fear Leonora felt a renewed stab of guilt for the way she had behaved. She felt so confused and unsure of herself, all too conscious that somehow she had allowed herself to stray into territory she didn't know and where she felt very vulnerable.

It had simply never occurred to her that she would be so attracted to Alessandro, or so helplessly unable to resist the tug of that attraction. The Alessandro Leopardi she had built up inside her head from what Leo had told her about him and, more importantly, from what she had decided he must be like after he had repeatedly rejected her job applications, refusing to acknowledge how well qualified she was to work for him, bore no resemblance to the man who had held her in his arms earlier or the man she was with now.

She tried and failed to imagine either her father or her brothers making the kind of offer that Alessandro had made just now with regard to her arachnophobia. They loved her—of course they did. But their father's robust, competition-focused parenting had affected them all—as Leonora had come to recognise once she had gone out into the wider world to earn her own living. Watching the fathers of her pupils, it had become obvious to her that many of them treated their young daughters very differently from the way they dealt with their young sons.

It was, of course, to her father's credit that he had insisted on treating all of them absolutely equally—he had done his best for them, and it couldn't have been easy losing their mother when they had been so young. They had all suffered. How could they not have? But Leonora suspected that her loss had been the greater. Without a female role model to guide her and teach her how to grow into her femininity she had felt so sad, and even a little envious of the way other fathers parented their little girls. Leonora had come to recognise, as she had watched small girls flirting outrageously with their fathers, that they were being gently taught the appropriate ways of using their feminine gifts in a way that she never had.

It was true that she had learned to moderate the straightforward and outspoken directness her father had taught them all, and it was true that doing so had made her feel more comfortable within herself. But when it came to flirting she felt as clumsy as a would-be juggler, trying to put on an act and having everything come crashing down all around her instead of keeping everything spinning effortlessly in the air. And that sent her straight back to the defensive habit of playing the brash tomboy, and watching men recoil from her.

Watching her, and seeing the shadows chasing one another through her eyes, Alessandro discovered that he wanted to know what was causing them. Uniquely, in his experience with her sex, she said very little about herself. He knew the basics, of course—he should, given the number of times she had submitted job applications to him—but even in the section allowed for personal comments about aspirations and hopes her words had been blunt, sometimes to the point of aggression, and had focused only on her fierce professional desire. And yet earlier tonight in his arms her response to him had been intense; her passion had meshed with his own desire instead of competing with it.

She had not, as he might have expected her to do, tried to control their intimacy. Instead—surprisingly, given what he knew about her—she had waited for him to take the lead. Why? Because she'd believed she would have a better chance of getting her own way later if she did? She was going to be disappointed if she thought he would change his mind and give her a job. Yes, she was well qualified— far better than many of his pilots—but her presence amongst them would cause trouble.

Had she been plainer in looks or less plain in opinion he might have been tempted to break his own rule, simply because of her qualifications, but it was obvious to him that she would create chaos amongst his existing pilots. There would be those who would champion her because of her looks and those who would oppose her because of the competitive streak in her nature which came across so clearly in her applications. Either way it would have led to the kind of fall-out that wasn't just divisive but was also, in his opinion, potentially dangerous. When he hired a pilot he needed him to be totally focused on his work. Not focused on a woman like Leonora.

If she could get under *his* skin, when he prided himself on being immune to any kind of female manipulation, then what chance did his pilots have?

But what he wanted to know even more was why she was so intent on securing a job with his airline, and if he was right to suspect that, having failed to do so via her professional pilot's skills, she was now attempting to do it via a very different set of skills. What would happen if he *did* try to dig a bit deeper?

There was only one way to find out, Alessandro told himself as he thrust back the bedclothes and stood up. Normally he slept completely naked, but tonight after his shower he'd put on fresh underwear—not that he had imagined for one minute that he would be called upon to take on anti-spider-invasion duties, he thought humorously.

He started to make his way towards the window, stopping at Leonora's side of the bed to say, in a deliberately light voice, 'You never mentioned your arachnophobia on your many CVs, as far as I can remember.'

'My brothers have teased me so much all my life about it that I've developed a second phobia about admitting it to anyone.' Leonora tried to joke back as she sat up in the bed, drawing up her knees protectively, just in case the spider was about, but it was hard to concentrate on exchanging light-hearted banter when Alessandro was standing so close to her wearing so little.

His body was superbly muscled, tapering downwards from his shoulders in an athletic male V shape. His chest was lightly covered with the dark hair she had already seen, which she could now see also arrowed downwards across his flat belly to disappear beneath the top of his underwear.

Underwear which, though perfectly respectable, neverthe-less revealed just how very much of a man he was. Her eyes rounded slightly and she tried to drag her gaze away. He was *magnificently* male, she thought, gulping back a treacher-ous sigh of longing. What would it be like to be the kind of woman who felt confident enough to touch him there inti-mately—to hold him and know him? Her face burned hot at the danger of her own out-of-control thoughts. She prayed that he hadn't noticed she hadn't been able to help looking at him.

Alessandro had noticed, but he was more concerned about controlling his body's reaction to her look than he was about the look itself. How could one look from a woman he had every reason to suspect was trying to ma-nipulate him arouse him so immediately when he normally had no difficulty whatsoever in resisting women coming on to him far more strongly?

As he turned away from her towards the window, he reminded himself of what he was supposed to be doing and said, 'I know that most boys go through a stage when it affords them a huge amount of pleasure to tease girls, but I should have thought that your parents—especially your mother—would have intervened once they realised you had a very real phobia.'

'Our mother died when I was eight. She was killed by a speeding car when she was on her way to collect us all from school. Dad thought the best way for me to get over my fear was to be embarrassed into not being afraid. He always encouraged us to be competitive with one another, and I think he thought that if the boys teased me—espe-cially Piers, because he's the eldest—then I'd do anything to prove that I wasn't afraid. I did try.' She gave a small defeated shrug of her shoulders. 'I hated conceding defeat and being called a cry-baby. But I just could not stop being afraid.'

Alessandro was glad that he had his back to her—and not just because her earlier visual focus on his sex had aroused him. Now he had something else he didn't want her to see for his own protection. Pity and anger filled him in a fierce surge of unexpected and unwanted emotion. He had to bite back on an instinctive criticism of her father for not handling things better. Even if she herself was not aware of how much she was giving away, he had heard in her voice a defensive awareness that she knew she had been let down, but equally he knew that she would defend her father and her brothers against anyone's criticism.

'It must have been hard for you, growing up without your mother,' he commented, when he had control of himself.

'No harder than it was for my brothers, or than it must have been for you and your brothers,' Leonora responded instantly.

They looked at one another. How well he understood what she was feeling, Alessandro recognised. For reasons he didn't want to analyse too closely, he couldn't bring himself to push her any harder. Not because she aroused any kind of tender feelings within him, he assured himself. No, it was because he believed he owed it to himself not to take an unfair advantage of her when she was so obviously vulnerable. He had a far too clear mental image of her as a girl, all sharp-angled pre-pubescent limbs, and with the defensive competitiveness that would have come from the parenting she had described—a girl growing up in a male environment without her mother.

Grimly Alessandro forced it away. That wasn't how he wanted to think of her. After all, no doubt at some stage she would have learned to twist her father round her little finger, and her brothers too. And yet he couldn't quite banish his awareness of how difficult her childhood must have been. Just like his own? No. They were two very different people with nothing in common. Nothing? So they were both second children—motherless second children. That meant nothing. Nothing at all.

He pulled back the curtain to check the window, which was slightly open. He closed it firmly and then checked the wall and the floor around it, before turning to tell Leonora, 'It's closed now, and I can't see any sign of an intruder.'

Leonora nodded her head, and let her breath escape on a leaky sigh of relief.

'Thank you. I know that you must think me foolish, even though you haven't said so.'

'Foolish for being afraid of spiders—no. But foolishly reckless in other ways, perhaps yes.'

That was as close as he was going to get to warning her that he had his suspicions about her. If she had any sense she would immediately abandon any attempts she might be thinking of making to start a battle between them that she was not going to win. He would never, ever let anyone manipulate him into letting them win—at anything. And she was no exception, shared family position or not.

Foolishly reckless in other ways? What exactly did he mean by that? Leonora didn't know, but she did know that he wasn't paying her a compliment. The tough façade Leonora usually presented to the world should have her challenging him and arguing with him, whilst affecting not to care what he thought, but the private inner Leonora was acutely sensitive to his criticism, and unwilling to risk further hurt by asking for an explanation of it.

Alessandro dropped the curtain and was just about to head back to the bed when, without intending to do any such thing, he stopped and said, 'I can't see any sign of your friend, but if it would make you feel more comfortable I'm quite prepared to swap sides of the bed with you and sleep on your side, seeing as it is closer to the window.'

What on earth had made him make *that* offer? He shouldn't be pandering to her fears. She'd think that she had some kind of hold on him, that he wanted to please her, and that wasn't the case at all.

Astonishment and gratitude had Leonora staring at him, unable to conceal how she felt. She wasn't used to being treated like this, and she certainly hadn't expected to be treated in such a way by Alessandro.

'Would you?' She couldn't conceal her wonderment. 'That would be really kind.'

She was overdoing the wide-eyed 'you are wonderful' stuff so much that if he could have done he would have withdrawn his offer, Alessandro decided. Instead he simply shrugged and told her brusquely, 'Hardly that. I'd simply like to get some sleep.'

Instantly the light died from Leonora's eyes, to be replaced with self-conscious chagrin. Of *course* he wasn't doing it for her—and of *course* he wanted to get some sleep. She didn't trust herself to apologise. She knew he'd be able to tell from her voice how mortified she felt. Instead she moved over to his side of the bed and then tensed, immediately aware of how the scent of his skin clung to the place where he had been lying. Surely if her fear of the spider didn't keep her awake then having to sleep here, lying in Alessandro's body warmth and scent, was bound to do so.

Deliberately she lay with her back towards Alessandro, but of course that didn't stop her from knowing the minute he got into the bed from the dip in the mattress. Closing her eyes, she fought not to be conscious of him—which, oddly, was even harder now than it had been earlier. Perhaps because the verbal intimacy they had shared had in its own way made her feel every bit as vulnerable as the sexual intimacy between them earlier?

She felt the bed dip again. He was moving towards her. Was he going to carry out the threat he had made earlier, about proving to her that she wanted him? Breathless anticipation seized her, obliterating the anxiety she knew she should feel. He was right next to her. She could feel the heat from his body. In fact she could feel his body too, where his leg touched her own. A shower of lava-hot longing spilled through her.

He reached round her, his head above her own as he lifted his hand—to turn her to him? Molten desire stirred the heavy arousal in her lower body, and instinctively she started to turn towards him. Only to hear him say, 'You may want to sleep with the light on, the better to spy on your friend, but I'm afraid I do not.' He reached up and switched off the bedside light she had forgotten was on, and then moved away from her.

It could have been worse, she reassured herself after he had returned to his own side of the bed. He could have realised how she was feeling—or, even worse again, she could actually have turned to him and reached out for him. How humiliating *that* would have been. At least this way all she had to contend with was the ache of her desire, not the ache of a bruised heart. A bruised heart? How could Alessandro bruise her heart? He didn't mean anything to her. Did he? No, of course he didn't.

But lying beneath him as he'd reached over her to switch off the light had filled Leonora with the most potent surge of longing that just would not go away. All she could think about was what it would be like not just to share the sensual intimacy of sex with him, but also to feel the tender warmth of his arms and the security of his protection. What was the matter with her? Such thoughts were inappropriate and unwanted—and what was worse they were also dangerous and painful.

What the hell was the matter with him? Alessandro asked himself angrily as he lay staring into the darkness, fighting down his need to cross the distance that separated him from Leonora. No matter how much he hated having to admit it, he ached to take her in his arms and caress her back to the responsive, eager woman he had held earlier in the evening.

It was an intensity that was wholly unfamiliar to him. He wasn't some callow youth. The fact that he was sharing a bed with Leonora should not have been a signal to his body to hunger for her. He'd been too long without sex— that was his problem. There was nothing personal in the potent mix of emotional and physical need that was now gripping him. He'd spent too much time working and not enough time playing, and he'd let her get under his skin and arouse a dangerous curiosity about her—something he would normally never have allowed to happen. Something that would *not* have happened if he hadn't been obliged by family duty to come here to the *castello* in the first place.

Returning to his childhood home had brought back too many unwanted memories. That was how Leonora had been able to arouse his sympathy. Listening to her talk about her childhood had taken him far too close to the misery of his own. At least her father had loved her in his own way—unlike his father, who had never loved him and had said so. Nothing had changed there. His father's hostility towards him was still there, underpinned by angry contempt. With his own sons he would behave very differently, Alessandro thought. They would all be loved equally and individually, each one of them uniquely precious to him and valued by him, and so would his daughters.

Sons and daughters? What on earth was he thinking? He'd already decided that it was unlikely that he would be a father, since he doubted that he'd ever meet a woman he could trust enough to make the kind of commitment that would lead to them having children. Perhaps it was old-fashioned of him, but he'd want his children to be born into a marriage that would last a lifetime—for their sakes more than for his own. He liked beautiful women, and felt no shame in his preference, but it seemed to him that modern women treated their beauty as a commodity they could sell to the highest bidder for their own advantage, going from marriage to marriage and collecting an impressive portfolio of divorce settlements on the way—just as Sofia had done.

Leonora Thaxton was less ambitious. No doubt she would be content to exchange her body for a pilot's job with his airline. And the way he was aching for her right now, maybe it would be worth giving her a job, Alessandro thought grimly. He knew, of course, that he would do no such thing. His pride would never allow it, and more importantly neither would his duty towards his passengers and customers. He had been too long without a lover—that was all. It was impossible for him to allow himself to want a woman he *knew* was simply using him.

It was a long time before Leonora finally fell asleep, and an even longer time before Alessandro did the same, promising himself that he was going to play Leonora at her own game. Before the weekend was over he intended to prove to her that he could make her want him far more than she could make him want her. No matter how hard she tried to manipulate him she wasn't going to win—and she wasn't going to get a job with his airline either.

CHAPTER TEN

THE bed on which they both lay naked was high, draped with richly sensuous silk fabric. But its touch against her flesh was nowhere near as sensuously erotic as *his* touch, nor could the whisper of the fabric's kiss compare with the fierce passion of *his* kiss.

His face was in the shadows, but she knew its features by heart—from the burning intensity of his dark eyes through the arrogance of his profile to the explicit sensuality of his mouth. Excited pleasure curled and then kicked through her. Simply looking at him awoke and aroused the woman in her in a way and at a level that no other man ever could. Just as she was the only woman who was woman enough to truly complement him as a man. They were made for one another, a perfect match, and they both knew it. Only here, with him, could she truly be herself and let down her guard to share her longing and her love.

He made her ache for him in a thousand—no, a hundred thousand different ways, and the way his knowing smile lifted the corners of his mouth told her that he *knew* that her whole body shuddered in mute delight at the slow, deliberate stroke of his fingertips along the curve of her breast.

He turned his head and looked at her. Joy ran through her like quicksilver as she reached up to him, knowing how much she loved him.

'Alessandro…'

The sound of her own voice woke Leonora from her dream, shocking her into reality, as her cry hung on the morning air of the bedroom. Alessandro her dream lover? How could that be? It couldn't.

She looked towards the other side of the bed. Thankfully it was empty. A glance at her watch told her that she had slept later than normal. She was surprised that she had slept at all, given the events of the evening. There was no sound from the bathroom or the dressing room. She was obviously alone in the bedroom, and of course she was glad. Of course she was. Why had she dreamed about Alessandro like that? She had never even dreamed her fantasy before while sleeping, never mind substituted a real-life man for her imaginary lover.

It didn't mean anything, she reassured herself as she pushed back the bedclothes and stood up. It was only because of what had happened last night before they had gone to bed. It might be true that the more she learned about Alessandro the more she wanted to learn, but that was just because of his airline. It didn't mean that she was foolish enough to think of him as her soul mate. That was ridiculous.

She showered quickly and slightly apprehensively, not wanting either the return of the spider or the return of Alessandro. How awful it would be if he ever got to know about her silly fantasy. But of course he would not get to know. How could he? She certainly wasn't going to tell him, Leonora thought wryly as she dressed casually in her new jeans and one of the T-shirts.

Having brushed her hair and applied a discreet touch of make-up, she made her way across the courtyard to the main entrance to the house. She was standing in the hallway, wondering what to do about finding some breakfast, when Falcon walked into the hall from the opposite direction, smiling warmly at her when he saw her. Like her, he was dressed casually in jeans, looking younger and less austere than he had done the previous evening.

'No Sandro?' he asked.

'I overslept, I'm afraid, and he must have got impatient for his breakfast,' Leonora responded.

'Most ungallant of him. But most fortunate for me, as it means that I can have the pleasure of escorting you to the breakfast room. With so much going on it will only be a buffet-style affair this morning—although if you wish for something more…'

'No, a light breakfast will be fine,' Leonora assured him.

Alessandro's brother was charming, and handsome, and she felt more comfortable with him than she did with Alessandro himself, but it was Alessandro who made her heart thump against her ribs—just as it was doing now, at the mere thought of him.

'The *castello* is so big I'm sure I'm going to get lost before the weekend's over,' Leonora told her host.

'If you would like a guided tour then I would be happy to be your guide.'

'Oh, no. I didn't mean—I mean, I wasn't…' Flustered, and feeling that she must have sounded as though she was angling for a personal tour of the *castello*, Leonora was aghast. But instead of looking grimly at her, as she was sure Alessandro would have done, Falcon gave her another warm smile and laughed.

'You would prefer Sandro to be the one to escort you,

I can see,' he said. 'No, there is no need to deny it. That is just as it should be.'

Alessandro frowned as he stood at the opposite end of the long salon, unobserved by either his brother or Leonora, watching them both. Falcon was smiling warmly at Leonora—too warmly, Alessandro decided—and she was smiling back. Falcon had placed his hand on her arm and she was looking up at him. Out of nowhere a sledge-hammer blow fell across Alessandro's heart, momentarily stopping it and then setting it thudding with a fierce, possessive alpha-male anger. Leonora was his, and she was going to stay his.

He was halfway across the room before logic cut in, warning him of the danger he was courting in giving way to his emotions. But by then it was too late, because both Falcon and Leonora had seen him and were looking at him. It was impossible for him to turn back—either from crossing the room or from what he had just learned about himself and his real feelings for Leonora.

'Ah, there you are, Sandro. I found Leonora in the grand hall, looking hungry and alone.'

'I left her in bed, and hungry, I had thought, only for my return.'

Alessandro's response to his brother, his words and their implied meaning, caused Leonora to take a sharp breath at the deliberate sensuality and his implication that there had been an implicit promise between them that he would return to the bed where he had left her to make love to her.

'I did offer to show her round the *castello*, but she made it plain to me that she would rather you were her guide,' Falcon told his brother without commenting on Alessandro's own words.

Falcon's comment caused Alessandro to look directly at Leonora for the first time since he had joined them. She looked flushed and uncomfortable, as though embarrassed by their conversation, but Alessandro told himself that she was simply putting on an act, that secretly she was relishing the opportunity to make him jealous because Falcon had shown an interest in her. Even so, he had no intention of leaving her on her own with Falcon—or anyone else.

He had risen this morning tired and frustrated, after a largely sleepless night, having at one stage woken up to discover that he had moved to lie so close to Leonora that she'd been within arm's reach of him. His thigh had ached to be thrown over hers, to claim his male possession of her. Of course he had let it do no such thing, moving back to his own side of the bed instead, but the ache had still tormented him—and it was tormenting him now, Alessandro admitted angrily. Of course the only reason he wanted her so fiercely—the only viable reason why his emotions were involved—was because she had challenged him and then rejected him. There was no other permissible reason.

'I thought you might like to see something of the island whilst we're here,' he told Leonora. 'So I've arranged for us to pick up a helicopter at the airfield in half an hour's time. We won't be able to see everything, of course, but I'll do my best to show you the highlights.'

Leonora's face lit up immediately. Unable to conceal her pleasure, she smiled up at Alessandro, her eyes sparkling with excitement.

'I've never piloted a helicopter—' she began, but Alessandro shook his head.

'And you won't be piloting one today either,' he warned her. 'You aren't licensed to fly them.'

'Are you?' Leonora couldn't resist demanding.

'Of course,' Alessandro responded. 'So, either you can have your breakfast now, or we could have brunch at a hotel I know with the most spectacular views of the Ionian Sea.'

'Let the poor girl at least have a cup of coffee, Sandro,' Falcon protested, but Leonora shook her head.

'Brunch sounds perfect,' she assured Alessandro happily.

In the end she did get her coffee, and some delicious fresh bread and honey, brought to her by Alessandro himself after she had returned to their suite to collect everything she thought she might need.

When he walked in, carrying a tray on which there was a cafetière of coffee, two cups and fresh bread and preserves, she did feel a small sweetly sharp heartbeat of self-conscious uncertainty, brought on as much by her own private dream fantasy as by what had actually happened between them.

The sight of Alessandro dressed like her in jeans, but wearing a soft white short-sleeved linen shirt with them, which somehow emphasised the breadth and masculinity of his torso, heightened her already acute awareness of him. What would happen if she went to him now and told him with the openness and the sexual confidence she knew she ought to have that she could not stop thinking about him and that she wanted them to make love? He had been angry with her last night when she had retreated from him, but he had wanted her then. Did he still want her now?

What was the matter with her? Her virginity might be a burden to her, but that was not a valid reason for her to feel the way she was doing right now. Wanting Alessandro merely physically would have been bad enough, given her ambition to work for him, but the need and the hunger she was battling contained an emotional longing to connect with him.

That was simply because they shared certain aspects of their childhood. She would have felt the same way about any man she met who, like her, was a second child and had lost a parent.

'Here you are.'

She had been so engrossed with her own thoughts that she hadn't noticed that Alessandro had poured them both a cup of coffee. As she took hers from him their fingertips touched, and she had to fight not to reach out to him, to make that touch even more intimate. This was crazy—and dangerous. Anyone would think she'd never been so close to a man before.

She hadn't, though, had she? Or at least not to a sensually powerful and compelling alpha male like Alessandro. He was unique, but her response to him was far from unique, she reminded herself firmly, turning away from him to face the window. She clasped her coffee and pretended to be interested in the view beyond the window in order to avoid having to look at him and further increase her unwanted vulnerability. No doubt hordes of other women had felt about him as she did. But they, unlike her, had no doubt had the sexual confidence to show him how they felt. What would his reaction be if he knew the truth? Would he be as repulsed as she dreaded? Or would he simply laugh at her? Either way, she wasn't going to risk finding out. Not when she already knew that what he certainly *wasn't* likely to do was sweep her up into his arms and carry her to bed. He wouldn't do that, would he? Not after the way she had stopped him last night.

Leonora tightened her grip on her coffee cup, all too aware of the betraying tremors of longing threatening her body. From the place deep within her memory where she had locked it away came a teasing comment made to her by Leo, when she had first insisted that she wasn't going to give up her dream of working for Alessandro's Avanti Airlines.

'Are you sure it's the job you want and not the man, sis? After all, there are dozens of airlines who'd jump at the chance to take on someone as qualified as you, but the only one *you* seem to be interested in is Alessandro Leopardi's.'

Her response had been immediate. She had repudiated his brotherly teasing, insisting with flags of anger flying in her cheeks that the only reason she was so determined to get Alessandro Leopardi to back down and take her on was to prove a point, that it had nothing to do with the man himself. Or at least not in the way Leo had been implying.

The reality was that her determination to force Alessandro to concede that she was more than up to being one of his pilots had everything to do with the fact that she had been so deeply resentful of his professional rejection of her, and intensely determined to make him change his mind.

'You'd better have something to eat—unless you're one of those women who doesn't do breakfast?'

Alessandro's cool voice, tinged with a mix of disapproval and contempt, broke into the chaotic confusion of her private thoughts. Glad of an excuse not to have to pursue them to a conclusion she already knew she wasn't going to like, Leonora answered him by going over to the table and putting down her coffee before selecting some bread and spreading it with honey.

'Food is fuel for the human body. I wouldn't expect or want to fly an aircraft that wasn't properly fuelled, and the same applies to my body. Besides,' she added wryly, 'it just isn't possible to grow up as the only female in a houseful of men and not eat breakfast. My father used to insist on us all having a huge bowlful of home-made porridge on winter mornings, and to tell the truth it's still my favourite comfort food.' She stopped speaking abruptly, conscious of having allowed him to see a softer side she'd normally have kept hidden.

'Mine is spaghetti with tomato sauce. Falcon used to make it for us—we were often sent supperless to bed by our stepmother, but our old cook taught Falcon how to make a few simple dishes,' Alessandro told her.

They looked at one another, both of them wondering what had prompted them to give away an aspect of themselves they normally kept very carefully guarded. For Alessandro, the unplanned giving of such a confidence about his childhood left him with a need to explain to himself why he had done so. He picked up a piece of bread, spooning fresh preserve onto it and biting into it with strong white teeth in a way that had Leonora's stomach muscles clamping down hard against a surge of sensual heat that caught her off guard.

All he was doing by exchanging such confidences with her was working towards getting her off guard and keeping her there until he was ready to show her which of them was the stronger, Alessandro assured himself, finishing the bread and then telling Leonora crisply, 'I'm surprised you haven't tried for your own helicopter pilot's licence.'

Had he deliberately chosen the word 'tried' to annoy her? Leonora wondered. If so, he had succeeded.

Defensive colour flushed her face as she told him fiercely, 'I had planned to, but tuition is expensive. I don't have the luxury of your kind of wealth. I have to work to support myself—plus, as I don't have a job as a pilot, I have to find the money to keep my licence up to date. Not a lot left over to indulge myself with helicopter piloting tuition.'

'And that's my fault, is it? Because I wouldn't give you a job?' Alessandro mocked her, quickly picking up on what she hadn't said. 'There are other airlines,' he pointed out.

'Not for me. For me there is only you—I mean only Avanti.'

Now Leonora's face was scarlet. What on earth had prompted her to make such a *faux pas* and substitute that far too personal and intimate 'you' for the name of his airline? Her face burning, she looked at Alessandro, but he was looking away from her, casually picking up his coffee as though he hadn't registered what she had said.

Oh, very clever, Alessandro thought cynically, as he pretended not to have registered Leonora's deliberately accidental 'you'. He might not have allowed her to see that he had registered it, but he certainly wasn't fooled by it. She was obviously a member of the 'the best way to a man's heart is via his ego' club, but Alessandro had learned not to trust his own ego a long time ago—and the hard way.

'Mandarin lessons don't come cheap,' he retaliated smoothly. 'And you are, I presume, self-employed?'

Leonora could feel her face burning again, but this time the heat was caused by anger. The parents who paid her to teach their children and the businessmen and -women eager to add Mandarin to their CVs *did* pay well, but she worked hard to fit in as many pupils as she could without prejudicing her own ability to teach them well.

Something her father had taught them all was the need to 'pay back' to society—from being young they had all run errands for elderly neighbours, as well as worked at home for pocket money—and now she took that early lesson a step further and gave as many free lessons as she could fit in to her timetable, travelling to various schools to teach groups of financially disadvantaged children several nights a week. Not that she would dream of defending herself from Alessandro's cutting jibe by telling him that. It wasn't something she had felt any need to put on her CV, so why should she feel the need to seek his good opinion by telling him now?

Unless, of course, there was another reason she wanted him to approve of her, and like her? Such as what? She had dreamed about him, hadn't she? Imagining him as her soul mate. But that had simply been because of last night, and didn't mean anything. Heavens, she'd be trying to tell herself she was in danger of falling in love with him if she carried on like this.

Her heart did a cartwheel reminiscent of the first slow spin of a washing machine. Falling in love with Alessandro? Oh, that would be something, wouldn't it? The joke of the year. And she'd be the fool—the one everyone was laughing at. But what if it wasn't a joke? What if she was actually falling in love with him? What if she had already fallen in love with him?

Panic gripped her. Her heart went into full washing machine spin cycle. She put down the bread and honey she had been enjoying only a minute ago, unable to finish eating it. Of *course* she hadn't fallen in love with Alessandro. She was panicking over nothing. Just because she had wanted to go to bed with him it didn't mean she loved him. But she had wanted him to hold her. She had wanted—

'We'd better make a move if you're going to see anything much of the island before we have to get back for tonight's ball.'

It was a relief to have Alessandro's voice cutting through the painful confusion of her thoughts.

'Look, I've been thinking.' Leonora gave him her brightest smile. 'If you've got things to do, and I'm going to hold you up, I'm perfectly happy to stay here.'

She wasn't in love with him, but it might be wiser and safer not to spend the day on her own with him.

She wanted to stay here—without him? Alessandro's mouth hardened. Did she really think he was so easily taken in that he didn't know what she was up to? Did she really believe she had a chance with Falcon, or was she simply trying to make him jealous?

'In the hope that Falcon will make good his offer to show you the *castello*?' he asked cynically.

'No,' Leonora denied truthfully.

'Like I said, it's time we made a move,' Alessandro told her, ignoring her denial. Did she really think that he was going to leave her here alone?

They were in the car—a dark green Maserati, all discreet paintwork outside and expensive-smelling leather inside—with Alessandro at the wheel, heading back to the private airstrip along a road Alessandro had told her was a shortcut.

Changing gear to take a series of stomach-churning hairpin bends, his focus was on the road ahead of him as he warned her, 'You are here for one reason and one reason only, and that reason is *not* so that you can flirt with my brother. Remember what I told you about your brother's future if you disobeyed my orders? That still holds good.'

Leonora refused to say anything, looking out of the window and gulping when she saw how steeply the narrow single-track road was dropping as they left the *castello* behind them.

Alessandro held all the power. For Leo's sake she could not defy him. What would she do if he should demand that she give herself to him? He was perfectly capable of making such a demand, she was sure, and of justifying why he had done so. But if he did… The swiftness of her intense physical reaction shocked her. She couldn't possibly *want* him to make such a demand. It would be archaic, appalling, feudal and beyond unthinkable. But if he did, and if she had no option but to let him lead her to his bed and once there command that she give herself over to his will, his touch, his full possession, then what would she do?

What was she thinking about? Or rather *who* was she thinking about? Alessandro wondered grimly as he caught Leonora's small gasp—surely one of anticipation and pleasure, caused by the privacy of her own thoughts, if the look softening her face was anything to go by. Such a look could not be faked. She probably thought that he was concentrating on his driving too much to be aware of it, but there was nothing about her of which he was not aware— not a look, not a sound, not a scent or a breath, not anything. Everything about her was imprinted into his own senses to irritate and torment him.

Torment? Because she annoyed him so much. Nothing more. His torment was *not* the torment of a man so hungry for a woman that she invaded not just his every thought and feeling but the primary code of his entire being. If he felt anything it was anger—because he knew instinctively that she was thinking about a man she wanted, a man who had already given her sexual pleasure and with whom she was aching to re-experience that pleasure. He was angry that she should think him stupid enough to be taken in by her, and he felt contempt for her as a woman because she clearly could not remain faithful to a man with whom she obviously already had a relationship.

Who was he? *What* was he? The aviation equivalent of a surf bum? One of life's players rather than one of its workers?

Alessandro cut back the speed of the powerful car. He liked well-made pieces of machinery, but he never took risks with them. In his book only a fool did that. The Maserati was one of a kind, adapted from its specifications specifically for him, with a top speed worthy of a race track, but unlike his now-dead half-brother Alessandro had no love of speed for the sake of showing off. And right now the emotions he refused to let himself admit, never mind express, might be urging him to give the car its head and those emotions an outlet, but even with a couple of miles of straight road ahead of him he refused to give in. Alessandro measured himself by a hard code, and he wasn't going to allow any woman to get under his skin enough for him to break it.

They'd reached the airfield, driving past an open hangar in which Leonora could see Alessandro's private jet. The helicopter was standing out on the tarmac, its Avanti Airlines paintwork of silver on white gleaming in the brilliance of the morning sunshine.

Alessandro brought the car to a halt outside the impressive architecture of a modern and chrome building that somehow, despite its stylish and almost urban modern look, seemed to fit perfectly into the landscape.

Alessandro noticed Leonora studying the building. Falcon, who had trained as an architect, and who shared his own love of structure and design, had incorporated many of Alessandro's own ideas into his design for the small terminal and office building, which also had its own air traffic control unit. Alessandro did a substantial amount of business with various concerns on the island, and for a variety of reasons had decided to construct his own private airfield rather than be dependent on the island's public airport facilities.

In addition to keeping the helicopter permanently based on the island, Alessandro also funded an air ambulance service, and provided the air ambulance itself. He and his brothers were united in their determination to do what they could to offset the effect of their father's feudal grip on his land and on the people who depended on it and him for their livelihood.

Falcon worked tirelessly behind the scenes to try and improve the lot of young people who otherwise would have no future ahead of them other than that endured by their parents and their grandparents. And in addition to the building work he was already doing on the island Rocco— helped by funds from Falcon and Alessandro—was building what would eventually be a college that they all hoped would be a gateway for at least some of the island's young people to a different way of life. Alessandro already had on his payroll several young men from his father's villages, whom he had trained at his own expense as aircraft technicians. All the staff working at the airfield came from local families and were paid well.

'I just want to check over everything with the ops crew,' he informed Leonora, before he opened the door of the car.

A smiling member of the ground staff opened Leonora's door for her. Not sure whether she was supposed to stand around and wait or follow him, Leonora opted for the latter course, hurrying to catch up with Alessandro as he strode across the concrete apron.

Inside the building air-conditioning cooled the air to exactly the right temperature and a smartly dressed and very pretty receptionist welcomed Alessandro. Leonora's attention was focused on the Leonardo da Vinci prints decorating the off-white walls opposite the tinted glass frontage of the building.

Seeing her looking at the prints, Alessandro told her, 'They are copies of Leonardo's sketches for various forms of flight.'

'Yes, I know,' Leonora responded, nodding in the direction of the prints as she told him, 'Whilst other girls were putting pin-ups of pop stars on their bedroom walls, mine were decorated with those. I found a set in a second-hand shop and badgered the poor shop owner until he eventually agreed to let me have them in exchange for working there on Saturdays.'

Alessandro looked away from her.

'I bought my first set during a visit to Florence to see my mother's relatives. My stepmother ripped them down from my bedroom wall and burned them as punishment for my not bringing back a gift for Antonio.'

'Oh, how cruel.' Her indignation made Leonora's voice shake, and instinctively she reached out and put her hand on Alessandro's arm—only to remove it as quickly as though she had been burned.

Stiffening, he drew back from her, and walked towards the pretty receptionist without a backwards look. Did she really think that he was taken in by her false sympathy?

Alessandro shrugged aside the warning slamming his heartbeat into his chest and telling him that his reactions to Leonora were both illogical and dangerous.

CHAPTER ELEVEN

THEY'D been in the air for nearly two hours. She'd seen Mount Etna from above, holding her breath as Alessandro took them in close to the volcano, and the remains of architectural wonders built by the many civilisations that had come to this island and left their stamp on it. Alessandro had given her a potted history of the island's differing cultures, and she'd heard the cynicism in his voice when he'd touched briefly on the feudal aspects of his own family's role in Sicily's history.

They'd flown over Palermo, spread beneath them in all its faded glory, with its groves of citrus fruit and olives, and now they were heading for the coast and the hotel where they were going to have what would now be lunch rather than brunch.

'Falcon was chief architect for the hotel to which we are heading, and Rocco, my younger brother, was the builder. It is part of a new fraternal venture—of sorts—a luxury resort on Capo d'Orlando, close to the town of Cefalù and overlooking the Tyrrhenian Sea. My contribution was the helipad and direct helicopter access from the island's airport to the resort. We are also looking into providing helicopter access to the Aeolian Islands offshore. If you look to your right now you should see the headland.'

Obediently Leonora did as Alessandro suggested, exclaiming, 'Oh, how beautiful!' when she saw the small cape, its sandy beaches lapped by turquoise waves. Cefalù resort itself was a picturesque tumble of clusters of Mediterranean colour-washed buildings, basking in the sunshine.

'This part of the island has known many civilisations, but for this development it was decided that we would follow a Moorish style of architecture. Here is the helipad, coming up now,' Alessandro added, in between speaking to the control unit, giving his position and getting clearance for landing.

He circled a tall tower that rose high above the rest of the sand-coloured complex below them, skilfully hovering over the landing pad before dropping the helicopter perfectly onto it. The tower and its landing pad combined both the beauty of ancient architecture and the near miracle of modern aero science, Leonora recognised, as she listened to Alessandro finishing his touchdown procedures with the control unit.

Outside, the ground staff were waiting to go through their checks, and as soon as Alessandro had stopped speaking he opened his door and got out of the helicopter. Leonora went to open her own door, but before she could get out Alessandro was there, offering her a helping hand. Initially tempted to refuse it, she reminded herself instead of the role she was supposed to be playing. And of course that was the *only* reason why she was allowing Alessandro to hold her. Her decision certainly had nothing whatsoever to do with that cartwheel of her heart, followed by the dizzy burst of pleasure engendered by his touch. Not at all.

So why was she almost leaning into him, and so delaying the moment when he could release her?

She wanted so badly to stay where she was, leaning into him, free to breathe in the scent of him, free to place her hand just above his heart and feel its strong, fierce beat. When a woman truly loved a man this was all she wanted: his closeness, their oneness, the knowledge that no other man could take his place. But she did not *love* Alessandro—truly or otherwise.

How could this woman get beneath his guard so easily and so disruptively? Alessandro wondered grimly. How could he possibly be thinking that he was sorry their flight was over because he had enjoyed the intimacy and the conversation they had shared so very much?

'This way.'

Alessandro might not be holding her close any more, but he was still holding her hand.

'There's a lift down to the hotel foyer over here,' Alessandro informed Leonora, guiding her towards an elegant limestone staircase that descended from the floor of the helipad into a smart forecourt.

Within seconds of stepping into the lift they were stepping out of it again, into the hotel foyer, beyond which Leonora could see a very smart restaurant and cocktail bar, and beyond that a wide terrace overlooking the sea.

Several tables were already occupied, but the one to which they were shown had by far the best position, Leonora noted. A tall, impeccably groomed woman, whose appearance—in Leonora's opinion, at least—was slightly marred by the amount of clanking gold jewellery she was wearing, turned her head to look at them.

'Alessandro!' she exclaimed. 'But how wonderful. I was only just talking about you to Luca, saying how much I was looking forward to seeing you again.'

Ignoring Leonora, the woman embraced Alessandro, lingering over the exchange of supposedly merely polite friendly kisses, and then retaining her hold of Alessandro's arm.

'It was such a wonderful surprise when your father invited me to attend the ball. I am looking forward to it so much. You will remember Luca, my cousin, of course?'

Alessandro inclined his head politely but distantly. Sofia was the last person he had been expecting to see when he had walked into the restaurant. How typical of his father that he should have invited *her* to attend tonight's celebratory ball. No doubt he had hoped to add a fresh sting of pain to old wounds, but he was wasting his time. How typical of him to do such a thing—and how pointless. Looking at her, and listening to her now, Alessandro could only marvel that he had ever found her in any way attractive. He could see the avarice in her gaze, could feel it in the possessive clutch of her hand on his arm.

Her cousin, he seemed to remember, had a long history of being her escort when she had no husband in tow, and the gossip was that they slept together as well, when neither had anyone else to share a bed with. Luca, a decade older than Sofia, which took him close to fifty, with a perma-tan and flesh like a snake's, was focusing his attention on Leonora. Instantly Alessandro stepped towards her, ignoring his ex-lover's possessive drag on his arm to say curtly, 'Please excuse us, Sofia, but we have had a busy morning, and I know that Leonora is ready for her lunch.'

'Leonora?' Sofia questioned—for all the world as though she hadn't even noticed that she was there, Leonora thought grimly, as the other woman smiled up at Alessandro.

'My…partner,' Alessandro informed Sofia firmly.

His *partner*? In what? In lies and deceit, yes. But in the real sense of the word, as Alessandro was quite obviously implying, then she was no such thing.

But Leonora was speedily adding two and two together, from the broad hints Sofia had given as to the nature of her old relationship with Alessandro and the comment Alessandro himself had made to her about a past love who had let him down. And she was coming to the natural conclusion that at one time Alessandro and Sofia had been lovers. Alessandro now—no doubt out of male pride—wanted Sofia to think that Leonora was enjoying her old position in his life—and in his bed. Had Alessandro known that Sofia was likely to be attending the ball? Was that the main reason he had blackmailed Leonora into partnering him?

What if it was? What did it matter to her what his reason was? But it *did* matter, Leonora admitted miserably, unable to stop comparing herself to the elegant and self-confident Sofia, who was now holding on to Alessandro's arm for all the world as though they were still a couple, forcing Leonora to one side. Leonora found herself wanting. Sofia had an air about her that said quite plainly that she was a very sexually experienced and knowing woman. The kind of woman Alessandro would much rather have in his bed than an inexperienced woman like her.

'I'm sure Leonora won't mind if we join you for lunch. This is a wonderful hotel. Your father was kind enough to recommend it. He told me that you and your brothers own it, Alessandro.'

Alessandro part owned the hotel too? Well, that was more than he had told her, Leonora reflected. But perhaps she should have worked that out for herself, after what he had told her about their fraternal input into it. Just as she should also have worked out that there was more to his insistence that she partner him to the weekend's events than he had told her.

How his father would have loved seeing the result of his meddling, Alessandro thought grimly as he was forced to allow Sofia to thrust her unwanted company on them. He knew that he had been emotionally and physically naive when he had first met her, but now meeting her again after so many years, he acknowledged wryly that he must have been even more naive than he had thought for ever having found her remotely attractive. Seen side by side with Leonora she looked tawdry and cheap, as fake as the 'designer label' handbags sold in the street markets of Florence to gullible tourists. Her gossip as they waited for the table to be enlarged was littered with references to people and places favoured by the celebrity culture he so despised and loathed, and by the time they were finally seated Alessandro was longing for the pure, clear bite of Leonora's far more varied and interesting conversation.

'So, Leonora, how long have you known Sandro? He and I were close for a long time, and I don't think it's any secret that he would have asked me to marry him if I'd let him. We were so young then, though—too young to know how lucky we were to have met one another. And of course as I was still modelling then I travelled a great deal, and poor Alessandro became very jealous of all the handsome rich men who wanted to take me out—didn't you, darling?'

'I'm afraid I don't remember,' Alessandro told her. 'After all, as you said yourself, it was a long time ago.'

'Oh, come on, Sandro,' Luca put in. 'You were mad for Sofia and we all knew it. I remember that diamond bracelet you bought her from Cartier. You desperately wanted to buy her a ring as well, but I told you you should talk to her first.'

Leonora, who *had* been feeling hungry, discovered that she had lost her appetite. It was ridiculous to feel so painfully jealous of a relationship that was in the past and a man she could never have, and yet she did. And it hurt—dreadfully.

'They serve locally caught fish here. I can recommend it,' Alessandro advised Leonora, ignoring Luca's comment. He had forgotten all about the Cartier bangle— bought not on a whim, he remembered now, but because Sofia had hinted so very broadly that she wanted it. There had certainly never been any discussion about a ring. Not that he could claim that he would *not* have bought her one during those early months of their relationship, before he had realised the truth about her.

'What is your costume for tonight, Sandro? I'm so excited about the ball. It's such a hugely prestigious event, and so exclusive.'

'Hardly, Sofia. It is a private celebration of a historical family event, that's all. Not one of your celebrity affairs.'

Sofia pouted.

'*Caro*, you are being far too modest. I understood from your father that at least two top-magazine society-page editors had been invited.'

That was news to Alessandro—unwelcome news. He suspected that it would be equally unwelcome to Falcon. Yet another example of their father's love of meddling. He'd have to warn Falcon to check the guest list.

'Who are you impersonating?' Alessandro asked Sofia, adding, 'No—let me guess—Lucretia Borgia?'

She gave a sharp trill of laughter.

'That is so naughty of you, Sandro—you always did have a wicked sense of humour. No, actually, I shall be Napoleon's sister Pauline—the bride your ancestor wanted for his son. Has Alessandro told you anything of the history of his family yet, Leonora?'

'A little—' Leonora began.

But Alessandro spoke over her answer, saying coolly, 'We've been far too busy talking about our own future to delve into the ancient past.'

'Ah, *caro*, do you remember the plans we had for our future?' Sofia asked Alessandro softly, placing her hand on his arm.

They deserved one another, Leonora decided crossly an hour later, as she sat pushing her lunch round her plate and trying not to feel sorry for herself. She listened to Alessandro and Sofia. For all that Alessandro's responses to her were blunt and dismissive, plainly Sofia believed that he still cared about her—otherwise surely she would not be so persistent. Leonora certainly believed that he did—even if for his pride's sake he was trying to pretend that he did not.

They were the last to leave the restaurant, Sofia having insisted on extending their lunch well into the afternoon, although having failed to persuade Alessandro into agreeing that she could move from the hotel to the *castello*. She had also failed to persuade him to go up to her suite with her so that she could show him how much she still treasured the Cartier bangle, which she apparently had with her.

Alessandro and Leonora flew back to the *castello* almost in silence, and when Alessandro told her that he had something he needed to discuss with his brother Leonora was glad of the opportunity to escape to their suite on her own, so that she could deal in private with the discovery she had made before they had left the hotel.

They had been in the foyer, saying their goodbyes after lunch. Sofia naturally had been all over Alessandro, but it had been when Leonora had seen the other woman kissing Alessandro on the mouth with a deliberate sensuality that had had his hands lifting to grip her arms that the hideous truth had torn through her. She loved him. How, when and why were all questions she could not answer. But they didn't affect the reality and its unbearable truth. Somehow, without her wanting it to happen and without her knowing how it had happened, he had taken her heart as effortlessly as his ancestors had taken their people's lands.

Leonora had always believed that she possessed both common sense and determination, but neither of them were strong enough to prevent the flow of some very painful tears in the privacy of the suite, as she lay curled up on the bed she had shared with Alessandro as his blackmailed pretend mistress. She would never share it with him as a woman who loved him, and who was loved by him in return.

She should take the opportunity to shower and wash her hair and ready herself for the evening before Alessandro returned. What would happen tonight? Would they still share this room or, despite all that he had said to Sofia over lunch, would Sofia be the one sharing his bed tonight?

CHAPTER TWELVE

As ALESSANDRO headed for the West Tower Suite his mind was on the conversation he had just had with Falcon. He had gone to find his brother, to warn him about what their father had done, and Falcon had been every bit as angry about their father's surreptitious invitation to Sofia as Alessandro had known he would be.

'I don't want her here tonight,' Alessandro had told Falcon. 'In fact I'd even go and tell Father that if I'd known she would be here then I would have refused to attend the ball if it weren't for the fact that he'd be bound to assume that I couldn't bear to be in the same room as a woman I once loved and lost. The only feelings I have left for Sofia are those of disbelief that I was ever taken in by her, and a certain dislike of admitting that I didn't recognise what she was in the first place so you had to rescue me from her.'

'I know that has always rankled, Sandro,' Falcon had surprised him by saying. And then he had gone on to surprise him even further by adding, 'I have often regretted my interference, and my inability to control the desire to play the big brother who knew what was best for you. You have always had the most carefully honed instincts of all of us, and it is my belief that in your heart you were already aware of what Sofia really was. But of course in those days my ego did tend to push me into interfering where my interference wasn't needed. No doubt an attempt to assert my position and to comfort myself that, even though you were an adult, you still needed me. For so long you and Rocco were my *raison d'être* so to speak—the purpose of my determination not to give in to our father. I became very good at telling myself I was doing things for your sakes and not my own, and with your adulthood came the fear of what my purpose in life would be other than my tethered goat status as eldest son and heir. With every step you took towards independence from our father I felt my own status crumble a little more.'

Falcon had reached out and put his hand on Alessandro's arm in a loving fraternal clasp. 'I have never said so before, and I have blamed myself many times for not doing so, but I needed you, Sandro—I needed your strength and your support and I was very afraid of losing them. Foolish of me, since those things we shared as boys still bond us together today, even though we seldom speak of them, and I still think of you as my strong right arm, and in fact as my true strength.'

Alessandro stopped in mid-step, as overcome by emotion now as he had been when he had heard Falcon say those words—miraculous, beneficent, humbling words that had filled him with love and given him a truly precious gift.

In answer to Falcon's emotional speech he had reached out in turn, placing his free hand on Falcon's arm and clasping it, as Falcon had, so that they were locked together. Then they had released one another and come together in a fierce, loving hug.

'I have looked up to you all my life, Falcon—and, yes, envied you as well. Not because you are the first-born, and certainly not because of what you will inherit, but because of your great courage and everything that you are. You are my hero, the person I have always longed most to be.'

'I doubt that your Leonora would be very happy to see the man she obviously loves so much changed in any kind of way. I envy you that, Sandro—a woman who loves you for what you are and not what you have, but also a woman with whom you have so much in common and can share your life. Be happy, my brother, for happiness is the greatest gift life can give us, and it is the one you deserve more than most. We must none of us repeat our father's mistakes. His bitterness and resentment mark him like a physical brand.'

'He has accepted now that Antonio did not father a child?'

'Reluctantly. As you know, I have looked thoroughly into every relationship Antonio had at the time, that would have allowed a child to have been conceived—in the period when he claims the child *was* conceived—even those lasting no more than a matter of hours. The facts prove beyond any doubt that there is no child.'

They had embraced again, but it hadn't been the breaking down of barriers that had allowed them to reach out to one another and show their love for one another that had occupied Alessandro's thoughts as much as Falcon's comments about Leonora. She didn't love him. Falcon was wrong about that. But they did have a great deal in common, he did desire her and he was certain that she desired him.

What if he suggested to her that they started again as two people who shared a mutual interest and a mutual desire that could, if they chose, go on to the mutual and exclusive intimacy of them becoming lovers who might ultimately commit to one another? Inside his head he had a mental image of the two of them together, of him holding her naked in their shared bed. She was smiling at him, her hair spilling over his body, her expression soft with love and happiness. An extraordinary sense of freedom and joy filled him, softening all the hard, painful edges of doubt and suspicion.

They could be lovers. Lovers who could meet equally in the neutral territory of shared honesty—a territory where they could put aside the contentious issues that kept them apart.

To do that, though, he would have to reveal to her his feelings and his desire, and in doing so risk appearing vulnerable. He would have to be the one who took the first step and showed his need and his weakness. Did he want her enough to take that risk?

As he continued to stride down the corridor, Alessandro knew the answer to his own question.

As for Sofia, he and Falcon had come to a decision to have an immediate message sent to the hotel where Sofia was staying, bluntly telling her that her invitation had been rescinded, and warning her that she would be refused entry if she attempted to attend the ball.

Their costumes were hanging ready in the dressing room—Alessandro's that of a fierce Norman warrior and her own that of a Saracen princess. Was she going to be able to get through the evening ahead of them without humiliating herself because of her love for Alessandro? She had felt so desperately jealous this afternoon, forced to sit and watch and listen whilst Sofia flirted with him, knowing that once they had been lovers and that Alessandro probably still loved her now.

She might not be free to announce that she was leaving, but there was one decision she could and had made—and that was that she no longer intended to pursue her dream to work for Alessandro's airline. How could she, now that she knew how she felt about him? She would never be able to concentrate properly on her work, and if she ever had to fly *him* anywhere she would be so wrought up with longing for him that she simply would not be able to be professional. Her dream was over. The harsh reality of her uninvited and unrequited love had destroyed it.

When Alessandro opened the door into the suite, Leonora was standing by the window, looking out.

'Checking to see if your spider friend is making a return trip?' he asked her.

The gently teasing note in his voice brought the swift sting of too-emotional tears to Leonora's eyes. Blinking fiercely, she half turned round, shaking her head.

'There's something I want to discuss with you,' Alessandro told her. 'It's about your desire to work for me.' *And my desire for you*, he was tempted to say. But he didn't want to antagonise her by rushing things.

'I've changed my mind about that,' Leonora told him simply. 'I don't want to work for you any more.' *Because I love you too much to bear the pain of seeing you but not being with you.*

Her statement was so unexpected and so obviously heartfelt that it made him pause and look searchingly at her. She looked pale and strained.

'Why not?'

'I'd really rather not say.'

'You've bombarded me with applications and your CV for two years, and now suddenly, just like that, you don't want a job with me after all and you won't say why?' He shook his head. 'If this is some kind of change of tactic, designed to make me—'

'No, it isn't.'

There was a catch in her voice that checked him. Something was very wrong. She wasn't simply trying a new strategy.

'What's wrong?' he asked her. 'You don't look well.'

'Nothing's wrong.'

'Liar,' he said, going to her and putting his hands on her shoulders.

He had intended to turn her in to the light, so that he could look at her more closely, but immediately she pulled away from him with a small gasp, retreating into the shadows and then saying too quickly, 'Our costumes are in the dressing room. You are to be a Norman knight, and I am a Saracen princess according to the labels on them.'

'Yes,' he agreed. 'When my family first came to Sicily as Norman knights my ancestor took as his mistress the daughter of the Saracen lord who held this land before he was vanquished.'

Leonora looked at him, and then looked away again, but it was too late. Alessandro had seen the desire in her gaze.

He moved closer to her, wearing his confidence with ease, backing her into a corner as he told her softly, 'I want us to have a fresh start, Leonora—I want us to be lovers.'

Her heart was a single, tight, unbearable ache inside her chest. To be offered what she so much desired and to know that she must refuse was truly a pain in a class of its own.

'No.'

'You want me,' Alessandro insisted.

'It must have been a shock for you to see Sofia at lunchtime.'

'My father would have liked to think so.'

'She's the woman you told me about, isn't she? The one you loved?'

Alessandro frowned. Why were they discussing Sofia, when all he wanted to do was take her in his arms?

'I may have thought once that I loved her, but I was wrong. And I don't want to waste time talking about Sofia when I could be holding you.'

She couldn't bear this. She really couldn't.

'No,' she protested, but Alessandro shook his head and framed her face in his hands, kissing her slowly and thoroughly. When he felt the sweet, sensual shudder grip her he kissed her more deeply, his tongue finding hers, his body closing in on hers.

Please, just let me have this, Leonora begged fate. Just these few kisses, and the erotically powerful weight of his body backing her own against the wall whilst his hands slipped from her face to hold her body and shield it from any discomfort. Somehow—how?—her thighs knew how to part for his even whilst her arms wrapped round him. His hands stroked from her back to her breasts, caressing them slowly and rhythmically until she was near mindless with a pleasure that could only demand more, wanting the intimacy of his touch on her bare skin.

She had no words for her need, only the frantic pleading of her lips against his jaw and then his throat, her tongue-tip tasting the male saltiness of his skin and tracing the swell of his Adam's apple. She pushed away his shirt, her hands trembling as she explored the shape of his back, smoothing her whole hand, palm flat, over his flesh, wanting to absorb the feel of every single cell of him, to commit that sensation to her memory.

She pressed her lips, open and hungry, to the bared vee of flesh exposed by his shirt, burying her face against him, shaking with a need that was as intensely emotional as it was physical. She could feel the swollen hard jut of his sex pressing against her softness. The ache of her own need pierced her, making her want to cry. In her mind's eye she could see him and feel him, taking that ache to an unbearable intensity with the slow and then fast thrust of his body within her own flesh, soothing it, satisfying it, filling her with a pleasure so perfect that it lifted them both to another dimension.

He was her soul mate. Not a fantasy lover any more, but a real man—far more perfect in every way than the shadowy figure she had once imagined.

The touch of Leonora's hands and mouth on his skin was pushing Alessandro beyond the limits of his self-control, taking him to a place with a promise of pleasure he'd never known or imagined might exist.

Alessandro tugged up the hem of the T-shirt Leonora had changed into after her shower, pulling it over her head and exposing her braless breasts. Bending his head, he captured one hard, swollen nipple with his lips, caressing it with his tongue-tip as he cupped her other breast in his hand, licking and sucking on her nipple until she was crying out in frantic pleasure. His fingers drew the same delight from her other breast, rendering her mindless and helpless, but when he unfastened the button on her jeans and unzipped them, sliding his hand down over her quivering belly and against her sex, Leonora knew she had to stop him or face the humiliation of him discovering she was a virgin and then rejecting her.

She had to stop him—yes. But please not yet—not now, when he was touching her with such unbelievable erotic intimacy, his fingertip finding the quivering eagerness of her clitoris.

She was velvet and roses, the scent of night and the eternal lure of the tide that moved the sea. She was woman, *his* woman, and he loved her more than he thought possible.

This was too much. She had to stop him now, whilst she was still able. Frantically Leonora pushed at Alessandro's chest, her heart thudding with a mixture of exertion and unbearable grief, heavy with love and longing, and with the dread of what she must do.

She wanted him to stop. She didn't want him. She didn't love him.

Alessandro had thought he knew the meaning of despair and loss, but he realised now he had not known them at all. He could feel his hands trembling as he released her. His throat was raw and his voice harsh as the plea he had promised he would not make burst from his throat in an agonised plea.

'Why? You want me! I know you do. If this is some game...'

Leonora shook her head. She didn't want to tell him, but the intimacy they had just shared could not be put aside—and besides, she was incurably honest.

'It isn't a game. Yes, I do want you. But you wouldn't want me if you knew the truth about me. I'm so ashamed. It's so humiliating. No man would want me if they knew, but especially a man like you.'

Tears thickened her voice.

What had she done? What secrets were there in her past that caused her such shame?

'If there have been others then that is only natural. But—'

Leonora started to laugh almost hysterically. She couldn't help it.

'Of course it is only natural. That's the whole point. There *haven't* been any others. I am not natural. I'm *unnatural*. What else can I be when I'm still a virgin?'

The air in the room seemed to thicken and go still. Alessandro looked at her, his heartbeat thudding, quickening from arousal to disbelief.

'You're a virgin?'

'Yes,' Leonora told him in a brittle voice, tossing her head. The defensive tomboy was stirring back to life. 'Ridiculous, isn't it? Perhaps I should wear a sign saying "Men beware. Virgin at large". It's all right, you don't have to say anything. I know how you feel. After all no man of your experience wants to go to bed with a virgin past her sell-by date. You want a woman you can enjoy having sex with—someone who can pleasure you as much as you can her. Not a…a woman like me who isn't even a proper woman…'

A virgin. She was a virgin. And she was hurting because of it, fearing his mockery and his rejection.

'You're right,' he told her softly. 'I *do* want a woman in my bed I can enjoy having sex with—a woman who can pleasure me as much as I intend to pleasure her, a woman who loves and desires me as much as I do her.'

He reached for her hand and she let him take it, unable to do anything other than let the pain roll down over her, crushing her and yet leaving her alive to experience even more pain.

'You *are* that woman, Leonora—my woman.'

'No,' she protested, not daring to believe him and certain that what he was saying was some kind of cruel joke.

'Yes.'

'But I'm not sensual, or skilled, or experienced like Sofia.'

Alessandro made a dismissive contemptuous sound deep in his throat. 'Sofia is as hard as nails and just about as sensual. True sensuality does not come from sexual experience but from within, from being with a partner who arouses it and shares it. Falcon was saying to me earlier how much he envies me because you and I share so much in common. I am not a virgin, but there is within me because of my childhood a desire—a need, in fact—to know that what is mine belongs only to me. Had you had ten lovers or a hundred it could not and would not have changed my love for you. But knowing that you have not, and that you will be exclusively mine, is a gift I never hoped to have. It is a soothing balm against a running sore within my psyche, the existence of which I have never been able to admit to myself until now, never mind to anyone else. Knowing I will not have to compete with any other man in your past...' Alessandro shook his head. 'I am ashamed to admit these things to you because of what they say about me.'

'No, you mustn't be,' Leonora assured him.

She *did* understand. She knew what he was revealing to her didn't spring from mere male ego or vanity but instead was something that went much deeper—a vulnerability within him, some might say a flaw, that only made him all the more human and loveable to her.

Even as her heart sang with the revelation that he loved her, she said, 'I don't want to disappoint you.'

'You will never disappoint me.'

He undressed her slowly and tenderly, encouraging her to undress him and then touch him, taking pleasure in her pleasure, taking time to reassure her. And in the end she was the one who urged him to possess her, crying out as she arched up against him, wrapping her long slim legs around him, her body knowing instinctively what it wanted from him and how to elicit it.

He thrust into her carefully, with the pad of his thumb finding her clitoris and caressing it as the pace of his rhythmic thrusts increased. Leonora clung to him, her breathing fast and shallow, her chest flushed with sexual desire, her whole being focused on their shared pleasure.

The convulsions began as he thrust deeper, making her cry out to him, imploring urgently, 'Deeper, Alessandro. Deeper and harder—yes, like that. Just like that.'

The convulsions gripped tighter and the thrust of his flesh within her own carried her over the threshold into full womanhood without her knowing anything other than the spiralling exploding miracle of her orgasm and the rhythmic surge that took him to his own completion.

Breathless, satiated, brimming over with joy and triumph, Leonora clung to Alessandro's naked and sweat-slick body, her head resting on his shoulder whilst her heartbeat raced, her heart itself filled to overflowing with the strength and the power of her love for him.

Never had she imagined that she might feel so blessed, so complete. There was no past nor any future, no doubt and no fear, only the wonderful and perfect rightness of the shared here and now.

She reached up and touched Alessandro's face, her own illuminated with all that she was feeling.

Alessandro was looking down at her, his face shadowed.

Her 'thank you' lilted, caught with the sweetness of her joy.

'We should get ready for the ball, otherwise we're going to be late,' Alessandro warned her, withdrawing from her, knowing that if he didn't it was unlikely they would put in an appearance at all. 'I don't want to let Falcon down.'

'No, of course not,' Leonora agreed valiantly.

She wasn't going to allow herself to feel disappointed or to regret anything just because he hadn't said anything about them sharing a future. It would be naive of her to think that his words of love to her earlier had been intended as a commitment. She must just be happy with what she had with him now, the fact that he loved her now, and not think about anything else.

Two hours later, with Alessandro on one side of his father and Falcon on the other, as she stood with Alessandro in the receiving line, greeting the arriving guests, Leonora was torn between pride and pain. Pride because she was Alessandro's, and pain because she knew that their shared time together might only be short.

The last of the guests had been received and welcomed. The quartet who had been playing in the background went to join the rest of the musicians in a specially designed alcove in the ballroom. The ballroom itself shimmered in the light of dozens of candles in elegant silver-gilt candelabra on the walls between the matching silver-gilt-framed mirrors. The scent of the white lilies and the greenery that made up the stunningly beautiful floral decorations filled the air.

The musicians struck up the first notes of a waltz and the guests, who had fallen back towards the walls, to leave the length of the ballroom floor free, turned expectantly to look towards their hosts. To Leonora's surprise, Alessandro turned to her, making her a small, formal half-bow.

He looked magnificent, in a medieval-style tunic of crimson cloth embroidered with the Leopardi arms worn over a grey undershirt, and a short cloak of scarlet lined with gold flowing from his shoulders. On a man of less male and athletic build such a costume would have looked ridiculous, but on Alessandro it looked magnificent. He was the first Leopardi, the powerful virile conqueror who had captured her heart and demanded his right to her body.

Leonora felt the breath lock in her lungs as he reached for her hand. Her own costume of several layers of the sheerest silk in varying shades of gold and bronze seemed to move with the thud of her heart. Eyes downcast, she allowed Alessandro to lead her onto the floor, hesitating only when he fully claimed her, taking her into his arms. Her gaze flew to his and she felt her body trembling as though she really was the Saracen princess whose virginity he had taken—as though in giving him her hand in public view she was like that princess, allowing him to show his people that he had claimed her for himself.

They danced alone, and Leonora was more conscious of the intimacy of his hold and her own fierce longing for it than she was of the whispered comments of their audience. Her gaze never left his face, her every breath saying how completely and proudly she had given herself to him and how totally she trusted him.

Alessandro drew her closer. She was *his*. He had claimed her in the privacy of his bed, and now he was claiming her in public.

After they had finished dancing, and the guests had clapped their performance enthusiastically, the musicians struck up again and the floor filled with dancers, allowing Alessandro to talk briefly and politely with some of the guests, whilst always keeping Leonora at his side.

For Leonora the evening passed in a daze of golden joy, highlighted by precious private moments carefully stored in her memory.

She must have talked, eaten, drunk at least some of the champagne she had been served, although she had no real recollection of doing so. All she knew and all she wanted to know was Alessandro.

'It will soon be midnight,' he told her, 'and Falcon is planning to make an important announcement. It's been too long since I kissed you. Will you be cold if we go out on the terrace?'

Leonora shook her head. What did it matter how cold she might be if Alessandro wanted to kiss her?

The doors to the terrace were locked, but Alessandro had the key, and Leonora noticed that he locked the doors behind them, so that they wouldn't be interrupted. The sky was so clear that she felt she could almost have reached out and touched the stars.

'You look lovely. You *are* lovely, Leonora—in every single way. I felt so proud tonight, having you at my side.'

'No. I was the one who felt proud to be with you,' Leonora told him.

She could see him smiling as he drew her close and kissed her, slowly and tenderly.

'I wish we could go back to our room,' Leonora whispered.

'You're a temptress—you know that, don't you?' Alessandro's voice was thick with passion. He squeezed her hand and told her, almost unsteadily, 'You remember I told you that my ancestor took the daughter of the Saracen he had vanquished as his mistress?'

Leonora nodded her head.

'What I didn't get round to telling you,' he informed her, shifting her weight in his arms so that he could look down into her face, 'was that he also made her his wife. You see, he fell in love with her—just as I have done with you. Marry me, Leonora.'

'You want to *marry* me?'

'Yes. And you've got exactly five minutes to make up your mind, because if the answer is no then I shall have to find Falcon and stop him announcing our engagement. I told him earlier that I love you, and that I want you to be my wife, and I can't think of any better way to tell the world than to make an announcement here tonight of our commitment to one another. If you are willing?'

She pretended to look grave.

'There's a condition,' she warned him.

Alessandro didn't care. She could make any condition she liked—including insisting on being the one to fly them when they travelled. All that mattered to him now was that she was his. She completed him, made him whole, and he had been a fool not to realise that the very first time he had read her job application and looked at her photograph.

'Mmm,' he murmured, as he lifted her hand to his lips and kissed her palm and then each finger in turn. 'What condition?'

'You must promise never, *ever* to tell my brothers about that spider.'

'What spider?'

'And I want us to have an even number of children so that there is no middle child.'

'Two, you mean?'

'Or four, or maybe even six.'

It was two minutes to midnight. Just enough time for Alessandro to kiss her with fierce exultation and commitment, and then reach into his pocket for a worn leather jeweller's box.

'If you don't like this then you shall have something else of your own choice,' Alessandro told her, opening the box. 'But this ring belonged to my great-great-grandmother on my mother's side. It is said that she married the man she loved and that their marriage was long and happy.'

The flawless single diamond on a plain gold band caught the light and captured it, holding it deep in its heart.

'It's beautiful and I love it,' Leonora told him truthfully.

When Alessandro slid it onto her finger the gold felt warm, almost caressing her finger, making her feel it was a true symbol of their love.

There was just time for one more all too brief kiss, and then Alessandro was guiding her back into the ballroom. Waiters were already circulating with trays holding glasses of champagne, and Falcon was waiting to lead them into the centre of the room.

'Ladies and gentlemen,' he began. 'Honoured friends and guests. It is my delight and my privilege to announce the engagement of my brother Alessandro Leopardi to Miss Leonora Thaxton. Please raise your glasses with me to Alessandro and to his wife-to-be, Leonora.'

When Alessandro held out his own glass to her, in a symbolic gesture of intimacy and promise, so that she could drink from it, Leonora trembled from head to foot with happiness.

'Your father is watching us,' Leonora whispered.

Alessandro turned his head to look at him.

'He looks so old and alone,' Leonora told him.

'Yes, but it is a situation of his own making. I don't want to talk about the past. I want to live in the present and in the future—with you, Leonora. I love you so much.'

'And I you.'

Leonora's breath quickened. Suddenly all she wanted was for them to be able to slip away to the privacy of their suite, where they could make their vows of love to one another in private.

Falcon watched them. It was obvious that they were madly in love with one another. Alessandro had eyes only for Leonora and she for him. Both his brothers had found love and wanted nothing more than to marry the women who had claimed their hearts. Falcon found it not just hard but virtually impossible to imagine that *he* would ever fall in love—even though he accepted that it was his duty to marry and sire an heir…

* * * * *

FALCON

PROLOGUE

FALCON LEOPARDI grimaced in distaste. This was supposed
to be a memorial gathering to mark what would have been
the birthday of his late half-brother Antonio. It was their
father's idea, and one that strictly speaking Falcon did not
approve of—especially not an excuse to get drunk. But
then the majority of Antonio's so-called friends obviously
shared his late half-brother's love of over-indulgence just
as they had shared his love of a louche lifestyle.

One of them was breathing alcoholic fumes over Falcon
now, as he leaned drunkenly towards him confidingly and
spoke to him.

'Did Tonio ever tell you about that woman whose drink
he spiked in Cannes last year? He swore to us all that he'd
get his revenge on her for turning him down, and he did
that, all right. Last I heard she was trying to claim that he'd
fathered the brat she was carrying.'

Falcon, who had been about to move away in disgusted
irritation, turned back to look at the unpleasant specimen
of manhood now reeling unsteadily in front of him.

'I seem to remember him mentioning something or
other about the situation,' he lied. 'But why don't you
refresh my memory?'

The drunk was more than happy to oblige.

'We'd seen her at Nikki Beach. She wasn't joining in

the fun like the other girls there, even though she was with one of the film outfits. Always turned up in a blouse and skirt, looking like a schoolteacher. Antonio soaked the shirt with champagne for a joke, trying to get her to lighten up, but she wasn't having any of it. Really got his back up, she did—the way she treated him. Rejecting him like she was something special. He told us all he was going to have his revenge on her, and he certainly did that. He found out where she was staying, then he bribed one of the waiters to slip something into her drink. Knocked her out flat. It took three of us to get her back to her room. Of course Antonio swore us to secrecy, threatened us with a whole lot of bad stuff if what he'd done ever got out. 'Course, me telling you now is different, 'cos he's dead and you're his brother.' He hiccupped and then belched, before continuing. 'Tonio made us keep guard outside. He told us afterwards that she was so tight she must have been a virgin.'

The man's expression began to alter and his manner changed from one of swaggering confidence to something far more sheepish as Falcon's cold silence penetrated his drink-befuddled state, bringing home to him the true shameful reality of the horrific tale he was relating. 'Not that Tonio got away with it,' he rushed to reassure Falcon. 'He told me that her brother came after him, saying that he'd got her pregnant. But that there was no way he was going to do as she wanted and provide for the kid she was carrying.'

Falcon hadn't said a word whilst his late brother's friend had been speaking. He found it easy, though, to accept his late half-brother's role in the nasty, sordid little incident the other man had described to him. It was typical of

Antonio, and underlined—if any underlining had been necessary—exactly why Falcon and his two younger brothers had so disliked their half-brother during his short life and had not mourned his passing.

'What was her name? Can you remember?' he asked the drunk now.

The other man shook his head, and then frowned in concentration, before telling Falcon, 'Think it might have been Anna or Annie—something like that. She was English—I know that.'

As though Falcon's cold contempt chilled him, the drunk shivered and then staggered away. No doubt keen to find himself another drink, Falcon reflected as he looked across to where his two brothers and their wives were seated with his father.

Their father, the Prince, had worshipped and spoiled his youngest son, the only child he had had with the woman who had been his mistress during his marriage to the mother of his elder three sons' mother—his wife once she was dead.

He had claimed, after Antonio's death in a car accident, that Antonio's last words to him had been to say that he had a child—conceived whilst Antonio was in Cannes—and he had demanded that this child be found.

Falcon had believed that he had left no stone unturned trying to do this—without any success—but now realised that he had overlooked the fact that his brother had lived his life among the slimy waste of humanity that was expert at scuttling away from the too-bright light of overturned stones.

He knew what he had to do now, of course. The only question was whether or not he told his brothers before or after he found the woman his half-brother had drugged, raped and impregnated with his child—because find her he most certainly would. Even if he had to turn the whole world upside down to do so. His honour and his duty to the Leopardi name would accept nothing less. On balance, telling them first would be easier....

CHAPTER ONE

ANNIE rubbed her eyes. Well shaped and an intense shade of almost violet-blue, with thick long eyelashes, they were eyes any woman could be proud of—if they hadn't been aching with tiredness and feeling as though they were filled with grit. She lifted her hand, its wrist so slender that it looked dangerously fragile, pushing the heavy weight of her shoulder-length, naturally blonde and softly curling hair off her face. Normally she wore it scraped back in a neat knot, but Ollie had grabbed it earlier when she had been giving him his bath, and in the end it had been easier to leave it down. She loved her baby so much. He meant everything to her, and there was nothing she wouldn't do to protect him and keep him safe. Nothing.

She had been reading all evening. Part-time freelance research work didn't pay very well—certainly not as well as her previous job, which had been working as a researcher for a novelist turned playwright. Tom had paid her very well indeed, and he and his wife had become good friends. Annie's face clouded. The lighting in her small one-bedroom flat didn't really give off enough light for the demanding work she was doing—even if it was energy-efficient.

Next to her work on the cramped space of the small folding table there was a letter from her stepbrother amongst the post forwarded from her old address. She shivered and looked over her shoulder, almost as though she feared that Colin himself might suddenly materialise out of the ether.

Colin was living in the house that had originally belonged to her father, which should have been hers. He had stolen it from her—just as he had stolen... She flinched, not wanting to think about her stepbrother.

But there were times when she had to do so, for Ollie's safety. Her stepbrother disapproved of the fact that she had kept Ollie, instead of having him put up for adoption as he had wanted her to do. But nothing could make her willingly part with her baby—not even Colin's attempts to make her feel guilty for keeping him. He had insisted, that someone else—a couple—would give him a better life than she could as a single mother. Colin could be very convincing and persuasive when he wanted to be. She had been desperately afraid that he would win others over to his cause.

Sometimes she felt that she would never be able to stop looking over her shoulder, afraid that Colin had tracked them down and that somehow he would succeed in parting her from her son.

She would never even have told him about her pregnancy, but Susie, the wife of the author she had been working for when 'it'—her rape by Antonio Leopardi—had happened, had thought she was doing her a favour by writing to him and telling him what had happened. Susie had been thrilled when Colin had offered her a home after Ollie's birth, and all the support she needed.

Annie had refused his offer, though. She, after all, knew him far better than Susie did. Instead she had stayed in her flat, using the excuse that she wanted Ollie to be born at the local hospital because of its excellent reputation.

Colin had refused to be put off and had insisted on continuing to visit her. Initially he had even pretended that he agreed with her decision to keep her baby once it was born, but that pretence had soon vanished once he'd realised that Antonio Leopardi was not going to respond to Colin's demand for financial support for his son.

Not that Colin had said anything of this to Susie and Tom, who had been so kind to her.

In the end Annie had begun to feel so desperate and so pressured, afraid that somehow Colin might succeed in forcing her and her baby apart, that a few weeks after Ollie's birth, whilst Colin had been away in Scotland, sorting out the affairs of an elderly cousin of his father's who had recently died, she had decided not to renew the lease on her existing flat and to move away instead, to start a new life for herself and Ollie.

Without telling anyone what she was doing—not even Susie and Tom, who had so obviously been taken in by Colin—she had found herself a new flat and new work, and then she had simply disappeared, leaving strict instructions that her forwarding address must remain confidential. It had been easy enough to do in a big city like London.

That had been five months ago now. But she still didn't feel safe—not one little bit.

She had felt guilty not saying anything to Susie and Tom, but she couldn't afford to take any risks. They didn't know Colin as she did, and they didn't know what he was capable of doing—or how intensely single-minded he could be. She shivered again, remembering how unhappy she had been when their parents had first married, and how she had tried to explain to her mother how apprehensive and ill at ease Colin had made her feel, with his concentrated focus on her, watching everything she did.

He had been away at university then, aged nineteen to her twelve, but after their parents had married—he had decided to change courses, and had ended up living at home and travelling daily to his new university.

Colin had taken a dislike to her best friend Claire, and Annie's mother had suggested to Annie that it might be better if Claire didn't come to the house any more after an incident during which Colin had nearly reversed his father's car into Claire whilst she had been riding her bike.

And now Colin had taken a dislike to Ollie. Annie shivered again.

She had never known her own father. A soldier, from a long line of army men, he had died in an ambush abroad before she had been born. But Annie had been very happy growing up with her mother.

Her father had left them very well provided for—there had been money in his family which had come down to him, and Annie's mother had always told Annie it would ultimately come down to her. But now it was Colin's, because her mother had died before her second husband, meaning that the house had passed into his hands and then into Colin's. The home that should have been hers and Oliver's was denied to them.

Automatically she looked anxiously towards her son's cot. Ollie was fast asleep. Unable to resist the temptation, she got up and went to stand looking down at him. He was so beautiful, so perfect, that sometimes just looking at him filled her with so much awe and love that she felt as though her heart would burst with the pressure of it. He was a good baby, healthy and happy, and so gorgeous—

with his head of silky dark curls and his startling blue-grey
eyes with thick black lashes—that people constantly
stopped to admire him. He was bright too, and full of curiosity about the world around him.

They adored him at the council-run nursery where she
had to leave him every weekday whilst she went off to her
cleaning job—the only other work she had been able to get
without too many questions being asked. Most of the
others on the team of agency cleaners she worked with
were foreign—hard working, but reluctant to talk very
much about themselves.

Her present life was a world away from the world in
which she had grown up and the future she had expected
to have. Ollie's childhood, unlike hers, would not be spent
in a large comfortable house with its own big garden on
the edge of a picturesque Dorset village. The area of the
city where they lived was run-down, with large blocks of
flats—once she would have been horrified at the thought
of living here, but now she welcomed its anonymity and
its fellow inhabitants, who neither welcomed questions
nor asked them.

Ollie opened his eyes and looked up at her, giving her
a beaming smile. Annie felt her insides melt. She loved
him so much. What an extraordinary thing mother love
was—empowering her to love her son despite the horror
of his conception.

She flinched again. She tried never to think about what
had happened to her in Cannes. Mercifully she had no
memory of her ordeal, thanks to the drug that had been
slipped into her drink. Susie, who had found her in her
room, still drugged and dazed late in the morning after the
night of the rape, had wanted her to go to the police but

she had refused—too much in shock and too fearful to trust them to believe her. Susie had been wonderfully kind to her. Annie missed her kindness and her friendship.

Like Colin, Susie had felt that her rapist should be forced at least to financially support his child, and it had been Susie who had supplied her stepbrother with Antonio's name—something Annie herself had refused to do.

Annie hadn't been surprised when Antonio had refused to do anything, and she had felt relieved when she had read in the papers about Antonio's death. Now there would never be any need for Ollie to have to learn about his father or how he had been conceived. Unless Colin found them.

Her stomach clenched. He couldn't. He mustn't. And she mustn't think about him doing so just in case somehow her thoughts enabled it to happen.

She thought of herself as a logical, realistic sort of person, well aware of the harsh reality of life, but sometimes at times like this, when she felt so dreadfully alone, she wished that there were such a thing as fairy godmothers who, with one wave of a magical wand, could somehow transport her and Ollie to a place where they could be together and safe, where Colin simply couldn't reach them.

If she believed in fairy godmothers, guardian angels and wishes then that would be her wish—but of course she didn't. And wishes couldn't come true just because one wished them.

The foyer of the five-star hotel was empty of any of its wealthy guests as Annie got down on her hands and knees to remove a piece of trodden-down chewing gum from the marble floor. Her shift was actually over, but the reception-ist—who seemed to have taken a dislike to her—had insisted that she pick up the litter dropped, Annie was sure quite deliberately, by the woman who had walked through the lobby a few minutes earlier. Her high heels had clacked on the marble floor, and her look of contempt for Annie had been all too plain as she'd smoothed down the skirt of her no-doubt expensive outfit and then dropped the chewing gum on the floor.

The sun was shining outside, its brilliant rays getting in Annie's eyes and dazzling her. She blinked, raising her head in an attempt to avoid the too-bright light.

Falcon wasn't in a very good mood. He had flown into London earlier in the week and had gone straight to a meeting with the head of what was supposed to be the country's best missing person tracking agency, only to be told that whilst the agency had initially managed to identify Annie Johnson as the mother of Antonio's child, she had disappeared five months ago, taking her baby with her, and they had not as yet managed to find her.

Falcon had spent a fruitless afternoon with Annie's stepbrother, to whom he had taken an instant dislike, and now he had received a message from his youngest brother Rocco, telling him that their father's health had suffered a sudden decline.

'He's stable now, and back at the *castello*.' Rocco had told him. 'But the hospital says that he is very frail.'

He needed to be in Sicily, Falcon knew, he had a duty to his family to be there. But he also had a duty to this child conceived so casually by his half-brother, and denied by him as though he was no more than a piece of detritus.

Falcon had never liked Antonio. He hadn't thought it was possible for his contempt for him to increase, but he had been wrong.

As he stepped into the foyer of his hotel, his eyes shielded from the glare of the sun by gold-rimmed discreetly non-logoed Cartier glasses, the first thing he saw was a cleaner, kneeling on the floor beside her bucket of dirty water. She was wearing a body-shrouding, washed-out blue overall and her hair was scraped back from her make-up-free face, but when she lifted her face to avoid the sunlight glaring into her eyes, Falcon's heart turned over inside his chest and his heart started to race.

It was her. There was no mistake. After all, he'd only just left the office where her photograph had been pinned to the file in front of him. There was no mistaking those intensely blue eyes, nor that elegantly boned and beautifully structured face, with its small straight nose and its softly full mouth—even if right now her skin was drained of life and her expression etched in lines of exhaustion.

The hand she'd reached out to remove the flat grey-white pat of chewing gum that someone had left on the otherwise immaculate floor was red and swollen, her wrist thin and fragile, and her scraped back hair was out of sight beneath some sort of protective cover. But it was her. By some miracle, it was her.

The receptionist was still glowering at her, causing Annie to feel a sudden rush of anger. She had worked over her allotted hours, time for which she would not be paid, and the chewing gum wasn't her responsibility. She stood up abruptly—and then gasped as her action brought her into immediate physical contact with someone. Not just someone, she recognised as male hands came out to grab her, somehow sliding up under the gaping arms of her overall to fasten round her bare skin. His intention was to fend her off, she imagined, rather than save her from stumbling, since such a man was hardly likely to care about the fate of someone like her. He was wearing an expensive suit, his eyes shielded from her inspection by dark-lensed sunglasses, and his hair were dark and his skin tanned.

He was still holding her—waiting for her to apologise for daring to breathe the same air as him, she thought bitterly. She tugged away from him, only to have his grip on her arms tighten. She looked up at him. A discomforting feeling was running through her body, its source the point of contact between his hands and her skin. Her pulse had started to jump and she was breathing too fast as her heart raced. She felt dizzy, her lungs starved of oxygen as though she had forgotten how to breathe and yet she *was* breathing—although very unsteadily.

Sensations like the mechanics of a long-unused piece of machinery were coming to painful life inside her. She wanted, she discovered in bemused disbelief, to lean into him, to have his arms come fully around her so that she was held against his maleness. A shudder ripped through her, and her body was hot with guilt and shame.

The most extraordinary feeling had Falcon in its grip. He didn't know what it was or where it had come from. The only comparison that came readily to his mind was a memory of being young and standing on the edge of one of Sicily's most dangerous clifftops in the middle of a fierce storm, feeling the wind buffet him, knowing that it could take him and do what it wished with him. He had both wanted to fight its power and give in to it. What he'd felt was a mixture of awe and exhilaration, an awareness of a great power and a desire to test himself against it. It was a sense of being alive, heightened and stretched taut, of being on the edge of something dangerous and compelling.

The receptionist had left her desk and was coming towards them. Somehow Annie managed to wrench herself free and pick up her bucket so that she could make a speedy exit. She could hear the receptionist apologising as she did so.

CHAPTER TWO

SACKED. She had been sacked because a hotel guest had—shock, horror—had to *touch* her. The hotel receptionist had obviously reported the incident, and a complaint had then been made to the firm that employed her. Her manager had been waiting for her when she had returned with the other workers to the depot, to give her the news. As a part timer she had no comeback. She was now out of a job.

It was supposed to be summer, but the morning's bright sunshine had now gone and it had started to rain. As she stepped out into the street Annie hunched into her raincoat—a good-quality trenchcoat that belonged to her previous life, a life before the death of her mother and the birth of her son.

She was twenty-four years old, she reminded herself. Far too old to cry because she was alone and vulnerable and desperately worried about how she was going to hold everything together without her cleaning job.

The city streets were busy now, and she didn't want to be late collecting Ollie from his nursery. There'd been a notice pinned up in the nursery asking for teachers' assistants at the nearby primary school. Annie would have loved to have applied, but it was too dangerous. They'd check up on her and discover that Antonio's clever lawyers had threatened to sue her for claiming that he'd raped her, saying that in reality she had consented to having sex with him. Her reputation would be ruined. She had no proof that she had been raped. It had been her word against his and she couldn't even remember what had happened. She knew beyond any shadow of a doubt, though, that she would not have consented.

Her stepbrother had been furious when he had received that telephone call from Antonio's solicitors. He had been so sure that Antonio would pay up. She shivered, even though it wasn't cold, and then pinned a forced smile to her face as she climbed the short flight of stone steps that led to the door of the nursery.

The sunny yellow-painted hall walls were decorated with the children's brightly coloured artwork, and Mrs Nkobu, one of the more senior staff, greeted her with a warm smile.

'There's a man waiting to see you. Mrs Ward wasn't for letting him—she told him it was against the rules—but it's plain to see that he's the kind that doesn't pay attention to anyone's rules but his own,' she told Annie conspiratorially.

Fear iced down Annie's spine.

Colin had found them.

Strictly speaking the nursery wasn't supposed to allow anyone not authorised by a parent to have access to any of the children, but Annie knew how persuasive Colin could be. Nausea curdled her stomach. He would try to take over her life again. He would say it was in her best interests. He would remind her that their parents had left their assets to him because they trusted him to look after her—even though her mother had told her that the house would come to her, because it had belonged to her father.

She mustn't think about any of that now, she told

herself. She would need all her energy and strength to survive the present; she mustn't waste it on the past.

'He's in the carers' room,' Mrs Nkobu informed her, referring to the small fusty room with a glass wall through which parents and guardians could watch the children whilst waiting to collect them.

Annie nodded her head, but instead of going to the carers' room she went to the nursery, busy with other mothers collecting their children. Ollie was sitting on the floor, playing with some toys, and as always when she saw him Annie's heart flooded with love. The minute he saw her he held out his arms to her to be picked up. Only once she was cradling him tightly in her arms did she feel brave enough to look through the glass panels into the room beyond them.

There was only one person there. He was standing with his back to the glass and he was not Colin. But any relief she might have felt was obliterated by the shock of recognition that arced through her, sending through her exactly the same tingling sensation of deadened sensory nerve-endings awakened into painful life as she had felt earlier in the hotel lobby, when he had held her.

A long-ago memory of herself as a young teenager came back to her. Inside her head she could see herself, giggling with a schoolfriend over a handsome young teenage pop idol they had both had a crush on. She had felt so alive then—so happy, and so unquestioningly secure in her unfolding sexuality. She held Ollie even tighter, causing him to wriggle in her arms at the same moment as the man from the hotel lobby turned round.

He wasn't wearing his sunglasses now, and she could see his eyes.

The breath left her lungs with so much force that it might as well have been driven out by a physical blow. She knew who or rather *what* he was immediately. How could she not when the eyes set in the scimitar-harsh maleness of his face were her son's eyes? That he and Ollie shared the same blood was undeniable—and yet he looked nothing like Ollie's father, the man who had raped her. Antonio Leopardi had had a soft, full-fleshed face, and pebble-hard brown eyes set too close together. He had been only of medium height, and thickset. This man was tall with broad shoulders, and his body—as she already knew—was hard with muscles, not soft with over-indulgence. He smelled of clean skin, and some cologne so subtle she couldn't put a name to it, not of alcohol and heavy aftershave.

He was clean-shaven, his thick dark hair groomed, whereas Antonio had favoured stubble and his hair thickly gelled.

Everything about this man said that he set the highest of standards for himself even more than for others. This man's word, once given, would be given for all time.

Everything about Antonio had said that he was not to be trusted, but despite their differences this man had to be related to her abuser. Ollie was the proof of that.

She wanted to turn and run, fear tumbling through her as she felt her defences as weak as a house of cards; but her fear was not fear of the man because he was a man, Annie had time to recognize. It was a different fear from the one that lay inside her like a heavy stone. Instinctively she knew that this man was no threat to *her*, and that *she* was in no danger from him. His focus wasn't on her. It was on her son—on Ollie.

Her mouth had gone dry and her heart was pounding recklessly, using up her strength. There was no escape for her. She knew that. Still she tried to delay the inevitable, her hands trembling as she strapped Ollie into his buggy and then reluctantly pushed it to the door.

He was waiting for her in the corridor, one strong, lean brown hand reaching for the buggy, forcing her to move her own hand or risk having him close his hand over her own.

Falcon frowned as he registered her reaction to him. Was her recoil part of the legacy Antonio had left her? He had been struck when he had seen her earlier by her vulnerability, and by his unfamiliar desire to reassure her. Now that feeling had returned.

Falcon wasn't used to experiencing such strong feelings for anyone outside his immediate family. He had never denied to himself his protective love for his two younger brothers, nor his belief that, as their elder, in the absence of their father's love and their mother's presence in their lives, it was his responsibility to protect and nurture them.

He had grown up shouldering that responsibility, but he had never before felt that fierce tug of emotional protectiveness towards anyone else.

It was because of the child, of course. There could be no other reason for his illogical reaction.

It had taken him several hours of impatient telephone calls and pressure to track her down via the agency that had employed her—thanks to that wretched receptionist preventing him from following her at the hotel.

This morning he had felt sorry for her. Now he was motivated solely by his duty to his family name to make amends for what Antonio had done, he assured himself.

And of course to ensure that Antonio's son grew up knowing his Leopardi heritage. It had taken him longer than he had wished and a great deal of money to track him down, but now that he had there could be no doubting that the child was a Leopardi. He had known that the minute he had seen him at the nursery. The boy's blood was stamped into his features, and Falcon had seen from the woman's expression when she had looked at him that she knew that too.

They were outside now, with no one to overhear them.

'Who are you?' Annie demanded unsteadily. 'And what do you want?'

'I am Falcon Leopardi, the eldest of Antonio's half-brothers from our father's first marriage.'

Colin had mentioned Antonio's family to her—or rather he had tried to. But she had refused to listen. Antonio had, after all, refused to acknowledge his son.

'You are Antonio's *brother*?'

The tone of her voice betrayed disbelief, and Falcon detected a deeper core of something that sounded like re-vulsion. He could hardly blame her for that. In fact, he shared her revulsion.

'No,' he corrected her grimly. 'We were only half-brothers.'

How well she understood that need to differentiate and distance oneself from a supposed sibling. But how ridicu-lous of her to allow herself to imagine that she and this man could have anything in common, could share that deep-rooted antipathy and guilt that had been so much a part of her growing up.

Even now she could still her mother saying plaintively, almost pleadingly, 'But, darling, Colin is just trying to be friends with you. Why can't you be nicer to him?' She had tried so hard to tell her mother how she had felt, but how could you explain what you did not understand yourself? In the end it had driven a wedge between them—a gulf on one side of which stood Colin, the good stepchild, and on the other side her, the bad daughter.

Where had she gone? Falcon wondered, watching the shadows seeping pain as they darkened her eyes. Wherever it was it was somewhere in her past, he recognized. The quality of her silence held a message of her helpless inability to change anything.

It was the present and the future that he was here for, though.

She must resent Antonio—more than resent him, he would have thought. Although her love for her child was obvious, and backed up by all the information his enquiry agents had been able to gather. She was an exemplary and devotedly loving mother. Apart from the fact that for some reason she had turned down her stepbrother's offer of a home under his roof. Colin Riley had not been able to furnish him with a logical explanation for that, although he *had* implied that there had been some kind of quarrel which she, despite all his attempts to repair the damage, had refused to make up.

'She's always been inclined to be over-emotional and to overreact,' he had told Falcon. 'All I wanted to do—all I've *ever* wanted to do—is help her.'

'There was no love lost between the three of us and Antonio.'

Falcon's voice, his English perfect and unaccented, brought Annie back out of the past.

'I will not seek to hide that fact from you—nor the fact

that Antonio was our father's favourite son. I can also assure you that Antonio's choice of lifestyle was not ours. It could never have been and was never condoned by us.'

Annie looked at him, and then looked away again, her heart jumping as it always did whenever she had to think about Ollie's conception. Falcon Leopardi was obviously trying to tell her that he and his brothers were not tarred with the same brush as their younger half-brother. His choice of the word *'assure'* suggested that convincing her that his morals were very different from his half-brother was something he was determined to do. But why?'

'As to what I want…'

He paused for so long that Annie looked at him again, hard fingers of uncertainty and unease tightening round her heart when she saw that he was looking at Ollie.

'Before his death,' Falcon continued, 'Antonio told our father that there was a child. But he died before he could give more details. Such was the love our father felt for Antonio that he demanded that this child be traced. When no child could be found we assumed that laying claim to its existence had been another example of Antonio's enjoyment of deceit.'

Falcon paused again. She'd kept her gazed fixed straight ahead of her whilst he was speaking, but he could see from the way her grip had tightened on the buggy how tense she was.

The tale of what had been done to her was one of breathtakingly callous cruelty that would fill any decent person with revulsion. The only merciful aspect of it was that she herself apparently had no recollection of what had occurred. There was no doubt in Falcon's mind that the rape had been a deliberate act of punishment, intended to humiliate her—

not conducted because Antonio had hoped to arouse her to passion and desire for him. That fitted in so well with everything Falcon knew about his half-brother's warped personality.

'Naturally, when it came to my knowledge that there might after all be a child, I had to find out the truth.'

He had stopped walking now, forcing Annie to do the same.

'How…how did it come to your knowledge?' She had to force the words out.

Falcon looked at her. He believed strongly in telling the truth. The truth, after all, was the only worthwhile foundation for anything that was worth having.

'A friend of Antonio's told me about your drink being spiked, about what he did, and I put two and two together.'

Annie had a childish desire to close her eyes, as though somehow by shutting everything out she could magically make herself disappear. Just to hear him say those words was as searingly humiliating as though she had been stripped naked in the street. Worse, because they ripped away her protection, laying bare her private shame.

'I know you contacted Antonio to tell him of the birth of his son—'

'No.' Annie checked him immediately, her pride reasserting itself. 'I didn't contact him. I would never— It was my stepbrother who did that. I didn't know about it until… until Colin told me that Antonio was denying that—that anything had happened.'

Falcon frowned. Was this perhaps the cause of the quarrel between them?

'Your stepbrother didn't mention anything about Antonio denying he had fathered your child when I spoke to him. He was most concerned about you, and asked me to keep him informed of any progress I might make in my search for you.'

Annie felt as though her heart had stopped beating.

She turned towards Falcon, imploring him. 'You haven't…you haven't told him where I am, have you?'

Falcon's frown deepened.

'He told me that his sole aim is to help and protect you.'

To help and protect *her*, but not Ollie. Colin didn't want anything to do with her baby, and if he had his way, Ollie would be removed from her life for ever.

How long did she have before Colin found her and started waging his relentless war to make her have Ollie adopted all over again? Panic clawed at her stomach. Everyone had always said how lucky she was to have such a devoted stepbrother, but they didn't know him as she did.

'He mustn't know where we are.'

In her panic she had revealed more than was wise, Annie recognised as she saw the way Falcon Leopardi was watching her. He was waiting for her to elaborate, to give him a logical reason as to why she didn't want Colin to find them.

'Colin believes that it would be better if Ollie was adopted,' she eventually managed to tell him.

Because he had not been able to get Antonio to pay up? Or because he felt it was the best option for the child? Falcon didn't think he needed to spend much time considering the two options. Colin had asked him specifically if there were any assets likely to come to Oliver from Antonio's estate or his family.

'But you don't agree with him?' Falcon asked now.

'No. I could never give him up. *Never*. Nothing and no one could ever make me do so.'

The passion in her expression and her voice changed her completely, bringing her suddenly to life, revealing the true perfection of her delicate beauty.

Falcon felt as though someone had suddenly punched him in the chest, rendering him unable to get his breath properly.

'I agree that a child as young as Oliver needs his mother,' he told her, as soon as he was back in control of himself. 'However, your son is a Leopardi—and as such it is only right and proper that he grows up amongst his own family and his own people in his own country. It is my duty to Oliver and to my family to ensure that he is raised as a Leopardi—and that you, as his mother, are treated as the mother of a Leopardi should be treated. That is why I am here. To take you both back to Sicily with me.'

Annie stared at him. His talk of duty was a world apart from the world she knew. Such a word belonged to another time, a feudal ancient time, and yet somehow it resonated within her.

'You want to take Ollie and me to Sicily—to live there?' she asked unsteadily, spacing out the words to clarify them inside her own head and make sure she had not misunderstood him.

His 'yes' was terse—like the brief inclination of his head.

'But you have no proof that Ollie is—'

The look he was giving her caused her to go silent.

'The evidence of his blood is quite plain to both of us,' he told her. 'You have seen it yourself.' He paused and looked down at the stroller before looking back to her. 'The child could be mine. He bears the Leopardi stamp quite clearly.'

His! Why did that assertion strike so compellingly into her heart?

'He doesn't look anything like Antonio.' He was all she could manage to say.

'No,' Falcon agreed. 'Antonio took after his mother, which I dare say is why our father loved him so much. He was obsessed by her, and that obsession killed our own mother and destroyed our childhood, depriving us of our father's love and our mother's presence. That will not happen to your child. In Sicily he will have you—his mother—the love and protection of his uncles, and the companionship of his cousins. He will be a Leopardi.'

He made it all sound so simple and so…so right. But she knew nothing of him of or his family other than that he had taken the trouble to track them down because he wanted Ollie.

How could she trust him—a stranger?

As though Falcon sensed her anxiety, he asked, 'You love your son, don't you?'

'Of course I do.'

'Then you must surely want what is best for him?'

'Yes,' Annie agreed helplessly.

'You will agree, I think, that he will have a far better life growing up in Sicily as a Leopardi than he could have here?'

'With a mother who works as a cleaner, you mean?' Annie challenged him.

'I am not the one who makes the rules of economics that say a financially disadvantaged child will suffer a great deal of hardship in his life. And besides, it is not just a matter of money—although of course that is important. You are alone in the world—you no longer have any contact with your stepbrother; you are all the family Oliver has. That is not healthy for a child, and it has been proven that is especially not healthy for a boy child to have only his mother. In Sicily, Oliver will have a proper family. If you love him as much as you claim, then for his sake you will be willing to come to Sicily. What, after all, is there to keep you here?'

If his last question was brutal it was also truthful, Annie admitted. There was *nothing* to keep her here—except of course that you did not go off to a foreign country with a man you did not know. You especially did not do so when you had a six-month-old beloved child to protect.

But in Sicily there would no Colin to fear. No dread of waking up to find her stepbrother leaning over Oliver's cot with that fixed look on his face, as she had once found him when he had visited her shortly after Ollie's birth.

Something—she didn't know what, other than that it was some deep core instinct—told her that in Falcon Leopardi's hands her precious son would be safe, and that those hands would hold him surely and protectively against all danger.

But what about her? What about the disquieting, unwanted, dangerous reaction she sensed within herself to him as a woman to his man? Panic seized her but she fought it down. It was Ollie she had to think of now, not herself. His needs and not hers. Falcon Leopardi was right to say that Ollie would have a far better life in Sicily as a Leopardi than he ever could here in London alone with her. When she added into that existing equation the potential threat of her stepbrother there was only one decision she could take, wasn't there?

As she struggled to come to terms with what the surrender of herself and her son into Falcon's care would mean, she reminded herself that only this morning she had laughed at herself for wishing for the impossible—for the magical waving of a wand to transport her somewhere she and Ollie could be safe.

That impossible had now happened, and she must, *must* seize the opportunity—for her son's sake. For Ollie. Nothing mattered more to her than her baby.

A strange dizzying sensation had filled her, making her feel giddy and weightless, as though she might almost float above the pavement. It took her several seconds to recognise that the feeling was one of relief at the removal of a heavy weight.

People would think she was crazy, going off with a man she didn't know, trusting her son to him. If she confided in Susie and Tom, who had been so kind in drumming up research work for her among Tom's writing friends while she was pregnant, they would ask questions and warn her to be careful. Susie would remind her of Colin's offer and look reproachfully at her. Susie had never understood why she hadn't accepted Colin's offer of a home. She had thought him kind and concerned. She had agreed with him about the benefits of having Ollie adopted.

How desperately she regretted letting slip to Susie in a moment of weakness that she had a stepbrother, and then letting Susie coax his name and address out of her. Susie had meant well when she had contacted him behind her back, believing that she was doing the right thing, and Colin had behaved in an exemplary fashion—playing the role of caring stepbrother to the hilt during her pregnancy, taking charge of everything.

'What happens if I refuse?' Annie asked now.

Falcon had been expecting her question.

'If you refuse, then I shall pursue my rights as Oliver's blood relative through the courts.'

He meant it, Annie recognised.

'You're asking me to accept a great deal on trust,' she pointed out. 'I have no reason to trust your family and every reason not to do so.'

'Antonio was never a true Leopardi. By his behaviour he dishonoured himself and our name, just as he dishonoured you. It is my duty to put right that wrong. You have my word that you will come to no harm whilst you are under my protection—from anyone or anything.'

Feudal words to match his feudal mindset, Annie thought, more affected by what he had said than she wanted to admit. He was offering her something she already knew she craved: respite and safety. What option did she have other than to take them when they were offered?

She sucked in a steadying breath, and then asked as calmly as she could, 'When would we have to leave?'

She had given in far more easily than Falcon had expected. Was that a reason for him to feel suspicious of her? Suspicious? No. After all, he knew all there was to know about her. But curious? Perhaps, yes.

'Soon,' he answered her. 'The sooner the better. My father isn't well. In fact, he is very frail, and it is his greatest wish to see Antonio's child.'

'There are things I shall need to do,' Annie began.

The reality of what she had committed to—not just herself but more importantly Oliver too—was only just beginning to sink in. But she could tell from Falcon

Leopardi's expression that he would not allow her to have any second thoughts.

'Such as?' he questioned, confirming her thoughts.

'I shall have to notify Ollie's nursery—and the council. And I'll need to check to see if Ollie needs any special injections for Sicily.'

'He doesn't. And as for the nursery and your flat, you can safely leave all that to me. You will, however, both need clothes suitable for a hot climate. It is high summer in Sicily now.'

New clothes? How on earth was she going to afford those?

Humiliatingly, as though he had guessed what she was thinking, Falcon continued smoothly, 'Naturally I shall cover the cost of whatever is needed.'

'We aren't charity cases.' Humiliation made Annie snap. 'I'm not letting you buy our clothes.'

'No? Then I shall have to telephone ahead to one of my sisters-in-law and ask them to provide a suitable wardrobe for you both. They are both English, by the way, so I expect you will find you have a great deal in common with them. My youngest brother Rocco and his wife already have one adopted child—a boy the same age as Oliver.'

His brothers had English wives? She would have other female company? A little of Annie's anxiety receded— only to return as she wondered how his brothers' wives would react to her.

'Do you all live together?' she asked uncertainly. She had only the haziest knowledge of Italian family life—and none at all of aristocratic Sicilian family life.

'Yes and no. Rocco has his own home on the island, whilst Alessandro and I both have our own apartments within the Leopardi *castello*, where my father also lives. A suite of rooms will be made ready for your occupation.'

'Mine and Ollie's?' Annie checked.

'Of course. His place is with you. I have already said so. Now—' Falcon flicked back his cuff to look at his watch '—we shall meet tomorrow morning in order to do necessary shopping. I shall call for you both at your flat and then with any luck we should be ready to leave for Sicily tomorrow evening. I shall request Alessandro to have a private jet made ready for us. As for all the necessary paperwork with regard to your life here, as I said, you may safely leave all of that to me.'

'And you won't tell Colin that you've found me?'

She hadn't meant to ask, and she certainly hadn't meant to sound so pathetically and desperately in need of reassurance, but it was too late to wish the plea unspoken now. Falcon was looking at her, searching her face as though seeking confirmation of something? Of what? Her fear of Colin?

'No, I won't tell him,' Falcon confirmed. She was afraid of her stepbrother. He had guessed it already, but her reaction now had confirmed his suspicion. But why?

'If he finds me, he'll only try to persuade me to give Ollie up for adoption.' Annie felt obliged to defend her plea.

Falcon nodded his head and repeated, 'I won't tell him.'

It was well into the early hours when Annie woke abruptly out of an uneasy sleep, her heart thudding too fast and her senses alert, probing the darkness of the unlit room for the source of the danger that had infiltrated her sleep. Outside in the London street beyond the flat a motorbike backfired, bringing a juddering physical relief to her tensed nerve endings.

She looked towards the cot where Ollie lay sleeping, and prayed that she had done the right thing in agreeing to go to Sicily—that she hadn't exchanged one form of imprisonment for another. As long as Ollie was safe that was all that mattered. Nothing else. *Nothing*.

CHAPTER THREE

TRUE to his word, Falcon Leopardi had arrived at the flat early in the morning to collect her and Ollie in the chauffeur-driven car he had hired. He had taken them to Harvey Nichols, where they had spent over an hour and more money than Annie liked to think about equipping Ollie with suitable clothes and a large amount of baby equipment for his new life.

Now, surveying what looked like a positive mountain of small garments, Annie felt guilty. She had been enjoying herself so much, choosing everything for him.

'I'm sorry.' She apologised to Falcon. 'I've chosen far too much, and it's all so expensive. Perhaps we should think again?'

'I shall be the judge of what is and is not expensive—and we don't have time for second thoughts. You still have your own wardrobe to attend to—although, I imagine that is something you can do far more comfortably without my presence.'

He pushed back the cuff of his suit jacket—a habit of his, Annie had noticed. In a different suit this morning, in a light tan that looked very continental, he had had all the super-thin and super-pretty salesgirls turning their heads to look at him.

'I've booked a personal shopper for you, so I'll leave you to it and come back in an hour.'

Annie nodded her head. He was leaving her to her own

devices because he had other things to do—not because somehow or other he had known how on edge the thought of him standing over her whilst she selected hot weather clothes had made her. She mustn't start elevating him to the status of something approaching a mind-reading saint. But she did feel more comfortable knowing that he wouldn't be standing there, silently assessing her choices, ready to point out all the reasons why it wasn't suitable.

As a little girl she had loved pretty clothes and going shopping with her mother, just the two of them, but all that had changed once her mother had remarried. Colin had complained that she wasn't giving their new extended family a chance to work when she told her mother that she didn't like shopping with her stepfather and Colin in tow. He had always had the knack of knowing when she had complained to her mother about him—and the knack of making sure she regretted doing so.

The personal shopping suite was a revelation to someone who couldn't even remember the last time she had shopped for clothes for herself. To her relief Ollie, who had earlier been torn between enchantment and excitement, surrounded by all the toys in the babywear department, had now fallen asleep in his buggy.

Her personal shopper looked as though she was around her own age, although she was wearing clothes far more fashionable and body-hugging than Annie would ever have felt comfortable wearing.

'I'll measure you first,' she announced, after she had introduced herself as Lissa.

'I've always been a size twelve,' Annie told her, causing the elegantly arched eyebrows to arch even further.

'Different designers have differing ideas of what a

specific size is, which is why we prefer to take proper measurements,' Lissa informed her with a soothing smile. 'And as for you being a size twelve—I'd bet on you being closer to a size eight. A ten at the very most. We find a lot of customers experience a change in their body weight and shape post-baby—although not many of them actually drop a size without working at it. Have you any specific designers or style in mind?'

'No. That is, we're going to be living in Sicily, so I shall want clothes suitable for a hot climate—but nothing too expensive, please. I prefer simple, plain things.'

'Daywear and evening things? Will you be entertaining? What kind of social life—?'

'Oh, no—nothing like that,' Annie interrupted her quickly. 'No. I'll be spending all my time with my son. Just very plain day things.' It was hard to sound as firm as she would have liked to with Lissa encircling various bits of her body with the tape measure.

'Just as I thought,' the other woman declared triumphantly once she had finished. 'You are an eight. Now, if you'd like to help yourself to a cup of coffee—' she gestured towards the coffee machine on the table '—and then get undressed and put on a robe, I shall go and collect some clothes. I shan't be long.'

She wasn't, soon returning accompanied by two other girls and a rail packed with clothes.

Two hours later Annie felt like a small and very irritating child. Even worse, she was humiliatingly close to tears. Lissa was very much out of patience with her, she could tell.

She was back in her below-the-knee A-line denim skirt, under which her cheap tights shone in the overhead lights.

The skirt was worn with a short-sleeved cotton blouse that she had bought in the latter stages of her pregnancy, which covered her from neck to hip. She felt hot and uncomfortable, and she was longing to escape from the store and from Lissa's obvious irritation.

'I'm sorry,' she apologised miserably, for what felt like the umpteenth time, 'but I just couldn't wear any of them.'

She had, she recognised, lost Lissa's attention—and the reason for that was because Falcon had just walked into the room.

'All done?' he asked, quite plainly expecting that it would be.

Annie had to say something.

'Well, not really…' she began—only to have Falcon frown.

'Why not?' he demanded.

'It seems that everything is "too revealing",' Lissa answered smartly for her, very plainly wanting to voice her sense of irritation and injustice.

Annie couldn't blame her. The clothes Lissa had shown her were beautiful—sundresses in perfect colours for her skin, with tiny straps and softly flowing skirts, well-cut narrow-legged Capri pants in white and black and zingy lime, and a shade of blue that almost matched her eyes, strappy tops, sleeveless V-necked dresses… Clothes meant to allow as much sun as possible to touch the skin. Clothes that would catch the male eye. Clothes that women wore when they wanted to attract male attention. In amongst them had been swimsuits and bikinis, wraps, sandals with no heels and high heels, underwear in cotton so fine that it was transparent—everything that any woman could reasonably need for a long sojourn in a hot climate. But

Annie had rejected it all. Even the heavenly white sundress with embroidered flowers that had—ridiculously, given its sophistication—reminded her of a dress she had had when she'd been about six years old.

'Too revealing?' Falcon looked at the rack of clothes that the salesgirl was now gesturing to with her hand. He was Italian, and an architect by training and desire. Good lines were important to him, and he couldn't see anything in the clothes he was being shown that in any kind of way merited the description 'too revealing'.

He turned from the clothes to Annie, his eyebrows snapping together as he studied her appearance in the over-large dull top and the denim skirt, his frown deepening in disbelief as he realised that she was wearing thick-looking tights.

'The temperature can rise above forty degrees centigrade in Sicily in the summer. You will need clothes that are cool and loose. It will be impossible for you to continue wearing the kind of clothes you are wearing now.' He turned to the salesgirl and told her firmly, 'We will take everything.'

Everything? All of it? He couldn't mean it. But quite patently he did.

Was this how things were going to be from now on? Was he going to continually tell her what she could and could not do? Automatically she stiffened in rejection of allowing that to happen. Perhaps she had acted too impulsively and in doing so had jumped from the frying pan into the fire? Perhaps…?

'We need go get moving. My brother has arranged for one of his fleet of jets to fly us out to Sicily in four hours' time, so I suggest that we now return to your flat. I have spoken with the council, by the way, and cancelled your tenancy.'

'Cancelled it? But what if I change my mind and I want to bring Ollie back?'

'Back to what? Your stepbrother rang my office this morning, and left a message for me asking if I had managed to trace you as yet.'

Had he told her that deliberately, to put her off insisting that she might want to come back? Was he trying to manipulate her? Had she made a terrible mistake?

How her mood now contrasted with and mocked the gratitude she had felt towards him last night. Why was she such a fool? Her mother had often said that Annie was a bad judge of character. Those had been her words to Annie as she had shaken her head over a boy from university who had asked her out, and over Rachel, a schoolfriend her mother had said was a bad influence on her. And clearly she had misjudged the extent of Antonio's malice towards her, and what it would lead him to do.

She had made more than enough mistakes, enough bad judgements, and had paid the price for doing so. She wasn't going to let Falcon Leopardi browbeat her into making yet another mistake.

She lifted her chin and challenged him. 'What will you tell him?'

'Nothing. He is your stepbrother, and so it is up to you to decide what you do and do not want him to know.'

His answer took the wind out of her sails, completely deflating the hard bubble of anger inside her and leaving her feeling foolish.

'I'll have you dropped off at your flat, so that you can pack everything that you want. Don't bother about packing any baby stuff. I've phoned Rocco and asked his wife to order everything you're likely to need to be ready for you. You'll need your passport, of course. I don't expect you have one for Oliver, so I've arranged for the British passport office to get one rushed through. They'll need a photograph, needless to say, so we'll get that done now, and we can go before I drop you off.'

Falcon had thought of everything, Annie admitted tiredly later, when the chauffeur-driven Mercedes limousine came to a halt on the runway, only a matter of yards from where a sleek jet was waiting for them.

The last time Annie had flown anywhere had been when she had gone to Cannes with Susie and Tom, in her capacity as Tom's researcher. He had been attending the showing of a film based on one of his books, as well as using the trip to source some background information on his new book, set against the backdrop of the jet set. That was why she had been on Nikki Beach—because Tom had felt that she could get a better insight into a woman's perspective of the scene there than him. She had tried to protest that she wasn't that kind of researcher, and that she preferred working amongst the books of the British Library, but Tom had refused to listen.

He had been devastated after what had happened to her, blaming himself until she had begged him not to do so. Both he and Susie felt that it was for the best that she couldn't remember anything of what had happened after she had swallowed her drugged drink until she had started to come round, when Susie had found her, but Colin didn't share that view. He had pressed her over and over again, insisting that she *must* remember something.

* * *

He had never known anyone whose eyes were so extraordinarily expressive when she didn't realise she was being watched, Falcon acknowledged. He could see quite clearly the pain and fear darkening them, and he wondered who or what had caused them.

'Let me take Oliver for you,' he offered, reaching for the now awake baby as the chauffer opened the car door.

Immediately Annie recoiled, holding her baby tightly.

'I can manage, thank you,' she said, stiff and uncompromising.

She was very protective of her child, Falcon admitted, and told her dryly, 'I *am* his uncle.'

'And I am his mother,' Annie pointed out, quickly and defensively.

'You will find that in Italian families it is expected that babies are passed around amongst the relatives, so that everyone in the family can share in the joy of having them there,' Falcon informed her calmly.

Stupidly, his words made her eyes sting with emotional tears. There was nothing she wanted more for Ollie than a large and loving family who would take him to their hearts and accept him and love him. And her with him?

The chauffeur helped her out of the car, and a uniformed steward came forward from the plane to greet them, followed by the pilot. Neither of them seemed curious about her. Too well trained, Annie decided. They were probably used to Falcon Leopardi boarding private jets with a woman in tow. But not a woman like her, Annie thought, uncomfortably aware of her shortcomings. Falcon's women would be soignée and confident. They would wear designer clothes that showed off the sensuality of their bodies. They would definitely not be dressed as she was, nor holding his disliked late half-brother's child.

What was she doing, comparing herself to them? The type of woman Falcon dated and Annie Johnson were worlds apart—so very many worlds apart. Suddenly out of nowhere she felt a sharp stab of almost physical pain for all that she had lost, all that was denied to her. It was so intense that it almost made her cry out loud. *Was* there a woman in his life? A special woman? A woman who he planned would ultimately bear his children? The pain intensified, seizing her in its claws and mauling her so badly that she almost cried out.

What was the matter with her? She had everything she wanted. The sexuality and happiness of some unknown woman meant nothing to her. Her life was what it was. It was for Ollie's sake and not her own that she had even felt what she had, she defended herself. Because he would never know what it was to be the child of two people who had created him out of their love for one another, who were there with him to show him that love. She knew what it was like to grow up without a father, and she hated knowing that Ollie would suffer that same loss.

'Let me take him now.' Falcon reached for Ollie, taking from her before she could stop him, and leaving her no option other than to allow the steward to guide her up the steps and into the plane.

She tried not to be impressed, but it wasn't easy. She had never imagined that the interior of a plane could be like this—furnished more like a sitting room than the kind of aircraft interior with which she was familiar.

Falcon had followed her into the plane, and was pointing

out to her the sky cot that had been prepared for Ollie. The baby was wide-awake now, and gazing round in wide-eyed delight.

He really was the most beautiful baby, Annie thought on a wave of love. She had dressed him in one of his new outfits—little chinos, with a blue and green checked shirt and a V-necked pullover, matching socks encasing his small baby feet. He looked adorable, and she suspected he knew it. She, on the other hand, was still wearing her dull top and her denim skirt—although she had put on her trenchcoat, as well, even though the early evening was mild and dry.

Oh, yes, his new family were bound to love Ollie she decided after the steward had discreetly shown her how to fasten herself into her armchair-like seat and they had begun to take off.

They would love *him* but how would they feel about *her*? How much did they know about her?

She was worrying about something, Falcon thought as he watched the now familiar darkening of her eyes. Although obviously it wasn't her appearance. He had never known a woman less concerned about how she looked. Antonio's drunken friend had mentioned her buttoned-up appearance, but Falcon hadn't paid much attention to his description until now. What made a young and potentially very attractive woman dress in such a way?

The seatbelts sign went off and Falcon unfastened his. What did it matter what motivated her to dress the way she did? It was her child who was his concern, and the duty he owed was to him. But what about the duty he owed *her*, being the brother of the man who had abused her?

* * *

Annie couldn't contain her anxiety any longer. Her fingers trembled as she unfastened her seatbelt and leaned towards Falcon Leopardi.

'Your brothers and their wives—what...what do they know about me?' she asked, her body tense with her anxiety.

'They know that you are Oliver's mother and that he is a Leopardi,' he answered her.

Colour now stained her skin, but she ignored it, pressing him determinedly, 'Do they know how I came to have Oliver? Do they know...?'

'That Antonio drugged and then raped you?' Falcon finished for her.

His voice was harsher than he had expected, scored by everything he felt about his late half-brother, and his loathing of the damage he had done to their family name, but to Annie his harshness was an indictment of her, and she flinched from it.

'Yes, they know,' Falcon confirmed.

Before he had even found her he had told them what he had discovered, and that it was his intention to find the woman Antonio had so badly wronged and bring her child within the protection of their family.

Annie's immediate gasp alerted him to her reaction.

'They know and they share my views on the subject,' he elaborated with deliberate emphasis.

'Because you have told them to?' Her voice wobbled, betraying very easily, Annie thought, what she was really feeling, and how apprehensive she was about meeting his family and being judged by them.

Falcon, though, seemed oblivious to what she was

thinking, because he asked bluntly, 'What is it you are trying to say?'

'Isn't it obvious? Your brother denied that—what happened. He refused to accept that Ollie was his. How do I know that your brothers and their wives accept what really happened?' When he didn't speak she added wildly, 'Do you think I *want* people knowing what happened to me? Do you think that I *want* Ollie to grow up with people knowing how he was conceived? It was bad enough that Susie and Tom knew even before—' She broke off, suddenly realising that she was saying far more than she had intended.

Her anguished outburst brought to the surface issues Falcon had already considered and then put to one side to be dealt with once he had dealt with the most urgent necessity—which had been to find Antonio's victim and her child.

It would have been hard for her to speak as she had, he acknowledged, and something inside him ached for her whilst at the same time registering her bravery.

His brothers had already discussed with him their concern over Oliver being Antonio's child, and what he might grow up to be.

'The last thing we want is another Antonio,' Rocco had told him bluntly. 'And if our father has his way, that is exactly what he will turn the boy into.'

'I shall not allow that to happen,' Falcon had assured him. 'The child will receive his fathering from me.'

Both his brothers had looked at him in such a way that he had felt obliged to continue.

'I know what you are thinking. My fathering of both of you contained more good intention than it did skill.'

'You are wrong, Falcon,' Rocco had responded. 'What we are thinking is that there could be no one better to parent this child than you. We are both eternally grateful to you for all that you did for us.'

It had been an emotional moment, and one that still moved him. He had been so young when their mother had died and their father had remarried—too young in many ways to shoulder the responsibility of protecting his younger brothers.

'Admit it, Falcon,' Rocco had teased him, in an attempt to lighten the mood, 'you want to have this boy under your wing because you miss having the two of us there. You should find yourself a girl to love, brother—marry her and produce sons of your own to father.'

Sons of his own.

Falcon had seen his mother wilt and then turn her back on life beneath the burden of being the wife of the head of their family. And then he had seen his father's second wife glory greedily in that position, revelling in the wealth and power of her status. He envied his brothers their marriages, and the love they so obviously shared with their wives, but their situation was not his. His personal desires must always come second to his duty. Ultimately he would be the head of the family, and it would be his duty to take the Leopardi name forward into the future.

If he married then his wife would have to understand and share his goals, and acknowledge the fact that his duty would always be a third presence in their marriage. He doubted that it was possible to find a woman with whom he could share true love and who at the same time would understand his ultimate role as Prince.

He looked at Annie, who by his own actions he had now made a part of his responsibilities.

'You speak as though you fear being shamed,' he told her evenly. 'But it was Antonio who should have borne that shame. It is we who bear it now, as his family. Not you. It is for us—for me as the eldest—to see to it that Antonio's shame does not contaminate either you or Oliver. You have my word that my brothers feel exactly as I do.'

It was impossible for her not to believe him, but he had spoken only of his brothers, Annie recognised. What of their wives? Would they look down on her and question the veracity of her version of events?

The steward appeared to ask what she would like to drink.

'Just water, please,' she answered.

There was something else that Falcon knew he had to say—since she herself had raised the issue.

'If Oliver learns to feel shame, then it is from you he will learn it if you wear it like a hair shirt—as you seem to wear your clothes.'

Anger flashed in Annie's eyes.

'There is nothing wrong with my clothes.'

'On the contrary, there is a great deal wrong with them for a woman of your age.'

His forthright response left Annie feeling taken aback and defensive.

'Well, I like them. And I am the one who has to wear them.' Annie's voice was becoming as heated as her emotions.

'That is impossible. No woman of your age could possibly *like* such incredibly ugly garments. And I remind you that I am the one who has to look at them.'

Annie was outraged. Outraged and—although she was reluctant to admit it—hurt, as well.

'Just because the kind of women *you* favour—just because your…your girlfriend dresses in fashionable designer clothes—that doesn't mean—'

'I do not have a girlfriend.' Falcon stopped Annie's outburst in mid-flow.

He didn't have a girlfriend? Why was she suddenly feeling oddly light-headed, almost pleased? She wasn't. At least not because Falcon didn't have a girlfriend.

'The summer heat in Sicily is such that it will be impossible for you to dress as you are dressed now and be comfortable. Sicily's young women go bare-legged in the summer, and wear sleeveless tops.'

'They may do as they wish, but I prefer to wear clothes that are not revealing and do not draw attention to me.'

'To wear clothes as inappropriate as the ones you have on now *will* draw attention to you. So maybe secretly, for all that you deny it, that *is* what you want?'

'No. That's not true. It isn't true at all. The last thing I want is for men to look at me.'

Annie stood up as she spoke, so agitated and upset that all she could do was look wildly around for an escape.

Falcon hadn't meant to provoke such an extreme reaction. And so far as he knew he hadn't said anything about his own sex looking at her. But she was trembling from head to foot, her eyes huge in her delicately shaped face—huge, and haunted with something that looked like fear.

'I didn't intend to imply that you are deliberately courting male attention,' he tried to assure her, but Annie shook her head.

'Yes, you did. I suppose you think secretly that I encouraged Antonio—that I deserved what happened to me?'

The words were bursting out of her now, like poison from a deep wound. The sound of her pain filled him with pity for her, awakening his own deep-rooted sense of responsibility towards the vulnerable, honed during the years of his youth, when he had tried to protect his younger brothers from the results of their father's lack of love for them.

He stood up himself.

'I think no such thing. I know that you were totally blameless.'

He had her attention now. Her lips parted and the hot pain died out of her gaze.

'You...' Annie gasped as the plane was suddenly buffeted by turbulence, throwing her off balance.

Falcon caught her as she stumbled and fell against his body, her cheek pressed against the pristine cotton of his shirt whilst his arms wrapped tightly around her. She could feel the strong, even beat of his heart. Her own pulse was racing ahead of it, fuelled by a mixture of panic and shock. She was feeling light-headed again, Annie acknowledged dizzily. It must be something to do with the atmosphere in the cabin—not enough oxygen or something... Or something? Perhaps something such as too much proximity to a certain man? He was wearing the same cologne he had been wearing before, its scent slightly stronger this time, because she was closer to his body.

Something kicked through her lower body. Shame, of course; it had to be that. She wasn't allowed to feel anything other than shame in a man's arms. She knew that. Her body shuddered and the arms holding her tightened around her.

'It's all right, keep still. It's only a bit of turbulence.'

It took her several seconds to recognise that the turbulence to which Falcon was referring as he murmured those words against her ear was outside the plane and not inside her body.

It was only natural that she should be wary of men, given what had happened, Falcon acknowledged. She needed his reassurance and his protection; she needed to feel safe so that she could enjoy her womanhood and her beauty. And he would provide her with that reassurance—just as he would provide Oliver with a secure home, and just as he had tried to provide his brothers with a strong protector. The instinct to give his protection to others was a deeply embedded part of his character and his destiny.

What must it be like to know that when a man's arms enfolded you like this you were safe and you could trust him? What was it like to lean your head against a man's chest and know that your vulnerability would be respected and your need answered?

Just for a second Annie allowed herself to let those questions into her thoughts—let her own response to them into her heart. Such a storm of unfamiliar feelings was surging through her, and at such a pace, that she felt too weak to move away. Something within her that was stronger than her learned fear, some deeply buried instinct, was pushing small, exploratory tendrils of new emotion and sensation through her fear with an unexpectedly powerful urgency, carrying to her feelings and needs within herself she didn't recognise. The urge to turn her head and breathe in the scent of Falcon's skin; the heavy pounding of her heart that did not have any association with fear; the aching urgency that seemed to have infiltrated and permeated every part of her body right down to its most intimate core. All of those things were new to her—and yet somehow known to her, as well.

The plane had levelled off and was flying smoothly again.

Ollie woke up and gave a small cry.

Brought back to reality, Annie tried to wrench herself out of Falcon's hold. She was trembling violently, fear of her own reaction to him darkening her eyes.

Seeing that fear, and mistaking the cause of it, Falcon asked in disbelief, 'You are afraid of me?'

Annie couldn't speak. Guilt and shame gripped her.

'This is what Antonio has done to you, isn't it?' Falcon demanded. 'He has left you with a fear of all men.'

Annie couldn't look at him.

'You have nothing to fear from me,' Falcon told her gently as he released her. 'I give you my word on that, and I give you my word that in Sicily, on Leopardi land, you will be treated only with respect.'

Should she believe him and trust him? She wanted to. Just as she had wanted him to go on holding her? Guilt burned through her. *No!* That was not true. She had not wanted that. She had not been in danger of shaming herself by behaving provocatively.

Panic flared through her and her hands trembled as she reached for Ollie.

Silently Falcon watched her. She had felt so vulnerable in his arms. And it was because he had recognised that vulnerability and had wanted to reassure her that he had wanted to go on holding her. Nothing more.

Antonio had damaged her very badly. Like a small bird with a broken wing, she needed protection until she was fully recovered and able to fly once again.

He had thought originally that his only duty was to her child, but he had been wrong; he realised that now. She was just as in need of his care in her own way as her son. Now that he was aware of it he could not ignore that fact.

He had a duty of care towards her, and he would fulfil that duty. No matter what.

CHAPTER FOUR

THE heat of the Sicilian night wrapped round them like a moist blanket when they left the plane, and by the time they reached the waiting car Annie, in her heavy clothes, was drenched with perspiration.

'Rocco.' Falcon greeted the brother who was waiting for them with obvious affection and warmth, and the two men exchanged fierce hugs before Falcon somehow managed to catch hold of her arm before she could stop him, to draw her forward to be introduced to the tall, good-looking man standing alongside the waiting Mercedes.

She expected him to shake her hand, but instead he hugged her, enveloping her in an embrace which oddly did not have anything like the effect on her that being held by Falcon had.

He then admired Ollie, picking him up out of his buggy with such obvious expertise that all Annie's maternal fears were immediately soothed. He made her son smile widely as he held him high in the air with an expert male care that said that Rocco was familiar with the needs of a young child.

'He is a true Leopardi,' she heard Falcon saying as proudly as though Oliver was his, whilst his brother laughed and teased him.

'I can see that he has your eyes, brother.'

Somehow it was Falcon who took charge of Ollie when

they got into the car, fastening him into the waiting baby seat whilst he made conversation with his brother.

The road to the *castello* was dark and winding—in contrast with the *castello* itself which was ablaze with lights.

'My wife is very anxious to meet you and welcome you,' Rocco told Annie before she got out of the car. 'She wanted to come with me tonight, but Falcon forbade it because he thought you would be too tired. She will be calling to see you tomorrow, though, and I dare say bringing our little one with her.'

He then kissed Ollie soundly on the forehead and gave him a firm hug, before passing him to Falcon who fastened him in his buggy whilst two men removed the cases from the back of the car.

She was then swept inside the *castello* and introduced to the housekeeper and two very young maids.

She had learned during the drive from the plane that Rocco and his wife lived in a villa some miles away from the *castello*, and that Rocco was a property developer, who travelled a great deal with his work, whilst Falcon's middle brother owned an airline. He apparently had his own apartment within the *castello*, but spent most of his time in Florence, which was where his business was based. What had surprised her most was learning that Falcon too had business interests independent of his responsibilities as his father's heir. He was an architect and conservation expert, who also had a home in Florence, as well as his own wing of the *castello*.

'So you don't live here all the time?' she questioned him now they were inside.

'Not normally, but you need not fear that I shall abandon you and Oliver.'

'I wasn't thinking that,' Annie lied. She didn't want him thinking that she needed him, because then he might start thinking that she had a personal interest in him—and she didn't.

'Maria has prepared rooms for you both,' Falcon told her, ignoring her fib. 'She will show you to them now.'

It was late, and she was tired—so tired that the minute she saw the huge, comfortable looking bed in the bedroom Maria took her to all she wanted to do was lie down on it.

She was a mother, though, with responsibilities. Although one brief look was enough to reassure her that the room into which her bedroom opened, which had clearly been turned into a nursery, was expertly quipped with everything Ollie could possibly need—including facilities for making and heating Oliver's bottle.

'The wife of the *signore*—she choose everything,' Maria told her in broken English.

'The *signore*?' Annie queried uncertainly, whilst trying not to look too yearningly at the waiting bed.

'Sí. The *signore* who is the brother of Signor Falcon. She will come tomorrow to see you.'

Maria must be referring to Rocco's wife, Annie recognised.

She woke up to find that someone must have come into the room earlier and left her a breakfast tray, with coffee and fruit and soft breads. They had also pulled back the curtains to allow the most glorious sunshine to stream into the room.

She got out of bed, wrapping herself in the towelling robe she had found in the bathroom the previous night, and went first to check on Ollie who was lying happily in his cot, watching the mobile hanging above his head.

She then poured herself a cup of coffee, drinking it with one eye on the open door to the nursery and the other on the view from the elegant French windows of her room, which opened on to a balcony large enough to contain a small table and two chairs, protected by railings high enough to make it safe for Ollie.

Already it was hot. The sky was a brilliant matt blue and the realisation that she could see the sea beyond the walls of the *castello* thrilled her with delight. Directly below the balcony were formal gardens enclosed by ancient walls over which roses climbed and tumbled. In the distance, beyond the walled garden, jagged mountain peaks rose up to meet the sky, their lower slopes cloaked in what looked like olive groves.

She could hear Ollie gurgling to himself. Finishing her coffee, she started to smile. It would be wonderful to be free to be with him and enjoy his every small development. He had loved nursery, but she had envied the nursery carers. She just hoped he wouldn't miss his little companions too much.

An hour later, with Ollie bathed, changed, fed and dressed and safely in his playpen, she went to get dressed herself. Her confusion when she couldn't find the clothes she had been wearing when she had arrived at the *castello* last night turned to suspicion and then an anger so intense that it made her shake from head to foot. She discovered that not only were last night's clothes missing, but that the suitcase containing the rest of her own things was missing, as well.

Her clothes had gone. Taken away, no doubt, on Falcon's orders, so that she would be forced to wear the clothes he had bought for her—clothes which he deemed more suitable and which—surprise, surprise—were not missing.

She would not have his choice imposed on her. She would not be bullied and controlled. But she had no option other than to wear one of the new outfits or remain in her bedroom, since she most certainly could not go downstairs wearing a bathrobe.

She could not bear to look at herself. She would *not* look at herself, Annie decided as she tugged up the zip of a pair of cotton Capri pants and slid her bare feet into a pair of pretty flat shoes. At least she'd managed to find a long-sleeved cotton wrap to wear over the strappy top she'd been forced to wear. Against her will she caught sight of her pale skin, its paleness making it look very bare.

Picking up Ollie, she hurried towards the bedroom door.

She was not going to put up with being controlled like this—and the minute she found Falcon she was going to tell him so.

The *castello* seemed to be a warren of long corridors, and she had been too tired last night to pay much attention when Maria had shown her upstairs to her room. When she had still not found the stairs, after traversing what felt like miles of corridors that led to dead ends, Annie was beginning to panic—until she turned a corner to find that she had finally reached a large landing from which the stairs swept downwards into an imposing hallway.

She was just about to go down when a door opened further along the landing and Falcon came out.

'I want my own clothes back,' Annie told him angrily, before he could speak. 'I suppose you thought you were being very clever, arranging for them to be taken away, knowing that I'd be forced to wear what you bought me. But—'

'Your clothes are missing? The ones you arrived in?'

Annie had to fight to suppress a desire to grind her teeth.

'You know perfectly well they are—and my case, as well. *You* are the one who arranged for them to be taken, You, after all, are the Leopardi heir.'

Ignoring her sarcasm, Falcon held out his hands for Ollie.

'You are wrong in your accusations. I have given no orders concerning your clothes whatsoever. Nor would I do. Personally I think that you will be far more comfortable in what you are wearing now, but the right of choice is yours. However, I think I know what may have happened to those you were wearing. Although, I have no knowledge of the whereabouts of your case. Come with me, please.'

Somehow or other he had managed to take Ollie from her, despite the fact that she had not intended to allow him to do so. Ollie certainly didn't seem to mind, beaming delightedly at his new relative and chattering away to him in his own brand of baby talk as Falcon strode down the stairs and across the hallway, leaving Annie to hurry to catch up with him.

From the hall he led her through several overpoweringly formal reception rooms, furnished with what Annie guessed must be priceless antiques, finally coming to a halt in a more comfortable-looking room where Maria was overseeing one of the maids.

The minute the housekeeper saw Ollie she beamed at him, and then greeted Annie herself.

'Annie wishes to know what has happened to the clothes

she arrived in last night,' Falcon told Maria, speaking slowly and carefully in English.

Maria beamed Annie a wide smile.

'I take them and put them in the machine,' she told her with delight. 'You like coffee now? And some food?'

'We'll have coffee on the terrace, thank you, Maria,' Falcon answered. 'Oh—and you had better bring extra cups for Rocco and his wife. They should be joining us soon.'

'You will have to blame my sisters-in-law for the absence of your clothes,' Falcon told Annie as soon as Maria and the maid had left. 'They insisted on revamping the *castello*'s kitchens, with the result that Maria cannot resist using the new washing machine, on the slightest excuse. As for your case—I shall make further enquiries.'

Annie felt mortified. It was blindingly obvious that she had jumped to the wrong conclusion. If she wasn't careful, he was going to start thinking she was paranoid. Despite the fact that the interior of the *castello* was a comfortable temperature, Annie could feel perspiration breaking out on her skin. The last thing she wanted was him asking questions about her reaction to the absence of her own clothes.

'I must apologise—' she began stiffly.

Falcon shook his head to stop her continuing.

'There is no need,' he told her. 'The fault is mine, in that I obviously made you feel under pressure with advice that was unsolicited.'

Annie was so astonished by his admission that she looked up at him, her gaze mutely questioning his in an act of openness that was so alien to her that the realisation of what she was doing caught at her breath. Allowing him to see what she was thinking, allowing herself to be vulnerable—these were acts she had thought she had trained herself not to risk a long time ago.

'Until they married, and I relinquished what I'd believed was my responsibility for their emotional well-being, my brothers berated me for my over-developed big brother concern for them. It was a habit I had fallen into when they were young, when the three of us were vulnerable to the moods of a stepmother who resented us and a father who did not care. If I sound self-pitying, that is not my intention. My brothers and I have led and continue to lead privileged lives.

'However, just as being their eldest brother does not give me the right to interfere in their lives, neither does my over-developed sense of responsibility give me the right to lecture you about the suitability of your clothes for Sicily's climate. I obviously went way over the top if you thought I had given Maria orders to remove your own clothes.'

There was that light-headed feeling again, Annie recognised. Experiencing it was becoming a regular aspect of being in Falcon's company.

'I probably overreacted,' Annie admitted.

The warm smile he was giving her was doing things to her heart that could have made it a contestant in an Olympic gymnastics team. Falcon was still smiling at her. He had a good smile—strong and real, with the curl of his mouth in amusement emphasising the fullness of his bottom lip. Something very reckless was spreading a dangerous heat through her lower body, its presence throwing her into frantic panic.

'My father will want to see Oliver, of course. He has a terminal heart condition which caused him to have a relapse whilst I was away. He has been very anxious that Oliver should become part of the family. He knows you are both here, and that has put his mind at rest, but his doctor has recommended that he needs to rest a little more before he sees the little one.

'I should warn you that my father idolised Antonio. He knows nothing of the circumstances surrounding Oliver's conception. He will not hear a word against his favourite son, and in view of his condition I thought it best not to try to force him to accept the reality of what my half-brother was. I should also warn you that my father does not treat your sex with the respect he should, and that you are likely to find his attitude offensive. I assure you that his offensiveness will not be personal in any way. If you wish, I will take Oliver to meet his grandfather.'

Falcon was trying both to warn her about his father and to protect her from him, Annie recognised, but on this occasion his concern was welcome. What was it that made the difference between care that was controlling and care that instilled in her the sweet swell of inner warmth that Falcon's was doing now?

Was it a matter of degree, of intention, or was it all down to the man offering the care?

Annie was relieved when the sound of other voices prevented her from pursuing her thoughts.

The couple coming into the hall quite plainly had so much love for one another that Annie felt a small lump of envy lock her throat. She saw the looks Rocco Leopardi was exchanging with his wife as together they strapped a happily smiling little boy who looked Ollie's age into a buggy.

Immediately the children saw one another, neither had eyes for anyone else.

'It's amazing, isn't it, how even small babies are drawn to one another? How they communicate their interest in one another without a word being said?' Rocco's wife laughed. 'I'm Julie, by the way,' she introduced herself, leaving the buggy with Rocco to come over and hug Falcon warmly, and then give Annie herself a briefer but still warm hug before admiring Ollie.

'Well, you'd certainly know that he is a Leopardi.' She laughed, adding, 'Oh, look at that, Rocco—you were right. He does have Falcon's eyes.'

'You must have been shocked when Falcon first made contact with you. I was terrified when Rocco did with me. I thought he was going to try and take my nephew away from me.'

The two women were sitting together on the terrace whilst the babies played happily on rugs at their feet. Falcon and Rocco had disappeared to attend to some family business, and in the hour during which they had been gone Annie had learned a huge amount from Rocco's wife—including the fact that at one stage the Leopardi family had thought her nephew, Josh, might be Antonio's son.

'It's very courageous of you to come here. I know how vulnerable and alone you must have felt after Oliver was born. But you've got Falcon to protect you both now, and you can trust him to do exactly that. He is honourable and strong. Rocco pretends not to, but I know that secretly he puts Falcon on a pedestal—and when you know how Falcon protected and looked after his younger brothers when they were growing up it's easy to understand why.

Their father was dreadfully unkind to them, you know, and to their mother. Rocco says that it's only Falcon's sense of duty to the Leopardi name that keeps him on speaking terms with his father.

'What I admire him for most of all, though, is the way he taught his brothers to value their individuality. He encouraged them to become independent of him and of the Leopardi wealth and status. All three of them are successful in their own right, and Rocco says that is because Falcon showed them by example the importance of earning self-respect. It must have been so hard for him. After all, he was only very young himself when their mother died after Rocco's birth—not even in his teens.

'You're obviously very fond of him.' Annie smiled.

She badly wanted a change of subject. Hearing about Falcon's childhood, imagining him as a boy, hearing about his emotional pain, was bringing her own emotions too close to the surface.

'I am, yes, and I want to reassure you that you can trust Falcon, that you and Oliver will be safe in his care.' She frowned and adjusted the folds of her skirt, then played with the sunglasses she had removed and put on the table, plainly not quite at ease. 'I don't like being disloyal, but I've already told Rocco how I feel. Whilst you can trust Falcon one thousand percent, I would warn you to be wary of the old Prince. I don't know if Falcon has told you anything about their father?'

'He's told me that he idolised Antonio,' said Annie.

Julie nodded her head.

'Yes, he does. I don't think there's anything he wouldn't do to have Antonio's son growing up here, where Antonio grew up.'

There was a warning in the other woman's words, Annie felt sure. But before she could ask her more directly what it was, Falcon and Rocco had returned.

CHAPTER FIVE

ANNIE grimaced to herself as she felt her body's reluctance to return to the heavy and uncomfortable constriction of her own clothes, washed and returned by Maria, after the freedom of wearing lighter things for two full days.

The only occupants of the *castello* were the old Prince, Falcon and the servants—so surely it was safe enough for her to continue to wear her new clothes? Playing with Ollie in a shady part of the garden, she had actually felt so safe that she had even removed her wrap top.

Rocco's wife's words had gone a long way to reassure her that she could trust Falcon, and had boosted her confidence in her own judgement. Once she had settled in properly, Julie had promised, she would take her round and show her something of the island. She'd said how delighted she was that Josh, her nephew—now her and Rocco's adopted son—would have another child to play with.

'It'll be lovely to have another woman with whom I've so much in common so close,' Julie had told her warmly.

Annie hoped that they would become friends. Having friends had always been so difficult for her at home and even at university, since she had still been living at home and her mother had always been so anxious about her mixing with the 'wrong kind' of people.

It had only been after the shocking accidental deaths of

her mother and her stepfather in a minibus crash whilst they had been on safari that she had finally moved away from home, helped by one of her university lecturers to get a job in London at the British Library. She had been lucky enough to rent a room in a house owned by a widow—but that, of course, hadn't been anything like as much fun as proper flat-sharing with other girls.

As it was, Colin had been concerned for her, reminding her that her mother had left the house and the responsibility for her welfare to *him*. They hadn't exactly fallen out over her decision to move to London, but Colin had let her know that her decision had upset him.

It had been a shock for her to return home from work one day to find him sitting in her landlady's front room, drinking tea with her, having—as he'd told Annie—explained to Mrs Slater that Annie's mother had made him promise that he would always keep an eye on her.

'Annie has a tendency to get involved with the wrong sort,' Colin had continued. 'Young men who aren't the type a mother wants to see her daughter associating with.'

Annie's face burned now, remembering the humiliation and her sense of helplessness at being trapped by his judgement, unable to escape from it as she had sat there listening to him.

Half-heartedly, she started to reach for her old clothes. Her case had now been found. It had been placed in a storeroom—no doubt because of its shabbiness, she suspected. However, now having been reunited with her own clothes, Annie discovered—guiltily—that she had no real wish to wear them. They reminded her of Colin. She had chosen them because of him.

The sun was striking hot bars of sunshine across the

polished wooden floor and the silky antique rug that covered it. As she moved the sunlight touched her arm, gilding her skin. Julie had the most lovely light tan. Her skin, like her eyes, almost seemed to glow with good health and happiness. Her own skin looked washed out and almost sickly pale in comparison.

Julie was so obviously happy and in love. Her happiness shone from her. She had confided to Annie that she and Rocco were now expecting their own child.

'Our second child,' she had made a point of saying to Annie as she'd hugged her nephew lovingly.

What must it feel like to be so happy and have the confidence to know you had a right to be the person you were, that no one would try to change you?

More than anything else what she wanted for Ollie was for him to grow up with that freedom, and in the knowledge that he was loved. She wanted him to have confidence and to know joy.

Before she could change her mind she dressed quickly in another of her new outfits—a pretty sundress with a neatly cut square neckline, the blue cotton edged with white. The dress was decorated with a row of white buttons that ran down the front, all the way to its dropped waistline. Annie looked at the little cardigan she had put on the bed to cover her arms, and then determinedly put it back in the drawer.

Ollie had now been introduced to his grandfather—who, Annie had sensed immediately, was not in the least bit interested in *her*. She had not taken to him at all; especially when he had wept emotionally over her baby, referring to him as the son of his own best beloved son.

She hadn't been able to stop herself from looking at

Falcon when the old Prince had spoken of his preference for Antonio, but it had been impossible to gauge what Falcon was thinking or feeling from the shuttered harshness of his face.

She had just reached the hallway with Ollie when Falcon appeared from one of the formal reception rooms opening off the hall, announcing when he saw her, 'Ah—good. I was just about to ask Maria if she knew where you were. Can you spare me a few minutes?'

'Of course.' Annie smiled. She felt more relaxed with him now that Julie had assured her that she could trust him, but not relaxed enough not to flinch when he put his hand under her elbow to guide her towards the terrace.

It wasn't the first time she had reacted with betraying intensity to either his touch or his proximity, and she could feel him looking at her—although to her relief he didn't say anything.

He was formally dressed in a summer-weight tan-coloured suit and a striped shirt. His clothes somehow emphasised his lean masculinity, making her stomach muscles tighten in response to the female awareness of him that a few days ago would have sent her headlong into panic but which now had become so familiar that she was able to control the urgency of her need to escape from what she was experiencing. It meant nothing other than that she knew Falcon was a very masculine and sexually powerful man. She was allowed to recognise that fact after all.

Once they were sitting down, and one of the maids had brought them coffee, and Oliver was happily engrossed in trying to roll over on his blanket, Falcon spoke.

'Since the *castello* is now to be yours and Oliver's home, we need to discuss providing you with something more comfortable and suitable than the two rooms you are occupying at the moment.'

'Our rooms are fine,' Annie assured him, but Falcon shook his head.

'No. I have my own apartment within the *castello*, my father has his rooms, and it is important that you too have somewhere that is your own—where you can make a proper home for yourself and Oliver. Besides, ultimately there will come a time when you may well want to entertain friends here privately. You are after all a young woman, and it is only natural that one day you will meet a man...'

Annie was so agitated that she would have stood up and run out of the room if it hadn't been for the fact that she couldn't leave Oliver.

'I don't want to meet a man. I will never...' She was too upset to be able to continue to speak, but Falcon could guess what she must be thinking.

'What my half-brother did was unforgivable, but you cannot let his behaviour deprive you of the right to enjoy your womanhood. If you do, you will be allowing him victory. And besides, you have Oliver to think of. I don't wish to lecture you, but I have seen at first hand the effects that my own mother's victimisation by our father has had on the emotional development of my brothers and I. It can be hard to recognise love as an adult when one has not witnessed it as a child. I fully intend to provide Oliver with a male influence in his life, but that cannot replace what he would learn from living with two people who love one another. I know that letting go of the horror of what Antonio did to you and learning to trust my sex again demands courage, but I believe that you have that courage.'

Annie couldn't let him go on. To do so would be unfair and dishonest. His comments about the duty she owed Ollie had hit home very sharply indeed. After all, she knew all about the long-lasting effect of emotional damage that could be caused in childhood. She sat down again, folding her hands together in her lap so that he wouldn't see how badly they were shaking. She couldn't look at him. She knew if she did that she'd never be able to get through saying to him what honesty compelled her to say.

'I… It isn't just because of what Antonio did to me that I don't want to meet anyone.'

Falcon studied Annie's downbent head. There was absolutely no mistaking the intensity of her reaction.

Suddenly he was very sharply aware that he had walked into a potential minefield and must tread extremely carefully indeed.

Mentally he rapidly reviewed everything he knew about her, double checked it, and then said as casually as he could, 'It seems to me that someone must have given you your dislike of men. Perhaps you didn't like it when your mother remarried—which is not an uncommon reaction after all? You were twelve at the time, as I recall. A difficult age for us all. If your stepfather wasn't kind and understanding…'

'No.' Annie shook her head fiercely. 'No. That was not the case. In fact, both my stepfather and Colin were…they were both very kind. Colin especially.'

Colin. Colin her stepbrother. The man Falcon had disliked so very much on sight and who had been so insistent that Falcon informed him if he managed to track Annie down. Immediately and instinctively, with a gut-twisting kick of certainty, Falcon knew exactly who had damaged her beyond any kind of doubt!

'It's because of your stepbrother, isn't it?'

'No!'

Now Falcon could hear the fear in her voice.

She was on her feet, her agitation ten times stronger than it had been before, her hand beating the table as she reinforced her denial with another forceful 'No!' that sent her cup of coffee flying, soaking into the skirt of her dress.

Falcon reacted immediately demanding, 'Are you all right? Has the coffee scalded you? It was hot.'

Annie could see Falcon coming towards her, snatching up the bottle of water that had been on the table as he did so. Another minute and he would be touching her, and she couldn't bear that now—she really could not.

'No...' She drew out the word like a frightened child, holding out her hands to keep him at bay.

'It's all right, Annie,' Falcon told her calmly. 'I won't touch you or come near you, I promise. But I need to know if you have been burned.'

His voice was so calm that it brought her back to reality and sanity.

'No. I'm fine.'

'Good. Now, can we sit down and talk?'

Talk about what she had just said—what she had just admitted, he meant. Annie knew that. She was beginning to feel slightly sick and uncomfortably light-headed. She tried but could not stop herself from looking anxiously over her shoulder towards the doors leading on to the terrace.

Again Falcon realised that he could interpret her thoughts as clearly as though she had spoken them.

'Colin can't hurt you here, Annie,' he assured her. 'He won't ever hurt you again. Because I won't let him.'

Her mouth trembled as she sat down and told him, in a mechanical voice, 'He'll tell you that I'm a liar, and that all he wants to do is protect me. He'll tell you that I make the wrong kind of friends, just like he had my mother.'

The past was threatening to drag her back into its possessive embrace. Heroically, Annie pushed it away. She wasn't a child or a teenager any more. She was an adult. Falcon was watching her, quite plainly awaiting a proper explanation. There was no point in trying to pretend to him that there was no reason for him to require one. Not now, after what she had already betrayed.

'I know what you must be thinking,' she acknowledged. 'But it wasn't like that. There was never anything sexual about...about the way Colin spoke to me or behaved towards me. It was just that he was... Well, he called it being protective, but to me it felt as though I was being smothered. There wasn't anything he was doing that was *wrong*, and it was hard for my mother to understand. She thought I was being difficult and unreasonable. I'd just started senior school, and I was making friends, but Colin insisted on meeting me from school. I had one particular close friend, but he didn't like her. There was nearly an accident. She was on her bike and he was reversing his car.'

Now that she had started to speak the words wouldn't be stemmed, and the fears and doubts poured out of her in relief at the release of finally being able to speak without the fear of being reprimanded, as her mother had always done.

'I tried to tell my mother how I felt, but she liked Colin. She said that I was being difficult.'

Something about the quality of Falcon's intently listening silence made Annie look at him. The angry contempt she could see in his eyes made her flinch.

'You think the same as my mother. I can see it from your expression—' she began, only to have him cut across her.

'My *expression*, as you call it, is for your mother,' he said harshly. 'Your stepbrother may not have touched you sexually, but his behaviour towards you was abusive.'

Falcon believed her. He understood. He was taking her side.

A huge dizzying wave of relief and gratitude surged through her. *You can trust Falcon,* Julie had told her, and now Annie knew that to be true. She *could* trust him. For the first time in her life there was someone prepared to listen and understand and believe her.

'It can't have been easy for my mother.' Annie felt duty-bound to defend her parent. 'She was grateful to Colin for accepting us both in his father's life, I suppose. He often used to say to me that his father would never have married my mother if he hadn't wanted him to. My mother was the kind of woman who needed someone to lean on. She'd been very angry with my father for dying, and sometimes I felt that she wished she didn't have me—that it would have been easier for her to remarry if she didn't have a child.'

Deep down inside himself Falcon was aware of the most extraordinary sense of rapport stretching between them. He didn't like talking about his own childhood, and rarely did so, but now—with Annie—inexplicably it felt both natural and easy to do so. Because he wanted to help her—not because he needed to share his own pain, he assured himself, as he told her quietly, 'It's hard for a child to come to terms with the fact that the person who should love them the most does not do. It makes it very difficult for them to recognise and accept love as adults. My brothers have both been lucky in that respect, meeting women who are prepared to help them recognise what love is.'

'I think they were also lucky in having *you* to love and protect them,' Annie found herself saying hesitantly, but very truthfully.

It was a new experience for her to be able to speak honestly about what she thought and felt—an empowering freedom after years of having to cautiously monitor what she said, as well as what she did, in case Colin pounced on it and used it to accuse her of some fresh wrongdoing.

His brothers had had him, Falcon acknowledged, but for Annie there had not been that all-important older someone to give her a true sense of her right to be loved and valued, to show her what true self-esteem was. That was a lack they shared, and he knew very well the effect that lack could have.

'Your stepbrother treated you very badly.' It was all he could trust himself to say to Annie.

'It probably wasn't all Colin's fault,' Annie felt bound to say. 'I probably was difficult. Sometimes teenagers are. But…but when he started to criticise me, telling me what I should and shouldn't do, what I should and shouldn't wear, warning me about…about the consequences of my behaviour, I started to feel scared.'

Which was exactly what her stepbrother would have wanted, Falcon recognised.

The more he learned about Annie's stepbrother the more he despised and disliked the other man—and the more challenged he felt to free Annie from the prison in which her stepbrother had put her.

'It was the way he manipulated the truth to make it

seem as though *I* was the one at fault that frightened me the most. Sometimes I even wondered if I *had* done the things he was accusing me of doing.'

'He was trying to destroy your right to make your own moral choices and judgements.'

With every word Falcon said he was lifting from her the terrible weight she had been carrying.

'Colin told my mother that I'd got in with a wild crowd at school—just because he'd seen me giggling with other girls and some boys when he came to collect me. It was all completely innocent, but he was awful about it. He said things that at thirteen I wasn't really able to deal with— things about boys and sex, suggesting that I was leading boys on, and that I wanted...'

She couldn't go on, but it seemed she didn't need to— because Falcon understood. She knew that because he was speaking evenly.

'He said things to you that made you feel ashamed of your sexual curiosity and of yourself?'

'Yes,' she agreed. Falcon had put it so simply, eloquently putting into words exactly what she had felt. 'He must have said something to my mother, as well, because she gave me a lecture about provocative behaviour and... and the danger of wearing provocative clothes. She took me out shopping and bought me longer skirts. I hated them, didn't want to wear them—they made me look so different to the other girls. But Colin said that if I didn't wear them it must be because I wanted boys to look at me.

'He used to come to my room at night after I'd gone to bed, and sit on the end of the bed to question me. He'd keep asking me over and over again who I talked to at school, and if I talked to any boys, if I *wanted* to talk to them.

Sometimes I lied and said no, just to make him go away, but one day he'd been watching me and he knew I was lying.'

Annie started to tremble.

'It was awful. He was so cold, and yet so angry. He took the little china ornaments that I'd been collecting and threw them on the floor one by one, until they were all broken. He said that he didn't want to be angry with me but that it was my fault, because I'd lied to him. He said that all he wanted to do was look after me because he cared about me, and he didn't want boys thinking I was cheap.

'My mother was always saying how lucky I was to have such a loving stepbrother. She didn't understand. No one did. I wanted to go to university, and when I was offered a place at Cambridge, I was over the moon. But my mother started saying that she didn't think I was mature enough to live away from home, that it would be much better if I did what Colin had done and went to the local university so that I could still live at home. I know it was his idea—just as I know that the dent Colin put in the car belonging to the boy who took me to the school prom wasn't an accident at all.'

Annie couldn't have stopped the torrent of words now even if she had wanted to. 'Before she met Colin's father my mother always told me that ultimately our house, which had belonged to my father's family, would come to me. But when she and my stepfather died I found that the house had been left to Colin, and that he'd been appointed my guardian. Luckily I was well over eighteen by then, and one of my lecturers at university—I think he understood a bit of what Colin was like, because Colin had been difficult with *him* when he'd given me some extra tuition—helped me to get a job in London.

'Colin was dreadfully upset. He begged me to go back home, but I wouldn't. I knew he'd have to stay in Dorset because his business is there. It was wonderful, living and working in London. But somehow I still couldn't let myself be the person I wanted to be. Every time I looked at a pretty dress or a short skirt I'd see Colin's face inside my head, or hear his voice.' Her own voice trailed away into drained exhaustion.

Annie recognised distantly that she felt very weak and slightly dizzy—and also, more importantly, semi-shocked and unable to fully comprehend what she had done.

'I shouldn't have told you any of that.' The words slipped out before she could snatch them back.

'Because your stepbrother wouldn't like it? You shouldn't have *had* to tell me. Because none of it should have happened,' was Falcon's response.

Did she have any idea of the grim picture she had painted of a childhood ruined by the bullying tactics of her obsessive stepbrother and her own mother's apparent inability or unwillingness to recognise what was happening to her?

His own childhood and the childhoods of his brothers had been rendered miserable by their father's lack of love for them, but what Annie had gone through was something of a different order altogether.

There was a sour taste in his mouth, a male anger on her behalf in his heart, and a steely determination in his head. Annie was now a member of his extended family. In Falcon's eyes that meant that in addition to recompensing her for the damage Antonio had done to her it was also his duty to restore to her what had been taken from her.

'After what you have just told me I can well understand why you would have ignored and tried to avoid Antonio.'

'I knew that he was making fun of me by pretending to be interested in me. I didn't like him at all. Thankfully I can't remember anything about...about what happened,' Annie told him truthfully. 'When Susie—the wife of the author I was working for—found me, I was still half-drugged.'

'You never reported what had happened to the police?'

'No,' she agreed. 'I was afraid to—in case they didn't believe me.'

Because she had been told so often by her wretched stepbrother that she was guilty of promiscuity simply by being female that she was still unable to trust men to believe her or protect her, Falcon guessed.

'It was a terrible shock when Susie asked me if I could be pregnant. That had never occurred to me. Stupid of me, I know, but I just assumed that Antonio would have... Well, that he wouldn't want there to be any risk of a child.'

'As proof of what he had done, you mean? It was typical of Antonio that he didn't think of that.'

'Originally, when...when it had happened, Susie saw from my passport that I'd given Colin's name as my next of kin. I begged her not to say anything to anyone but... She meant well, I know. And when Colin arrived in London he was so concerned that naturally...'

'He worked the same trick on her that he had on your mother?' Falcon supplied for her.

Annie nodded.

'He wanted me to have a termination. He said it would be for the best. But I wouldn't. I couldn't. So then he started saying that I must have wanted it to happen. I told him that of course I hadn't, but he said that if I couldn't even remember what had happened I couldn't say that. He said that I'd probably encouraged Antonio—otherwise I'd want to get rid of his baby. I think Susie and Tom agreed with him, although they never said so.

When Ollie was born Colin tried to get Antonio to acknowledge responsibility for him—even though I'd begged him not to. When Antonio refused Colin started pressuring me to have Ollie adopted. He even managed to persuade Susie to side with him.' Annie shivered. 'I was so afraid that somehow he'd separate us.'

As he had successfully separated her from everyone else who might have loved her or helped her, Falcon recognised. 'That's why, when you...'

'That's why you agreed to come to Sicily?' Falcon completed her sentence for her.

'Yes. I thought Ollie would be safe here.'

'You thought right,' Falcon confirmed grimly.

'You must understand now why I don't want to get involved with anyone,' Annie told him tiredly.

For a few seconds she thought he wasn't going to respond. But then, when the silence had stretched for long enough to make her feel she had said the wrong thing, he asked quietly, but with open confidence in his own correct assessment of things, 'There's never been anyone special for you sexually, has there? Someone who, when you look back, you recognise as the person you shared sexual intimacy with and who gave you the foundation stone of understanding and appreciating your own sexuality?'

For some reason Annie discovered that she wanted badly to cry. She had spent so many years cut off from what it meant to be a woman that she had grown to accept it as her fate. She was alone with it, and with the secret burden of its grief. Now, with a few simple words, Falcon had shone a light on that dark secret place within her, illuminating it so brightly that the brightness hurt unbearably, making her feel that she wanted to retreat back into the safety of the dark. She felt ashamed, she recognized. Ashamed and afraid.

She couldn't answer his question. She just couldn't. The truth hurt too much, made her feel too raw and vulnerable, and yet to her own disbelief something deep inside her was struggling against her shame and her fear, making her give Falcon an answer.

'No. Never,' she heard herself admitting shakily. 'I was too young when…when Colin first started making me feel uncomfortable about…'

She had to stop now. She had already said too much, betrayed too much. It was shamefully ridiculous and humiliating that she, a woman of twenty-four, a *mother* of twenty-four, had never known what it was to experience the pleasure of good sex.

'About being attracted to the opposite sex? About liking boys and exploring the sensations thinking about liking boys aroused?'

Annie wanted to cover her ears with her hands, just as though she was still twelve years old.

'There is nothing to be ashamed of,' Falcon was telling her. 'That is how it starts for all of us. With curiosity and awareness, with excitement and a dread of making a fool of oneself.'

'I can't imagine *you* ever feeling like that. Worrying about making a fool of yourself, I mean,' Annie explained hastily. She didn't want to think about the first part of his description. It caused too much dangerous tumult inside her body, and she already had more than enough problems to deal with.

'I can assure you that I did. Everyone does. It's a natural and normal part of growing up—but you were denied that.'

'I couldn't bear the thought of someone thinking about me in the way Colin told me that boys—men—thought about women who allow them sexual intimacies. I couldn't let myself even *think* about being attracted to anyone,' she admitted.

It was disconcerting to realise how shocked and ashamed she would have been such a very short time ago to have said those things to him—things that now she could speak of so easily and openly.

'So you suppressed your natural inclinations along with your desirability and your right to your own sexuality?' Falcon prompted her.

'I just wanted to feel safe.'

'From boys, or from your stepbrother?'

Annie's eyes widened in silent recognition of how well he understood just what she had felt.

'I suppose I could have tried to…to be more normal when I came to London, but all the other young women I saw were so…so everything I knew that I wasn't. I couldn't imagine that anyone… That is to say I thought that if I did start to go out with someone, when they found out they'd either be put off or laugh at me. It seemed easier somehow not to bother. And now, of course, it's too late. I couldn't start a relationship now even if I wanted to. What man these days wants a woman like me. A single mother, who doesn't know the first thing about how to give and receive sexual pleasure, or what it's like to enjoy sex? How would I explain to them? I couldn't tell them…'

'Why not? You've told me?'

His words had her lifting her head to look at him, caught in the shock of her realisation not just of what she had done, but more importantly of how easy it had been.

'That's different,' she told him weakly. 'You aren't... We aren't... I know I can trust you because...'

Because what? Because of what he was or because of *who* he was? Annie wasn't sure. She just knew that Falcon was different, one of a kind—a man who embodied qualities that in the modern age were very rare.

'It must have been very hard for you to live as you have lived—to live—such an unnatural life for a young and attractive woman.'

Falcon thought she was attractive? Or was he just saying that because he felt sorry for her?

'You needn't feel sorry for me,' Annie defended herself. 'I'm perfectly happy as I am.'

'No, you are not,' Falcon corrected her. 'You merely think that you are happy. But you are so afraid of being punished that you have completely disowned your sexuality. That is no way for you to live—in constant denial and fear of such an essential part of yourself.' His voice had changed and become sternly autocratic.

'It is the way I *have* to live,' Annie told him. 'I don't have any other choice.'

'But you would like that choice? You would wish, if you could, to be restored to your sexuality? To be reunited with it? So that armed with it you could have the freedom and the right to find someone with whom ultimately you might share your life?'

'I...' She desperately wanted to hang on to her pride and deny that she wanted any such thing, but Falcon's words had awakened inside her such a sharply painful, yearning pang of longing for all that she could not have that it shamed her into telling him the truth. 'Yes,' she admitted.

Falcon looked away from her. He had come to a decision. It had been there all the time he had been listening to her. Initially it had been more of an awareness that had now coalesced into the decision that he now realised he had somehow known he must make right from the beginning.

'There is something I have to say to you,' he told Annie. 'Your right to your sexuality has been stolen from you by a member of my sex, and the damage that he has done has been compounded by a member of my family. As a Leopardi, and the eldest of my brothers, I have a duty to make recompense to you and to restore to you what has been taken away. That is the law of the Leopardi family and the code by which we live.'

'That's nonsense,' Annie told him unsteadily.

Something dark and steely glinted in the depths of his eyes as he turned his head to look at her.

'It is my duty,' he repeated. 'A duty I owe not just to you but to Oliver, who shares my blood. He has the right to grow up with a mother who rejoices in her sexuality instead of fearing it, and who can thus show him a good example of all that a woman who values herself should be. How can he choose a partner who is worthy of him if he does not know what to look for? It is your duty as his mother to provide him with a template for that woman.'

With every word he said Falcon was making her feel more guilty.

'It's all very well you saying all this,' she told him helplessly. 'But I can't become the kind of woman you describe.'

'Yes, you can. With me as your guide and teacher.'

CHAPTER SIX

WITH him as her guide and teacher? Did that mean what she thought it meant? Annie's heart started to thud unsteadily.

'Give me your hand,' Falcon demanded.

Reluctantly Annie held out her hand, stiffening when he took it and held it between his own.

'Five minutes ago you said to me, "What man these days wants a woman like me? A single mother, who doesn't know the first thing about how to give and receive sexual pleasure, or what it's like to enjoy sex." I believe that deep down inside you *do* want to take back to yourself what has been stolen from you, and that you *do* want to walk free as a sexually confident and happy woman. Isn't that so?'

'I don't know,' Annie answered uncertainly. Her heart was racing. She felt as though she was confronting something she knew to be dangerous but that she also found enticing and exciting.

'Yes, you do,' Falcon corrected her. 'You love Oliver, and you know that ultimately, in order to give him the right to grow up confident in his own sexuality, you need to be confident in yours. I can teach you how to be what you want to be. You said earlier that you trusted me?'

'I…'

'I promise you that you can. I promise that I will not hurt you or abuse you, or do anything that you do not wish me to do. But I also promise you that I will show you and teach you that you have the right to own your own sexuality, to take pleasure in it and give pleasure through it.'

He meant what he said, Annie recognised weakly. He was a crusader, a motivator, a man with a mission—and he meant to restore to her what she had thought was forever lost.

'If you wish, step by step, I will help you to rediscover what has been stolen from you. You do not have to accept. I would be as bad as your stepbrother if I coerced you verbally or emotionally to accept my help. All I will say to you is that you should ask yourself what you really want and be brave enough to take it. Once you have made that decision I promise that I will be here for you and with you. There won't be anything you can't tell me or ask me.'

'What you're saying is that for Oliver's sake and my own I need to learn what it is to enjoy sex. But we don't... we don't...'

'We don't what?'

'We don't *love* one another,' Annie told him.

There was a gleam in his eyes that made her heart thud as though it was flinging itself against her ribcage.

'It is not necessary to love to enjoy good sex. It *is*, though, important to share a mutual attraction.'

He paused whilst her heart somersaulted and thudded so much that she had to lift her hand to her chest, in an attempt to steady its frantic beat.

'It is my belief that we share such an attraction.'

'No...I mean, I don't think...'

'You don't think what? That I find you attractive? I assure you that I do.'

Falcon was still holding her hand, and now to her shock he turned it over, then gently ran the pad of his thumb over her inner wrist.

Lightning surges of reaction hot-wired up her arm, causing her to gasp out loud and try to pull away.

Falcon was watching her closely, and Annie knew that her reaction had been plain to him and had given her away.

'You gave me a shock,' she told him feebly. It was the truth—even if the reality was that the shock he had given her had been entirely sexually charged rather than mentally.

'I gave you pleasure,' Falcon corrected her softly. 'And your pleasure gave me pleasure. Imagine, if the touch of my thumb can give us both that pleasure, how much more intense it would be if I followed up the touch of my thumb with the caress of my lips.'

Oh, to be a Victorian virgin and free to swoon, Annie thought feverishly. Because that was the only guaranteed way she could think of escaping from her present situation. And by her present situation what she meant was the sheer extent of the feeling of longing that surged through her at the mental images Falcon's soft words had created.

'It is entirely possible to enjoy sex without loving someone, you know,' he was telling her now. 'Just so long as there is mutual respect and understanding, and a mutual desire to give and receive pleasure. There is nothing shameful in that—no matter what your stepbrother may have tried to make you think.'

He had released her hand now, and she was delighted that he had done so. Totally delighted. And relieved that he hadn't thought it necessary to show her just what the caress of his lips could do. Absolutely. Definitely.

'You don't have to make up your mind right now. I have to fly to Florence later this afternoon, for a meeting about a building I'm involved in helping to renovate,' Falcon told her. 'I shall be back by tomorrow evening. You can give me your decision then. I'm not your stepbrother, Annie. I might tell you what I think would help you, but only *you* can make the decision as to whether or not you agree with my assessment of the situation and want to accept my help.'

Annie leaned over the still, sun-warmed water of the fish pond in the middle of the formal garden, dropping in some crumbs of bread for the fat lazy goldfish and then trailing her fingers in the water. Ollie slept in his buggy. By now Falcon would be in Florence. The *castello* felt empty without him.

When he came back— Her hand jerked, disturbing the basking fish, her skin burning. She didn't want to think about his return, because that meant she would have to think about the decision she had to make before that return.

There was no decision to make, she reassured herself determinedly, standing up and taking hold of the buggy, preparing to take Ollie back inside. She was happy as she was.

She was happy as she was. Was she? Then why was she repeating those words to herself as though they were some kind of mantra she needed to use to reinforce her belief in her own words? Annie asked herself later than evening as she prepared for bed. She wanted to escape from the disconcerting pressure of the increasingly rebellious thoughts that were trying to undermine the sensible decision she had already made.

Although thankfully she had no memory of Antonio's abuse, he *had* stolen something from her. And that was her right to give her body freely to the man of her own choice for that first special time. Deep down inside it *did* hurt to know that her body's only experience of sex was such a cruel one. If she was honest, didn't she feel cheated of something very special? Of something that could have been and should have been very sweet? Nothing and no-one could give her back what she had lost, but what Falcon was offering her could be a very special gift to her body. Didn't she owe herself that for what Antonio had taken?

Falcon was man enough to offer to recompense her—was she woman enough to accept? A frisson of something that could have been dangerously close to excitement raced down her spine.

Falcon. Even his name sounded strong. *He* was strong. Strong enough to conquer her past and her pain? Could she afford to let him try?

For Ollie's sake, could she afford not to?

She felt so restless and on edge—so buoyed-up and... and filled with conflicting feelings.

It was only half past nine. No doubt in Florence Falcon's evening would only just be beginning, Annie acknowledged as she ran a bath for herself, hoping it would soothe her and help her to sleep.

Falcon might be stepping into the shower, before going out for the evening. Unbidden and definitely unwanted, out of nowhere she had a mental image of him standing beneath the shower, water cascading down onto his broad shoulders, and from there down over his chest, smoothing and flattening the dark hair on his body, running in rivulets that arrowed downwards.

Annie gasped, and tried to sink beneath the water of her bath to hide her shocked chagrin. What was the matter with her? She had never thought about a man like this before—imagining him naked, imagining him aroused, imagining that arousal giving her a feast of varied sensual pleasures. It was an imagining which now had a very real physical effect on her own body, in the tightening of her nipples and in the slow, grinding ache that had taken possession of her lower body.

What would Falcon think of her body? Would he think it attractive? Would it arouse him? Her breasts were firm and full. She had been so embarrassed when she had been the first girl in her class to need a bra—and even more uncomfortable when Colin had started asking her if boys ever tried to touch them. After that she had taken to wearing tops that were big and loose to disguise them.

If she accepted Falcon's offer he wouldn't expect her to do that. He'd want her to take pride in them. He'd want to see them and touch them—kiss them, perhaps. What was she doing, allowing herself to think like this? She'd already decided that she wasn't going to accept his offer—hadn't she?

She tried to think about something else—anything else. She didn't need to rediscover her lost sexuality. She was happy as she was. She had her adored son, and she felt she was on the verge of making a good friend in Julie. She and Rocco were so obviously happy together, and they loved one another very much. Anyone could see that. Every smile and every touch they exchanged showed their feelings for one another. Wouldn't *she* secretly like to be like that? To have a partner, someone with whom she shared that kind of bond of love and commitment? No, she wouldn't.

They might be lucky enough to love one another, but couples made commitments to one another every day of the week and then regretted them. She didn't need anyone else in her life, she didn't need Falcon to teach her to let go of the past, and most especially she didn't need Falcon to show her how to reawaken her suppressed sexuality. Because it was already awakening of its own accord. And she was afraid that if it awakened any more she might be in danger of enjoying her lessons way too much.

That was ridiculous.

But so was trying to lie to herself that she would be happy to spend the rest of her life alone. Everyone needed and wanted love.

She had Ollie.

Who one day would want to live his own life, find his own personal happiness. How would she feel if he was unable to do that because of her?

Her bathwater was growing cold, and her head was beginning to ache with the weight of her confused and contradictory thoughts.

Don't think about it any more.

She wasn't going to.

She stepped out of the bath and reached for a towel.

What was Falcon doing now? Was he thinking about her at all?

Why should he be thinking about her. She didn't *want* him to be thinking about her. Because if she did then that would mean…

What? What would it mean? Certainly not that she had some private ulterior motive for wanting to agree to his suggestion. Those almost forgotten frissons of sensation that had stoked her body into renewed sensual life from the first minute she had seen him meant nothing other than that her body was one step ahead of her head, that it was already eager to become the body of a woman who knew and understood her own sensuality.

Freedom was beckoning her. It was freedom that was causing such an intoxication of her senses, overwhelming the barriers of her anxiety and fear.

There was nothing personal in those unsettling little surges of sensation that pulsed through her and gripped her every time she allowed herself to acknowledge that Falcon was a very male man. It was just the same kind of natural response to a situation as the tingling that came from blood returning to numbed flesh.

Pulling on her bathrobe, Annie walked through her own bedroom and into the nursery, where Ollie lay peacefully asleep in his cot.

With a mother's instinct she knew it wasn't just her imagination that her son was thriving in his new environment. He had put on weight. And already his skin—despite the copious amounts of sun protection cream in which she smothered it—was warming to what she suspected was really its natural colour. It hadn't escaped her that the colour was closer to Falcon's skin tone than it was to her own. Already he seemed to be taking a much greater interest in his surroundings, smiling more readily at the strangers who had come in to his life than he ever had at strangers in London. Did he somehow, with his baby instinct, sense that these new people were *his* people, of *his* blood?

What she would be doing if she accepted Falcon's offer wouldn't be so much for herself as for Ollie. Annie felt love for her baby gripping her heart. When he grew up she wanted more than anything else what surely every loving parent wanted for their child. She wanted his happiness and his joy in life. She wanted him to know and share love, and to build good relationships out of that knowledge. She wanted for him all that she had not known but must for his sake learn.

But could she do it? Could she find the strength to thrust herself into the fire and endure more, much more, of what she already felt when Falcon touched her?

CHAPTER SEVEN

'I'VE been thinking,' Falcon announced, leaning forward across the wrought iron table on the terrace, where they'd been sitting, drinking a pre-dinner aperitif.

He had arrived back from Florence just over half an hour ago. Annie had seen him drive up to the *castello* and then into the paved courtyard. She had watched him uncurl his lean height and muscular shoulders from his car, and then reach back inside it to gather up his suit jacket and a small laptop case, hooking the jacket over his shoulder before mounting the flight of marble steps that led up to the main entrance of the *castello*.

His shirt had been unfastened at the throat, just by one button, but the brilliance of the late-afternoon sun had struck through his shirt so clearly that she could almost have traced the dark shadowing of male body hair that crossed his chest and bisected his flat six-pack. There was something very sensually male about that dark shadowing. Something so strongly intimate that it had set off a reaction inside her that curled mockingly round her prim self-consciousness, silencing the voice that had said it was wrong for her to watch him and be so aware of his masculinity.

It wasn't as though she had been waiting for him to return. The only reason she had been on the first floor of the *castello*, and thus able to witness his arrival through one of the windows of the line of formal salons on this side of the building, was because Maria had insisted on giving her a tour of them.

The *castello* was enormous, with cellars and attics and three and sometimes four full floors in between. It had three towers, a huge ball-room, and was in fact a combination of the original *castello* and an eighteenth-century *palazzo* which one of Falcon's ancestors had built to extend the original building.

He'd changed out of his suit now, and was wearing a pair of faded, well-washed jeans and a soft white linen shirt, his bare feet thrust into soft shoes. He looked casually relaxed, whilst she felt tensely uncomfortable in one of her new dresses. She didn't want him to think that she had deliberately tried to make herself look more attractive for him. That wasn't the case at all. She had simply grabbed the first dress that had come to hand after he had strolled into the salon where she had been with Maria, to ask her to join him on the terrace for a drink before dinner.

Tonight would be the first time she had had dinner with him since she had come here. Previously she had eaten alone—and happily—she assured herself, in her room, content to be safe and with Ollie, and not wanting anything or anyone else.

It wasn't her fault that the dress she had grabbed turned out to be a sleeveless tube of honey-coloured jersey. It had looked so nondescript on its hanger that she hadn't given its suitability a second thought when she had pulled it on over her head, before slipping on a pair of kitten-heeled sandals. As the mother of a six-month-old baby she had no intention of wearing high stiletto heels in case she stumbled and Ollie came to harm.

She hadn't even looked at her full-length reflection before leaving her bedroom, simply running a brush through her hair and then sliding on a soft slick of lipgloss, before spraying herself with the admittedly delicious light scent the personal shopper had recommended, and scooping up Ollie.

In fact, it had only been when she had been about to leave her bedroom that she had caught sight of herself in the mirror and had realised how very slender the jersey dress made her look—how faithfully it followed the lines of her body, despite the stylish pleated ruching that swept from the bust right down to her hip, which she had naively assumed meant that the dress would be suitably unrevealing.

It had been too late to go back and get changed, but she had comforted herself with the thought that she would be sitting down and the dress's neckline, whilst slashed across her throat, did not reveal very much flesh.

That had been before she had realised that Falcon was already on the terrace and waiting for her—or realized that he would come towards her to take Ollie from her, and then survey her in such a silent and yet at the same time very meaningful way. Her heart kicked off in a flurry of little beats now, just thinking about the way he had smiled at her before he had come to put Oliver in the highchair that was pulled up at the table, waiting for him.

It wasn't the way Falcon had smiled at her five minutes ago that she ought to be concentrating on, Annie warned herself. It was what he had just said to her. What had he been thinking? That he had changed his mind about his plan to turn her into a fully functioning modern sexual woman? Of course, if that was the case she would be relieved in many ways. Very relieved. Wouldn't she?

She took a quick sip of her drink. She didn't normally touch alcohol, but the chilled light rosé wine Falcon had persuaded her to try was delicious. She could feel it relaxing her tense cramped stomach muscles as she tried to breathe evenly, as though she wasn't in the least bit apprehensive and most particularly as though she hadn't hardy slept at all last night for thinking about what he had said to her, what she would say to him, and how she felt about…about everything.

'Whilst I was in Florence I was speaking with a member of my late mother's family. One of the old family houses is currently being emptied of its treasures, including the books from its library and a great many family letters. He has asked me if we could house the books here, to which of course I have agreed.

'My mother's family history is an interesting one. They were originally silk merchants in the fifteenth century, who bought themselves into the nobility and ultimately became very wealthy and well connected. The marriage between my parents was one brokered between my father and my mother's uncle, for reasons of mutual financial benefit and social prestige. However, my father never allowed our mother to forget that, whilst his family line descended directly from nobility, hers descended from the merchant class.'

'Your mother must have been so hurt,' said Annie sympathetically.

'She suffered very badly because of my father's cruelty to her. As children we all felt that our mother must not have loved us enough to want to live, but of course that was not the reality. The reality is that she died from complications after Rocco's birth.'

Annie could see the three bereft children, desperately longing for their mother, all too easily. Her heart ached for those boys, and inside her head she saw herself as a mother, gathering them close—especially Falcon, who she knew would have been proud and brave and determined to hold back his own tears in order to comfort his brothers.

'Growing up without your mother must have been awful for you.'

'As growing up without your father must have been for *you*. The understanding of what that means is something we share. It may be that, should you decide to learn Italian, you will one day read the story of my parents' families for yourself. The library here at the *castello* holds many personal diaries.'

Immediately Annie's eyes lit up with excited anticipation.

'There's nothing I'd like to do more,' she admitted.

'Then I shall make some enquiries and find a teacher for you. Or if you prefer you could take a language course in Florence. My apartment there is large enough to accommodate you and Ollie.'

He was being so kind. Whilst she had been listening to him she had, she realised as Falcon reached for the bottle of rosé and leaned across to top up her glass, almost emptied it.

'Oh, no. No more for me. I don't drink at all normally—' she began, but Falcon ignored her and continued to pour.

'I am most certainly not in favour of anyone drinking more than they should, but it is important that you learn to drink a couple of glasses of wine without it going to your head. It will give you confidence in social situations. Now,

I have also been thinking about you and Oliver whilst I was in Florence.'

Annie's heart gave another furious flurry of too-fast beats, so she took another sip of her wine. It did taste good, and a lovely warm, mellow and relaxed feeling was beginning to creep over her.

'If you are to have any quality of life of your own then you will need someone who you can trust to look after Oliver in your absence.'

'I don't want anyone else to look after him,' Annie protested. 'I love him and I want to be with him.'

'It is not healthy when mother and child have only one another. Normally in Italian families there is always someone for a mother to turn to for help. She is not left alone to bring up her child. I have spoken with Maria already, and she has a cousin who trained as a nursery nurse. She and her husband have recently returned to live on the island, and I have arranged for her to come up to the *castello* when you feel ready to speak with her. You can interview her. If you decide she is suitable then you will be doing her a favour, as well.'

Noblesse oblige, Annie thought ruefully, but she knew that what he was saying made sense, so she nodded her head and then said, 'Ollie's falling asleep. I'd better take him upstairs and put him to bed.'

Falcon's answer—'I'll carry him for you'—had her denying that there was any need for him to do so, but Falcon simply stood up and went to lift Ollie out of his chair.

'I have a distinct feeling that if I let you disappear upstairs alone you won't come back down again. And as you know we have an outstanding matter to discuss,' he told her.

Annie was glad she wasn't holding Ollie, because she suspected that if she had been she would have been in danger of dropping him, so great was the effect of Falcon's words on her.

It didn't take her long to put Ollie to bed. He was such a good baby. She smiled lovingly as she kissed his forehead, and then gave a small gasp as she realised that Falcon had come from the small sitting room that opened off her bedroom into the nursery, and was standing watching her.

'Oliver is a very lucky child to have such a devoted mother.'

Was he thinking of his own mother, and how he and his brothers as children had mistakenly felt that she had not loved them enough to fight death to be with them?

Instinctively moved to comfort him, she told him gently, 'I'm sure your mother did love you all, Falcon—and that she wanted to be with you. Even though to you as a child it must have seemed that she had chosen not to live.'

She had lifted her hand to his sleeve as she spoke, touching his arm in the kind of tender gesture that came unbidden and naturally, but now—as he moved closer to her and she felt the hard, muscular warmth of his flesh beneath her fingers— a very different feeling from the one that had originally motivated her surged through her, causing her to snatch back her hand and quickly turn towards the door, her face hot.

'You have a very compassionate nature,' she heard Falcon saying as he followed her. 'And I think you are right. Certainly as an adult it is pity I feel for my mother, rather than the despair her death caused me as a boy. She used to say that producing us was her duty and that she herself was a sacrifice.'

Annie had to fight hard not to betray her shock. Poor

woman. She must have been dreadfully unhappy to have spoken to her son like that, instead of protecting him from her own unhappiness. She would never do that to Ollie. *Never!* She wanted him to grow up whole and happy, and free of any sense of guilt about her or about himself.

They had dinner. Warmed goat cheese with tomatoes and herbs to start with, and then a roast chicken and pasta dish that was mouth-wateringly delicious.

Annie had already learned from Maria that most of the staff at the *castello* were local, and that their families had lived and worked on Leopardi land for countless genera-tions—even the chef.

She had drunk another glass of wine with her meal, and now she and Falcon had finished the piping hot coffee the little maid had brought them. Although Annie had regret-fully had to refuse the chocolate *petit fours* that had been with the coffee—not just because she was full, but because she was also feeling very nervous. All through the meal Falcon had answered her curious questions about the ob-viously feudal nature of the area, and the relationship between his father the old Prince and the people who looked on him almost as though he were still their ruler. Not once had he made any reference to the fact that she had not as yet given him her decision.

'My father's attitude towards the land and the people *is* feudal,' Falcon told her now. 'And that is a matter of great concern to me and to my brothers. We have all been fortu-nate in having benefited financially through our mother's family, and we have all become financially successful in the modern world. The opportunity to live in that modern world is one I am committed to giving to our people, despite my father's wish to keep them locked in the past. And speaking of people being locked in the past…' He stood up. 'A walk in the gardens will, I think, help us to digest our dinner. And whilst we are walking you can give me your decision on the offer I made before I left for Florence.'

Annie's breath escaped her lungs in a leaky gasp.

'What is it?' Falcon asked as she too stood up.

'I thought that perhaps you'd changed your mind about that, and that that was why you hadn't mentioned it,' Annie confessed.

'You thought or you hoped?' he challenged her, even as his light touch—and it was merely a touch, quickly removed—guided her towards the steps that led down into the gardens.

It was darker here than it had been on the terrace. A prickle of sensation quivered over her skin. The night was full of hidden dangers—or were they hidden promises? What on earth had made her think *that*?

The moon, new and bright, gave off just enough light to show the outline of the mountains, silvering Leopardi land, the olive groves and the fields closer to the *castello*. Her son was part of all of this—but he was part of her, as well. Somewhere unseen a bird screeched, making her jump and miss a step. Instantly Falcon moved closer to catch her, one hand splayed across the middle of her back the other encircling her wrist.

Had he turned her in towards his own body or had she done that for herself? Annie didn't know. She did know that she was acutely aware of him. She could smell the scent of his skin, its familiarity immediately transporting her back to the first time they had met.

'Are you warm enough?'

Had he felt the rash of goosebumps that had suddenly come up under her skin? He must have done. They weren't caused by cold, though. The evening air was wonderfully balmy and warm.

'It's late,' she told him unsteadily, as she looked imploringly towards the *castello*.

'Too late to change your mind,' Falcon told her.

He *had* moved closer to her—much closer. They were standing face to face. One of his hands was still splayed out across her back, its firm pressure bringing her towards him, whilst the other hand…

Annie had to swallow very hard. The fingertips of the other hand were slowly stroking her bare arm in a caress that drifted from her inner wrist all the way up to her elbow. Tongues of fire licked through her veins. She was trembling openly now, completely unable to conceal her reaction to him.

She still made a brave attempt to face him down, though, reminding him shakily, 'I haven't given you my decision yet.'

He was so close to her that she could feel his chest shaking as he laughed. The warmth of his amusement gusted round her, his breath grazing her cheek and making her turn and lift her head as though she wanted to capture it with her lips.

'Yes, you have,' he corrected her. 'You told me when I refilled your wineglass and you trembled; you told me when you looked at my mouth over dinner; just now when you shivered when I touched you. You told me then that you are ready to be aroused by me. Your body has signalled to mine its curiosity and its interest.'

Annie opened her mouth to object, to tell him that he was wrong, but the unseen bird screeched again and instead she gasped and moved closer to Falcon.

It was the wrong thing to do. His arm was encircling her now, holding her against his body, whilst her own body trembled helplessly beneath the slow caress of his fingertips on her arm.

Somehow, without her knowing what she was doing, she had gripped his other hand, curling her fingers into the muscle as she clung to him.

'How does this feel?' he asked her softly as his knuckles brushed her arm lightly.

'I don't know,' Annie lied. But of course she did. It felt shockingly and dangerously erotic.

Beneath her dress she could feel her nipples tightening, whilst heat curled through her lower body and the insides of her thighs began to ache, the feeling there spreading from deep inside her body.

She badly wanted to close her eyes and simply lean into Falcon, so that he could hold her and caress her, those magical knowing hands of his touching all those places that were now aching for his touch.

Panic hit her and she pulled back from him. Everything that Colin had told her and warned her about suddenly flooded into her head, filling her with self disgust and shock. The woman she wanted to be and the girl she had fought relentlessly with one another for possession of her mind.

Falcon had stepped back from her, his hand holding her own as he directed her deeper still into the garden. The danger had passed and she was safe. But was safe what she really wanted to be? Hadn't there been a moment back there—more than merely a moment—when she had been anticipating the touch of his mouth on her own with greedy longing?

'You are a woman it is extremely easy for a man to want,' Falcon told her.

His voice reached her out of the darkness and had her stopping, walking to turn and confront him with her emotional response.

'You don't have to say things like that to me. In fact, I would rather that you didn't. I'm not a complete fool, even if I am laughably sexually inexperienced. I know perfectly well that you're just trying to be kind and to…to boost my confidence. A man like you would never find me extremely easy to want.'

The moonlight fell directly on Falcon's face, highlighting its sensually male structure and sending a flood surge of aching, sweet need pounding through her. What was happening to her? Whatever it was it, was happening far too fast.

'By your own admission you know nothing about the needs and desires of my sex. Therefore you are not qualified to know that I would never find you extremely easy to want.' Falcon swept aside her argument, his voice sharpening as he added, 'The discovery that you have the ability to arouse me simply by doing nothing other than letting me see and feel your response to me is as unfamiliar to me as it is to you.'

'I…I'm flattered that…that you…'

'That I find you desirable? That being here in the moonlight with you arouses me? We must take things slowly if I am not to lose my head and thus lose my efficacy as your teacher.'

His face was shadowed and hidden from her now, but Annie could tell from his voice that he was smiling—which must mean that the eventuality to which he was referring, namely him losing his head, was simply not going to happen. And that was a relief to her. Of course it was. The last thing she wanted was for Falcon to become so aroused by their intimacy that he lost control and made proper, real passionate love to her—wasn't it?

'I ought to go in. I don't like leaving Ollie on his own.'

'Don't worry, I asked Maria to keep an eye on him. I knew that maternal heart of yours would be anxious.'

Before Annie could thank him he continued.

'In a week or so's time, once you have settled in and if you are agreeable, I thought I would take a day off to show you and Oliver something of the island.'

A week or so's time seemed a safely vague distance away, so it was easy for her to say, half shyly, 'Thank you. I would like that.' After all it was the truth. She *would* like to see something of the island.

They were deep in the garden now, hidden from the moonlight by the branches of a tree, and yet Falcon still managed to find her forehead accurately as he deposited a light kiss there, and told her, 'Now you can relax. Because the first lesson is almost over.'

'I just hope you don't mean to set me any tests,' Annie responded feelingly, in her relief, and then realised her mistake when Falcon laughed.

'Oh, I fully intend to do that,' he assured her. 'And to see how much you have been paying attention to what I have been doing by getting you to repeat my caresses for you on me. But not yet.'

He was going to expect her to caress him—to send

those same quivers of helpless mindless physical delight zinging through his body that he had sent through hers. Impossible!

'There is just one thing more I intend to do tonight, before I let you escape from your instruction.'

One more thing? Annie's head jerked towards him, and as though that was exactly what he had intended he cupped the side of her face with his palm and then stroked his thumb across her half-parted lips, brushing softly to and fro against them whilst her senses reeled and her mind slipped away, allowing her body and her sensuality to take control.

Falcon's arm was round her, supporting her, whilst his thumb probed between her parted lips. Without even having to think about it Annie touched his thumb with the tip of her tongue, exploring its texture and its taste, circling it and stroking it, growing bolder as she realised how powerful it made her feel to take that control.

Lost in the excitement of what she was doing, she didn't even realise at first that Falcon had removed his thumb and replaced it with his mouth until he started to kiss her.

There was no chance for her to deny him and no point, either. Her lips, she herself, were both already open to him, and to the raw sexuality of his kiss. He was cupping her face with both of his hands now, caressing her skin as he took the kiss deeper, his tongue probing the soft sweetness of her mouth whilst his fingers spread to her ears and the responsive area just behind them.

Annie heard herself moan into Falcon's kiss. She felt herself writhe and then press eagerly into his body. She suffered the savaging of disappointment and a sense of loss when he removed his mouth from her own—and then was flung headlong into the sweetness of the pleasure that came when his lips caressed their way along her throat from her ear to her shoulder, and then back along her collarbone. His dark head bent over her, encouraging her to slide her fingers into the heavenly thickness of his hair.

It was like being on a roller coaster.

She could feel her heart thudding so heavily that it seemed to be beating outside her body. And then she realised that the beat she could feel drumming so hard wasn't coming from her own heart but from Falcon's. The sweetest pleasure and triumph pierced her, catching her off guard with its intensity. Falcon was *enjoying* kissing her. Her—a woman who had thought herself not a proper woman at all.

Gratitude and exhilaration filled her, but was quickly forgotten when Falcon kissed her again, taking her mouth and covering it with his own, finding her tongue and teasing it into an erotically intimate dance with his own whilst his hands moved down over her body, his palms just skimming her breasts.

Immediately Annie tensed, her delight in the moment broken by the sharpness of her sudden recognition that things were moving too fast.

As though Falcon himself recognised that fact he released her, leaning his forehead against her own for a second before saying huskily, 'It is just as well this dress of yours does not possess a zip. Because if it did right now I'd be caressing your breasts, learning them with my hands and my lips. There is something almost unbearably erotic about the sight of moonlight on a woman's naked body, caressing it with silver pathways.'

Annie shuddered wildly and pulled back from him.

'I really must go in.'

'Yes,' Falcon agreed meaningfully. 'I think you must—unless you want me to take this evening's lesson far further than I had originally planned.'

He wasn't really asking her if she wanted what he had just described to her, was he? Annie thought dizzily. He couldn't be. Could he? Her senses swung between fear and excitement. They were a long way from that stage yet, she reassured herself. Indeed, she wasn't even sure she would be able to go that far.

Annie couldn't sleep. She had tried—she had tried very hard. But every time she closed her eyes it was as though she was back in the garden with Falcon. In fact, so vivid were the images conjured up behind her closed eyelids that she could almost feel him, as well as see him. His warmth against her own body, his touch on her skin, his scent, his kiss, his voice sensitising her already over-sensitised mind when he told her what he would do to her.

It was no use. Annie pushed back the covers and slid her feet out of the bed and onto the floor. It was so warm tonight that even the thin cotton tee-shirt-style nightdress she was wearing felt unpleasant and unwanted against her skin. Because what she really wanted was the touch of Falcon's hands?

This was ridiculous. She was glad, of course, that she was rediscovering her sexuality. She just hadn't expected that what she would feel would be so…so intense. She had imagined she would feel nervous and uncertain, too anxious to really enjoy what was happening, but it was as though somehow Falcon had cast some magic spell on her that had cut through those expected feelings.

She walked to the nursery, where Ollie was fast asleep—as she herself should be and no doubt Falcon was.

Falcon stared unseeingly at the computer screen in front of him. Unable to sleep, he had decided he might as well work on one of his new architectural commissions.

Falcon loved his work. His love of the beauty of Florence's buildings was, he believed, his mother's gift to him, since Florence had been her home. Annie would enjoy Florence, and he would enjoy her pleasure in it. As he had enjoyed her pleasure this evening...

It was no use lying to himself. The truth was that he had been caught off guard by the intensity of his own desire for her—aroused, no doubt, by the sweetness of her response to him.

He sat back in his chair and exhaled slowly. The object of the exercise was not his pleasure but Annie's rediscovery of her lost sexuality. And if he had experienced an arousal and desire with her tonight that he had felt might get out of control then he must ensure that he did not do so again. In future he must experience those things only to the extent that her knowledge of his response would aid her progress. If he could not do that then he would, in his own eyes, be as culpable and as guilty of abusing her as her stepbrother.

He stood up and walked over to the window. His private apartment was in the original part of the *castello*, which he had remodelled sympathetically to create for himself very modern living quarters in what was essentially a twelfth-century building. The walls had been stripped back to their natural stone, where appropriate, and limestone floors had been laid on the ground floor of the two-storey apartment. Damage to the outer wall in one area had allowed him, with modern building techniques, to replace the crumbling wall with a two-storey, floor-to-ceiling glass 'wall', which looked out onto a limestone patio, beyond which an infinity pool melted visually into the sea itself.

Within the area he had renovated there had been enough space to create an inner room, with glass and polished plaster walls, which contained a small modern kitchen again with views towards the sea.

A matt-finish metal staircase led up to a galleried landing and three bedrooms, each with its own bathroom and dressing room area. The apartment was furnished with the very best of modern Italian furniture in natural products like leather and wood, as well as steel and modern textiles, and artwork.

The apartment was a clean open space that breathed light and openness. As an antidote to his father's love of secrecy and control? Falcon frowned. He was digging too deep within himself when there was no need. Better that he thought about Annie than his own childhood.

He doubted that Annie would totally approve of his apartment. She would think it child-unfriendly. Her ideal would no doubt be somewhere more like the villa outside Florence his second brother had bought for his new wife—a large, elegant family home that would happily accommodate any number of children in safety and comfort.

It was his duty, though, as the eldest son to maintain a presence here. When their father died, the people would expect him to be here.

But it was Annie and Oliver and their needs that were preoccupying him right now, rather than those of his people.

Annie. She was invading his thoughts and his senses more deeply and more intensely than he had been prepared for. But that wasn't her fault.

It had been obvious to him that she was devoid of the least idea of how much it had aroused him to feel her body trembling so wildly just because he had caressed her. A reaction like that could go to a man's head far too easily, and could make *her* far too vulnerable.

His body was aching. It had been a long time since he had had a relationship. The effect of too many women throwing themselves at him rather too often and too hard during his twenties had left him picky about the women he dated, and cynical about the likelihood of actually finding love and the right kind of wife in one woman. On a practical level it was important that his wife understood his commitment to his people, and that she was willing to share that commitment with him. But it was equally important to him that his marriage should be one in which husband and wife were faithful to one another. His father's affair had left him with an abhorrence of marital infidelity. His brothers were lucky. They had had the good fortune to fall in love and be loved in return.

He, on the other hand, had to balance his own needs with the needs of the Leopardi name and its people. Passion and practicality. Could they ever go together? Or must one always be sacrificed in order to have the other?

If so, he must favour practicality for the benefit of others over passion for the benefit of himself.

His body still ached with unsatisfied need.

If he closed his eyes it would be all too easy to picture Annie—not as she had been in the garden, but far more intimately, here with him now, clothed only in moonlight, silvering her breasts and dipping shadows between them, turning her nipples as dark as olives, stroking silken pathways along her body. She would taste of night air and warm skin, her breathing shaken by tremors of desire. She would cry out to him as he kissed her and held her. And he would...

He would do nothing other than remember what his role was in her life, Falcon told himself harshly.

'I thought this evening we would concentrate on the small things a man might do to show that he is attracted to a woman.'

They had finished dinner. Ollie was asleep—Annie had been up to check on him—and her nerves were so on edge she was sure that Falcon must notice. It was five days since he had kissed her. Five whole days. And there hadn't been a single one of them when she hadn't relived that kiss over and over again.

'The small things?' Annie repeated. She must not feel disappointed. She must not wish that he would kiss her again. She must *not*!

'Yes,' Falcon confirmed. 'Such as the way a man might hold the gaze of a woman he admires for that little bit longer, looking at her like so.'

His hand under her chin gently turned her face towards his own and slightly upwards, so that his gaze fell directly onto her upturned face and she could see the slow, concentrated way in which he allowed it to almost physically caress her skin.

Tension prickled along her nerve-endings; her heart started to race. She could almost *feel* the heavy weight of his concentration on her mouth. It was impossible for her to stop her lips from parting, and impossible not to look helplessly into his eyes. He was looking at her in a way that made her catch her breath. The blood was pounding in her ears and a mixture of weakness and excitement was pouring through her.

Falcon knew he had to break the spell he himself had woven, which now trapped him within its sensual mystery. Just looking at Annie's mouth made him want to feel it beneath his own—to feel too the sweetness of her previous response.

This wasn't what he had planned. The object was to encourage her to explore and enjoy her sensuality—not for him to become aroused.

Somehow he managed to drag his gaze away. Although there was nothing he could do about the powerful thumping of his heart.

Annie watched him, torn between disappointment and relief as she saw him win his battle for control.

'I can see how…how erotic something like that could be,' she told him, striving to sound calm and business-like—after all, what they were doing was a sort of businesslike venture.

'It's amazing, isn't it, that something so…Well, something that's just a look really can have such a powerful effect?' She hesitated, and then told him honestly, 'You make it all seem so natural and…and that it's all right to feel…to want…' She couldn't risk putting into words exactly what he had made her feel, so instead she finished quickly, 'It's not shameful and wrong, like Colin used to say it was.'

'No man worthy of the name would ever make a woman feel ashamed of her sensuality.' Falcon's voice was constricted with the force of his feelings. Her trusting admission had reminded him of the role he had elected to play. His hand dropped away from her face. It might be better in future if he conducted at least some of her lessons in public, where he would surely not be in so much danger from his own reactions.

'Bring swimming things,' Falcon had said to her yesterday, when he had asked her if she still wanted to see a little more of the island. But it had simply not occurred to Annie that he would bring her and Ollie somewhere as achingly smart and exclusive as this hotel where they had had lunch, after a drive during which Falcon had not only driven at a safe and comfortable speed but had also given her an expert commentary on their surroundings and their architectural past.

She should surely be getting used to the intimacy of being around him now? she told herself. And to all those small touches that came when he pulled out a chair for her, or helped her in any way—the smiles that accompanied the compliments he paid her. All were designed, she knew, to boost her confidence in herself as a woman.

She *was* getting used to them, and she *did* feel comfortable in his presence—but at the same time she also felt confused by the way she herself so often felt. The way she ached inside for him to kiss her again, and her sense of loss when he didn't.

Today, though, they were having a day out with Ollie.

The hotel he had brought them to was close to the town of Taormina, famous for its historical buildings—including the ruins of a Greek theatre—and for its proximity to Mount Etna. Before lunch they had had time to walk down the main street, Falcon insisting on pushing Ollie's buggy, whilst he pointed out various sites of interest to her—including the glamorous Caffè Wunderbar, where Elizabeth Taylor and Richard Burton had sipped cocktails.

Falcon had even told her, leaning closer to her to murmur the words in her ear that, 'D.H. Lawrence holidayed here with his wife.' He had based Mellors the gamekeeper in *Lady Chatterley's Lover* on a boatman from the town, whom Lawrence's wife had seduced. 'Taormina was famous at one time for the effect it had on visiting Englishwomen. You must tell me later if there is any truth in that rumour.'

He had been smiling at her as he spoke, a lazy smile of such intimacy that she had quickly forgotten the small pang of aloneness she had felt earlier, glimpsing a couple ambling along the street totally wrapped up in one another. In fact, having Falcon's concentrated attention fixed on her had made her feel she was in so much danger of becoming dizzy that she had reached out to steady herself, placing her hand on the handle of the buggy, only to have it immediately covered by Falcon's hand closing around it.

It was strange, the effect such small gestures could have. She had wanted to pull her hand away—if only to stop her heart from pounding so heavily—but she had reminded herself that Falcon was trying to teach her what it felt like to experience all those things she should have experienced naturally as she grew from a teenager to a young woman.

Because he'd still had his hand over hers, Falcon had been forced to move closer to her as they'd walked along together, and that had meant that she had been acutely conscious of his thigh brushing hers and of his closeness to her. When they had had to cross a road he had released her hand, but her relief had been short-lived because instead he had placed his arm around her waist, guiding her politely across the road.

'You look terrified,' he had told her once they were safely across. 'This kind of physical intimacy is supposed to be a pleasure. When a man takes every opportunity he can to be close to you, in mundane everyday matters of life and in public, it signifies not just his physical desire for you but also his desire to claim and protect you. If you want his attention then the way to show him would be to lean in a little bit closer to him.' His arm had urged her closer as he had spoken.

'And relax your body so that it moves with his. Then he will probably do something like this.' His hand had moved to the curve of her waist, discreetly caressing it.

Discreet so far as any possible onlookers were concerned. The effect his touch had had on the internal workings of her body had been anything but discreet. Warmth from his hand had spread all over her body, making her breasts grow heavy and her nipples tighten and ache. It had pooled with devastating effect low within her, and her mind had created mental images and physical longings that had made her face burn with self-consciousness.

Was that physical desire? She had felt as though Falcon had unlocked a place within her—the turning of its key unleashing almost frighteningly powerful urges. Like the urge she had experienced during lunch, when Falcon had put his hand on her knee to attract her attention whilst she had been spooning baby food into Ollie's eager mouth, so that he could tell her something. It had been an urge that had meant she would gladly have turned to him in silent invitation for him to slide his hand along the bare length of her thigh.

And he had known what she had been feeling. She was sure of it, Annie thought now, from the shelter of their private tented poolside *cabana* at the same exclusive hotel where they had had lunch.

Annie had seen photographs of such places in the glossy magazines she'd flicked through in doctors' and dentists' waiting rooms, but she'd never expected to experience the reality of one of them for herself.

Their lunch had been served at a private table under the shade of an umbrella, on signature china with heavy designer cutlery, crystal glasses and beautifully laundered linen.

In the baby changing room provided for guests she'd found everything the most fussy and spoiled mother and baby could ever want—although she had noticed that the two other babies in the changing room were accompanied by uniformed nannies and not their mothers.

Now, having changed into her swimsuit whilst Falcon minded Ollie, she was lying in the shade on the most comfortable lounger imaginable, whilst Ollie played happily within her watchful view.

Falcon had gone for a swim—which was perhaps just as well, she admitted, given the effect the constant sight of him clothed in a pair of admittedly perfectly respectable brightly coloured shorts of the type most of the other men also seemed to be wearing had been having on her.

Her swimsuit and its matching prettily embroidered kaftan had been chosen by the personal shopper. Annie hadn't so much as tried them on, convinced that she would never wear *any* of the clothes the shopper had selected, never mind something as revealing as the swimsuit, but she was forced to admit now that it might have been wiser if she had.

In its elegant box the pewter-coloured swim-suit had looked innocuous enough, even a little dull, but once on it had wrapped itself around her curves in a way that, whilst covering her very respectably, had somehow or other managed to create the most sensual of body shapes—and surely a greater length of leg than she really possessed. It had been a relief to slip on the matching pewter kaftan, which thankfully covered her from her throat to her knees.

Now, though, the privacy of the cabana and the relaxing effect of her lunchtime glass of wine had combined to coax her into removing the kaftan and luxuriating in the wonderful warmth of the sun—easily felt despite the shade.

Tired out after his busy day, Ollie was starting to close his eyes. Smiling at her son, Annie got up off her lounger and picked him up, hugging and kissing him before settling him in his buggy for a sleep.

She had just finished tucking Ollie in when Falcon returned to the *cabana* from his swim, the sun catching shoulders surely as broad and powerful as those of any Olympic swimmer, tanned as his whole body was, in a beautiful golden brown. There was something about the close proximity of so much semi-naked masculinity that was making it very difficult for her to breathe, Annie admitted to herself.

Not wanting to be caught by Falcon gazing wide-eyed at his broad shoulders and powerful arms, she let her attention slide lower—only to realise her mistake far too late, when it became trapped in watching drops of water from the pool roll down his chest.

She couldn't breathe properly, couldn't move, couldn't think—but she could certainly feel, and what she was feeling was telling her in no uncertain terms that Falcon had well and truly unleashed her natural instincts. The weight of the water had pulled his shorts low down on his hips, and the sight of the dark arrowing of his body hair was making her feel slightly light headed. Or was it the thudding pound of her heart that was doing that? It didn't matter. All that mattered was her relief when Falcon reached for a towel and started to dry himself.

'I saw you putting sunscreen on Oliver earlier. I hope you've put some on yourself,' he said when he had finished drying his body and was rubbing at his hair.

'Yes. Yes, I have,' Annie told him quickly. She could feel her temperature soaring at the same speed with which her heartbeat was accelerating at the thought of having Falcon offer to perform that task for her.

'Good.' He reached down and picked up the sunscreen she had placed by her sun lounger and handed it to her, re-questing, 'Do my back for me, will you?'

What could she say? If she refused he was bound to want to know why—and besides, this was exactly the kind of thing that a woman of her age should be used to doing. Falcon would make allowances for her, she reassured herself as she nodded her head in acquiescence, her throat suddenly too dry for her to be able to trust herself to speak. He knew, after all, that she had no experience of this kind of personal intimacy.

He had presented his back to her now, and was standing with his hands on his hips, waiting.

Her hands were trembling so much she dropped the bottle of lotion, and then struggled to uncap it, causing Falcon to turn round and take it from her, telling her wryly, 'Hold out your hand.' He squeezed a small amount of the lotion into her palm, before turning his back to her a second time.

She started at the back of his neck, suffering the shock of the silky hot feel of his skin against her lotion-slick hands as she worked the cream into his skin as slowly and as carefully as though it had been Ollie's baby skin she was protecting. Beneath her fingertips his shoulders were every bit as strongly muscled as they had looked, and it was hard for her not to give in to the unexpected temptation to trace the shape of his bones with her fingertip. How extraordinary and amazing and life-affirming it was to know that one day her son, her baby, would be like this—a man whom women would admire and desire and love, just as they must Falcon.

Her body stiffened. How many women had there been? How many had he loved back? Why was that sharp pain skewering her heart?

Falcon's voce—'Something wrong?'—brought her back to reality.

'I've run out of lotion,' she told him.

The cap was still off the bottle, but strangely she felt no inclination to point that fact out to him when he picked it up and tipped some more into her waiting hand.

'I'm not Oliver, you know,' he told her. 'In a real man and woman situation there would be nothing wrong and a whole lot right in caressing me as a potential lover whilst you're doing that.'

Immediately Annie stiffened.

'I'm not used to things like this,' she reminded him defensively. It hurt to know that he thought her touch too clinical to be arousing, even though she told herself that it ought not to.

'Perhaps it would be better if I gave you a small demonstration?' Falcon suggested.

Before she could say anything he had poured some of the lotion into his own hand and was turning her around.

She was wearing her hair up in a knot for coolness, and she could feel the warmth of Falcon's breath as he leaned closer to her. Was he going to kiss her? Her stomach turned liquid with a longing that turned to disappointment when he didn't. Only for that disappointment to go up in flames of fresh sensual excitement when he eased the straps of her swimsuit down. Frantically she clutched the front of it to her breasts, whilst Falcon began to slowly stroke and circle trails of hot desire on the vulnerable flesh of her bare back.

How could something as simple as putting on sun cream be so unbearably erotic? Annie felt as though she had entered a whole new world of sensation and discovery. What Falcon was doing was giving her a master class in the art of sensual massage, she recognized, as her body took fire and her inhibitions were burned away.

Long before he had reached the base of her spine her body was urging her to beg him to remove her swimsuit completely and take her in his arms. Surely it wasn't possible for her to be feeling like this so quickly, so easily, and so…so intensely? Perhaps Colin had been right when he had warned her all those years ago that there was something about her that meant she needed protecting from her own too-sexual nature?

As though somehow her thoughts and fears had communicated themselves to Falcon, he turned her around to face him, his hands firm and cool on her upper arms, holding her safe, making her *feel* safe.

'You are aroused and that is exactly what I intended to happen,' he told her calmly. 'It's a completely natural reaction to my deliberately erotic stimulation of your body and your senses. It's nothing to feel ashamed of or concerned about. Rather, you should feel proud of your inbuilt ability to be the woman nature designed you to be. No matter what your stepbrother might have told you, responding sensually to a man who has aroused your desire does not make you bad or promiscuous or any of the other things I suspect he said to poison you against yourself.'

'Thank you for saying that.' Annie could feel tears threatening to sting her eyes. 'I was questioning how... how appropriate it was for me to feel what...what I was feeling so quickly and so—so very *much*.'

'It was entirely appropriate. And, if it makes you feel happier, I have to confess that I was equally aroused myself.'

Annie looked at him uncertainly before venturing to ask, 'Is that good or bad?'

'It's both good *and* bad,' Falcon answered enigmatically, slanting her one of those sidelong looks of assessment that made her bones melt and her pulse race. She had used up more than her allowance of courage for one day. She couldn't bring herself to ask him just what his response meant.

'Now,' Falcon announced briskly, handing her the lotion, 'it's your turn to practise on me what I have just shown you.'

'You mean, you want me to make *you* feel the way you

just made *me* feel?' The words were out before she could call them back, leaving her feeling wretchedly gauche and foolish, but Falcon seemed not to notice, simply nodding his head and agreeing.

'I certainly want you to try. I promise you that when you do meet a man with whom you want to have sex you will want not just to arouse him with your touch but to touch him simply for the pleasure it will give you. And you will feel much more confident doing so if you know what you are doing.'

She knew that he was right. But even so she could feel herself baulking at what he had told her he wanted her to do.

There was no point in arguing, though. Falcon had already stretched himself out full-length on his front on one of the loungers, his head pillowed on his forearms.

Annie tried not to feel alarmed, but to think instead of what she was doing as a practical exercise. Falcon had started at the back of her neck, causing delicious little thrills of pleasure to course through her and then to cascade down her body as he worked his way down it. She must try to mirror his movements.

She felt awkward at first, not sure how to touch him or where, simply copying what he had done to her. But within a very short space of time her own pleasure—the pleasure she was deriving from touching him—took over, totally obliterating her earlier self-consciousness.

When she heard Falcon exhale sharply as she stroked her fingertips down his spine, a thrill of triumph shot through her, emboldening her to slowly caress the taut flesh ether side of the base of his spine, using both hands as she moved out towards his hips, loving the feel of male flesh and muscle and bone beneath her touch.

In fact, such was her pleasure in what she was doing that at one point she leaned forward and pressed her lips to his skin, hesitantly at first, and then with more confidence as she heard the sound that escaped from his lungs—more of a slight groan than a mere breath, its pent-up sexual tension increasing the ache in her own lower body. If he'd been wearing briefer swimming shorts, or even just a towel, she'd have been able to move lower, to stroke the dark haired breadth of his powerful thighs.

That part of her that contained the mystery and the mechanics of the female orgasm quivered and fluttered and then ached into a pulsing life that froze her into complete shock—just at the same time as Falcon turned over and reached for her, lifting her with one easy movement from her position kneeling beside the lounger to lie against his body.

Like sheet lightning the most exquisite pleasure burst through her in an almost unbearable ache of delight that had her both appalled by her own runaway reaction to him, wanting to pull back, and yet so eager for more that she desperately wanted to press herself closer to him.

His lips were close to her ear, and when he murmured in it, 'Very good…' fresh quivers of arousal hurled themselves through her body. 'But one word of warning. When you do this for real, it might be better to ascertain how strong your partner's self-control is before you start. Especially if you are in a public place. Because right now you have aroused me to a very improper state for where we are, and I have to award you full marks and the continuation of your lesson this evening in my apartment.'

Did his words mean what she thought they meant? That tonight he would take things to their natural conclusion?

She wanted to protest, to tell him that things were moving too fast and that she wasn't ready, but his hand was over her heart, measuring its frantic beat. How could she deny that was what she wanted when her own heartbeat was giving her away and telling him the truth?

Fortunately she had a cast iron excuse to delay things.

'I can't leave Ollie,' she told him truthfully. Her son was her first concern at all times and in all ways.

'You won't need to leave him. You can bring him with you. I'm sure that he won't mind sleeping in a travel cot for once. I asked Maria to make sure that she ordered one just in case you ever wanted to accompany me to Florence.'

The gate was closed, the die cast, the decision made. Tonight she would lie naked in Falcon's arms in Falcon's bed, and he would teach her body all that it needed to know to be free. She had to say something.

She half stumbled into speech. 'You love Florence, don't you?' It was an attempt to cling on to some edge of social normality—a difficult task when she was lying half naked on top of him and his arm was holding her firmly against his body.

'Yes.' Falcon reached for her hand, closing her fingers over her palm and looking down at it as though he wanted to guard his words and his emotions. 'Which is why my father was probably right to claim when I was a child that I was not enough of a Leopardi to succeed him—that I was more my mother's child than his. Unfortunately for him, and for me, I am his eldest son. Therefore, no matter how much he would have liked to put Antonio in my place, nothing short of my death and the deaths of both my brothers could have achieved that. As a boy I used to fear that—'

He broke off, but Annie guessed what he had been about to say. 'You were afraid that your father might try to harm you?'

'I was afraid for my brothers,' he admitted.

His hand was still curled round her palm, and without thinking she placed her other hand on top of it in a gesture of silent comfort.

'That must have been dreadful for you.' She could easily imagine how dreadful. He had such a strongly developed sense of duty and responsibility towards others that it was only natural that as the eldest he should have felt protective of his brothers even if their family life had been a happy one. But when she added the burden of the tensions and fears he had just admitted to, it filled Annie with a protective surge of almost maternal emotion to think of what Falcon the boy had had to endure.

'My father would never have hurt them—or me, of course. He spoke merely out of the frustration of his excessive love for Antonio. It is not without irony, though, he felt that the son he did lose should have been his favourite. It is my opinion that the responsibility for Antonio's faults of character can be placed at our father's door. He spoiled and indulged Antonio from the moment of his birth—and, worse, taught and encouraged him to copy his own attitude of contempt towards the three of us. He allowed Antonio to grow up believing he was invincible, beyond any form of law or retribution. He was in many ways the orchestrator and the cause of Antonio's death, and it is my belief that he knows that.'

'Sometimes I worry that Ollie might have inherited some of Antonio's…failings,' Annie admitted, putting into words for the first time a fear that haunted the deepest recesses of her own heart.

'Oliver is himself,' Falcon assured her, immediately and with firm authority. 'He has you to love and protect him, and if you will allow me, until such time as you do find a man with whom you wish to share your life and bear more children, I would like to stand as his protector and the male influence in his life. You need not fear that my love for him will be tainted by his relationship to Antonio. He is a child of my blood—Leopardi blood—and that is all that matters to me. He will have my love for as long as I am alive to give it to him.'

Tears filled Annie's eyes. She had never imagined that a man as male as Falcon could speak like this, and be so in accord with her own emotions.

'My father had hoped to discover a grandson that he could mould in his lost son's image. But I am not a boy any longer, I am a man, and I will not allow him to ruin Oliver as he did Antonio.'

Annie moved imperceptibly closer to him, alarmed by the thought of the Prince trying to control her precious son.

'Maria told me that you are not expecting your father to live very much longer.'

'We were warned that he would not have much more time, but the new medication he is on seems to have give him a fresh lease of life. Despite all the pain he has caused us, I know that neither I or my brothers want his death.'

'No, of course not,' Annie agreed instantly.

Her hand still rested comfortingly on Falcon's. He looked up at her, and then said softly, 'I was right about you. You are a very seductive woman.'

Annie looked down at their hands.

'No, not that,' Falcon told her. 'It is your compassion and your tenderness that make you seductive—not just the passion you keep so firmly hidden away. But tonight we shall see it revealed as its own fiercely sweet self.'

Annie could feel herself starting to tremble. She didn't resist when Falcon released her hand and then lifted his own newly free hand to the back of her head, so that he could pull her down towards him to kiss her.

It was only the briefest of kisses—just the mere brush of his lips against hers—but it was enough to tell her just how eagerly her body would respond to him later.

CHAPTER EIGHT

ANNIE had had a full tour of Falcon's apartment, and was genuinely impressed, and filled with admiration for everything about it—especially the double-height floor-to-ceiling glass wall of the living room and the master bedroom.

'There are no curtains,' she had commented in surprise. She had noticed this lack as she and Falcon had stood side by side, looking out across the clifftop to the sea beyond. Falcon had insisted on holding Ollie, who had been grizzling a little bit—preparatory, Annie thought, to cutting a new tooth. He had smiled widely with delight the minute Falcon had taken him in his arms.

'No, this corner of the *castello*, very private,' Falcon had agreed. 'I like the freedom of lying in bed and watching the night sky—just as I like the freedom of being able to walk naked around my own personal space, and swim naked in my pool. They are simple pleasures, but very meaningful to those who cherish them. There is nothing to compare with the cloak of the night sky on one's naked body, like the touch of velvet, or the silken brush of water against bare skin.'

'I wouldn't know,' Annie had told him, uncomfortably aware of just what the images his words were drawing inside her head were doing to her body.

'Well, tonight you can know, if you wish,' he had said softly. Which had had her running for the safety of banal conversation rather than the bold acceptance of his offer which her body had demanded.

To her astonishment Falcon had cooked their dinner himself—a delicious fresh fish dish, served with stuffed vegetables and pasta in a delicately textured sauce, although he had freely admitted the chef had prepared it for him earlier.

'What will the staff think about me having dinner alone here with you?' she had asked, a little apprehensively.

His answer had been a dismissive, confident shrug.

'They will think that I have invited you to have dinner with me in my private quarters. Nothing more—nothing less.'

Did that mean that he regularly entertained women here? she had wondered. And had then had to question just why she had felt such a savage surge of emotion at that thought.

Now she had put Ollie to bed in his travel cot in the dressing room off Falcon's bedroom, so that she would hear him if he woke up. She knew that Falcon would be waiting for her to continue what they had started earlier, but inexplicably—or perhaps sensibly she didn't know—she felt self-consciously reluctant to go to him. But, having come this far, she must do so—there could be no going back. Not if she wanted to be the mother Ollie deserved to have.

Taking a deep breath, she opened the dressing room door and stepped into the bedroom—which was empty.

Confused, she looked uncertainly around the room—and then tensed as Falcon emerged from the bathroom, wearing a robe.

'I'm going to have a swim. Why don't you join me?'

Did he mean a naked swim? Was he wearing anything under that robe?

Her heart was thudding, and that fluttering, pulsing wanton aching that she had felt earlier had started up again.

'I'd better stay here in case Ollie wakes up,' she answered feebly.

A staircase led down from the bedroom to the patio and pool area below, and Annie vowed that she would *not* watch Falcon to see whether or not he was planning to swim in the nude. Instead she determinedly went back down the stairs to retrieve the white wine spritzer she had abandoned earlier, when she had come to put Ollie to bed.

Music was playing softly in the background of the living room, but it was impossible for her to relax. She went back upstairs, to be nearer to Ollie, and moved anxiously round the room, drinking her spritzer and determinedly not looking in the direction of the pool. Which was no doubt why she was taken completely off guard when Falcon came up behind her, relieved her of her almost empty glass and turned her into his arms.

'Now, where were we?' he said firmly, before he silenced her surprised gasp with the hard warmth of his mouth on hers.

He had kissed her before—more than once—so she should have known what to expect. And of course she did. But this time the effect of his kiss on her was magnified a hundred times—no, a thousand, she thought headily as his teeth tugged sensually at her bottom lip so that his tongue could run inside its softness. Then, when she was aching for it to plunge deeper, he withdrew to place tiny, nibbling kisses at the corners of her mouth and tease the pleading parted longing of her lips with the slow, deliberate caress of his tongue.

Annie had no idea just when she had stood up on her tiptoes and pressed herself fiercely against him, her fingers digging into his arms, and then wrapped her arms around his neck to hold him as close to her as she could, whilst her frustrated senses tried to show him what she wanted in place of his teasing caress that was leaving her so hungry and so unsatisfied.

Somewhere at some deep level she knew she must have recorded his encouraging words.

'Yes, that's it—show me that you want me.' He had murmured them in her ear after disengaging his mouth from hers for a thankfully brief few seconds, before returning to reward her for her willingness as a pupil with the slow, soft pressure of his mouth on hers, speedily upgrading the intense and intimate meeting of lips and tongues she had longed for, leaving her to hunger for even greater intimacy.

Miraculously, as though somehow he knew of her desire, he stroked his tongue deep into her mouth, its thrusts long and slow, making her go soft and boneless, as though she was already accommodating him within her, her muscles closing eagerly around him.

Beyond the window the patio and the pool, which had been floodlit whilst Falcon had swum, were now almost in darkness. The only light was that supplied by the stars and the fattening curve of the moon as they sent trails of silver glinting and dancing on both the sea and the pool. That same light was coming through the vast expanse of glass window, turning their surroundings into monochrome mystery highlighted with silver, so that the shadows of the bedroom seemed alluring and enticing, something that belonged to another world—a world of fiction and fantasy into which she could safely step, leaving the harshness of reality unwanted and outside the special empowering sensuality of the here and now.

Or at least that was as close as she was going to allow herself to get to rationalising or analysing her sudden sense of freedom to do and be what she most wanted, stroked into her senses with each passionate thrust of Falcon's tongue against her own. It certainly had to be the reason she was as happy to shed her dress as though it were an unwanted skin she was sloughing off, leaving her wantonly free to be caressed by the night and the look that Falcon was giving her.

His soft words, 'Perfect—you are as perfect as I knew you would be,' Made her eye him boldly, longing to replicate his easy removal of her clothes so that she could repay the compliment. Her stomach muscles tensed with fierce excitement. She didn't need Falcon to remove his bathrobe for her to know that he would be total male perfection. After all, she had already seen most of him that afternoon. Most of him, but not all of him....

Wasn't that exactly the kind of thought Colin had warned her against? For a second Annie hovered between past and present, her old teenage fear chilling through her veins. But again, as though he knew what she was thinking, Falcon drew her towards him and wrapped her in his arms, murmuring against her ear.

'This is where what we started this afternoon ends and where what we both really wanted then begins.'

He was kissing the hollow behind her ear, trailing his fingertips down the side of her neck and then along her shoulder to her arm, kissing his way towards her mouth.

She was aware of him and of her own physical arousal

with every single cell in her body. There wasn't a particle of her that wasn't affected by his touch and responsive to it. She wasn't wearing a bra—it hadn't been necessary as her dress had its own built in support—and now the only support her breasts wanted was his hands cupping them whilst he kissed her and brought her tight nipples to even harder aching longing with the pads of his thumbs and the erotic pluck of his finger and thumb. That aroused such a firestorm of sensation within her that she was forced to cry out against it, feeling scarcely able to bear its intensity.

In response Falcon moved back towards the bed, drawing her with him as he sat down on the mattress, pulling her between his open legs and holding her there whilst he circled first one of her nipples and then the other with his tongue-tip, gently at first, so that the torment of her pleasure had her straining towards him, and then more fiercely, lapping at the stiff, swollen, moon-silvered flesh.

Her head thrown back, her spine arched, Annie was lost—a helpless prisoner to her own desire. She felt Falcon's arm supporting her, a sure, strong iron band against her lower back, holding her safe whilst he drew spirals of hot liquid longing on her taut belly with the fingers of his free hand, dipping lower to the barrier of her brief silky knickers, wet now with the excretions of her fierce desire, an unwanted restriction.

Falcon stroked the swollen mound of her sex through the fragile fabric—a light touch that sent Annie wild and made her long for something more intense, more intimate.

His lips opened over one of her nipples, his tongue probing and stroking, and then his teeth gently grating against her hot flesh. At the same time he slid his hand into the leg of her briefs and probed the fullness of the lips covering her sex.

Annie never even heard herself cry out—the sharp, high and wild woman's cry of aching unbearable need—but Falcon did.

Somewhere in the deepest recesses of his conscious he knew that his own arousal—his own need for this woman—was out of control. But for once he wasn't willing to listen to his own inner voice of warning. Annie's arousal, her complete and total offering of herself and her desire to him, in mute acceptance of her trust that he could and would satisfy it and her, overwhelmed him.

He wanted to know her completely—to take her and fill her with the result of his own desire for her. He wanted to hear her cries of orgasm. He wanted to touch and pleasure all of her, with his hands, with his lips, with words and in silence, until she was completely, totally and only his.

He slid down her briefs, breathing in the sweet, musky woman scent of her and feeling his whole body surge on a tsunami of arousal. He slid to the floor, still holding her, his hands spread wide against her rounded cheeks, kneading them erotically as he kissed the inside of her thigh.

Annie was lost, totally and completely, inhabiting a world she had never thought she would know—a world in which just the sensation of another's breath against her skin was enough to have the ache inside her threatening to burst out of control. The slow caress of Falcon's lips and tongue on the inside of her thigh was making her protest volubly against the growing pressure of her own need as she tried to hold it inside her.

It was too late though. It was the final unbearable pressure, Falcon's throaty words—'This is what I wanted to do this afternoon.' He sprang the dam of her desire, resulting in the convulsive contraction of her body into a flood of sensation she was totally unable to withstand.

So this was an orgasm—this was what she had been denying herself during all these years when she had woken from her sleep, aching, somehow knowing what was waiting for her but feeling too afraid to do anything about it because of Colin. Now Falcon had shown her what her own pleasure was.

He was scooping her up in his arms, her body limp with release and satisfaction, and her lips curved into a smile as she put them to his ear and whispered, 'Thank you.'

His skin tasted warm, tempting her to nuzzle deeper into it and then wrap her arms around his neck whilst she burrowed closer to him, driven by an instinct she was too relaxed to question to be close to him, to prolong their intimacy.

He should send her back to her own room. Things had progressed far enough for now. He might be aching with unsatisfied arousal, but the purpose of the exercise was not to satisfy *his* desire.

But she'd never make it back to her room under her own steam. She was practically falling asleep in his arms now, and he was damned if he was going to carry her naked all the way there when there was a perfectly good bed here, Falcon told himself. He pulled back the bedclothes and placed Annie on the bed, covering her up before going to check on Oliver.

The baby was contentedly asleep, twin fans of dark lashes lying on his cheeks concealing eyes that were a direct copy of his own. Falcon stood looking down at him for several seconds, mentally deriding himself for the fierce tug this small human being had on his emotions. Oliver wasn't even his child, and yet he felt as protective of him as though he had created him himself.

This child must not be damaged and spoiled by his father as Antonio had been. And the best way to ensure that that did not happen was for Annie to find a partner who would protect and rear Oliver as though he were his own. Something deep within Falcon felt as though it was being wrenched apart, causing a fierce stab of angry, denying pain to thrust through him.

What was the matter with him? That was, after all, in part the purpose of this evening's intimacy, wasn't it? That Annie should have the confidence to find herself a man?

It was because Oliver was a Leopardi that he was feeling the way he was. Because it was bred into his bones that Leopardi children—especially Leopardi children without their natural fathers—should be brought up here in Sicily, knowing their heritage.

He was getting as bad as his father, Falcon derided himself.

His body still ached fiercely with unsatisfied desire. He should go for another swim to rid himself of it. But instead for some reason, when he walked back into the bedroom, what he did was shrug off his bathrobe and slide into the bed next to Annie, drawing her sleeping body into his arms.

CHAPTER NINE

'It is so lovely having you and Ollie living here, Annie. Sometimes I have to pinch myself in case I'm dreaming. I feel I've been so lucky.'

Annie nodded her head and tried to look as though she was paying proper attention to what Julie was saying as the two of them sat drinking tea and watching their babies playing happily together on the shaded patio of Rocco's beautiful mansion. The reality, though, was that she was finding it next to impossible to drag her thoughts away from the intoxicating and guilty pleasure of reliving over and over again the events of two nights ago, when she had woken up in the velvet darkness to find herself in bed with Falcon.

Still buoyed up with the sweet physical satisfaction of her earlier orgasm, and the emotional high of feeling that she had finally broken free of her imprisonment and celebrated her sexuality, she had been filled with unfamiliar confidence and happiness.

It was those feelings, she felt sure, that had somehow led to her not only stretching luxuriously against Falcon, savouring the sensuality of being in her own skin and at one with her sensuality, but also being proactive enough to decide that the rush of pleasure it gave her to stretch out and feel Falcon's skin against her own was a pleasure that needed further exploration.

From that thought it had only been the merest heartbeat of a step—the simple raising of her hand to place it palm-down flat against Falcon's chest so that she could absorb the simple but delightful pleasure of feeling his heart beat against her touch—to discovering the temptation to do far more than that.

The fact that Falcon had been asleep wasn't something that had even registered with her. She had been on such a high of thrilling confidence and sensual joy. Her new sense of freedom had swept away all normal rationality. She had been lost, totally and utterly, in a daze of such sensual delight and arousal, so pleased with herself for being able to feel that way, that she simply hadn't been able to stop herself from letting her new-found womanhood have its way.

She had stroked her fingertips along Falcon's bare arm, kissed her way from the place where her head had rested on his chest close to his heart right up to his throat—spending endless absorbed and entranced minutes, or so it had seemed, exploring the hollow at the base of his throat with her tongue-tip, painting swirls of delighted gratitude there for all that he had given her. And then, when the languorous, relaxed happiness she had been feeling started to transform into an aroused ache, she'd continued to stroke her tongue over his Adams's apple and then upwards, diverting towards his ear, leaning across him as she did so. Every movement of her lips had seemed to necessitate a similar movement of her already tight breasts against his chest, the friction caused by the movement of her still-sensitised nipples against his body hair rekindling a powerful surge of the need she had experienced earlier in the evening.

Quite how or when her hand had drifted down to his hip, her fingertips itching to stroke lower, she had no idea. All she did know was that even now, nearly two full days later, just recalling the moment when Falcon had moved, turned his head and murmured in her ear, 'Either you stop right now, or you accept the consequences of what you are doing,' brought back a tumultuously intense echo of what she had felt then, accompanied by an all too familiar dragging ache low down in her body.

Of course she should have stopped. She had found her sensuality, after all, so there had been no real need at all, absolutely none, for Falcon to continue with his teaching programme. But she hadn't stopped. Wild horses, if available, would not have had the least impact on her desire *not* to stop. And not only had she not stopped, she had deliberately moved her hand lower, stroking her fingers through the thick, slightly damp heat of the hair above it until she had reached Falcon's firm erection.

How a woman who had had no knowledge of the intimacy of a man's body could have known such a fiercely possessive female desire to caress and control such maleness she had no idea. All she knew was that she had done so.

Falcon had suffered her caressing exploration for a handful of heat-charged minutes, during which her heartbeat had raced to match the thunder of his and the air between them had become filled with the heightened sound of their mutually unsteady breathing. His flesh, already firm beneath her fingertips, had grown harder and wider. And then he had groaned out loud—a raw, guttural, utterly visceral sound that had thrilled through her, reaching deep into her body to turn its already aroused flutter into a driving, urgent pulse. Then he had reached for her, pulling her down on top of his own body, his hands pressing her hips down against his hardness and then sweeping possessively up over her back and into her hair whilst he held her against his mouth and kissed the breath out of her.

He had broken his kiss only to tell her in a semi-tortured, throaty voice, 'I want you. I want you right here, right now.'

'I want you too,' she had whispered back.

She had been the one to tug urgently on his hands, shivering with raw delight when he had rolled her beneath him. The moonlight had been a silver, sweat-slick pathway over his skin, revealing to her the male desire burning in his gaze, its intensity mirroring the dangerous heat licking at her own nerve endings.

She'd had a child, rejoiced in his birth, unconcerned then about the effect that physical experience might have on her body. But suddenly she had been acutely aware of how much that process might have changed her. And not just that process. She might have no memory of what had happened with Antonio, but it had happened.

Somewhere deep down in her most secret self she had felt a pang of something primitive she hadn't really wanted to admit to: a mixture of longing and grief and recognition of the fact that Falcon was the man, the lover, was, given the choice, she would have wanted to be her first.

He had kissed her face and then her throat, moving over her, touching her sex with his fingers as he had done before. This time the rush of sensation that had filled her was stronger and deeper, arching her up towards him.

He'd kissed her breasts and then asked softly, 'Are you sure you want this?'

She had, she remembered, laughed a little unsteadily before telling him truthfully, 'Yes—and a thousand times more than I have ever imagined I could want it.'

In the moonlight she had seen his chest expand and then contract.

'I'll need to take precautions,' he had told her. 'I won't be a second.'

She had known that what he was saying made sense, but suddenly the thought of him leaving her was one she hadn't been able to bear. She had clung to him, wrapping her arms tightly around him, pressing her pelvis into him with aching need as she had told him, 'No.'

Would he have stayed if she hadn't rubbed herself against him so provocatively, her body convulsing in open and delirious pleasure and need as she'd felt his hardness against her sex? She didn't know. What she did know was that the pleasure of her own wanton sensuality had been so intense that she had repeated the movement—not once, but several times.

His control had broken then, and he had positioned her, lifting her slightly so that he could thrust slowly and deliberately into her.

'If you want me to stop—' he had begun, but she had shaken her head, showing him rather than telling him how little she wanted that by wrapping her legs around him and rising up to meet his thrust.

After that the world had become a whirligig of different pleasures, each one more intense than the last. A kaleidoscope of shared need and movement. Her flesh had clasped itself greedily around him as each thrust took him deeper into her, taking her higher and higher.

Having him inside her had felt so right—like nothing

she could ever have imagined. He had filled her and completed her, and the pleasure had grown and kept on growing, leaving her so lost in the marvel of it that her orgasm had caught her unawares, overwhelming her so swiftly that she'd wanted to hold it back so that she could enjoy the sensation for longer.

The echoes of it had still been shuddering through her when Falcon had arched and tensed before thrusting one last time, the agonised joy of his male triumph reverberating through the silver night.

She had cried a little afterwards, for no good reason at all, and if that hadn't been shameful enough she had then compounded her silliness by telling Falcon emotionally, 'That was wonderful. I just wish that you had been the first.'

The first, the last and the only.

Ollie's protesting wail as he and Josh reached for the same toy brought her abruptly back to reality.

'When is Falcon due back from Florence?' Julie was asking her.

'Not until tomorrow evening some time.'

She saw the look that Julie gave her and tried not to blush. Her words had betrayed all too clearly that she was missing Falcon and wanted his return.

She'd only learned that he'd left the *castello* and gone to Florence when Maria had told her. Annie had returned to her own room to sleep, of course. After all, she and Falcon weren't a couple in the normal sense. But her bed had seemed empty and cold after the warmth of his and his presence in it. The whole *castello* felt empty and cold without him, in fact.

Like the rest of her life would be without him?

Annie jumped as though she'd touched something that had given her a small electric shock. What kind of silly thinking was that? How could her life be empty when she had a son and now, thanks to Falcon, the ability to find herself a proper partner and to make a commitment to that partner? But the only man she wanted to make a commitment to and with was Falcon.

No! She must not think like that. She could not and would not. Having her fall in love with him had most certainly not been the purpose of Falcon's plan to help her recover her repressed sexuality. He would be horrified if he were ever to discover how she felt. It had to remain her secret.

'I worry about the Prince when Falcon isn't here,' she said, excusing her reaction to Julie. 'Especially after your warning to me.'

It was the truth in one sense. She had felt distinctly anxious earlier in the day, when Maria had told her that the Prince's manservant had said that his master wanted to see 'the child', and that he—the manservant—would come and collect Ollie, to take him to see his grandfather. Her presence was not required.

It was silly to feel so afraid and vulnerable because Falcon wasn't there. After all what could his father do? He was a frail elderly man, and Ollie was *her* son.

Falcon pushed to one side the plans he had been studying. It was no use. He was only deceiving himself if he thought he was actually going to do any work. There had only been one place his thoughts had been since the evening Annie had shared his bed, and that had been with her.

Falcon had always considered his attitude—no, he corrected himself harshly, he had *prided* himself on his attitude to others and their needs, but now he recognised that he had been guilty of hubris. In his arrogance and his inability to recognise his own human vulnerability he had not seen the danger of what he was planning to do—for himself and, even more unforgivably, for Annie.

There was no point telling himself that his motives had been altruistic, based on a genuine belief that he had a duty to help her. He should have known and factored in the risk of his own weakness. He was human, after all. Very human— as the evening he had spent in bed with Annie had proved.

He had believed that he was doing the right thing, and that there was no risk to either of them. No risk? When he had broken the golden rule of modern sexual relationships by not using a condom? How much more evidence of his own reckless risk taking did he need to be confronted with before he admitted his fallibility and his error?

He had challenged fate, thoughtlessly and arrogantly, and now he was having to pay the price. But worse than that, with his behaviour he had broken the bond of trust he had assured Annie she could depend on. The plain, un-varnished truth was, as he had now been forced to concede, that he had wanted her from the minute he had first held her. Something had been communicated then, from the feel of her in his arms, that had seeded itself directly into his senses—and his heart. Wilfully he had ignored all the warning signs along the way, and deliberately he had en-couraged her to believe that he would be her saviour.

Her saviour! He was no better than Antonio in what he had done, even if in his arms she had learned and discov-ered true sexual pleasure. Just as in hers *he* had learned and discovered what it was to love?

A shudder ran through his body, causing him to push back from his desk and stand up. From the window of his office in his Florence apartment, in the beautiful eighteenth-century *palazzo* that had come down to him through his mother's family, Falcon looked down into the elegant courtyard garden.

He had stolen from Annie, abused her just as surely as his half-brother had done—even if Annie herself was not aware of that as yet; even if before she had finally fallen asleep in his arms she had whispered to him her joyful thanks for what they had shared.

Somewhere, somehow, during their intimacy, a line had been crossed that he had had no right to allow her to cross. He owed her an apology and an explanation. The former he could and would give her, but as for the latter...

What would he explain? That he had concealed the truth from himself and thus by default from her when he had not admitted to himself that his actions were in part motivated by his own desire for her? That admission should have been made, and with it a choice given to her. He had not been honest either with her or with himself, and Annie would have every right to treat him with anger and contempt. Those were certainly the emotions he felt towards himself. And was he really sure that his motivating need right now to be with her stemmed from a desire to admit his failings to her? Was he really sure that the reason he wanted to be with her wasn't that he wanted to repeat the intimacy they had already shared?

What he had done was, in his own eyes, a gross violation of all that he believed his duty to Annie to be.

He had seen his brothers fall in love and find their love was returned, and he had envied them their happiness. Now he envied them even more.

Because he was falling in love with Annie?

He could not, must not, *would* not do that. He had after all promised her the freedom to make her own choice. He must never burden her with his feelings. From now on they must be his secret and his alone.

He had a dinner engagement here in Florence tonight, with a fellow architect and his wife.

But there was only one place he wanted to be right now, and one person he wanted to be with.

CHAPTER TEN

THEY were within sight of the *castello* when a taxi coming away from it passed them on the road, causing Annie to feel a fierce spiral of joyous anticipation, and the hope that it meant that Falcon had returned earlier than planned.

But after Rocco's driver had dropped her off, she asked Maria if Falcon was back, and the housekeeper shook her head and said that no, the taxi had brought a visitor—the second that afternoon—for the Prince. She grumbled that she suspected Falcon knew nothing of these two visits, and that she hoped that two visitors in one day would not be too much for the elderly man.

Nodding her head, Annie was more concerned about the danger of her disappointed reaction to the fact that the taxi had *not* brought Falcon back to the *castello*, than curious about the Prince's visitors.

Now, having fed and changed Ollie, she was walking round the enclosed courtyard garden adjacent to the terrace with him. He lay back in his buggy enjoying the warmth of the late-afternoon sunshine.

She was totally oblivious, until she happened to catch sight of her own reflection in the tranquil goldfish pond beside which she had stopped, of just how accustomed she had become to her new clothes, and how relaxed she now felt about the way they subtly enhanced her womanliness.

It was a sweet moment of true female pleasure and one that made her smile.

She had Falcon to thank for that, of course. He had given her the confidence to accept that only *she* had the right to decide what she would wear, and to believe that she was perfectly capable of deciding for herself what was and what was not appropriate. Her skin had begun to develop a light tan, and her hair was loose on her shoulders. She lifted Ollie out of his buggy and, holding him securely showed him the goldfish pond, sitting down at the side of it with him on her lap and disturbing the smooth surface of the water so that he could see the fat goldfish swimming off. This was an idyllic place for him to grow up. He would have the company of Rocco and Julie's little boy, and no doubt there would be other children to come. He would be surrounded by love, and best of all he would have Falcon to guide and protect him.

Falcon. She let her lips form his name, savouring the luxury of the heady pleasure of doing so, knowing that he wasn't here to witness and object to her folly.

The evening stretched out ahead of her, lonely and empty without Falcon's company, just like the previous two evenings had been. She missed him so much. It made no difference that she had known him for such a short space of time. How much time did it take to fall in love? No time at all. A mere heartbeat was enough to change the whole course of a person's life. And Falcon had done that for her. She already owed him so much. She must not add another burden to those she had already given him. Motivated as he was by duty, and his sense of responsibility toward others, no doubt if he found out she loved him he would be concerned on her behalf.

She could see Maria coming towards her through the garden, no doubt to ask her what she wanted for dinner, Annie decided.

But when Maria reached her she announced breathlessly, 'The Prince wishes to see you and Oliver in his apartment.'

'What? Now?' Annie questioned the housekeeper uncertainly.

'Yes. Now.'

He asked for me too?

Previously it had been Falcon who had taken her son to see his grandfather, the Prince having shown no interest in her after their initial meeting.

'You must hurry,' Maria told her, looking anxious. 'The Prince does not like to be kept waiting.'

Ideally, Annie would have preferred to be given an opportunity to freshen up—to make sure that both she and Ollie, especially Ollie, were looking their best before they were subjected to what she suspected would be a very critical inspection by the Prince. But Maria was making it very plain that there would be no time for that kind of luxury.

Indeed, the housekeeper had put out her hand to the buggy, quite obviously wanting to hurry them along.

There was nothing Annie could do other than go along with what was happening, and she wheeled Ollie in his buggy over the immaculately polished floors and priceless antique carpets of the *castello*'s succession of formal reception rooms until they reached the discreetly tucked away lift that went up to the Prince's private apartments on the first floor.

Maria went up in the lift with them, and once it had

stopped and the doors had opened handed them over to the
manservant who was waiting for them.

The old Prince was a stickler for tradition, Annie had
learned from Julie, and lived very much in the style of the
early nineteen-hundreds, waited on by a formidable retinue
of equally elderly retainers.

This part of the *castello* felt and looked very different
from Falcon's modern apartments. The decor of the two
empty salons she was almost marched through was very
baroque—the ceilings intricately plastered, gilded like the
heavily carved woodwork, the wall panels hung with silks
that matched those used for the curtains and the soft furnish-
ings. These rooms felt more like a museum than a home,
Annie reflected, shivering a little in her sleeveless sundress.

A liveried footman stood on guard outside the final pair
of double doors which he and Annie's escort drew back,
so that she could enter the room beyond.

Here, if anything, the decor was even more imposing
than it had been in the two previous salons. Huge paintings in sombre colours dominated the walls, whilst over
her head the ceiling fresco could, she thought, have rivalled
the Sistine chapel.

The heavy velvet curtains either side of the room's four
windows shut out almost all the natural daylight, so that
the room was ablaze with chandeliers, whilst a fire burned
in the enormous fireplace.

The air smelled of old age—both human and non-
human—but Annie no longer had the luxury of assessing
her surroundings. She was unable to drag her shocked,
disbelieving gaze from one of the two dark-suited men
standing beside the shrunken figure of the Prince, wrapped
in a rug and seated in his wheelchair beside the fire.

Colin! What was he doing here?

Her heart started to jolt sickeningly inside her chest, thudding with familiar fear, and she began to shiver and then tremble as her stepbrother's familiar disapproving gaze focused on her bare shoulders and arms.

How much she wished now that she had insisted on having time to go to her room and get herself a cardigan to cover herself with—or even better to change completely.

She knew—just knew from the way Colin's lips were thinning—what he was thinking.

'Colin. What…what are you doing here?'

The words were out before she could silence them. Uttering them, she recognized, angry with herself, had made her sound like an immature schoolgirl, caught out in some forbidden activity.

'It's all right, Annie.'

How soft and reassuring Colin's voice always sounded. So kind and caring and reasonable. No wonder her mother had never understood her fear of him.

'No one's going to be angry with you. I'm here to make sure of that. You know I've always had your best interests at heart.'

No one was going to be angry with her? But he already was. She mustn't let him do this to her. She must *not* slip back to being the fearful creature she had been before Falcon had rescued her. *Falcon.* If only he had been here…

'I don't understand why you are here,' Annie told him flatly. She must be strong and firm. She must behave as though Falcon were standing at her side, guiding and guarding her.

'I've come to take you home.'

Fire, like a petrol-soaked rag to which someone had just

applied a flame, shot up inside her, ravaging and out of control.

But she *must* control it.

'This is my home now. Mine and Ollie's.'

Colin was smiling at her now—the triumphant, gloating smile she remembered so well, and which before he had only shown her in private. Her heart turned over in a sickening lurch of fear when she realised how confident he must feel if he was showing it to her now, in public....

'This is Oliver's home now, yes. But your home is with me, Annie. You know that. It always has been and it always will be.'

'Let's get this over with.' The Prince spoke for the first time. His English was good but his voice was shaky and unsteady. 'Where are the papers?' he demanded turning to the third man, who had not spoken as yet. 'She must sign them, and then he can take her away. He must take her away before she hurts my grandson. Bring the child to me.'

Hurt Ollie? What was the Prince saying? What was going on?

As the third man came towards her Annie snatched Ollie up out of his buggy, holding him tightly. As though her fear had communicated itself to him, Ollie suddenly started to cry.

'See,' Falcon's father announced fiercely. 'Her brother is right. She is not fit to have charge of the boy. He is afraid of her.'

Ollie afraid of her? Colin her brother? What was going on?

Confusion, horror and fear—she felt them all. Instinctively she tried to escape, turning towards the doors through which she had entered the room. But they were closed, with the two manservants standing in front of them.

Her fear increased, pounding through her, filling her and all but drowning out the courage Falcon had given her. *Falcon*. Just thinking his name steadied her, calmed her. Desperately she clung to it, willing herself to be strong and to remember that she was no longer a child in thrall to Colin; there was no need now for her to fear him.

But what about the Prince? He obviously wanted to take Ollie away from her, and Colin would encourage and help him to do that. Colin had never wanted her to have Ollie. She must not be afraid. She must try to be strong.

'It's all right, Annie,' she could hear Colin saying, in his best kind voice. She struggled not to panic. 'Everything's all right. We know how much you love Oliver. But the best place for him is with his grandfather. And the Prince's solicitor will ensure that the courts think that, as well. We all saw the way you held Oliver over the pond earlier, and I've already given testimony as to how you wanted to abort him before his birth. No one blames you for wanting to do that—not after what happened to you. It's perfectly natural that there should be times when... when what happened to you overwhelms you. We're only trying to protect you and Oliver. To protect you from doing something that you would later regret. It's for your own sake and for his. Imagine how you would feel if you were to hurt him.

'Now, if you're sensible and sign these papers that the Prince's solicitor has prepared, giving the Prince guardianship of Ollie, everything will be much easier for you. I'll take you back to England with me and we can forget about all of this....'

'No!'

The denial was ripped from Annie's throat. Fear was

crawling all through her. Surely she could only be imagining this? It couldn't possibly be happening? But it was.

'I'm sorry about this.' It wasn't her to whom Colin was apologizing, but the Prince. 'As I've already confirmed to you, the breakdown Annie had after Oliver's birth has left her very mentally and emotionally fragile. Which is why—'

'She should be locked up with other madwomen, where she can't hurt or harm my grandson.'

The Prince turned to his solicitor and said something to him in Italian, glaring at Annie as he did so.

Colin was responsible for what was happening to her. Instinctively Annie knew that. Somehow or other he had managed to put into action the train of events that had brought her here now, to this room and this horrifying situation.

'I'm not signing anything,' she told the three men firmly. 'And I'm not going anywhere. Not until I've spoken to Falcon.'

Whilst the Prince and his solicitor exchanged looks that resulted in the solicitor giving a small shake of his head, Colin took a step towards her.

As though he sensed the danger they were in, Oliver started to cry in earnest.

'Give me my grandson,' the Prince demanded, setting his wheelchair in motion and heading for Annie. 'He is a Leopardi, and there is no court in Sicily that would deny me my right to his guardianship. Especially when they know of the wickedness of his mother—a mother who tried to deny him life.'

'That is not true,' Annie protested.

'Annie, it's no use. I've already told the Prince everything. He knows that you wanted a termination, and that you tried to have Oliver adopted once you knew that Antonio wanted him.'

Annie gasped. 'That's not true.'

'No, it isn't.'

None of them had heard the doors open, but now all four of them turned to look towards them, to where Falcon was standing.

'Falcon!'

Annie could hear the relief in her own voice. She could just imagine the way Colin was looking at her as she half ran and half stumbled across the room, all but flinging herself into Falcon's arms, but she simply didn't care.

'They're trying to take Ollie from me. They're trying to say that I'm a bad mother.'

'The child is a Leopardi,' she could hear the old Prince insisting, 'His place is here with—'

'With me, Father.' Falcon stopped his father in mid-rant. 'And that is exactly where Oliver will be from now on. With me and with his mother—since she has agreed to be my wife and I shall be formally adopting him as my son.'

Falcon's arm was round her, supporting her, tightening in warning as she made a small shocked sound of protest.

'I should warn all three of you that there is no law in this land or any other that will remove from me the right to be the guardian of my stepson, a child of my own blood, and protector of both him and his mother.'

'You can't do this. You can't marry her—a whore who your brother—'

Whilst Annie flinched, Falcon stood firm.

'An innocent virgin whom your son—thankfully only my *half*-brother—abused and defiled, but who, out of the sweetness and goodness she possesses in abundance, has given to this family the sacred trust of a new life—a child that I will never, *ever* allow to be damaged and corrupted in the way that his father was. However, I cannot blame Antonio alone for his shortcomings. He inherited the weakness and the love of vice that eventually destroyed him from his mother. So Oliver will inherit from his mother great courage and true strength of character.'

As he finished speaking Falcon lifted Oliver from Annie's arms, nestling him in the crook of his own arm, from where the baby smiled up at him. The look of love the two of them exchanged made Annie want to weep with gratitude.

Putting his free arm back around her, Falcon guided her towards the buggy and deftly secured Oliver in it, before straightening up to say calmly and evenly to his father, 'I should hate you for all that you have done to hurt and harm those I love over the years, but instead I pity you, Father. For all that you could have had and have thrown away.'

Her ordeal was over and she and Oliver were safe. Safe here in Falcon's apartment. Safe from the Prince and from Colin perhaps, but she was not safe from her own feelings— from her love for Falcon, deeper and burning even more fiercely now, after what he had done to rescue her.

'I'm really grateful to you for what you've done,' she told Falcon emotionally as she sat opposite him on the comfortable U-shaped arrangement of leather sofas. A coffee table on which she had placed her now-empty cup of restorative coffee was between them, whilst Ollie lay fast asleep on the middle sofa.

Falcon inclined his head in acknowledgement of her

words. Her voice was still tremulous with the shadow of the fear she had been through. He couldn't trust himself to speak as yet. His anger was still churning savagely inside him, twisting his guts and locking his heart against his father.

'I'm so glad you came back when you did, earlier than you had planned. I was so afraid.'

'I completed the business I'd gone to Florence to do earlier than I expected,' Falcon told Annie brusquely.

It was a lie. He had been sitting in a café in the square next to his apartment when out of nowhere he had been filled, driven by a sudden conviction that he had to be with her. He'd tried to ignore it at first, but it had refused to be ignored and he had been forced to give in to it.

He'd telephoned his second brother Alessandro from the square, demanding and insisting that Alessandro organise a private jet to fly him back to Sicily, then driving as recklessly as though he had been Antonio and not his normal conservative self from the airport to the *castello*, shocking Maria with his unexpected arrival and learning from her not just where Annie was but also about the two men who were with his father.

After he had rescued her, Maria had fussed over Annie, bringing her the coffee he had ordered for her and staying with her behind the safely locked doors of his apartment while he had gone to speak with his father, demanding an explanation of his behaviour and piecing together what had happened.

Now they were on their own, just the three of them in the peace of his apartment. His suit jacket was flung across the back of the sofa, the top button of his shirt was unfastened.

This was how he wanted his life to be, Falcon realised; with Annie and Oliver, in the love he bore them both.

'I have spoken with my father,' he told Annie. 'And I have demanded from him an explanation of his unforgivable behaviour. It seems that your stepbrother and he made contact with one another—and very quickly both of them realised that the other had a purpose that fitted in well with their own. My father wanted to gain control of Oliver's life, and your stepbrother wanted to gain control of *you*.

'I doubt that my father believed for a second that you intended any harm towards Oliver. However, it suited him to pretend that he did—just as it suited your stepbrother to claim that you were mentally unstable and therefore unfit to have control of your child.'

'Colin tried to do that before. That was part of the reason why I tried to hide from him,' Annie told Falcon. 'He threatened to tell Social Services that I wasn't fit to look after Ollie. It wasn't true, but I was afraid that they'd believe him. That's why I moved flats.'

Falcon nodded his head.

He'd already informed Colin that he would be taken to the airport in the morning and put on a flight. He had also told him that he, Falcon, would be taking legal steps to ensure that Colin was forbidden to make any future contact with Annie or Oliver, and that he would never again be allowed to put so much as a foot on Sicilian soil.

He would never tell Annie about the filth and innuendo that her stepbrother had come out with, or the accusations he had made against her: that she was a wanton flirt who enjoyed encouraging men and had done since her early teens, when she had first begun flaunting her body in unsuitable clothes and encouraging boys to take liberties with her; that Antonio had merely been one of a string of men she had led on; that he, Colin, had been asked by her distraught and shamed mother to do everything he could to put a stop to her promiscuous lifestyle. All were accusations Falcon would have known to be untrue even if the intimacy he had shared with her hadn't already proved to him how innocent she was.

'I expect you've told your father that he needn't worry and that you aren't really going to marry me?'

Annie had spent the last hour, whilst she waited for Falcon to come back from seeing his father, picking over and discarding a wide variety of ways in which she could bring up the subject of his statement about marrying her in a way that would let him know immediately that she fully understood his words had simply been a means of protecting her, and that they had not been intended to be taken as a genuine proposition on his part.

'No. I haven't told him that.'

Annie had sworn to herself that she would not look directly at Falcon, no matter what—because she was so afraid that if she did he would see in her eyes how much she loved him. But now she could feel her gaze being pulled towards his as though it was being moved by powerful magnets. Or as though he was somehow compelling her to look at him.

'Well, I dare say he'll find out anyway in time—once we don't. That is to say, when he sees that we aren't...'

Falcon briskly cut across her floundering. 'I haven't told him for the simple reason that I believe it would make very good sense for us to marry.'

Now Annie couldn't have dragged her gaze from his, no matter what power had been put at her disposal—because she simply had to look at him and go on looking at him, just to make sure she wasn't imagining things.

'You think that we should get married—to one another?' she questioned Falcon feebly.

'Yes. It's the best and simplest way of both protecting you from your stepbrother and securing Oliver's future within your guardianship. Once you are my wife no one, least of all my father, can make any claim to usurp your role in Oliver's life.'

'But one day you will succeed your father. You are his eldest son. You will be Prince and head of the Leopardi family. You can't marry someone like me.'

'I can marry whoever I choose to marry,' Falcon corrected her arrogantly. 'And if you are worrying that some people might choose not to accept you as my wife, let me reassure you they will accept you—or risk losing their relationship with me.'

'I can't let you make such a sacrifice,' Annie protested. 'You should marry someone you love.'

Falcon hesitated. Should he tell her? Should he admit to her that he loved her? No! He had no right to burden her with his feelings—especially when she was still so vulnerable and upset by her confrontation with her stepbrother.

'Doing my duty is more important to me than love,' he lied firmly. 'And it is my duty to protect both you and Oliver. I can think of no better way to fulfil that duty than to marry you. That does not mean that you have to say yes, though.'

He had at the very least to say that—offer her an escape route. He couldn't leave her trapped and forced to accept him with no way out. His honour and the love he felt for her demanded that much.

Not say yes! When she loved him so much? But perhaps

for his sake she *should* refuse. He might say that love wasn't important to him, and she might have taken into herself in silence the pain that careless statement had caused her, but what if one day he *did* fall in love? How could she allow him to be trapped in a marriage with her when he loved someone else?

But if she left him where would she go? How would she ever be safe? Colin would hunt her down—she just knew he would. And Ollie—how could she protect her son from her stepbrother's dangerous malice if she was on her own?

'It does seem to be the sensible thing to do,' she agreed.

Falcon felt his heart slam into his ribs in a mixture of relief and longing. Relief because she had said yes, and longing because right now more than anything else he wanted to take her in his arms and tell her how he felt about her—tell her how happy he wanted to make her.

Instead he forced himself to agree coolly, 'It *is* the sensible thing to do.'

He started to stand up, and Annie's gaze slid helplessly to the movement of the muscles in his thighs. Like sand washed clean by the tide, everything she had felt over the last few hours was suddenly swept away, leaving only that now familiar deep inner ache that told her how much she wanted him.

'From now on you and Oliver will live and sleep here, in this apartment. I'll give you a key, so that if for any reason I'm not here and you feel the need to do so you can lock yourselves in. Although you have my word that my father will not attempt a repeat performance of today's events.'

She was going to share Falcon's apartment. Her whole body quivered in something that was far more sensual than mere relief.

'There is a spare guest suite,' Falcon continued.

A guest suite!

'Does that mean...?' Annie stopped, her face going pink.

'Does it mean what?' Falcon invited.

'If we are to be married, does that mean that we'll be...erm...sleeping together?'

'It is customary for married couples to sleep together,' Falcon told her. 'But if what you are really asking me is if our marriage will include a shared sexual relationship, as well as our shared love for Oliver, then the answer is that I would certainly like it to do so. But that decision must be yours.'

Hers? Well, she knew what she really wanted to say, of course. She loved him, and there was nothing she wanted more than for them to be lovers in every way there was.

She was hesitating—reluctant to give up her freedom of choice to share her life and her body with a man of her own choosing, Falcon recognised grimly. Well, what had he expected? That she would fling herself into his arms now, as she had done earlier, and this time tell him that she loved and wanted him?

'There is no need to make a decision on that right now,' he told her, as casually as he could.

'Has...has Colin left yet?' Annie asked, deliberately changing the subject just in case she burst out with what she was really thinking and feeling and embarrassed them both.

Falcon frowned as he was reminded of an issue that had irritated him.

'No. The first flight I can get him on is not until tomorrow morning. I'm reluctant to allow him the freedom of the island in the meantime, for obvious reasons. Plus there is the matter of my lawyers applying to the courts for an emergency restraining order, to ensure that he is stopped from coming anywhere near you or Oliver ever again. Unfortunately he will have to stay here in the *castello* for now. You need not worry, though. You and Oliver will be safe in here, whilst he will remain in my father's quarters. A fitting extra punishment for both of them, I think, that they should be forced to endure one another's company.'

Falcon wanted to keep Colin here at the *castello* prior to his flight back to the United Kingdom in case Colin went to ground and was then free to hound her and threaten Ollie, Annie knew, so she nodded her head in understanding.

Could he win her love? Falcon wondered. Was it truly fair of him to even try? In marrying her, was he protecting her or imprisoning her just as surely as her stepbrother had done? Was he doing his duty or was he simply greedily and selfishly seizing what he wanted more than anything else?

He looked at Annie, who had leaned across the sofa to check on Oliver. The look of tender maternal love warming her face made his heart turn over in his chest.

He had to put her first.

'It is my view that for Oliver's sake it is necessary that we marry now. However, if our marriage doesn't work out,' he told her curtly, 'or if at some future date one of us were to fall in love, then we can and will be divorced.'

Annie's heart contracted with fiercely sharp pain. Only one of them could fall in love outside their marriage, and it wasn't her. How would she be able to bear it if Falcon did fall in love with someone else? Was he perhaps already regretting his decision to marry her?

'We don't have to get married,' she forced herself to say.

'Yes, we do,' Falcon corrected her. 'Apart from anything else, there is also the chance that we may already have created a child together.'

Annie swallowed hard against the tight knot of guilt blocking her throat. That had been her fault. He had wanted to take precautions but she hadn't let him. Even more guilt-inducing was the knowledge that she was *glad* she had been able to enjoy the precious and wonderful sensation of his body filling her own without any barriers between them, however reckless that intimacy might have been.

'I'm going to go and tell Maria that you're moving into the guest suite here, so that she can get the maids organised.'

Annie nodded her head, but as soon as Falcon reached the door the knowledge that she was going to be left on her own filled her with so much panic that she stood up.

'Could that wait until tomorrow?' she begged. 'I know that you said I could lock myself in here, but… But I don't want to be on my own whilst Colin's still here. He makes me feel so afraid.' She tried to laugh and make a joke about her fear, adding, 'I don't even think I could *sleep* on my own.'

The minute she realised what she had said, her face burned.

'I didn't mean that the way it sounded. I just meant…'

'I know what you meant,' Falcon assured her. 'And there's no need for you to sleep alone. I am perfectly happy to share my bed with you.'

His bed, his body, his life, his heart and his love—everything he had to give, all of it. But of course, he couldn't tell her that. It would only add another burden to those she already had to carry.

CHAPTER ELEVEN

WHY was being in Falcon's bed tonight so very different from last night? Annie wondered miserably, as she lay alone. It was over an hour since Falcon had suggested that she must be tired—only to tell her that he had some work to finish the minute she had agreed that she was, but that she should go ahead and go to bed. In that time she had showered and dried herself and curled up in the large bed, her heart pounding with excitement and love, her body on fire with intoxicated longing and desire, but Falcon had not come to join her.

Now he was in the bathroom, where he had been for what seemed like for ever, and the unwelcome and unwanted thought was creeping over her that Falcon might be delaying coming to bed because he was hoping that she would be asleep when he joined her. After all, she was the one who had asked to sleep with him, not the other way round.

But the last time he had been in bed with her he had wanted her.

Had he? Or had he simply been doing what he had promised and showing her what it was like to be wanted?

He was going to marry her.

To protect her and Ollie and because he thought it was his duty. Not for any other reason.

The joyful anticipation that had filled her began to drain away. Annie turned on her side, to face away from the middle of the bed. If Falcon didn't want her then she wasn't going to embarrass them both by making it look as though she wanted *him*.

Falcon pushed his hand through his damp hair, having wrapped a towel around his hips. He had just spent an hour desperately trying to pretend that he was working when the only place his thoughts were was in his bedroom and in his bed—with Annie. Now he had been forced to endure the supposedly arousal-dousing ritual of a cold shower to ensure that when he got into bed with her he would have no reason to be tempted into waking her up to take her in his arms.

His body was quite obviously not aware of the purpose of a cold shower, since it was showing every evidence of its physical desire for Annie not having abated one iota. As for his emotional desire for her—his love for her seemed to be increasing with every second he spent with her.

Falcon had believed that he had put in place within himself emotional and mental back-up systems for dealing with every situation that life could throw at him. But he had neglected to prepare for anything like this. Love was something that wasn't going to happen for him, he had decided. It was something he could not allow to happen.

Everyone assumed that in due course he would marry and produce an heir, as countless eldest Leopardi sons had done before him. Deep down inside himself, though, Falcon had questioned the whole concept that being the eldest son meant he must marry and provide an heir. He had two brothers, after all. Then there had been the conflicting natures of the kind of traditional marriage entered into by his parents and a modern twenty-first-century marriage. One thing they shared, though, was that neither of them guaranteed a mutual commitment to a shared lifetime of marital happiness.

He had grown to manhood loathing the thought of making a woman as unhappy as his father had made his mother—the result of their traditional dynastic marriage— but neither had he felt able to trust the longevity of a modern marriage. Especially one that would have to endure the pressures that came with his position as head of the Leopardi family, custodian of its present and future good name, as well as the history of its past. Falcon took those responsibilities very seriously.

Without a really strong, enduring love he doubted that it would be possible to give any children of his marriage the inner emotional security and strength his own eldest son would ultimately need if he was not to feel burdened, as Falcon had from a very young age, with the knowledge of what lay ahead of him. It was, he had decided, better— and easier—to stay single.

When his brothers had married for love their happiness had reinforced his private decision. But that had been before Annie had come into his life and he had fallen in love with her.

Even if they had met 'normally', and fallen mutually in love, he would not have wanted to burden her with the life that must be his. Hand in hand with Falcon's strong sense of duty went an equally strong awareness that his life involved making sacrifices. There was no way that he would have wanted the woman he loved to share those sac-rifices.

He believed passionately in Annie's right to her personal freedom of choice—in her right to define her own boundaries and live her own life. The actions of those who had deprived her of those rights filled him with contempt, and an almost missionary zeal to counter them.

And yet now *he* was the one who would be taking them from her by marrying her.

What choice did he have? Without his protection she would be at risk from her stepbrother for as long as Colin lived. The only way Falcon could give her his protection was by marrying her.

Marrying her, taking her to his bed as his love, impregnating her with his child, even loving her—surely these were all forms of imprisonment every bit as bad in their way as the behaviour he had so criticised and condemned in her stepbrother, who also claimed to love her? Love could be a terrible prison when it wasn't reciprocated— for both parties, but especially for the one who hadn't asked for it and didn't want it.

So what was he to do? Not marry her and leave Annie and Oliver vulnerable to the machinations of a man who had already made it very clear that, whilst he would go to any lengths to keep Annie in his life, he would equally go to any lengths to remove her child from her life?

Marry her but ensure that the marriage was in name only, so that he was only violating his promise to preserve her right to freedom on one issue?

In his arms she had wanted him; she had responded to him with passion and pleasure.

Because she had never known anyone else. Because he had sprung for her the trap which had been set over her. The sensuality of her response to him was merely the beginning of her journey into her own womanhood, not the end.

She would continue that journey in his arms.

But because their marriage forced her to do so. Not because she wanted to.

Annie felt the bed depress beneath Falcon's weight, and then the cool rush of air as he disturbed the bedclothes. She waited, desperately hoping beyond hope that he would reach for her, or even say something to her—some words of comfort and tenderness that would offer her the solace of knowing that it wasn't *her* he was rejecting but simply their current situation. But instead all she had was the cold pain of an empty silence.

How could she marry him knowing that he was only marrying her out of some misplaced sense of duty and honour? Where was her pride? Her self-respect?

The same moonlight that had silvered Falcon's body so erotically only a few nights ago was streaming in through the windows tonight, but now it was reinforcing her pain in lying here alone and longing for him.

She forced herself to close her eyes, in the hope that she would be able to escape into sleep, but before she could do so Ollie started crying.

He had been grizzly earlier in the day, his right cheek flushed and slightly swollen, indicating that he was cutting a new tooth. Poor baby—no wonder he was crying in pain, Annie thought sympathetically as she slid carefully out of the bed, praying that the sound of Ollie's distress wouldn't wake Falcon.

She hurried into Falcon's dressing room without stopping to pull on her robe. She was wearing one of the nightdresses that had been included with her new clothes, full-length, in fine pleated sheer soft peach-coloured silk, with darker ribbons that cupped her breasts and then tied at the front. The side seams were split almost to her hipbone, and tied with more ribbons at the top of her thigh. Not exactly practical for night-time nursery visits—but then, she admitted ruefully, she hadn't been thinking of its suitability for that purpose when she had put it on so much as of the speed with which Falcon could divest her of it when he pulled at the ribbons.

As the dressing room did not possess a window, a small nightlight had been left glowing, to give some light without disturbing Ollie, and now, as he saw Annie, he stopped crying. His poor little cheek looked very red and sore, and Annie winced as she lifted him out of the travel cot and then sat down in the chair that had been put next to it, with him on her knee.

A quick inspection of his mouth confirmed he was indeed cutting a new tooth. The moment he felt her touch on his raw flesh he clamped his gums together, in an attempt to relieve the pain, the edges of the new tooth sharp on Annie's finger.

'Poor little boy,' she comforted him. She had got some soothing gel and some medicine in his baby bag, but she'd have to put him back in his cot so that she could get them out, and she knew from past experience that the minute she did that he would start roaring in protest. The last thing she wanted was for him to wake Falcon, so she pushed the door closed with her elbow and then put Ollie into the cot, gently shushing him whilst she searched frantically in his bag for the teething gel and the baby pain relief.

Five minutes later she was congratulating herself on having both soothed Ollie and not woken Falcon—and then, as she straightened up from kissing the baby's sleeping face, she caught the side of the slightly unstable butler's tray she'd been using as a worktop, sending an empty glass crashing to the marble floor, where it immediately smashed into zillions of pieces.

By some miracle Ollie didn't wake up, but the combination of her shock and her desire to steady herself had her stepping backwards, in her bare feet, straight onto a piece of broken glass.

She had barely begun to cry out in automatic reaction when the dressing room door was flung open, and the room itself illuminated by the light from the bedroom. Falcon stood in the doorway, instantly taking in what had happened. Unlike her, he was wearing soft leather slip-on footwear, along with a thick bathrobe.

'Don't move,' he told Annie, stepping into the dressing room and then lifting her bodily into his arms to carry her through the bedroom and into the bathroom, ignoring her protests about the damage that would be done to the bedroom carpet by the blood dripping from her cut foot as he did so.

Once they were in the marble bathroom he placed her on the top step of the short flight of limestone stairs that led down to the large shower area, warning her, 'Keep your foot off the floor, in case there's still glass in it.'

'It's nothing—just a small cut,' Annie protested. She felt so guilty about waking him up and causing all this trouble, but Falcon wasn't listening to her. Instead he was crouching on the hard limestone floor with her cut foot resting on his knee whilst he studied it carefully in the bright light.

'I can't see any glass there,' he told her.

'I'm sure there won't be.' Annie tried to remove her foot, but his left hand was cupping her heel, spreading an unwanted and very dangerous heat through her body.

'Maybe not, but I'm not prepared to take any chances that there is.' Very gently Falcon worked his way round the cut and into its centre with his fingertips.

When he had stopped, and Annie had eased out a long, fractured pent-up breath, Falcon mistook the cause of her relief, looked up at her and said, 'Yes, it does seem to be free of glass.'

Thank goodness Falcon didn't realise that it hadn't been the cut on her foot that had caused her anxiety, but her fear of betraying to him just what his touch was doing to her.

'Stay like that and don't put your foot down on the floor. I'm going to get a bowl from the kitchen, so that you can bathe the cut in antiseptic, and then I'll go and clear up the broken glass.'

He was only gone a matter of seconds, returning with a large plastic bowl which he half filled under the basin tap before adding to it some antiseptic liquid from the bathroom cabinet.

'It will sting,' he warned as he placed the bowl on the floor next to her foot. 'But keep it in the bowl until I come back.'

He was right. It did sting, Annie acknowledged, after he had left her to go and clean up the broken glass. But the pain was nothing compared with the pain of loving him.

The stinging sensation had worn off by the time he came back. He checked her foot after she had obediently lifted it from the bowl, and then frowingly pronounced that the cut was glass-free and clean.

'I can do that,' Annie objected, when he removed the bowl and placed a towel on the floor for her to put her foot on.

'You could, but it will be easier if I do it.'

Easier? To have him gently but firmly drying her foot? One hand cupping her heel as he had done before, the sensation of his touch arousing a wild frenzy of inappropriate images and longings? No way. Sitting there, her hands gripping the edge of the step for fear that she might reach out towards him, was one of the hardest things she had ever had to do.

She had to say something. She couldn't bear the thick, tense silence between them any longer.

'I'm sorry I disturbed you.'

Falcon looked up at her. There was an expression in his eyes she couldn't define—a darkness edged with something fierce and proud.

'So am I,' he agreed flatly.

His response to her apology made her recoil. What had she been hoping for? A gallant remark to the effect that he didn't mind?

He was still holding her foot. Apparently a final inspection had to be made of the cut, a dressing applied to it, followed by a plaster. And then, just when she had thought her ordeal was finally over, and had stood up, ready to make the excuse of wanting to check on Ollie—anything other than get into that bed again—Falcon told her brusquely, 'It might be a good idea not to walk on it yet.'

He was going to *carry* her back to bed. Annie didn't think she could endure intimate physical contact with him that was no intimacy at all—or at least not the kind she so desperately wanted. Her heart was thudding as though she'd been running. Her senses were filled with their awareness of him, their longing for him. She'd managed to hang on to her self control this long—surely she could hang on to it for a few more seconds? Held in his arms? Close to his body? Not a chance.

Panic galvanised her.

She backed away from him, uttering a half-choked, 'No!' that had him frowning and flustered her into hurried speech.

'That is—I mean—there's no need to carry me. I have to go and check on Ollie anyway.'

'I've already done it. He's fast asleep.'

There was to be no escape. He was bending towards her. Annie closed her eyes.

Perhaps if she couldn't see him it would be easier for her?

Big mistake. With her eyes closed, and thus denied the sight of him, her other senses were immediately flooded with an increased awareness of how much she loved him.

She loved him and she wanted him, now and for ever, in her life as he was already in her heart, holding her, loving her, sharing with her the wonderful magic of her sensuality that he himself had shown to her.

Annie opened her eyes.

They'd reached the bed, and Falcon was leaning down to place her onto it. Another few seconds and the contact between them would be broken. Another few seconds and the opportunity now facing her would be gone. Was she brave enough to seize it and risk the consequences? Consequences that could easily include rejection?

She could feel the mattress beneath her. Falcon was releasing her. Already it was nearly too late. Another heartbeat and she would miss her chance. He had wanted her; he was marrying her; he would be Ollie's protector and guardian. Why shouldn't he be her lover, as well? Even if he could not and did not love her? She had enough love for both of them.

Annie took a deep breath, inwardly begging for time to smile on her as she reached up to clasp her hands behind Falcon's head and pull him down towards her.

His, 'No!' cracked through the room like a pistol-shot.

Annie could feel him tensing against her, and she could see the darkness in his gaze. Once such a rejection would have had her releasing him immediately and cowering back in humiliated, shocked pain. But Falcon himself had taught her to take pride in her sexuality. He had even advised her to use her sensuality to choose herself a mate. But of course he had not had himself in mind when he had spoken those words to her.

His hands had left her body and his arms had dropped to his sides. He was standing at the end of the bed, held there by her embrace, whilst she kneeled on the bed facing him.

She could feel a wildness racing through her, smashing everything in its way, filling her with a surge of powerful female determination.

The hands she had clasped around his neck stayed there and tightened together. Her heart, her mind and her body were unified in their purpose.

'Yes.' She rejected his denial fiercely.

And then she reached up and placed her lips against his. Just for a second she allowed herself to savour their heart-wrenching familiarity as her own softened and moulded to them.

She could feel him resisting her, mentally and emotionally fighting her, denying her. But, incredibly, his silent hard muscled tension only increased her determination to achieve her goal.

She kissed one corner of his mouth, and then the other,

and then lovingly, with great sensual pleasure, she slowly traced the sharp cut of his upper lip with her tongue-tip, and the full curve of its partner.

In the silvered darkness her own accelerated breathing sent her pulses racing, whilst her heart thundered in a wild, passionate tempo. What she was doing thrilled her and shocked her in almost equal measure.

Her tongue-tip stroked the closed line of Falcon's mouth and then probed it.

Falcon groaned and then seized her, kissing her with a passion that drove her back onto the bed, his body following her own and pinning her there, his hands tangling in her hair whilst he held her mouth beneath his own. His kiss was all that she had longed for and more, and she responded to its command with euphoric delight.

His capitulation had been so swift it had been like ice cracking and splintering, taking them both down deep into the darkness of the passion they were now sharing.

Their clothes, her nightdress and his robe, were removed with urgent hands. Falcon's hands were steady and knowing on her nightdress; her own were eager and excited on his robe.

Just the act of inhaling the scent of his skin was enough to send her over the edge and make her mindless with sensual arousal and longing.

This should not be happening, Falcon told himself. But he couldn't stop it. He was helpless in the face of his own love and longing—unable to deny Annie the control she had taken.

Her face was ablaze with joy as she touched him. 'I want you so much.' The words spilled from her as she opened herself to his possession, wanting it with a sharply sweet immediacy that could not be ignored or delayed. Her whole body quivered with delight as she felt Falcon answer her need, and then flamed with heat when he thrust slowly into her, then faster and deeper, taking her to that place where there was only him and their shared need for one another. All she could do was hold on to him and cry out her delight as each powerful thrust of his body took her pleasure higher.

It was over quickly and fiercely, leaving them both breathing heavily.

'That shouldn't have happened.' Falcon's voice was terse.

'I'm glad that it did—because I *wanted* it to happen,' Annie told him defiantly.

Falcon made a small restless movement, pulling away from her. 'That is because sex is a newly discovered pleasure for you. That is all.'

His casual dismissal of what they had just shared pushed her into saying fiercely, 'No, it isn't. What happened wasn't because I'm like some kind of suddenly sex-crazed teenager. It was because I love you and I wanted to show you that love. Because I wanted to create for myself another memory of sharing the intimacy of lovemaking with you to have for the future. I know you don't want my love, Falcon, and...'

Annie took a deep breath. She had come to a very important decision. 'And you don't have to marry me. Because...because what you've shown me and taught me has given me the strength to be the woman you told me I could be. I'm not frightened of Colin any more, and I'm not going to burden you with the responsibility of me or Ollie. Loving someone means wanting the best for them, and wanting their happiness above your own. You've given me freedom from my past. I want to give you freedom to meet someone and fall in love with them....'

'I already have.'

The pain was so intense that after the blow had fallen she thought she was going to pass out from the agony of it.

'You've met someone you've fallen in love with?' Her lips felt slightly numb, unable to form the words properly.

Because they didn't want to do so. Because she didn't want to confront what speaking them meant.

'Yes. And I love her more deeply and passionately than I ever imagined it was possible to love anyone.'

'That makes you even more admirable for offering to marry me.'

It was the truth, after all—even if saying the words nearly choked her.

'Offering to marry you doesn't make me admirable at all, Annie. It makes me selfish and weak, and subject to all the flaws I was so ready to criticise in your stepbrother. What was my offer of marriage other than an attempt to control your life and take away your freedom?'

'You wanted to protect me.'

'I wanted to keep you for myself. I wanted to bind you to me and keep you with me.'

Annie could feel her heart starting to race again.

Falcon had moved closer to her.

'I wanted all the things with you that a man wants with the woman he loves. But I was acquiring them—and you—through dishonesty. I thought myself so noble and dutiful, but the reality is that I was no such thing.'

'You were wonderful,' Annie told him passionately.

'You *are* wonderful. Oh, Falcon, do you mean it? Do you really love me?'

'You are stealing my question to you,' he answered softly, and she could see in his eyes the light and the love that were glowing there. 'But I am the first man—your first man. I don't want you to mistake...'

'Lust for love? Annie supplied for him, shaking her head as she told him, 'I'm twenty-four, Falcon—not sixteen. I could have broken out of my Colin-imposed cage of fear a long time ago if I'd really wanted to. But I didn't want to. Not until I met you. That first time we met in the hotel foyer, the minute you touched me, I knew that something inside me had changed.'

'It was the same for me,' Falcon admitted. He had taken hold of her hand, and his fingers were now entwined lovingly with hers. 'Although I didn't recognise what I felt for you at first as love. Had I done so, I would never...'

'Have become my sexual teacher and healer?' Annie suggested.

'That is what I should say—but I cannot do so since I have no idea if it is true. Where you are concerned I have no control over my feelings.'

'You certainly seemed to be able to control them earlier,' Annie pointed out.

'That wasn't control, it was desperation. I knew that once I touched you I wouldn't be able to stop. You are far too good a pupil—irresistible, in fact.'

He was reaching for her, and Annie happily snuggled closer to him.

'Mmm...' she encouraged him. 'How irresistible, exactly?'

EPILOGUE

'YOU May kiss the bride.'

Annie's face was alight with joy and love as Falcon raised the traditional lace veil which was a family heirloom back off her face and kissed her reverently.

The church was filled with Leopardi family and friends, all come to witness and celebrate their marriage—arranged so hastily, Falcon had put it about, because of the precarious state of the old Prince's health.

Annie smiled a secret smile of private happiness. She might not as yet have the same bloomingly pregnant figure as the wives of Falcon's two brothers, but her and Falcon's baby was already growing inside her—had, she was sure, been conceived that very first time they had made love.

'I love you,' Falcon whispered to her.

'I love you too,' she whispered back.

AUTHOR NOTE

The three books I have written about the Leopardi brothers have to be amongst my own all-time favourites, and yet initially I wasn't sure I could write them. What did I know about Sicily or about the emotions that might hold three alpha brothers together or keep them apart?

As always when I write I needed a strong underlying structure that would support the mindset of my heroes and I found that structure in Sicily itself. During a short visit to the island my research showed me the powerful loyalty to family and culture, handed down through the generations, that exists there.

I wanted to create three alpha heroes, all of them equally independent and equally alpha, but how would that work in a family set-up? How would the traditional Sicilian mindset of complete loyalty to, and reverence for, the head of the family sit with such independence?

My answer to these questions was to have my brothers give their loyalty to their family name rather than to an individual. Each of them was able to take charge of their own empowerment whilst respecting their inbuilt instinct to put loyalty and duty above the needs of their own ego.

When the brothers concerned belong to a proud aristocratic family, then the loyalty they receive from their "people" goes hand in hand with their sense of duty towards those people—in fact to all those who they see it as their duty to protect—and the mix takes on an intriguing potential for conflict.

Add into this mix a distant, cruel father whose unkindness forced my heroes, when young, to turn to one another for support; a dead half-brother whose lifestyle filled them with contempt; and an urgent need to find, and ultimately protect from their own father, the child that their half-brother might have fathered, and I felt I had the beginnings of "something" that could work.

The island, its history, its people and their culture gave me the framework that created the brothers' attitude to life. Their lack of parental love as children forged such strong bonds between them that I wanted to reinforce their sense of duty to their name and to one another whilst establishing a credible reason why they should feel so strongly about finding and protecting a child who shared their blood.

I was nearly there—and my own experience of the effect differing sibling positions have on the way we develop added the final element to the mix.

My first hero—the youngest of the three—would be creative, independent, and unafraid of taking risks and being open to the outside world (my own younger sister is like that—younger children can be more adventurous). Additionally though, the first hero carried the burden of feeling that his mother, having given birth to him, had chosen to die rather than to fight for life. This influenced his own emotional development, giving his character certain deep and complex barriers to personal happiness. As a Leopardi he believed that it was his duty to help find his hated half-brother's child, but as a man he finds that the woman he believes is that child's mother compels from him a love that goes against the demands of his Leopardi name. He must choose between duty and love. Rocco Leopardi is gorgeous—my take on a traditional alpha hero with a modern outlook, who can't help but respond to the needs and the vulnerability of the heroine. His strength protects and shelters her, his confidence inspires her, and his love for her heals all her emotional wounds. Rocco Leopardi stands tall as an alpha hero, even whilst he's cradling a baby in one arm and protecting the woman he loves with the other. This is a man who has the strength to put love first.

The second brother is a classical "middle child" and to add to the turbulence of this emotional mix I created for him a heroine who is also a middle child. They share a fierce determination to prove to the world that being a second child does not make them second best, that they can be "better" than the first born. As a couple they both automatically understand what drives the other, they know all about loving an elder sibling and yet at the same time hating being subservient to a first-born. They know about creating challenges for themselves, targets, goals, barriers to their own happiness in what they are.

I loved the emotional intensity of this book; the way my hero is torn between his sense of not being as good as his elder brother and the resentment that causes him, whilst at the same time loving him deeply.

This couple are so well suited for one another in their shared passion, and strength and vulnerability. Together they can teach one another how to be free of their childhood unhappiness.

I just love this book, and this couple. My heroine is so proud and yet so vulnerable, a girl growing up in an all-male household who has never really been able to be "feminine"—everything at first sight that Alessandro Leopardi most dislikes in a woman, and yet…heart to heart, birth position to birth position, he recognises something within her that touches his own emotions no matter how much he wants to reject that knowledge. He knows how she feels and how she thinks, he knows what she hungers for and he knows that more than anything else he wants her to hunger for him.

The third book relates to the love story of the eldest brother— Falcon Leopardi. A first born of three, an eldest child through and through who has always taken his responsibilities seriously, and for Falcon there is no greater responsibility as a Leopardi than that of righting all that his father has done wrong, and protecting the innocent, especially when that innocent shares his own blood.

Falcon knows what it is to be rejected and unloved. As a boy he tried his best to protect his brothers, to give them the love and security their parents did not, but he was only a boy himself then and he feels that there were many times when he failed them. He will not fail this innocent life, this child conceived in the most brutal of circumstances—nor its mother. He will find a way to make amends. He will re-write the failures of his earlier struggles to "make things right" for his brothers and he will restore all that has been taken from her. Only Falcon has not taken into account that his personal feelings will get in the way of his commitment to his self-imposed duty. Who can he turn to for help and advice? Only those who know him best can help him now. Even the most alpha of men sometimes has to ask for help. Even the eldest child sometimes needs the love and understanding of its siblings.

Falcon for me is all that I myself would want to find in an alpha man.

I have enjoyed writing these three books far more than I thought I would at the outset. I've tried within them to give a flavour of the "old" Sicily and its people's pride and courage; so many different peoples have influenced the island, and its history, and I hope you will find a flavour of this within these books.

As for the Leopardi brothers—I wish there were more of them for me to write about.

Penny Jordan

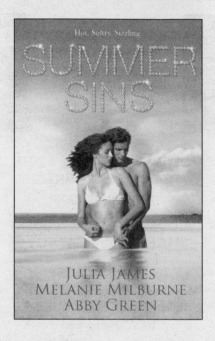

BAD BLOOD

A POWERFUL
DYNASTY,
WHERE SECRETS
AND SCANDAL
NEVER SLEEP!

VOLUME 1 – 15th April 2011
TORTURED RAKE
by Sarah Morgan

VOLUME 2 – 6th May 2011
SHAMELESS PLAYBOY
by Caitlin Crews

VOLUME 3 – 20th May 2011
RESTLESS BILLIONAIRE
by Abby Green

VOLUME 4 – 3rd June 2011
FEARLESS MAVERICK
by Robyn Grady

8 VOLUMES IN ALL TO COLLECT!

MILLS
BOON

www.millsandboon.co.uk